Forever in the Past

A NOTE ON THE AUTHOR

Lilian Roberts Finlay was born in Dublin and educated at Mount Sackville and at the Abbey Theatre School. She now lives in Dunsany, County Meath. Her published works of fiction include *Always in My Mind*, *A Bona Fide Husband* and *Stella*.

—LILIAN—
ROBERTS FINLAY

Forever in the Past

POOLBEG

First published 1993 by
Poolbeg,
A Division of Poolbeg Enterprises Itd,
Knocksedan House,
Swords, Co Dublin, Ireland.

© Lilian Roberts Finlay 1993

The moral right of the author has been asserted.

Poolbeg Press receives financial assistance from the Arts Council/
An Chomhairle Ealaíon, Dublin

A catalogue record for this book is available from the British Library.

ISBN 1 85371271 X

Cover illustration by Tom Roche
Set by Mac Book Limited in Stone 10/15
Printed by Cox & Wyman Limited
Reading, Berks

—LILIAN—
ROBERTS FINLAY

Forever in the Past

POOLBEG

First published 1993 by
Poolbeg,
A Division of Poolbeg Enterprises ltd,
Knocksedan House,
Swords, Co Dublin, Ireland.

Poolbeg Press receives financial assistance from the Arts Council/
An Chomhairle Ealaíon, Dublin

A catalogue record for this book is available from the British Library.

ISBN 1 85371271 X

Cover illustration by Tom Roche
Set by Mac Book Limited in Stone 10/15
Printed by Cox & Wyman Limited
Reading, Berks

In memory of Theo
For whom that which could not be carved
From the actuality of time
Was rendered down
In the rhythms of fiction

PRELUDE

Should I leave Lia out there in the sunset on Sandymount Strand, safe in Max's arms, secure in the knowledge that he would take care of the coming child fathered by his friend? She is happy with the thought that she need fear neither poverty nor loneliness ever again. It was not to be so easily foretold.

The days of her innocence were over. She was a woman awakened to the meaning of passionate desire. In Max's first kiss she felt herself ready to respond because her need had been created in the partisans' camp by the man she had loved since she was six years of age. Could awakened need for shared loving be transferred to Max or would the love for the child transcend that hungry lifelong love of Tadek? Could there be any love after Tadek? There could and there would.

Before the sun had set over the empty strand on that day, the reality of Lia's life had ended. From now on she would follow a script written for her before she was born. She would pick up the cues, she would learn the words, she would give her honesty to new meanings, she would assent to life and she would love in many different ways.

She would come to know for fact the truth she used

to question: love comes either too soon or too late. Hope would grow, very slowly, that somewhere at the very end there would be another strand, another ebb-tide, another sunset, when her lost choice would return.

CHAPTER ONE

A rm in arm they walked across the strand. The little puppy raced ahead and back and on again.

"Did your father find this little dog for you to give to me?" Lia asked.

Max pressed her arm closer to him. "It was his plan. He made enquiries about the exact breed and colour and he had the puppy kept in readiness. It was to be his present for your birthday."

"But he allowed you to give the present. Always he goes one step further in his generosity. When did he know you were coming home?"

"He did not know. I came as soon as I could. The partisans' camp is closed; those who were left are dispersed." Heavy grief was in his voice. Lia knew it was not the time for questions.

At the wall Max caught up the frolicking puppy. He turned back to look across the strand. The setting sun was gilding the incoming tide. "This space, this open space," his voice was constricted, "this clear water running into the ripples in the sand. I had forgotten the free wonder of it all."

In their time together, Tadek had talked scarcely at all about the concentration camps but then Tadek had fought free of those events to dwell only on the memories of which Lia had been a part. Tadek knew he would be free of all memory all too soon. Max must take his hellish memories with him into whatever future lay ahead. In this first hour of their reunion, his tense words told Lia that Max was not free of the camps and of all the despair that followed. In the months that Lia had been in the partisans' camp, she had become aware of the enormous burden Max had shouldered for those men, shattered by loss of identity, loss of their families, loss of hope and by the diseases of years of starvation. He had taken on himself the near-impossible task of restoring them to a world in which they had no place any more. Lia knew those stricken souls had thought of Herr Doktor Max as a miracle worker. Who would be the miracle worker for Max himself? Would he look to Lia? Was that the meaning of the words he had spoken when he came across the strand to her? "I have found you," he said. Lia wanted to be found, and helped and cherished. For her own sake. For the baby within her. For the sake of hiding safely from the eyes of the world. She remembered the faces of the men in the camp. She had seen the longing in their eyes and the blank extinction of light when a man had finally to accept that he alone of all his family had survived annihilation. Who would help Max to survive?

"Will you tell me again that you have found me?" Max could not speak. He ruffled the puppy's furry coat gently, abstractedly. "Let's sit on the wall for a little while, shall we?" Lia invited. Max's father had absorbed Lia's tears for Tadek; now it was her turn and she wanted to show Max that she was found indeed and here at his hand to help him. "Max, this is our very own place, our very own strand, Sandymount, just the same as if we had never gone away. We played crazy cricket here, like only yesterday. You remember, Sandymount Strand?"

"Sandymount Strand!" he repeated as if it were a place heard of only in a dream.

"And this is Lia," she reminded him, "the one who always dropped the cricket ball. You used to get so exasperated with me!"

His face cleared a little. He almost smiled but his voice was very husky. "I never got exasperated with you, Lia."

"Oh yes you did! But don't you dare now!" He looked at her, slowly his smile settled. "Am I back in your good book?"

"You were never out of it, *balibt*."

But Lia knew she was absent from his mind in those minutes and she knew Max was not even present in his body. He was back in the stinking hell of the concentration camps. This was a tragic abstraction that Lia would learn to recognise in the years ahead. She would have to deal with the past, for him as for herself, in ways that would avoid constant heartache. To talk of recent memory, as two old friends should be able to talk, was to bring Tadek back into their everyday talk, back into their company. For Lia, it was too soon. But long-ago memory was still too soon.

Max carried the puppy. He tucked Lia's arm in his as they climbed the steps to the road. He was a big man, and Lia remembered how she was nervous of how big he was when Tadek brought him to the strand. Those two became friends in their first year as medical students. Tadek was tall but slight, a little austere. In those days, Max was the comfortable one, and the one who could afford things. "You always brought the bats and the balls," she reminded him. "Was it rounders we used to play?"

Ted was waiting for them in the old man's limousine.

"You used to call the game mad cricket," Max said as he opened the car door, "and the dogs used to join in."

"Toozy and Silky!" Those two beloved old doggies shared the one little grave in Max's father's garden. "So what is the name of this puppy?"

"My father will give you the pedigree papers and if

you don't like the name, choose one for yourself—
that is what he said."

Lia was enchanted; she was whiffling the puppy's
silky ears. "I haven't owned a little dog for so many
years although I have often longed for one. Do you
think I could call her Silkitoo or is that a bit silly?"

Silkitoo became an instant part of my life. She was
to have a life-span of eleven years, a very special family
pet. She was joined by other little dogs and cats as time
passed and she was always the essential welcoming
hostess. To me, a small dog in the household is
indispensable. That long-ago day, chauffeured on the
Merrion Road, Silkitoo sat between us on the rear seat
as sedately as if she, too, were off to a special dinner.

"Have you been home from Vienna for a long
while, Max?" I had been occupied with Phyllis's
wedding, and the old man had not revealed anything
of his son's movements. Quite obviously this surprise,
including Silkitoo, had been well planned. That was
the way my old friend had always organised events.
He was my most beloved friend in all my life, and after
that day, he would become ever dearer.

"No, not home. I spent three weeks in the hospital
in Paris—the one in which I worked before the war.
Physically, I was not too bad but I needed new glasses
and some dental work. I was in touch with my father
by phone and I am home two days now."

I remembered my Gran used to say, "Now there's a fine young fellow, a massive build of a lad!" She never passed a like remark about Tadek, not even to say how handsome he was. Did she suspect I had given my heart to him? Were there times she feared for me? A Jew and a Catholic. She didn't practise any religion but she knew the traditional Irish way of looking on such an alliance. So the massive build of Max had stood up to the ghastly rigours of the camps. I dared not think, just then, of Tadek's fragile, slender form. I must show joy and pleasure in Max's homecoming. Smiling, I turned to him. "And I thought your father insisted on this dinner for fear I would be upset for Phyllis's departure. It is for your homecoming. How wonderful—but how well he keeps his secrets!"

"We must go first to Terenure," Max said, trying to handle things lightly in tune with the spirit of the occasion. "My father insists on a dinner jacket to match with your lovely dress, and, of course, *he*'ll be dressed up to the nines!" We both knew the old man loved dressing up and living up to an occasion. "I should have guessed," Lia said.

In Terenure, Max's father was waiting in the long drawing-room. And now I cannot write of Lia. In that man's presence I was myself. He was my friend, my father, my fount of wisdom. To stand within the circle of his arms, to lift my head for his kiss, was to know pure love and I had basked in that love for a long, long time. It had become the custom for us to enter directly into a warm embrace; it had been so during all the years when he, and she, waited for Max's return. Now we stood apart as if in deference to Max. Was I to be handed over so soon? Surely not. Was I in my pregnant state still the prize he had once wanted for Max? These quick thoughts vanished. I had perfect trust in this man. I stood in front of him. I said softly, "You did not kiss me?"

"Do you wish me to?" Benign as always.

"Of course." We embraced and I was at peace. I turned to Max. "Since the first day I came here, the day Mrs Vashinsky died, your father has been my guardian angel." They smiled at the fantasy. Perhaps Jews do not have this idea of a guardian angel on one shoulder and a tempter on the other?

"You are smiling, both of you. Now I am not sure if I am thinking theology or mythology." I wanted to see them smiling, both of them, together in this house after the lost years of war. Her dependence on Max's father, and his on her, had rooted during those years when they had grown accustomed to the bitter word "annihilation" and the bitter dread that the two brilliant young doctors, Max and Tadek, had been swallowed up in Nazi Germany. The newspapers of that time were vague and unreal in their reporting.

The instant revelation of world news, so familiar to us today, was totally unknown in 1940. Max's father had never allowed his hope to die. He had made unstinting efforts to get news with a continuous search for contacts and an endless outlay of money on agencies and offices, often resulting in unfulfilled promises. I, weak and needing a man's touch, had given up, believed them dead, and engaged myself to Tony Lloyd.

The Shelbourne had always been the old man's favourite place for dinner, the Hibernian for lunch. To the Shelbourne he took special customers when purchasing or selling a picture or piece of sculpture. He had a unique knowledge of wines and cuisine. He expected the best from the chef, and in those days he was never disappointed. To me, his Shelbourne dinners were memorable feasts, which began when I was eighteen years of age and he booked a room for dinner with all my friends in the Abbey School of Acting. Memorable indeed! In the Dublin of the thirties and forties, we were unaccustomed to the grandeur of the Shelbourne, the glittering chandeliers, the sumptuous food. Were there very rich people in Dublin then? We thought only lords and ladies dined in the Shelbourne.

Walking into this famous hotel on that night of our celebration dinner for Max, I was very proud indeed of my escorts. About the older man, tall and heavily built, there was always an assured air of opulence, in the cut of his clothes, the crisp silver of his hair. Behind that elegance there was learning, wisdom, tolerance. A man to cherish. Max was very dear to me in a different way, and Max too was handsome. He was bearded before beards were popular on younger men. Beards were for grandfathers, or statesmen. Max was thirty-eight then, a big man with a beard and horn-rimmed spectacles. And I? I was wearing a long full dress, bought for Phyllis's wedding which had taken place in Ringsend Church that morning. My hair had been arranged stylishly for the wedding, piled up and caught with Spanish combs, as they were known then. Painting the face was not so much done by young women. In Dublin, a painted woman was a "jade." We used a little glycerine on the lips, and carried little notebooks of powder pages to pat the nose very discreetly. Funny old times when to own a powder compact and a lipstick was considered fast. When Max's father said, "You are a little beauty, Lia!" (he was always full of compliments for me) I preened myself contentedly, but I really did not believe him. He indulged me and I knew it.

They were seated. Max's father was discussing the menu with the waiter and smilingly consulting Lia and Max as to their preferences. Then the aperitifs were brought and they settled back to look on each other in that state of united relaxation which was unknown in all their years of perilous separation.

Max's father placed a hand on Lia's hand and a hand on Max's hand. "At last!" he said. "At last!" Still holding Lia's hand, he added, "I have a special request to make of you, little one. Close friends as we have become, you never address me by name. How do you think of me?"

I had always thought of him as "the old man" because when she was eighteen, he had seemed old. That was twelve years ago, and he seemed much the same now, not older at all. Tonight he looked splendid but I guessed he must not be far off sixty. At that time, sixty was considered to be "getting on."

"From now on, little one, would you please call me Theo? Max does sometimes, and we are three old friends after all, are we not?"

The tone was thus set for the celebration dinner. They chatted easily although they did not talk of anything special or important. Theo Randt had the gift of fluent conversation. He drew Lia out on the subject of Phyllis's wedding. She was able to make them laugh with her descriptions of Mr Daly's speech in praise of marriage and Luigi's response in broken English, prompted and encouraged by the bibulous Daly brothers, interrupted by Mrs Daly's good-humoured sarcastic remarks as she hurried in and out with fresh platters of food. If Max was a little silent, Lia included him in all the smiling glances. She dwelt on the comedy of the hilarious wedding and she said nothing about the tragic memories which were so poignantly part of the Ringsend scene.

Towards the end of their leisurely dinner, Theo asked if Lia would come back to Terenure for a nightcap. "Now that Max is home, you will move to Terenure?" He put it as a question, but of course he saw it as a conclusion. He had arranged to put Gran's old house up for sale, as soon as I could pack up and come to live with him in Terenure. I had promised to do this after Phyllis's wedding to her Italian, Luigi Martelli, when the married couple would go to Siena where Luigi's family were in the hotel business. As for me, I had resigned from the civil service to get married to Tony Lloyd—a wedding that was cancelled. So I was unemployed, not an enviable position in Dublin forty years ago, when every outgoing ship was full of emigrants. Unemployed, pregnant and unmarried, I needed friends and I needed shelter. Yet, suprisingly rebellious instincts were fighting for a hold on independence. At times, it was not easy to keep the social smile in place.

"Lia has promised to come and share our house," Theo was telling Max. "Your room is ready, little one."

"Oh, when may I see it?" It was only right to show

enthusiasm in the face of such graciousness, but I was still uncertain about leaving the house in the city street where I lived alone now that Phyllis was gone. Gran had been gone a long time.

"Tonight, of course," Theo smiled fondly at me, "just as soon as we go home." He went on to describe the pictures I might like. I listened to him amid the muted noise of the other diners, the faint clang of dishes and cutlery, but my mind had fled away from the Shelbourne. It was wrong and disloyal and unfaithful to sit here drinking wine while Tadek was to lie for ever in that awesome mountain graveyard. I was feeling the shadowy pressure within me of Tadek's baby. Only a few weeks ago I had lain with Tadek in an ecstasy of passion. This baby was begotten, this new life that Tadek would never see. I should not be here in an atmosphere of thoughtless festivity. I should be alone in a prison of recollection. I should be fasting and praying, not lightly responding to Theo Randt's plans to raise me up to his level. I was only me and I had sinned and I should make myself suffer. I should have said nothing and settled for the marriage to Tony Lloyd, a marriage into which ecstasy would never come. Oh, no! Oh, no! I had known ecstasy.

Under cover of the linen cloth, I felt Max's hand close over mine. I saw his eyes glisten behind the heavy glasses. As his father spoke to a waiter, Max leaned a little towards me. "Tadek will always be there, Lia. With you, but also with me. Remember his message."

And I was back in the Shelbourne. This sudden fixing of thoughts in the Matra mountains (far away from present company) was to become a very familiar experience, a kind of vision, sometimes misty, sometimes heartbreakingly vivid. Always I had to recall the message he had given to Max: "Tell Lia she is to be happy."

I did not need reminding and yet I did. I could forget and sink into an abyss of desolation—those years were still ahead. And yet I could never forget because Tadek's message went back, back, back into the utter aloneness of childhood. Tadek had nothing and it seemed I had so much. But Tadek had everything and I had nothing. Oh yes, he knew that. "Be happy, Lia. Think of the bright things. Think of the lovely bright home you are going to live in. Think of the great education you are going to be given." With solemn strokes, he brushed my hair each night, repeating the message. "Be happy. That is what I want for you, Lia. You were made for happiness. Remember that, Lia." In Auschwitz he said to Max, "If you get out, and if you find Lia, tell her to be happy. She will remember. I told her long ago in our dark cave."

Now Theo Randt was talking of pictures, "...and

you may prefer some that I have not considered. You will choose tomorrow?"

"Tomorrow I must go to the airport to say a final goodbye to Phyllis and Luigi. I promised them I would."

"Do you think they will be happy together?" Theo enquired. "Won't Siena and the strange language create a lot of problems for her?"

I considered that. "No," I said slowly. "Not for Phyllis. I don't ever remember a time without Phyllis. She was always singing her way through the scrubbing, and the polishing, and the cooking. She would not recognise a problem! Life in Italy is going to be wonderful for Phyllis. She will be mistress after all the years of being servant. I am so happy for her." I touched Theo's face gratefully. "Your wedding flowers in the chapel this morning were the most beautiful I ever saw." I paused and then I used his name with love. "Theo, you are the most generous person on earth! The puzzle for the Dalys for the year will be 'How could a Jew spend his money on Catholic flowers?'"

"Jews do many puzzling things," Theo smiled. "Just so long as you liked the flowers, little one."

They returned to Theo's house in Terenure, and Theo took great pleasure in showing her the room prepared for her. It was grander than any room Lia had ever seen.

"How absolutely lovely!" I exclaimed. "Oh Theo, you have given me two of your favourite paintings! And this gorgeous desk! Why, it is a sitting-room and a bedroom all in one!"

"You like it, little one?"

"I adore it. And what is this?"

Now it was Max's turn. "That is my contribution. It is the very latest thing in dog-basket-bed!"

Lia looked questioningly at Theo.

"But of course," he said, "when the puppy is trained—if you wish it. Max often told me how Silky used sleep on your bed, to Aunt Julia's extreme consternation!" Lia went across the room to Max. "You are a darling," she whispered, and to Theo she said, "But in those days I was a small girl and very lonely at times."

"Do not be lonely tonight," Theo said. "Why not stay and hansel the bed?"

Lia hesitated; it was not easy to refuse. There were so many questions still to be settled, questions not even yet faced. "You will forgive me, both of you, if Max takes me home in a little while?"

Theo was, as ever, gracious. "Then let us go downstairs and have our night-cap. I know exactly what Lia would fancy."

After a time, Theo left them to themselves in the long drawing-room. This was a room I had come to love. It was a room full of treasures, the fruits of Theo's lifetime of collecting. They sat comfortably by a table on which their glasses rested. It had always been Lia's way to wait for Max to talk and an instinct told her that his earlier silences had been reflective, a pondering on the words best to choose. She wondered what response should she give if he had it in his mind to propose marriage.

Up until that night, I had, as it were, left decisions to other people. Was I an agreeable person? One who liked to pass herself off? I wanted to be independent but always ended up by giving in. A change had come over my character; perhaps I was becoming an adult in becoming a bride, in holding a new life in my pliant body. I was beginning to question my passivity, thinking I should fend for myself and stop caring what the world might do to an unmarried woman with an illegitimate child. I almost smiled as the thought caught up with me that, once again, at that very moment, with the notion of a proposal, I was waiting for a man to speak, waiting for a man to solve all my problems, to provide a shelter, money, comfort. Provide a father for the child? Ah Tadek, Tadek, what was I to do?

"Do you love my father, Lia? Love him?"

"You know I do, Max. He is my tower of strength and sometimes he tells me that I am the solace of his spirit. Yes, I have loved him for many years."

"And did you love Tony Lloyd who wanted to marry you?"

This was a question I had asked myself often enough when I accepted Tony's affections. There were times, many times, when Tony was adorable. I would try to be honest and not brush the question diplomatically to one side as I was tempted to do.

"I suppose Tony came into his own when the news came that you had given up hope of finding Tadek and that you—and we—presumed him dead—after Sobibor."

"You loved Lloyd then? Enough to marry him?"

Now I chose the words carefully and slowly, supposing that it was as good a time as any to exorcise Tony Lloyd. It could sound incredible should I say now that indeed his image had very quickly disappeared out of my memory; I could not conjure up the sound of his voice nor the colour of his eyes. I knew he was very good-looking but that impression was all that remained of the original attraction.

"No, I never loved him as I now know love. Nor was there ever any love-making between us. He was deeply, rigorously religious in his Catholic faith and he was not a man to take risks of any sort. He thought highly of his own position in Dublin, among his colleagues and friends. No, I did not love him but I respected him, and perhaps I was depending on that to create love and maybe happiness in the marriage."

"Do you think he loved you?" It seemed that Max had wrought himself up to a cross-examination of the years unknown to him. This was unlike him, I thought, but then, did I really know this man? But I loved him as a brother and as a friend and I would answer.

"In a sentimental way, perhaps. Suitability and mutual attraction perhaps. Respectability weighed with him most of all."

"Did you tell him about Tadek?"

"I never told anyone about Tadek." I caught my breath with pain. "Tadek had forbidden me ever, ever to use his name with mine." My voice almost broke, but the time for tears was not yet. "Tadek never kissed my lips until the night you brought me to him in the partisans' camp. When I was little, I used to ask him to kiss me, and again I asked him when his father died, but he never would. He always said, 'Some day, some day.'"

For a while, Max said nothing and Lia sat back to wait reluctantly, longing to jump up and say something assertively. She never had, and now there were no quick handy words. At last, he drained his glass as if to give himself courage. "More than anything else on earth, I want you to be safe, Lia. I want you to be safe from prying eyes. Safe."

He paused again, and again Lia waited. She too wanted to be safe. That word was comforting.

"Do you remember the night I proposed marriage to you? Out on the Sugar Loaf mountain? The night we came home to hear that England and Germany were at war? The next day I left Dublin to join Tadek in the partisans. Only suppose (and I have thought of it so many times), only suppose that war had been postponed for a few more days, and that I had taken you away—and you wanted me to, don't you remember?—and suppose I was the one who had given you the child? Perhaps a son who would now be eight years old? That night on the mountain, I did not know you had loved Tadek since you yourself were less than eight years old. How could I know? In all the years that Tadek was my friend, I thought that his nature was too cold, too reserved to have much of a warm interest in a woman. There were plenty of easy adventures for both of us, in our student days, in Vienna and in Bucharest, and yes, in the camps. We had our chances and I took mine. To the male, such things are seldom love affairs, more often a vital necessity. In Auschwitz he told me of his love affair with you, his lifelong innocent love affair. I did not, and could not, tell him that you had come to me on the mountainside. When he said your name, he was almost—Lia, I do not mean to hurt you by telling you, he had been tortured—we both thought he would die before morning. I never told him when I had the messages from my father that you were going to marry a man named Tony Lloyd, and I never told him that if I were the one to survive, I would seek you out, married or not."

Max was bent forward, his face in his hands. "Most of all I did not tell him that I had loved you since the first day on Sandymount Stand. I wanted to protect you; you were so small and defenceless."

Still I waited, instincts and emotions jostling inside me, trying to guess at the outcome of all this telling, so unlike the Max of my perception. Was he offering his protective love now? Max raised his head. He took off his glasses with a gesture of weariness and laid them on the table. "You say nothing, Lia?"

"What can I say, Max, that would not make me a suppliant? I must learn to go forward on my own."

"Lia, may I give you a question to think overnight? To sleep on, as they say?"

Lia smiled unwillingly. "A recipe for no sleep at all? Max, hold me in your arms for this question. I feel it is going to be difficult."

Standing, he held her. "When I saw you on the strand today, I knew you were pregnant. My father forbore to tell me. I knew for sure. I could not ask you to marry me, not actually, not physically, although up to that moment, it was my intention, up to that very moment."

He rested his head down against her hair. "The question is, *balibt*, may I offer you my name in marriage?"

Lia stepped back. "Max, I..."

"No, Lia. Please think about it. Please, Lia." He called from the door, "Ted, Miss Lia is ready to go home now."

When Ted set me down at Gran's old house, I thanked him politely. "Please ask Mr Max to wait for my phone call." Ted looked mildly surprised at this formal tone, and I was surprised at myself. "I expect to be busy for a quite a while."

CHAPTER TWO

Phyllis had left Gran's little house in what she used to call apple-pie order, a phrase she had made her own. If I had thought to distract my mind by a frantic attempt at spring-cleaning, I was disappointed; there was very little to do. I washed each cup and plate as I used them. I did not light the range because I never cleaned it and I did not know how. In the evenings, I wrapped a shawl of Gran's around my shoulders. I sat in her chair with a pencil and a notebook, making vague lists and improbable minutes of passing ideas so aimless as to be now mysterious. I had no position, no wages. In those days of the 1940s, if you held down a sound, pensionable job, you stayed with it for life. When you resigned from the civil service, your job was gone for ever. In later years a case was made for widows. I was not even a widow. I was an unmarried pregnant woman, just over thirty years of age.

I wished with all my heart that I could be inspired to know what was best to do for my future and for the child's future. What was best...I knew what was easiest: to do as I had always done, to say very little and go along with what the others thought suitable for me. I knew they cared for me. I knew they had my interests in high regard. Money would be taken into consideration, and that was so important. On the note-book I wrote the magic letters *£sd, £sd, £sd,* which is how we referred to money in those days. Guiltily, I had taken money from the dwindling hoard in the Beckers' caddy which Phyllis had left for me, and gone out to the airport in a taxi. Saying goodbye to Phyllis was not easy but she refused to let it be sad. All the Dalys were there, their numbers swollen by more and more children and in-laws. Phyllis was radiant and very smart in her going-away outfit.

"We never got to bed at all! We sang all night! Poor old Luigi is buggered!" It was Phyllis's chosen word for all occasions, as far back as Lia could remember. If the word had a nefarious meaning, Phyllis was quite unaware of it. "Now, Lovey, you promised to come out to Siena the minute we are settled in."

"You should sleep on the plane, Phyllis. Better look lively for your mother-in-law!" She roared with laughter. This future mother-in-law had been the subject of joking speculation between us for weeks before the wedding day.

"Sure, Lovey, we are only going to Torquay, stopping over in London. A first cousin of Luigi's has a hotel in Torquay, and Luigi wants to see it and compare it with ours."

Ours! I smiled to hear that. As only Phyllis could, she had moved in and taken over long before she had even seen Siena and Luigi's *albergo*. *La madre,* the *albergo, la famiglia,* the *ristorante,* all would be under Phyllis's efficient hands within the week. A piano would be installed and Phyllis would be having singsongs. I hugged her fondly. "Drop a line—your usual postcard—to let me know your news. Now be sure to, Phyllis, when you have a spare minute. And I will write regularly."

Surrounded as they were by clamorous Dalys, it would have been impossible for Lia to whisper confidentially and Phyllis would have been troubled. In Phyllis's code Catholics and Jews never mixed in Ireland. She had always referred to Mr Randt as the "old Jewman" as if he were a rag-and-bone merchant. Why Lia's friend, the old Jewman, had Ringsend Church decorated with expensive flowers for Phyllis's wedding would have prompted discussion for many a day if Mr Daly had not come up with the simple explanation that "the money involved was the same as Catholic indulgences: the old Jewman was laying up riches in Heaven to save his soul." Lia had been fond of Mr Daly ever since she was taken in her pram for the quick trip home on Phyllis's day off from the shop in Ringsend. Mr Daly played the piano in the pit of the Azem, a little picture-house in Sandymount. In better times, Mr Daly would have risen to become a musician, but, with eleven children to feed, the piano-playing in the Azem and at weddings and parties kept the wolf off their backs. The Dalys used phrases as if they originated them and Mr Daly had passed on his gift of music to all the family. So Lia pretended to agree with him about the Jewman's hidden motives and saved the story for Theo who would be much amused.

It was just as well that I had much else to worry about. Phyllis's going out of the everyday scene left a great loneliness which I had to push to one side as I tried to concentrate on the immediate question of what was best to do. Each day, I counted out the money and bought milk and some biscuits—not in packets then but by weight. There were things still in the cupboard like tea and sugar and flour. Soon I would have to cook properly for the baby's sake. I persuaded myself that I was not full of self-pity, but that indeed I was developing pride and solitary independence, that it was well known such qualities grew in fasting and solitude.

I find it written in the little notebook, hoarded like everything I ever had: "There were hermits and holy women who survived in the desert on corn husks, lived alone and grew in sanctity." And after that I wrote, "An apple, washing powder, more milk, my father's stock bonds. Buy a newspaper. There are no jobs in the paper. Should you see a doctor even if you feel fine?"

Phyllis had made a sort of patio garden in the gloomy yard with some stone flags and a few veronica bushes. She had bought a small nondescript statue which she claimed to be St Anne and she had constructed a little altar with red bricks. Children used to skip in the street outside, keeping time with an old Dublin jingle:

Holy Saint Anne, send me a man,
With buckets of money, as soon as you can.

Occasionally, Phyllis would put a little bouquet of flowers in a vase on the altar. Was that in the month of May? Maybe Luigi was the answer to Phyllis's devotion. The sun never shone on this patio; it was overshadowed by an old derelict warehouse. For me it was a cold place, for grieving not for hopeful praying. When tears threatened to break, I went out into this patio as if to the graveyard in the Matra mountains. I would never be in that place again. I pictured the camp broken up, the huge gun dismantled, the gates of the graveyard locked for ever against intruders. The tangled windswept trees would grow down over Tadek's grave and in a year from now no one would find a way up the steep rocks to look at the once-white markers with the names inscribed. I had stood by while Max inscribed the words *Tadek Vashinsky*, and the date. I wanted to add my name but strangely, even then, only dead names were safe. There is a Victorian saying: "She cried to her heart's content," and I suppose that is what I did. Desperation had to create a place of mourning, and that poor patio was mine.

In his wisdom, Theo gave me time. There were public phones in the GPO, five minutes' walk away, but I did not phone the house in Terenure. Then, one sunny morning, I saw the big car drive into Creighton Street. When I opened the door, Ted was there with Silkitoo in her basket and behind him stood Theo, beaming with kindness. In our lowest days during the war, he had remained optimistic. He brought with him a spirit of good cheer. The perky little dog in the basket was guaranteed to bring a smile to Lia's face, a certain guarantee! For my friend there were no icicles...I put my arms high up around Theo's neck, I clung to him and we kissed on each other's cheek. Long ago, that kind of kiss was considered "foreign" and in Dublin, kisses were exchanged only between lovers and then, only in secret. Do I remember a girl being arrested for kissing her fellow in a Dublin street? In 1948?

Ted carried in the basket and a selection of little pots full of puppy food. "See!" he said. "This little girl has quite an appetite! She is twelve weeks old. She likes the basket and this rug, and this is the towel Shanlee sent for her."

Theo said, "She answers now to Silkitoo, although they were calling her something else in the beginning."

I held the little doggy on my lap. We took to each other immediately and from that moment she was undisputed queen. "Will Shanlee be lonely now?" I asked Ted.

"Ah no, Miss Lia," Ted smiled. "She has the two cats." Shanlee was Ted's wife. They had looked after Theo Randt since his wife died when Max was only two. Max always spoke of Shanlee with the utmost affection. She had been a mother to him. She and Ted had lost all their family in a pogrom when their village was set on fire. As in the case of the Vashinskys, Ted had hoped to get to the United States but the money was finished in London or Liverpool, and they managed to go as far as Dublin when the First World War started.

"Will you make coffee for me, Lia? See I have brought the coffee I like. We will talk a while the same as we did when your gran made the coffee. Ted will come back for me when it is four o'clock. Is that good with you?"

I remember I clutched my new spirit close to me. I made a decision when I walked on the strand and Max's finding me there must be regarded as a diversion, nothing more. The time had come to stop depending, stop clinging, stop looking over my shoulder, most of all, stop weeping futile tears. I had told myself to go forward into a future, even if I had not planned that future. I had my child, Tadek's precious gift to me. My life would not be for sharing.

"Lia, when I see that stubborn little thrust of your lips, my poor old heart sinks to the depths. You have been my dear child for so many years now that I cannot bear to lose you."

So well he knew. He was reading my independent thoughts. I put my hands in his. "You will never lose me, darling Theo. You are my dearest friend, my only friend. I owe you all I hold dear and had to keep secret for so long! Don't you know I love only you in the world?"

"Ah yes, I know." Theo's voice was tender. "I know. I feel your love when I am with you; your eyes so often sparkle love at me and I am so grateful. But, little one, you love your idea of independence more, and this is clouding your vision. You forget, too, that I worry. Even today when I see how this district is deteriorating, dangerously deteriorating, my child."

"But I have lived here so many years, Theo—the old neighbours have always been the same. You know that. They are protective; they watch out for me. And I own this house now and the rates are so cheap—a roof over my head!" Now I smiled for him. He was the one who had organised this roof when he arranged for my gran to sign the house over to me. Surely my security was here if all else failed. "And I will get a job, too!" I told him.

"Lia, you are making me cross. How will you get a job and look after the baby? And you do not need the money from a job. The arrangement I made with Phyllis is now in your name in the bank in College Green. No, Lia, allow me to continue. I *am* responsible. Yes, I am. If I had not insisted on your coming to Vienna with me you would be safely married to Tony Lloyd. He is a wealthy man and there is no doubt he loved you, valued you. He pursued you for years."

I came closer to Theo. "You never wanted me to marry Tony Lloyd. Now I believe I would not have turned up at the church…Go on, Theo, smile at me." Then I caught my breath. "If I had not gone with you, I would never have known, never have guessed…"I bit back the sob in my throat; Theo had endured enough of my tears and if I began to cry again, he would know how weak was this resolve on independence.

Now Theo was telling me his own thoughts. "I cannot deny that I had hoped, not knowing your secrets although I was sure I was in your confidence, and seeing your uncertainty about Mr Lloyd…Yes, Lia, I had hoped you would find happiness with my son, Max. I did not, and I presume he did not, know the full story."

"That story goes back too far for telling and I had despaired of the happy-ever-after long before I met Tony Lloyd."

"And Max?"

"Now you make me feel guilty, Theo."

"So he was the mutual friend? The bystander? He was going to come today to say goodbye." This surprised me. "But, Theo, Max is only now home with you. Surely he needs rest and relaxation?"

"He may find it in San Francisco," Theo said heavily. "He is going away tonight, first to Paris to collect papers and books, then to friends in America. He needs counselling, treatment, psychiatric help. He is tormented by nightmares, fierce headaches, tension."

"I thought, or I hoped, he had come out of the war almost unscathed. In the mountains he was so firm, so in command—so strong."

"He had to be." Theo's face and his voice were very sad. "No one who was in the camps will be unscathed. There have been already many suicides by those who could not handle freedom. Few will fully recover the health of the mind; fewer still will get back the prestige or the position enjoyed before the camps. The word "holocaust" is being used. Millions have disappeared, gone out of all knowledge."

"Will Max...?" I asked shakily.

Theo gave me that benign look on which I had learned to depend. "You and he are in much the same frame. I can see in you the same bitter resentment for lost causes. You have been crying, little one. Men do not cry easily."

"Theo," I asked, "if I had..."

"No, you both need time. He is not equal to demanding what his heart would plead for, and you have the baby. Without meaning to, you would shut him out. The last case would be worse than the first. Do you understand? Talk to me, Lia, about your day in this place."

So I talked, although it was probable that he had figured out for himself why I had taken refuge away from the luxury of his house in Terenure. In the first couple of months after we came back to Dublin, there was Phyllis to consider. She knew nothing of Tadek, his name was not uttered since I was six years of age. She never suspected my pregnancy; that would be the very last thought ever to come into her head. And if it had she would have abandoned Luigi to look after Lovey. That was certain. Her day of happiness had come. I entered into all her plans and I was careful not to let a tear stain my pillow for fear of her eagle eye in all household matters. Now she was gone. I could put on widow's weeds and mourn my dead.

Theo seemed to understand my need to cling to the old house. "I miss your gran in this kitchen," he said. "She was a comfortable little body."

And finally we compromised. He would give me another little while. On Thursday he would come again to see me. Meanwhile I could be alone but there must be no nonsense about money. "Here is your bank-book and your cheque-book. If you have no facility for cooking apart from the range, then please, Lia, go out and get a meal. And, as we are on the subject, the range is the only heat here and soon the weather will be cold. So that should determine your stay. Besides which, I am putting this house on the market." I never felt he was ordering me around, that was always his manner: the decisive words accompanied by the warm-hearted gesture. I think of him now on every hour and more often than that. Theo Randt had a quality of graciousness unsurpassed by anyone I have ever met.

I had been given time to shut out the world, to hold off the capitulation of my heroic (as I saw it) effort to be self-reliant. Deep down and a little way off, I could see the end in sight. Sometimes, the stray thought has come: would I have made a life on my own? Was I greatly influenced by the remembrance of Tadek telling me to go for happiness? Alone in Creighton Street, the choice, the future, was mine. In later years, the choice was bound in with others, but should I despise myself for making happiness the golden rule? There is an Irish proverb which says that nature comes out through the eyes of the cat. There is, too, a maxim of Theo's which I have pondered on many times: We come into the world with a certain capacity, and that exact capacity limits all contrary tendencies. Illimitability is one of the words that does not exist. There are others.

In Phyllis's patio, I was still very close to the Matra mountains. I could still feel Tadek in the air about me. In my bed each night I was free to let my imagination recapture the enchantment of his passionate caresses. I was able to touch his face, his hair, the slender lines of his beloved body. I could feel his hands finding me as they did on the night of our marriage. I sensed again the thrusting fulfilment of our intercourse. I could murmur his voice against the pillow: Tadek, Tadek. I knew very well that if I should leave here, and I knew I had to leave, that no poor ghost would come to the magnificent house in Terenure. It was then that I first began to answer myself in Tadek's message: But you told me to be happy, Tadek. You had a reason for telling me. You guessed, because you knew so much about me, all the tales I repeated to you about the things I heard...when I was the small child you befriended...things my gran used to say about Mama...poor Marie, she needs a strong man; she is only a weak woman. I really want to go on on my own, Tadek, so that no one will ever come between us. But you told me to be happy. You even told Max to tell me that. And their idea of my happiness is to take me into their home. I know they care for me, but, Tadek, will I lose you? Will I lose this closeness?

I took Silkitoo to bed with me of course, and perhaps her warm little body at my feet helped as the nights went by. One morning I found myself thinking about a future with the baby. I began to look towards Christmas and to imagine the face of a child under a Christmas tree. I was wondering if Silkitoo would be jealous. As I walked along the Liffey dock wall with Silkitoo on the lead I could picture myself with a pram and a dog.

When Theo came he commented on what he called a brighter face, a lighter voice.

"I have heard from Max in San Francisco," he told me. "We talk on the telephone."

"How is he?" I asked.

"He was surprised that I had not moved you out of Creighton Street. He assured me that you would come to live in Terenure now you know he is not there."

While I wondered how he could be so sure, I also knew it was becoming inevitable. There had been some drunken fellows in the street late at night and they had shouted noisy curses in a way that was frightening. This had never happened in Creighton Street before.

"You have seen your room, Lia, and you liked it. Now I have the adjoining room ready for the baby. There is a door between the two rooms and I have had it made into a glass door. It is stained glass, the picture is of the sheep and Bo Peep."

Now I laughed at him. "And will you change it into Humpty Dumpty if we have a baby boy?"

"Oh no," he said with mock seriousness, "Humpty Dumpty is too ugly. Besides we are going to have a little baby girl. I have read the signs!"

"Oh Theo, you are too good. You will spoil me with so much kindness."

"Sheer selfishness on my part, little one—although not so little as you once were!"

"Yes, I'm dreadful, aren't I?" He took me up into his arms and hugged me lightly.

"Come soon, child. I cannot do without you. Have I not told you often? You are the solace of my spirit."

"Theo, do not be hurt when I say that after the baby, some time after, I should try to rent a little place of my own." I showed him the stock bonds which Gran had hidden away. "These papers of my father—could you look at them? They are all I got from my mother's will. My stepfather contested the will and the money all went on litigation. Gran kept back these papers and they have always been here among her things."

Theo took the envelope and examined the flimsy pages. "They look like old bonds or share certificates," he said. "I will bring them to my solicitor and have him contact this name on the envelope: Montgomery. Do you know him?"

"He was the solicitor to whom my gran applied for money for my school fees, but that was years and years ago. He looked very old then."

"We will see," he said. Then he smiled at me. "This idea of a little place of your own? I think that is good. But, Lia, until after the baby, you will give me the pleasure of being responsible?"

"I am so lucky to have your friendship," I told him and at the same time, I was deploring how my vaulted notion of independence was being neatly set aside, as much by myself as by Theo.

"I will look out for houses in due time," he said, "and of course this little place will fetch something. Timing is important. Now the Government wants everyone out of the city. These slums will be condemned. If we could hang on for thirty years, the city will again be populated. All over the world, this has happened. Old cities wear out and old citizens take to the hills. But young, up-coming citizens revalue the city and rebuild it for young living. It is a natural cycle.

But with this old house of Gran's we cannot wait thirty years; there could be compulsory acquisition."

CHAPTER THREE

In all the stories in all the world there is one special name for that superlative period in a life when the elements come together like first love in a long hot summer: Nirvana, Valhalla, Shangri-la, Elysium, Camelot. In Ireland, the name is *Tír na nÓg*: the land of eternal youth, a paradise where the sun shines in all seasons and no one grows older even by a day. Theo Randt now created *Tír na nÓg* for Lia, and I must set those days down because not one of them has ever been forgotten.

It had long been Theo's wish that Lia should come to live with him in the big house in Terenure—preparatory to her marriage to his son, Max, of course. In the partisans' camp he had come quickly to realise that Lia had never been in love with Max but, always since childhood, in love with Max's close friend, Tadek. In the adolescent years, Max had told his father all about this young girl, Lia, as if he, Max, was Lia's special friend, the "one." During the long years of waiting for the war to end when Lia had come to his house and shared his vigil, Theo had, happily enough, believed that Max would find comfort with Lia or at least a chance of such comfort. When Tadek died, that hope had revived. In the camp, Lia had told Theo that Tadek had forbidden her ever to reveal her love, nor even to couple their names because of his being a Jew and for ethical reasons. "But you know," Lia had said sadly, "Tadek never used words of love until I came here. I often wondered if it was all in my own mind—a childish illusion impossible to forget." In the camp, Theo saw no illusion in the very adult passion Lia found for Tadek. A new lustre was shining out of her skin, glowing in her eyes, increasing her beauty every day. Theo saw in Max the dejection and the brave cover-up in Lia's presence. Now it was in Theo Randt's power to woo Lia for his son, to win her over to his own very powerful way of providing compensation, contented compensation if he could. Theo adored Lia but there were other considerations to be taken into account. To Tadek there was an immense obligation: Max owed his life to Tadek in the concentration camp of Auschwitz. That story had yet to be told. Let there be no talk of obligation, let Lia be loved simply because she was Lia. She must not be there to know the pathos of leaving Gran's old house. Whisk her away for a drive in the Wicklow Mountains and with kindly diplomacy install her belongings in her new bedroom in Terenure. Creighton Street must disappear for ever into the past.

"You will allow me to accompany you to the gynaecologist, my dear? I have made the necessary telephone call. He recommends a nursing home in Hatch Street. It seems a suitable street in which to give birth." Theo liked to try out a little joke at times, and later, he was amused to hear that this excellent nursing home was known to its patronesses as "the Hatch." He was relieved to have the doctor and the date and the place all established. Every two weeks we visited the doctor in Fitzwilliam Square and I responded to the name of Mrs Randt. Theo was not a man to do things by halves. I simply accepted that it was best to be a married woman for the present time. Every day Ted drove us to the Phoenix Park, a place familiar to me since schooldays, and we walked sedately under the autumn trees with Silkitoo on the lead. Ted stayed in the car reading his newspaper. Now, I remember that wives, largely expectant, were taken out by their husbands for short exercise walks after twilight. Was there a reluctant modesty in pregnancy, even respectable pregnancy? A kind of shame? Did they go walking at other times, apart from going to church? I recall being embarrassed when we walked through the National Gallery for fear of meeting an acquaintance of Theo's. I warned him that I would walk on ahead as if I were a stranger. "If you do," he smiled, "I shall call after you in an aggrieved voice. Any old dealer I might happen to meet would be mad with jealousy to see me with a beautiful woman half my age!"

He was an arrant flatterer but how I wish that we were strolling through Dublin today and I had in my pocket one of those little gadgets to record his words. He was never boring and he knew simply everything. Standing outside Trinity College, he was telling me the story of Goldsmith: "Did you know that he drank as much as twenty-three cups of tea at a sitting?" A little crowd gathered, assuming him to be an eminent professor from the college. He was very elated to attract an audience, but pretended not to notice. Afterwards, he told Ted that a woman selling apples had shouted out, "Jeez, will ya listen to the nob spouting!" That was so many years ago that you could count the number of people walking down O'Connell Street.

Quite often we went out to dinner in the evening, not always to the Shelbourne. Dublin was still a poor city. There was not a constant renewal of restaurants as there is today but if Theo read of a new place, he would insist we try it. Often we had supper after the theatre for a change. Then we could dissect the play and bisect the actors. Our shopping expeditions were most enjoyable. We were buying for the coming baby. Unlike today when babies have cosy stretchies, there were vests and nightdresses and day dresses to be bought—the same for a baby boy as for a baby girl. We bought dozens of matinée jackets and lacy shawls, far more than one baby would need. "Everything," Theo ordained, "everything, but everything, must be white— pure white. No pink! No blue! As for cream—banish the thought! Some smocking but no fiddly borders!" Cups of coffee in Bewley's or Roberts Roberts were an essential break in a morning's shopping. I often got tired before he did. The buying of the cot, the peram- bulator, the high chair, were events especially inter- esting to him, but again no coloured wood, no cheap transferred figures. "We will supply all the spectacle this baby will require in the surrounding area."

I often found myself looking and listening and hoping to God that the forthcoming child, for Theo's sake, would not be a little philistine rossy who hated great art and adored Tom and Jerry, nor a tough little barbarian who thought only of football and thumping other kids. I kept those ideas to myself. They were the relics of a child who longed to run out in South Lotts Road and play with the children called (by my mama) the "Ringsend gurriers." I had moved up in the world and I had better learn to adapt. I was pliable enough and I needed Theo. The gurriers, along with all the other Ringsend characters, were for the dungeons of memory.

Since Max had gone away he and his father talked on the telephone every week. For Lia there was the regular picture postcard. I look at them now. There are several of Sausalito, as if he did not look at the name but chose a scenic sunny place. The message on each card is the same: Keep well. Keep happy. I miss you. I think of you. Then one day there came a letter, from San Francisco, for Lia. It was from Max. Now I knew his way of writing. Unsure if I wanted to open it in the hall where Theo was glancing through the post, I carried the letter up to my room. I felt Theo's eyes following me on the stairs. He and I had come to the sharing of each small event of every day. I was aware of climbing the stairs slowly. I was seven months into my pregnancy and Theo was, more than ever, my constant guardian angel.

I had had a letter, just one, from Max when he was studying in Vienna. The letter was about the deaths of our two little dogs, Toozy and Silky. I cried that day, and my gran made much ado about comforting me. I cried for the little dogs but I cried more because the letter was not from Tadek. From Tadek I had never had a letter, never even one. This letter, from Max in San Francisco, I opened slowly, and I spread out the page, gazing at it without reading it. I thought I had not been expecting a letter from Max but now I knew I had been waiting for one. Not consciously waiting, but deep within there was an instinctual reaction to this letter. I tried to analyse this reaction before I began to read. Far back, out of her little theatre history came the answer: Lia had been waiting for the cue.

I would receive many beautiful letters from Max and I must not record them all in this story. This one, this very special first letter, I am going to copy out. It is not a revelation of the woman, Lia, rather does it tell everything about the man who wrote it.

Lia, where to begin?

I love your face because it is the face of a beautiful woman.

I love you when you smile because I must smile too.

I love you when you frown because I can forestall the question.

I love your eyes, I love your hair, I love the colour of your skin.

I love your forehead, it gives away the secret of your quiet love of learning.

I love your grace when you sit into a chair, your fingers linked and still.

I love your unconquerable air when you know you are giving in...amiably giving in.

I love your sincerity, I love your courtesy, I love your vitality.

I love your cleanliness and the sweet fragrance of you.

I love and even love the more because we share it,
your love of small dogs.
I love you for always tolerating me.
Most of all I love you because I have always loved
you and I cannot help but love you.

I know I read this letter many times. I know I folded it carefully, putting it back into the envelope, taking it out very gently, reading it again and again. If I did not yet desire the writer, with all my heart I desired to be the woman so loved by this man.

Holding the letter against my blouse, I went down the stairs to Theo's study. He would be there reading the morning newspaper. I said, "Max will come home soon."

"Does he tell you this in the letter?" Theo asked.

"No," but my voice was not negative. The "no" floated across the room as light as air.

"Ah!" Theo said softly and he smiled. I have sought for adjectives, all my life, to describe Theo's smile. It was a benign smile which must mean that the smile blessed me. His smile was much more than a blessing. His smile loved, it courted, it responded. His smile was entrancing, inviting. His smile always drew me into his arms.

Was it the night of that same day when Max telephoned? Theo handed the receiver to me. He left me alone to answer.

"How are you, Lia?"

"I am still glowing from all the beautiful things you wrote in your letter. Thank you a thousand times, Max." There was a little silence. Perhaps he waited for a word of love in return? "How are you? Max, please tell me."

"More settled, I think. Lia, did you think about my question? The question you were to sleep on?" Again, he paused. She could almost hear his thoughts sifting one against the other. Which words to say?

"Lia, we have both had time to think. I want you to know that while I am slow to push thoughts into actions, the reins are in your hands." Then only the humm of the long-distance wire. "Lia?"

She felt like a beggar at the gates. She longed to call out, Yes, yes, save me, save me. Equally she felt like a proud woman, slamming the gates, pridefully telling the world that she could take care of Tadek's child, without help from anyone. But she knew she could not. In that year of 1948, in Ireland, a woman with an illegitimate child had nowhere to turn. Oh yes, she had time to think of Max's question, and looming over all her thoughts was another question: Jew and Catholic? How deep was her faith, and even if she rejected her faith, would the Jewish community in Dublin reject her and her child? Would they reject Max as an apostate? Theo Randt, who talked to her about everything under the sun, had never discussed this problem. Tadek had sown the seed of doubt in her mind when he said, and said so arrogantly, "I am a Jew. Jews are set apart." Did he mean only in Ireland? In their bed, in the camp, Tadek told her of his plan to live in America where, he said, their different religions would not count against them. In Dublin everyone knew everyone.

"Perhaps," Lia said gently into the telephone, "you had better come home and we can talk about religion?"

If Max could be angry with her, he was angry now. His voice was tightly controlled when he said, "For my part, to hell with religion. Cause of all the trouble in the world. But yes, I will come home. You may finally decide against my question, but I will apply for the civil licence. It can be cancelled. Lia, I am putting down the phone."

Of course I could see that he must act out of conscience. He "owed" his friend, the debt would be paid with the life that Tadek had saved for him. I did not know the full story but I knew enough. I read the love-letter many times in the days after the telephone call; it was not only conscience that prompted Max to offer his good name to the fatherless child. I read again and again all the lovely compliments and I read myself into the letter. If I had misgivings, they were never on Max's account but on my own. His letter set a high standard and in due course he came back from San Francisco to ask for the answer, firmly and without hesitation from the deeply sincere Lia who lived in his letter.

Tír na nÓg continued. I was very much the centre of all attention for Max now as for Theo. They spoiled me. Like a fat kitten, I lapped it all up. I gave no further thought to the lonely idea of being an independent woman. Theo left us on our own and there were serious talks that I have not forgotten.

"Your father, Max. He does not go to the synagogue but he observes the sabbath."

"You mean he gives himself a day off. He reads the Book. He meditates. It is good for him."

"I mean he cherishes his being a Jew."

Max said, "We are all conditioned by our earliest years. His were spent in Zamosc. Mine were passed in Ireland in a secular society. Jews in Ireland had a few skirmishes with priests, hardly to be compared with a Russian pogrom. I am not imbued the way my father was, and now his blood is diluted. In Zamosc, the Torah was their daily newspaper, the outside world beyond the ghetto was not affordable. They became immanacled. I met them in the camps."

That day we were driving high up on the Feather Bed in the Dublin mountains. I asked Max to pull over and stop a while. Almost afraid to ask, my voice almost a whisper, I got out the words: "And what about Tadek? Was he not proud to be a Jew?"

Max pushed back the driver's seat. He rolled down the car window, and leaning back against it, he faced around to Lia.

"Yes," he answered slowly, "Tadek is at the centre of my question and not least his Jewishness. In the concentration camps he remained strictly orthodox. At first I saw it as sheer bravado against the Schutzstaffel. There was an element of that, but only an element. He had inherited the true fibre of a Jew. He observed the feasts. He recited the prayers. He could listen to old Jews commenting on the dialectics of some obscure point of Mosaic Law, even as they stripped for the gas chambers. He fought to give them an injection in defiance of the press-gangs, pleading the importance of the dialectical obscurity for his delay. 'Let them have a moment of joy,' he would say. Jews who had been shipped out of eastern Poland had never had joy in their lives anyway. In the fervour of their prayers, in their abandonment to pure study, they were able to forget their previous poverty, their present plight. They were so convinced of the efficacy of their calling on their God in total, absolute belief that they were able to close their ears to German lies. Tadek said it was better so...God was their inevitable goal."

Tadek had never mentioned God when she lay in

his arms murmuring love to him; now Lia waited for Tadek's friend to make up her mind for her, and as she waited, she studied his face against the high light of the mountains. Max was not strikingly Jewish in appearance as Tadek had been nor was he slimly, darkly handsome as Tadek had been. Max was a big man, his beard curled and was clipped closely to his face; he wore heavy horn-rimmed spectacles; the hair on his temples and around his ears was turning to silver. Lia liked his voice, always reluctant, seldom given easily to talk. Lia would always notice the long pauses in the search for the right words. Now his voice was full of pain.

"I had a woman in Vienna and I want to tell you about her. She was a student in the hospital. Lia, you must know that although a man has given his heart to one love, another woman can make his mind churn with desire. Viennese women may have that gift more than other women, I have found French women quite resistible. A woman, I said? She was a girl of nineteen."

It must be a step forward that Max could confide in her. It was difficult for him. It was an effort to go on.

"We had found a small flat and we were living together. I will never be sure but I think she was carrying my child. She had not said and she may have been considering an abortion. Afterwards, I was told by another doctor that she had asked him. He promised to send her to yet another. She did not ask me. She was always light-hearted, no problems. We were making love in our bed when the SS came, breaking down the doors. Her crime was that she was a Jew. We fought them on the staircase. They shot her through the head. She fell six flights into the stone vestibule. I spent three nights in a cell but my Irish passport saved me—on that occasion..." His voice broke, and he turned his head away.

Lia longed to touch him in consolation. She wondered if the girl was beautiful. What was her name? Lia would never know. That tragedy was never to be trivialised by repetition. After a long time gazing out across the furze, Max turned back to Lia. "That was a large part of my reason, that yearning for revenge, my reason for leaving you and my father and joining the partisans. Would you have come to me if I had not gone away?"

"I do not know. I never knew my own mind in those days."

"When my father, in those garbled messages, said you were thinking of marrying, I thought (in my confused ignorance) that you were taking revenge on me."

Oh God, Lia thought, we will never get rid of Tony!

"But you were not, were you, Lia?"

"Poor old Tony Lloyd! I used him shamefully as a

background in a make-believe world. I was afraid of
turning into a wrinkled old spinster when your father
told me that you and Tadek might be dead—although
he hoped on, I did not."

"So you would have married him if the report of
our deaths had been true? Perhaps I would have
married in Vienna if ..." He stopped, and Lia ended the
sentence for him: "...if she was to become the mother
of your child?"

"No," he said decisively, "not even then. Lia, have
I a chance at all? You will marry me, won't you? Under
the circumstances..." he added shyly.

Lia had made her choice when she had seen the tear
slip out from under the frame of his glasses. Whatever
of the best she could give him, he should have. He had
been through enough, and he was offering all he had
left. It would suffice. And all she had left must suffice
for him.

"Max, would you consider a real marriage, not a
makeshift under-the-circumstances sort of a marriage?"

"But Lia, what about the religion? Does that worry
you?"

"Could we talk about that another time? Just now
could we talk about loving each other and setting a
date? You have brought up Tony Lloyd several times.
It is a sort of unfaithful thing about me that you find
it hard to live with. Why?"

"Because I suffered agonies of jealousy. Never about Tadek but about this unknown hero. My father said this fellow was the handsomest man in Dublin. You went with him for years."

"Probably for that very reason, that he was so good-looking. It is easy to look kindly on good looks—you find it easy too, Max. But there were times I hated him for being a bigot. And, let me be honest as you have been, there were times when I wondered what it would be like to go to bed with him, and I never had the wish to. Neither did he ever suggest bed. He was, and I have said this before, the most rigidly, religiously, puritanical kind of Catholic. He even had what he termed his own special confessor, a Benedictine monk in Limerick. Most of the many years were spent evading setting the wedding date. Is that what we are doing now? Max, I am going to sing a little song for you to cheer you up. Phyllis used to sing this song and bang it out on the piano in the room above the shop in Ringsend, years and years ago, and after this, never mention Tony Lloyd again. Promise?"

The bridegroom at the church turned up.
His ma turned up and his da turned up.
His sister Gert and his brother Bert
And a parson in a long white shirt turned up.
But never a bride in white, a lovely sight.
A fellow on a trike brought a telegram that read:

She didn'

And you wou

With her toes tu

Years of singing-al... with ... had made ... tune-perfect; the words w... ... mixed up.

Now Max was laughing, rea... laughing for the ... time in ages. That was how we de... ... ...d. No down-on-the-knees proposal bu... in a big ... g and kiss out on the Feather Bed in Theo's ca... ...erwards we drove on out to Enniskerry to the little hotel where we had the first candle-lit dinner, our first proposal. I made sure to be the delighted (and delightful) fiancée. We talked non-stop of our plans. Max opened up about the time he had spent in San Francisco, the people he had met, the chances of taking an in-service course in the psychiatric clinic there, maybe next year when the baby would be old enough to travel. When the barriers were down, we were rapidly becoming great friends. In his eyes, I could see the joy: we had a future with each other, we were in accord.

But all the repeated references to Tony Lloyd had whipped up my previous terms of secrecy. Tony had raped Francesca and there was a child. I had run away from Tony into the arms of Burton only to find that my beloved Laelia, sister of Tadek, had Burton's child.

CHAPTER FOUR

A s on that other night long ago, Max and Lia
stood in the hotel garden to admire the full
moon shining on the slopes of the mountain. She said,
"I was never here in wintertime before. So many
glittering stars!"

"Would it be too cold for you if we drove up the old
Sugar Loaf road, *balibt*? I have often recalled that night
and wanted it to happen all over again. Would it be
too cold?"

And Lia said, "It is not cold at all. I, too, remember
that night."

When they were driving, Lia was going over the
memories for Max, and it came to her mind that this
talk was all too similar to the reminiscing talk with
Tadek in their marriage bed, in the long afternoons
when he was still well enough to join with her in
remembering. Ah well, now the talk was for Max who
had been an essential partner in the long ago days,
anyway.

"You always brought some nice things for us to
eat," she told him. "Vimto and twopenny packets of

Polo biscuits. Tadek and Laelia never had money for treats."

"Ah, Laelia." Max said. "I wonder what happened to Laelia—in her life, I mean. I know she is the star of the Metropolitan. In San Francisco, I read about her every day—but not much personal detail."

Lia had an idea that Theo would have told Max of Burton's role in Laelia's life in London. Of course, that might have involved Lia's name. A surge of gratitude lifted Lia's heart that Max had never heard of Burton. All her days, she had to remember so many secrets, hers and others.

Max pulled over the car. They stood out on the grassy path and leaning on the old remembered gate, they stared up at the Sugar Loaf peak.

"From here we used to trek up to the top, the two little dogs panting as if they would expire. Especially poor old Toozy." Max took a rug out of the car and wrapped it around Lia. "There!"

"It was always summer when we were young, wasn't it, Max? And you were the one whose generosity made our summers possible."

Max laughed softly. "And I was the one who used to cringe because I was the one with the rich father!"

Max held the rug about Lia's shoulders. His body was rampant with desire, an impossible desire which must be held in check for many weeks to come. He dare not kiss her although he longed to feel her soft lips against his mouth. Close to her like this, his thoughts spun chaotically out of his control, but he held his hands steady and his body rigid. He had witnessed the coming together of Tadek and Lia at the camp in the Matra mountains. He had seen the adoration in their eyes as the days went slowly by in the consummation of their love, their lifelong love. Beside Tadek's grave, he had held a desolate Lia in his arms. He let no one suspect the desolation in his own heart for the tragic death of his beloved friend and for the loss of this woman with whom he had fallen in love all over again. Lia had asked him if it was possible that she could be pregnant, and he had told her that miracles do happen. And all the time he was trying to convince himself that it was impossible for a baby to have been conceived. Tadek's heart was sustained by a mixture of drugs which would undoubtedly have side-effects. And Lia was so alone in the world that the temptation could be there for her to protect herself by marrying the man in Dublin to whom she was engaged. His father assured him that Lia was of greater strength than that. He had discouraged him from approaching Lia. Time was all-important. Lia would come around. "She has a practical streak," his father said. Max said he had never noticed it.

Now Max said, "I love you, Lia."

"Oh thank you, Max. You are a darling. I need so very much to be loved and loved and loved. That need can so easily betray me. Your father has rescued me from indulging that need..." Lia stopped short. Where would that revelation lead her?

"I am jealous of him, too. You love him more?"

"In a way, yes. I love him because he loves so...so...so decorously. You know? And you know all his virtues: he is so wise and so kind and so patient. He welcomes me each time he sees me. He tells me that I am the solace of his spirit. Oh yes, I love him."

"And me?" After that litany to his father, Max was humble. "I hope you will never have cause to regret...regret throwing in your lot with mine." Max was a little afraid of the too-intense, the too-dramatic.

"I loved you when you kissed me that day on the strand. I loved the feel of your beard on my lips."

Lia turned around in his arms, offering her face for his kiss. He whispered, "I must be careful of you, *balibt*." Lia understood; she whispered back, "But our time will come?"

"Our time will come, *balibt*," Max repeated fervently.

"You know, darling Max, the problem in my mind for weeks past? If I love you, and I wanted to, it would diminish my love for Tadek. All this stuff about Tony Lloyd meant nothing. Tadek was the only person you had to care about and you solved my problem in the beautiful letter. You knew you would, didn't you?"

Max did not know what she meant but he accepted the lifeline. "So do you think you could tell me now?" Lia wanted to get used to the words of love in a different language, in Max's language. She saw the words as rungs in the ladder towards their union. She had read herself into the idyllic Lia in Max's love-letter. She would talk herself into complete acceptance of loving Max, and now she understood what loving meant.

"I love you and I have loved you since I stopped being afraid of you when Tadek brought you to Sandymount. You were so huge, my gran always admired you, and I felt so inadequate with the cricket ball and all that."

Max was smiling broadly. "You made up for dropping the ball by all the shrieks you let out of you!"

"At least, I am bigger now?" Lia asked invitingly, and drawing his arms down to her rotundity.

"And more lovely every day," Max said. "Lia, I have a plan for the next six weeks. Get into the car. We must head for home. Do not mention to Theo that we went up the Sugar Loaf. He is like a mother hen where you are concerned. I want to see his face when we tell him our news!"

I leaned against his shoulder as we drove along. I wanted to be happy. I was determined to be happy. I watched every word. I would be the Lia he dreamed of.

Max's old memories had revived in our talk on the Sugar Loaf. "I remember driving along this very road with your gran sitting beside me in the old two-seater Citroën. She fed me little pieces of walnut toffee as we whizzed along. We used to have the canvas top down so I could shout back to you and Tadek and the dogs in the press-up seat. Come to think of it, your gran can't have liked all that windy gale rushing around!"

"She loved it," Lia said. "You were her favourite. She never forgot you." It was great to share my gran with someone who knew her. I never stopped missing her, never.

Theo hoped for definite news each night Max and I returned from an outing. When Max opened the hall-door he would come out into the hall, his face expectant. On that night—oh how well I remember—his eyes lit up with joy. Our clasped hands, our lively looks, told him everything. "A toast!" he said immediately. "This is the night for a toast!" Ted was despatched to the basement to fetch a special bottle, and Shanlee came hurrying with a tray. So quickly did she come, it was as if Theo was stage-managing an event already well rehearsed. Silkitoo emerged sleepily from her basket by the fire, where she had been keeping Theo company. He shared my love of small dogs, as he shared so much else in his wish to please me. "Lia, my dear, come sit here on the couch, by the fire. Oh now, look, Lia's hands are cold. Build up the fire, Max. For Lia, something hot, Shanlee. A hot toddy, Lia? Just a little?"

"She is fine," Max said with a new note of possession in his voice. "I gave her a good dinner."

"And so you should, my son!" and Theo gently rubbed my hands in his. His affectionate regard for my comfort was sweet. We were close on the couch, I rested against him. Afterwards when the toasts were drunk and Shanlee had gone away with the supper tray, Theo stood at the door ready to go upstairs but lingering to look back at us. "You may never know how pleased and happy I am. For all of us, this night is the new beginning. Come here, Lia, one more good-night, the very last good-night of the old days, the very first of the new. Come."

No description has ever fitted the familiar wonder of standing within the circle of Theo's arms, my arms lifted high to clasp him in gratitude, my face waiting to receive his kiss on the left and then on the right and returning my kiss to his face, bent down to mine. We stood always the exact number of seconds for our mutual affection to pass through the circuit holding us as in a vow.

"Goodnight, dearest Theo," Lia said, her voice unwilling to let him go even for a night. When Theo closed the door, the enchantment of the beautiful room was halved. Theo's ambience was Lia's cornerstone in the house.

Max took my hand and drew me down again to the warm couch. "My father is right, you know. We have to make a new beginning. New from this moment. Up to now, there has been only one sure mutual contact between us, and that is Tadek. No, Lia, do not turn away; we must use his name freely, at least until we enter into our own bond. Even then, he will always be with us. He is the father of our child. You will allow me to say, our child? He was dearer to me than a brother. You loved him all your life and I...almost as long. And perhaps he knew that I loved you. He must have observed how I hung on every word when he talked of your childhood in that awful dreary room; he must have noticed the endless questions I asked about you. Maybe he saw my face when we were in his room that first night you were in the camp. Lia, you were so beautiful that night. We had hidden ourselves in fear, for years. Can you imagine our thoughts when we looked on the child we loved, now a gorgeous woman?"

Max was silent for a long time and I was too close to tears to dare any sort of response. I began to hope we could cross all the hurdles tonight. Could I really want to leave the past to take care of itself? Did that mean I was faithless?

"I am not the greatest talker, Lia; you know that. Please help me. You wanted to talk about religion. There are things we both should say. If we do not, they will lie at the back of our minds, each not sure if, or what, the other thinks or knows."

At the back of our minds? All the years that Max had studied psychology in Vienna, all his father's high hopes and how he had seen those hopes threatened by the war and then by Max's involvement with the partisans. There was so much at the back of our minds for Max to sort out.

I took my courage in hands. "Tadek always saw an insurmountable barrier between a Jew and an Irish Catholic. Is there such an immense barrier?"

"Lia, is this our marriage we are talking about?"

"Yes," I said, and I repeated what I had asked. "Max, is there such an immense barrier?"

"There is no ready answer to that," Max said. "Who, of the two partners, would suffer in such an alliance? And what of the children? Into which faith would they be born? Surely there could be conflict."

We were quiet for a while. I felt our bodies were becoming accustomed to sitting side by side. Perhaps our minds were engaged in tunnelling through to an understanding. I longed for an accord in this very special aspect of our lives—this barrier always apparent to Tadek.

"Lia, may I ask you something? It is asking you to tell me something which perhaps I have no right to know."

"Whatever it is," I told him, "I shall answer honestly."

"If Tadek had asked you to marry him, forsaking all faith, all religion, yours and his, for the sake of family harmony—would you have been prepared for that?"

I had known the answer to that question since I was six years of age. If Tadek had lived to marry me, I would have gone through fire for him. That he might live, I would have died. I had practised my religion but it had meant infinitely less than my need to love and be loved.

"Of course," I said. I had not a moment's doubt.

"Lia, that is my position. To marry you, I am prepared to become merely humanist. It is not, for me, a sacrifice. I believe in many things: charity, hope, work, family. Many forms of religion have brought dissension into the world, but that is not a reason I wish to dwell on. Each human has a right of choice, I as well as all the others."

"Are you sure you want to marry me, Max, even though you know all about me? Or maybe you know only the nice things."

"In Auschwitz, when Tadek talked of you, I loved you more, if that is possible, than when you were a small girl of fourteen and your Aunt Julia had to give permission for you to come out to tea, to get into the old Citroën. You surely remember those days? Tadek told me how he taught you to read, how he brushed your curly hair, how he used to light the candle in his room so you would know he could cross the wall. Everything he told me made me love you more." Max's arm came around my shoulder.

"But, Max, you loved me the night we were out on the Sugar Loaf. And that was long before Auschwitz. But loving and marrying? Even with the religion question settled? Are you sure?"

"I am sure, Lia. I want you to be sure. I have a suggestion. May I tell you?" Now he hesitated as he always did when he wanted to choose the exact right words. "I should like...like to—it is an old-fashioned word—I should like to court you for the time up until the baby."

I had the immediate feeling that I wanted to be made safe now. I wanted to be a safely married mother-to-be. What if anything happened to Max in the next few months? What if the Randts changed their minds?

"Are you hesitating, Lia? You are uncertain?"

"I thought we would get married tomorrow!" I whispered. He smiled down at me. "And you would deprive me of sending you roses every day for courtship, of taking you out to dinner? Of buying presents—extravagant useless presents? Of choosing the engagement ring after endless consultation? After all, Lia, all those exciting adventures would be ours alone—mine alone."

Then I knew what he was thinking. With Tadek there had been no courtship. When he should have been courting, he was in the concentration camp. Death had already marked out Tadek's name when he took me to his bed. No roses. No presents. No diamond ring.

"And when would we marry then?" I asked.

"Lia, in your last few weeks before your time. Then Tadek's son will have a father's name."

"You have talked this over with your father?" The question was a gentle one. For years now I had taken all my problems to his father. He was my father, too, and my friend.

"No," Max said, "although he may very well read my mind. I have had this hope growing in my heart since the day in the camp when you came to me in the office there. You remember, Lia? You said you thought you had missed a period."

Now I could smile mistily. "And you told me that miracles can happen."

"I think you did not tell Tadek about the possibility of a miracle?"

"Oh Max, I wanted to. I wanted to share with him. Oh, how I longed to share with him!" The thought was stinging my eyes. "It seemed unfair to tell—his worry—his distress."

"But also his pride, *balibt*." Deep within, Max was glad that Tadek had not been told because Tadek was fully aware of the potency of the drug which kept his failing heart in action. In a normal time and place, Tadek would surely have protected Lia from pregnancy. Her instinct not to tell was good and right.

"On your next visit to the gynaecologist, may I take my father's place? And on all the visits from now on?"

I remember gazing into the flickering firelight as if each flame was taking another piece of my life away up the chimney to scatter it to the stars, the glittering stars we had seen from the Sugar Loaf. This Mrs Randt, or that Mrs Randt, it was one pretence or another pretence. I had left Creighton Street and now that little house had been sold. This was a fact almost more significant than which Mr Randt would accompany Lia to Fitzwilliam Square. Tony had his flat in Fitzwilliam Square. Lia had very good reason to remember that. And Tony and Creighton Street had been suddenly taken by flickering fiery passing time. Office blocks would occupy the old street where Gran's ageing neighbours used take their chairs to the front doors, to sit in the sun and pass the time of day with other neighbours. They took care of each other, those kindly Dubliners, passing on a message, keeping an eye out for strangers. Rarely and seldom do I drive along that quay of memory now, the assault on the emotions is too much. Gran lives always in my heart as surely as on those last days when I mourned for my lost love in the cold patio at the back of her little house. I realised, when I listened to Max's plans for the pleasant passing of the last weeks of my pregnancy, that if I had considered myself as a self-reliant, free, independent woman, able to earn and look after a child, a kind of effective twentieth-century woman— well I was very mistaken. I was like my mother, I needed a man to stand foursquare between me and trouble, between me and the rest of the world.

I should like to make excuses for the timorous creature that was a woman in Ireland fifty years ago. There had been two world wars—two within twenty-five years. The widows of the first war had reared the widows for the second war and, in that span of time, Ireland was struggling to take its place among the nations of the world. Neither war was Ireland's war. Nevertheless Ireland lost two generations of men in what they perhaps thought of as "the fight for freedom." Exactly whose freedom was never clear but there was no argument about that. As Lia saw it, the fight was against the merciless poverty and the spiralling cost of survival for the thousands without employment in the nineteen-forties and into the fifties. The untutored Government had few friends in a world crippled by war. The Irish people entered a new and terrible trend of emigration unknown since the famine a hundred years earlier.

I knew with certainty that I was one of the lucky ones. I had much to be grateful for: I had people to take me into their home, to shelter me from criticism of my plight. These people gave me love and I stand forever in humility before that wondrous gift. Never for a moment have I believed myself worthy of their inestimable generosity...I have never understood what it was in me that they found to love. I have been a recipient and they have been benefactors. Theo was my fount of wisdom, my Ark of the Covenant, since I was eighteen years of age in my first year out of boarding-school. I adored the very proper elegant stance of him. He could hold me in his arms, shower compliments and praise on me, kiss my head, tell me he loved me—all of those things always, without ever any tremor of fear in me that he, or I, would sense the male-female element in both of us. In its proper time, that day would come. Until then, there was a reverential stepping-stone in our relationship. I remember when I was young, I asked him, "How is it that I am more at home in your tradition than in my own?" And he had answered, smiling but serious: "Perhaps, a thousand years ago, my soul was the father of your soul." I hoped, then, that was true because his tradition was Tadek's tradition. When I moved out of Gran's house into the big house in Terenure, I transplanted easily; I had been ready since I was six years old.

So, that night by the fireside, I was able to lay any possible doubt to rest. I was continuing along familiar lines. Tadek had written the script years ago. By his own will he had taken his role away to end in another faraway place. He had left all the cues in place for Lia and many other actors. That is how I saw my part and I have never changed my mind.

I had been listening dreamily to Max, my imagination slipping back and forth into the bygone years. "You agree, don't you Lia? I am so completely out of touch with Dublin. I read the paper like a schoolboy. You love the theatre and the cinema, so you can bring me up to date, educate me, and we will go everywhere."

"But you like to ponder over a book, darling, and you like long companionable silences," Lia teased him.

"At least, tell me that I am not going to have to share you with my father every day of the week! He has a ten-year stretch of time over me where you are concerned. Not every day, Lia—jealousy is my worst failing!" I knew he was not serious. We were equally devoted to Theo and we could never resist his entertaining company. I recollect, however, that in the last few weeks before the birth, Theo found reasons for going to Paris and later to Rome. He had, undoubtedly, laid down certain rules and regulations both for Lia's care and for Lia's amusement. The content of living in *Tír na nÓg* continued unabated.

Many times in those weeks, Max and I took refuge in my very comfortable bedroom. He never found endless talk come easily, and I began to adjust to the long breaks when we fell into a meditative quiet, unthinkingly content, happy to be alone together. I sensed the days he needed to say things that were afflicting his mind and disturbing his sleep. Those times were still early days after the partisans' camp, and the camp itself had not served to blot out memories of the concentration camps. Those experiences had left a deep groove that was filled with a grievous, painful yearning for justice. There were times when he laid his head on my shoulder and almost wept for the lost years.

Max went into the war when his career as a brilliant psychologist was approaching the pinnacle of success. He was firmly established in Paris where his father had a famous gallery and a lovely house in Saint Cloud on the road to Versailles.

"When I went away from you and my father that morning in September 1939, I managed to get to Paris. My intention was to travel on to Budapest. I knew Tadek had an address there in 1938. It was impossible to get out of Paris; very soon all movement became chaotic. In May 1940, eight months after I left Dublin, the Germans had advanced into France as far as the English Channel and on 14 June they entered Paris. A few days before that Italy had declared itself an ally of Germany. I was able to join a hospital unit travelling to the Italian border. Here I succeeded in getting in touch with the resistance movement, then in its very early stages and active mainly in border areas. It took almost a year for me to work my way from the French–Italian checkpoint to Yugoslavia, Hungary, Czechoslovakia and the Polish border. We travelled any way we could, in small mixed groups, and a lot of the time we had no idea which country we were in. I made sure always to carry my medical affirmations and some supplies. I hid money in some strange places, leaving some available to thieves in less obscure parts! Having a smattering of the languages helped but I often wished my father was at hand to supply a word. He travelled extensively in Central Europe when he was a young man, but of course you know that, Lia."

"Go on Max, tell me more. We—he and I—spent so many years thinking and worrying and longing to know if you were still alive, if we would ever see you again."

"You know, he has upbraided me—well, just a little—for my inability to get news to him. I couldn't. Always moving on and never within town limits, often betrayed by the farmers in an out-of-the-way village which was, in its turn, obliterated by enemy forces. We became unaware of the changing seasons; a year could slip by like so many days. The small things became the important things—unbroken boots were supreme. They never left your feet until they fell off. For me, the most urgent need was to find Tadek, and for that I walked thousands of miles. I hate war. I hate dirt. I hate uncivilised action of any sort. Every day, every night, I wanted to give up—anything—jump in a river—lie down in the snow—and all the time I had to press on to find him. I had to know that I was not less a Jew than he was. Now I know I am less. I proved nothing."

At moments like that, I showed my love very tenderly. I had become very fond of Max and kissing his dear lips was a joy and a pleasure. I feel sure, now, that if I had not been so cumbersomely large with the coming baby, we would have tumbled into bed and made love all night. Years ago, passionate kisses were exchanged as wild promises of unbridled delights still in the future. So we kissed with unspoken vows and it was wonderfully reassuring. We were both intensely aware that Tadek's presence was with us. We both felt guilty at times and we both knew we would have uneasy moments of fearing infidelity in our hearts. It would be years before we could come to each other with open hands empty of remorse or regret or recall.

CHAPTER FIVE

Max did not allow the sessions of deep depression to last for long in the weeks before the baby. We were, all the time, each making up to the other. Loving Max was becoming easier for me each day as I grew to know him. Courting became a delightful way of life.

"Aren't you a little ashamed of me?" I would query. "I look so bloomingly significant!"

"So long as your doctor assures me that all is well, Lia, I feel content. In fact, I feel nothing but pride. And you must know, I did not think you could become more beautiful, but you have—your skin, your hair."

I loved compliments, and I had plenty of them. How could I not be cheered despite the shadow of Tadek's death. I was cheered and helped. We retraced our drives down into Wicklow, making sure of getting out of the car to walk a mile or two; around the lakes of Glendalough, high up on the Feather Bed, along the Sally Gap.

"Walking is very good at this time, Lia." I was reminded of Phyllis long ago: "Up to the Hanover

Basin and back, Lovey. Walking is good for you."

"You two should look out for a cottage up around Glencree," Theo said. "Useful in summertime and you are both daft about Wicklow. Property has never been cheaper. No one has any money now. In ten years' time, property will rise. Pictures, too."

So, to please him, we inspected any picturesque old ruined cottages we came across and there were plenty of them, usually with a few acres of gorse. We found nothing up in the mountains, but coming home one evening we saw a small perfect Edwardian villa for sale on the Dargle Road. The sign was stuck up in a high hedge that almost obscured the house. We walked up and down to spy out the garden, noting that the rear garden probably sloped down to the river from which the road got its name. We took down the telephone number of the auctioneer and chatted excitedly all the way home, laughing at ourselves for this sudden desire to become Mr & Mrs in a little house all our own. A day or two later we brought Theo out to see it. The owner was a widow. She wished to sell so that she could go and live with her daughter in England, also a widow, with three young children. The poor woman was almost in tears telling us this. It was all the fault of that horrible war. Her daughter had tried to manage but she would have to go out to work. Theo confided to us that the woman was not asking enough. It was a very sound house. However, when he talked to the auctioneer in Bray, he found that this man had several hundred houses on his books and, as he said, no one interested.

Theo bought the house. It is worth recording that in 1948 I became the owner of a villa with a lovely garden that ran down to the Dargle River. It had bow windows and a porch with stained glass, three bedrooms and two receptions, a large kitchen complete with a Stanley range, the usual conveniences in good order and all for the sum of eight hundred and fifty pounds plus five per cent commission. In 1948 a five-pound note was money.

"This house will be in Lia's married name," Theo said. When I protested that it was his house, he told us that the house in Terenure was now in Max's name. "Part of your wedding presents, both of you."

Some time around then, Theo announced that he had run to earth all the information about the papers I had given to him when I was in Creighton Street: my father's papers which Gran had hidden away from Burton's lawyer. There were thirty shares purchased at a few shillings each, a first birthday present for the little daughter he was destined never to hold in his arms. They were Hawker-Siddley shares, each one now worth a couple of hundred pounds. My father was not much older on the day he died than I was on the day Theo lodged that money in the bank for me. My father died when he, and many thousands like him returning home after the First World War, contracted Spanish flu. He is buried in Germany, in Göttingen. Thirty years after his death, he had ensured that his daughter did not go penniless into her marriage.

It never occurred to me to take the money and escape from a marriage I had never planned. By the day that Theo announced his delight in tracing the shares, I was beginning to fall in love with Max. I had difficulty in persuading myself that I was not being unfaithful. I questioned myself repeatedly whether I was in love with the man or with the idea of comfortable marriage or in love with all that Max represented. Or in love with Theo? I only knew I loved him. I did not realise then that I was in love with Theo. So small was my total experience that such an idea would have seemed absurd. Loving and being loved seemed enough, more than enough. All the time I was waiting for the birth of Tadek's baby. After that, would everything change? For worse? For better? The courtship was working its magic now but the anxiety to please in marriage and to be pleased, was hanging in a space of time. Endless questioning. The kisses of this courting were tender but often unemotional. Was he full of respect, or was he a temperate lover? I despised myself for wanting to know. So soon could a body betray its owner. I wanted to play the temptress, to prove the unknowable, but one glance in the mirror made me instantly more sensible. Of course Max could not show passion for a largely pregnant woman. I learned to be gently acquiescent, but my secret expectation was undeniable. Am I falling in love with Max? He *is* so lovable. Oh please let me fall in love; let there be another reality; don't let it be all in the past. I am sure I needed to pray, but how to phrase such peculiar pleas? What saint in Heaven would listen? There was another hidden anxiety which continued to haunt me. I missed my religion.

Long before I went to the boarding-school, Phyllis used to take me by the hand as we walked to Mass in Ringsend Church. There was no why; she had to go anyway—"solemn obligation to hear Mass on Sunday"—and she liked dressing up in the good coat Mama had given her. My small hand in hers trusted her always. The mysterious Latin language of the Mass, the candles glowing in the dim church, the shining vestments of the priest in contrast to the poor rags of the congregation all combined to make a lasting impression on Lia's awakening imagination. When Phyllis handed over a penny to light a candle, how could I have known that I was setting alight a small flame which would flicker while I lived yet never be snuffed out. Lighting a candle to pray had always been a consolation of sorts, an appeal to a higher authority for Tadek's safe return; and when that prayer failed, another prayer took its place for Tadek's safe-keeping until we would meet in Heaven, Valhalla, Shangri-la—wherever was the hereafter for a Jew and a Catholic. In the months of waiting for Tadek's baby to be born, and in thrall to the courtship of Max, I often needed to go down on my knees and pray. Was I forfeiting the right? I missed my religion.

We left the widow on the Dargle Road to take her time about packing up and going to England. Our baby was due in weeks and we were well content to stay in Terenure, close enough to the nursing-home should there be an emergency and (as Max thought fit) close enough to the gynaecologist for a weekly visit. Max concealed his foreboding about the baby. Afterwards he revealed his fearful anticipation of the possible side-effects of Tadek's cardiac stimulants— nikethamide, picrotoxin. I was not aware of extra danger. I basked in his care of me. I listened carefully to his little lectures on relaxation and deep breathing and the virtue of obeying the gynaecologist's instructions when the birth began to happen.

So, for a page or two, let me now go back to those days in Terenure and try to recapture the house as it was when Theo was king and we were his courtiers. No novel element had entered the house in Terenure for decades.

There is a south-going road which takes the traveller out of Dublin into Ringsend, through Sandymount, to Dún Laoghaire (which was Kingstown when I was young), on beyond that to Dalkey, up onto the Vico Road and, passing Bray, arrives into Wicklow, known then as the Garden of Ireland. That south-going road is, for me, the magic road of memory. Another road became equally familiar although, until I was eighteen, I had never taken the Terenure tram and Terenure was not the populous suburb it is now. It had, very lately, left the village status behind. There were few houses and few shops. There were elegant squares built at the turn of the century, similar to the great Georgian squares of the city itself. In one of these squares Theo Randt had his residence. I sought him out there on the day Tadek's mother died, because his son was Tadek's friend, and we knew no other Jews to enquire about burial rites. I knew, when I stood on the steps of the big house, that there had to be a staff of servants to run a place like this. As I have written earlier, Mr Randt had Ted and Shanlee Levitsky to look after him, the house, the garden and the car. They were always welcoming and when I came to live with Theo and Max, they became my friends. Shanlee was a mother to Max. Theo's young wife had died when Max was two years of age. Theo never spoke of her. I came to believe, or at least understand, that Theo Randt had a woman in

Rome or in Paris. Different women or the same woman, or perhaps he merely used a house of pleasure. He travelled frequently to those cities, presumably on his extensive business in the world of art galleries and antiques. During the years of war he could not travel. Those were my years when I went to the house in Terenure every Thursday. I cannot recall when I understood that he had a lover, or lovers. It would never have occurred to me in those days to wonder how a man got along without a woman to minister to his needs. I was very much a schoolgirl in my knowledge, and even when Tony Lloyd came into my life, he was careful to keep me that way. He was saving me for himself, and the day he suffered himself to assume that I had had a sexual relationship with Theo Randt was the day he fled out of my life. I was never intimate with Tony, even to entrusting him with the secret of Tadek. From the first moment I saw Theo, I belonged to him as a child, as a daughter, as a friend, and I loved him but neither did I tell him my secret. As I said, he was king. We worshipped at his court.

I would so like to describe that house in Terenure. It was two-storey above garden level at the back, and the garden was extensive. In the front, the house had two storeys above a basement whose windows had the security of iron bars. There was a substantial set of granite steps to the porticoed front door. Viewed from the area's railed ironwork the house was gloomy. Impressive but uninviting, and perhaps deliberately so. Within, all was light. All the walls were painted a creamy colour. In that time, heavy patterned wallpaper in decorative panels was the customary fashion, not so here. The ceilings, also creamy, were corniced and, in some rooms, sculpted in plaster. All the windows were full length to the floor. The fireplaces were beautiful, many of them in white marble with figures and flowers in bas-relief. From the picture-rails hung a collection of works of art, the fruits of a lifetime's pursuit. There were mirrors, cabinets, carved tables, antiques from many places. The furniture was heavy and gleamed from constant care. Console brackets held busts or vases of oriental beauty. The library was shelved from floor to ceiling. Here the couches were so enticingly comfortable that the snatches of reading, from the endless supply, were prolonged for hours. It was a favourite room of Theo's. The entrance hall was wide and curved, concealing the wide staircase. In some rooms there were lovely antique gas lamps, and in others newly installed electric shades in apricot silk. Electricity was for lighting in Theo's house, not for cooking.

The long drawing-room positioned to one side ran the depth of the house. The family room went from the front to end in a Victorian conservatory. Beyond the staircase there was a dining-room, a breakfast room and a very modern kitchen. In the mews, which had once held a carriage and horses, the Levitskys had their comfortable quarters. Upstairs in the main house were many rooms. That assigned to me, which was quite sumptuously appointed, overlooked a back garden of many tall trees and a stretch of lawn. The first thing I noticed, when Theo proudly displayed my room, was the large double bed. My surprise must have shown in my face.

"This will give you a choice when you are married, Lia." I looked at him questioningly. I had come out of a convent boarding-school into my little single bed in Gran's house. I had no experience at all of intimate family life. I suppose I assumed that a happy married couple slept happily together in one big double bed in one special room all their own. My mother and Burton had just such a room overlooking the strand at Sandymount.

"You will find I am right, my dear. A choice is always desirable." He emphasised the word.

"The room is very beautiful," I told him, "fit for a princess. And I love the pictures. You could not have given me any I liked more. I have always loved that Murillo." This is a picture of three ragged street urchins, two gambling with dice while the third bites into a piece of bread. They are little Spanish kids but I think of them as three little Dublin gurriers from Ringsend.

"I had that copied on canvas a few years ago. The young artist, who had great promise, was killed in the Spanish war in 1938. A pity. He was only nineteen years of age." That endeared the picture to me even more. I thought of Tadek at nineteen teaching me to swim in Greystones. One of these little gurriers has dark eyes like Tadek's eyes.

"Lia, you are dreaming! Do you like these curtains?" I came back to earth quickly. "They are lovely, Theo— so lacy and so frilly." He was pleased with this inept reply. He knew very well that my thoughts tended to fly off at a tangent and that it would be a long time into the future before I became a composed, serene woman, always in control. He knew the destination of my thoughts and he was patient with me.

"Then shall we have the same type of curtain in the nursery?" He always consulted but he had always arranged. In another person that might have proved irritating. Somehow, in Theo, decision-making was an attractive quality.

His taste was perfect. He never vacillated. Agreement was awarded with the smile of a blessing graciously bestowed.

When the end of my pregnancy was three weeks away, Max arranged for Mr Wine to come from Grafton Street with a tray of engagement rings.

"I should like you to choose a ring, Lia, when Ben Wine comes. Do not hurry over your choice. He will bring a selection. We could go into town, but from today, I am going to ask you to rest every afternoon." Max never forgot to show his professional as well as his personal interest.

"Please don't send me off by myself, Max. I like to be with you. It is lonely now on my own."

"Then I shall rest with you. I shall sit in the big chair in the window though I'll probably fall asleep!"

"Just so long as you are there, darling."

I chose a half-hoop of diamonds set in filigree, on a broad gold band. Max allowed me to buy a gold signet ring for him. Mr Wine took the rings away to have them engraved. Max wanted my name and his and the date to be on my ring. The date is still there as clear as the first day I wore the lovely thing : *1 January 1948*. On his ring I asked only for his entwined initials. Theo had to come into the picture, of course. He bought for me what Mr Wine called an eternity ring. This would be the third ring above the engagement and wedding rings. And of course Mr Wine joined us in one of Theo's toasts. Ted and Shanlee had come with wine and glasses. They, too, toasted the happiness of the engaged couple.

That night as Max escorted me to my bedroom door, I said to him that I felt a bit cheated. He knew I was teasing him a little. Our bond had been made on the day on the Sugar Loaf. "Did you ever go down on your knees, Max, and formally ask my hand?" I liked dramatic gestures.

"May I do that now?" he asked. He followed me into the bedroom. I sat in the big chair and he knelt on the floor. I wish I could remember the next hour. I know we talked of Tadek, of the baby, of the partisans' camp. I know I shed tears both for grief and for joy. I know he held me in his arms, and I was truly glad to be held. I cannot remember the formal words of his asking me to marry him, but at the end of an hour, when Max kissed me goodnight, we were promised to each other for life.

When the rings came, there was another toasting. A week after that, we were married very quietly, but very contentedly, in the Register of Marriages office. That arrangement had been made weeks before.

There was a blessed peace, a kind of satisfied span of time, while I waited for the baby. Max knew the exact moment to drive us to the nursing home in Hatch Street.

"Would you like me to stay with you, Lia?" he asked.

"Do you mean in the same room?" Long ago that was unheard of. Husbands were banished out of sight.

"They know I am a doctor," he said. "Are you

frightened?"

I was terrified. I had read of women screaming in childbirth. I did not want Max to see me screaming. Not that kind of drama!

"I'll be all right when we get there," I told him.

"Remember, I will be in the next room. If it gets too bad—after all it is a first time—please call my name."

"Tell me again that it is only the last couple of pains that are bad. What is happening now is not so bad. When does the hard part begin?" Then we were in Hatch Street. I felt very alone when Max was not with me but he had coached me well. The labour seemed hours long, but the end was wonderfully quick. There is no joy on earth to compare with the joy a mother feels when she looks on the face of her newborn child. When I heard the cry of the baby, sudden and strong, I thought, this is at last the new beginning.

Max was beside me very quickly. "We have a lovely little girl." He held the baby against me. "A daughter, Lia." I held him and the baby. He kissed my face repeatedly. "I am very proud of you," he whispered over and over. When they took the tiny infant away to bathe and dress her, Max went with them. When he came back, I was almost asleep but I have never forgotten his softly spoken, tender words : "She is perfect in every smallest detail, and, Lia, she is Tadek in miniature. How proud he would have been!"

That evening, Theo came. He filled the room with flowers. Then he sat by my bed, utterly solicitous for my health. He spoke softly as if I had become too fragile for any word louder than a whisper. Then the nurse brought in the baby.

"We will put the little one to the breast for a moment or two," she said.

"But first," I said to the nurse, "Mr Randt will hold his grandchild," and Theo held out his arms for my firstborn baby—this baby who was not at all his grandchild, this baby who had no drop of his blood in her veins. The strangest thing happened and I knew it happened in the very moment that Theo gazed on the baby's little face. She gazed back into his face, her dark, dark eyes wide open as if in welcome. From that very moment, she belonged to Theo and he belonged to her. In the years that followed, that moment remained photographed in my mind, and the strangeness never changed. They had entered into each other's inmost consciousness; they had recognised each other; they had come together. There was an unbroken silence when I took the baby to my breast. She had closed her eyes but her little mouth was open ready to suckle. I was afraid to look at Theo. I was afraid to speak. There had been an awesome moment in which there was some hidden meaning. The baby fell asleep and the nurse took her away to tuck her into the little cot at the end of the bed. Then at last I turned my head to him. He was visibly moved. "*A dank! A dank! Mazltov, mazltov mayn.*"

He had slipped into the language of his childhood, words I remembered from the Vashinskys' kitchen in Ringsend and from Tadek's mother when she lived with Gran. It was fitting that the greeting to Tadek's child should be Yiddish. The old man was thanking me. He was congratulating me. He was welcoming the baby.

He was emotionally so moved that he went away to stand at the window. Then he stood staring down into the baby's cot. He could not speak. When Max came, he went away very quietly, very reluctantly, looking back into the room he had filled with flowers.

When I was alone and holding my baby to examine every detail of her perfection, I could see that indeed, as Max had said, she was an image, a tiny statue, re-created out of the perfection of Tadek. Already the arch of the eyebrows, the depth beyond depth in the dark eyes, the close black hair, the delicate fingers, the slender structure of the shoulders and hips.

"She is not like me in any way at all," I said to Max.

"Are you disappointed?" Max asked.

"Well, no," I answered very slowly, "but you see, I was so full of joy and hope when I was carrying Tadek's baby. I don't want to start weeping, but you see, the baby was all I had left after twenty-five years of loving Tadek...so that I thought there must surely be some imprint of me on the baby when she came, even that she would turn to me, need me. Is it wrong to say that although she is so like Tadek, to me she is a little stranger? She means so much to me, but I seem not to exist for her! I am not jealous of Theo—I need him the way the baby needs him. I thought all the positions would be reversed. I have lost the connection; I feel almost bereft."

Max wanted to find consoling words. "Perhaps that is how a mother feels when she releases her child out of the intimacy of her warmth into an alien world."

"Perhaps," I said but I knew there was something more. I hid my obscure sense of disappointment from Theo in whom I had loved to confide secret thoughts. In the years we had waited together for news of Max and Tadek, I had let Theo think that the news was equal whether of one or the other, his son or my beloved. I did not mean to deceive, and perhaps he was not deceived. He never said. I never knew.

"Do you feel love for the baby?" Max was a little anxious.

"Oh yes, oh yes, and she is beautiful. She is a mirror image of Tadek. How could one not feel love for her!"

"It is important that you love her just for herself,

Lia. Be positive about it. The strangeness may go in a week or two. You are naturally in an emotional state, highly strung. You have been brave and gallant, but that has created a great strain. Your nature is pliant, unused to force." My nature had held on grimly to first love for many, many years. Yes, I loved her but not as I had loved her father. The all-encompassing love I felt I owed her, and which was there down through the years in readiness, was never put to the test. She loved me tenderly. We were to forge a loving relationship but the strangeness between us lay for ever like an evening shadow. Sunlight for her came from another direction. There has been a personal disappointment which I have fought always to rationalise. Rationalise was a word of which Tadek was very fond. "As time passes, Lia, rationalise the past: see it for what it is, experience that must be rationalised into maturity." When I think of myself in the early teens, I smile to remember his little lectures. All I wanted were passionate film-star kisses; all I got were little lectures for my betterment. Ah Tadek! I loved you so.

Theo Randt talked every day of a name for the baby. "Within the next week, the birth will be registered. Have you thought of a name for her, Lia?" She lay in his arms, their eyes locked into recognition, her tiny hand twined around his index finger. He would often say in after times, "She and I are hand in glove with each other." It was so from the beginning.

"Should we choose a Jewish name?" I asked. "Sarah, or Rachel or Miriam or Rebecca?" I had thought to please him, and the baby was undoubtedly a little Jewish princess. He frowned. I had not pleased him. "Have you a name in mind?" I asked, "because I have not." His would be the choice.

"Would you allow us to commemorate the fact that she is the child of Tadek Vashinsky? Some day you will tell her that. Some day, you will judge that she will not be hurt by our deception to shelter her while she was vulnerable." He knew I was fully aware that when he started by "would you allow," his mind was made up before the words were spoken.

"You must choose the name, Theo," I smiled at him. I owed this child to him, and so much more I owed to him.

"Yes," he said, "I believe it falls to me to choose her name, and I have given this matter a lot of thought. Her name will lead her into a recognition of who she is. I suggest we register her name as Vasha Victoria Randt. Vasha would be sufficient for the family, but for a school roll-call we will add Victoria because it is an accepted name." Theo never had a problem with long speeches. His enunciation was very distinct if very slightly European. No one ever dreamed of cavilling. I caught the ghost of Max's amused consent behind his glasses.

"Vasha is just perfect, Theo." My thoughts as always flew away to the Matra mountains, and I had to drag them back. "I have engaged help for Shanlee," Theo said. "There will be extra work. However, the young woman is not a nursemaid. We will look after Vasha; there are three of us. I could not trust a stranger in anything nearer than a clothes line."

Theo was enjoying himself; he was smiling. His life had been given a direction.

CHAPTER SIX

I n the months that followed, I often found myself reflecting that when Max was an infant, a little boy, a schoolboy, a student in medical college (when I met him with Tadek), he found a mother in Shanlee Levitsky. He spoke of her with deep affection. She was devoted to him and he to her. She redoubled her devotion to include me but she never became a surrogate grandmother to Vasha. An invisible net surrounded Vasha in the first weeks after we brought her home to Terenure. Shanlee would admire, touch, listen. She could never actually care for Vasha in the way one cares for, caters for, a baby's demands. I was allowed, Max was permitted, but Theo was in charge.

I was still sleeping in my own bedroom. I was recuperating, they said. Theo brought Vasha to me to be changed and suckled. If he spoke to me during feeding time, her little mouth would fall away from the breast and her eyes wander in search of the voice. His fingers would direct the tiny head back to the nipple. I murmured little phrases of mother love to the infant; Theo watched and timed: ten minutes each side, twenty minutes as she grew hungrier. Lifting the baby away, he would ask, "Does it hurt, Lia?" and I would shake my head. "Is it pleasurable, Lia?" and I would nod my head. I presumed he knew that feeding time was arousal time. He knew so many things, but perhaps he did not know that very special thing. When Theo had taken Vasha away to the nursery, he would go down to his study. After a while we would hear him. He was bringing his book up to the nursery. Then Max would stretch out on the bed beside me. He had perfected a very gentle kind of lovemaking, kisses, caresses, searching hands, promises that in a little while we would have a honeymoon.

"I want so much to love you, Max."

"You will get the chance, my darling. Now is too soon." We were adults, we were married and yet we were fugitives, having a hidden affair. Our feelings were too new to put on display. I had sworn a lasting fidelity to Max's friend. I had been delivered of the friend's baby. Max had sworn an oath to his dying friend that he would let no harm come to Lia, that he would find happiness for Lia. We married that the child might have a name, protection, a family. We knew we had always loved each other in all innocence. We had neither of us bargained on the proximity of the other causing passion's urgent need. We read each other's thoughts; we were each unfaithful to the ideal of fidelity, and we each feared to fall short in the other's eyes. We had seen ourselves as a couple who had been given a charge: the child. We would be a steady mamma and dadda. The situation was not as we envisaged. The child was Theo's child, not deliberately on his part, but she was, in some mysterious way, pre-ordained to be for him alone. As the weeks flew by we were accepting that situation without question. There was never confrontation. If we had misgivings we never allowed them to surface. We were beholden to Theo equally. Above all we loved him profoundly as our father and as himself.

"How many months do you continue to breastfeed?" Theo enquired.

I glanced at Max. "I think six months would be sufficient," he said, "if little Vasha continues to make a steady weight gain, and if Lia is not tired."

Theo turned to me for confirmation of this. "I am not tired at all," I told him. "I feel a fraud, idling so much time. Never was I so fighting fit. But according to the baby books which I have been reading, when a baby starts on semi-solids, the breast becomes just a comfortable habit, and weaning becomes increasingly difficult." I picked up a book and showed the page to Theo. "It states here that a baby overdue for weaning may become fractious. The book recommends six months and then a gradual withdrawal."

"Fractious!" Theo echoed. "That must not be allowed to happen. In another month then, I shall re-arrange the schedule." His son was a qualified doctor and I was the qualified breast-feeder but Theo was the high-priest of the schedule. If Max and I wanted to exchange looks, we did not dare. The unexchanged look became our unspoken symbol of agreement with each other and our acquiescence to him.

So it was arranged. Theo always brought Vasha to me at 6 a.m. for her change and feed. He sat on the bed watching, his face a study of delight. He would change the words a little each day: "This is the highlight of my day, Lia. Flushed with sleep, you are as beautiful as ever, as when you were eighteen. Do you remember?" When he had restored the baby to her cot in the nursery, he would come back with tea. We would murmur together, always about Vasha, I think. "Go back to sleep, my darling. I will see you at breakfast." He would cover me with a tender lingering gentleness, such as no other person ever had. Then he would kiss my head and go away. I would hear his footsteps pause at the nursery door. I could almost see his benign smile. The 6 a.m. feed was the last to be phased out. By that time, Vasha was able to sit up, and babble; she had produced two little teeth without any mention of the baby-books' teething troubles.

🍎🍎

"Vasha is almost nine months," Max said. "She is taking her first steps. She has six teeth. She eats well. She will soon join us for meals."

His voice was amused but I detected a talkative note. He was going to phrase a question. I was still sleeping alone in my own room. I knew there were good reasons why. Max had told me that he was tormented by dreams, often by hideous nightmares. Sometimes he woke drenched in sweat; sometimes he could not sleep at all for many nights. There were times he looked grey and worn although he was not yet forty years of age. (He did not talk about the concentration camp. If the name of Auschwitz appeared in the newspaper, the war still of recent memory, he would crush the paper in his hands and trample it underfoot. "What do they know! What do they know!" he would mutter.) "I was wondering, Lia, if we have postponed the honeymoon long enough?"

"You mean, a little holiday?" I asked. "You were talking about Vasha's progress. Would she be coming on the holiday?" Immediately, I pictured Theo's face. We could hear his voice in the conservatory, the special sweet note of cooing that he kept for Vasha. She would be sitting up in the very regal perambulator he had bought for her, and she would be listening to him relating some old rhyme as if she understood every word. The rhyme might be in English, or in

French or German, or any one of half a dozen Slavic languages, and sometimes in Yiddish. Vasha's dark eyes would glow and Theo's papery fingers would ripple her curls.

"How would your dad feel about our taking Vasha on a holiday?" I asked. It struck home to me for the first time: how would Vasha feel? Would there be tears and tantrums? There had never been but it had become clear to me that I was a very muted second fiddle in this family orchestra. And Max? Where Vasha was concerned, he was second fiddle to my second fiddle.

"I think Vasha would not miss us," Max said, "but I had not thought of going far. A phone call would bring us back within an hour. We could take Silkitoo."

I guessed immediately what he had in mind—the little house in Bray, our Edwardian villa. We had gone out every week to make sure the local contractor had made all the changes we had decided on. Forty years ago, the all-electric house was fairly new but that was what we had arranged, so that if we used the house just for a week-end holiday, all we had to do was switch on the power. No ordering of fuel and, as Theo pointed out, no endless dusting. Of course there was dusting and polishing, but in those early days of all-electric, the deal was a dust-free house. There were other reasons for this ideal conception of housework. After the war, the days of the lowly paid domestic drudge came rapidly to an end. It was not at once apparent, but indoor servants became impossible to get. In the fifties, the crowded emigrant ships were off as before to England, and now much further afield: Canada, Australia, America. A generation of men had been slain, and women were needed everywhere. Women's new importance was not called feminism, not liberation, but all unbeknown, that is what it was. In Ireland, the new technology of electrical gadgets played a significant role in the changing fate of women.

We were smiling at each other. "Our little house in Bray? But is it furnished?"

"Let's buy our own furniture," Max suggested. "There is a big emporium in Bray that sells furniture. I think it is called Lee's." To Max, this would be an adventure, a distraction not before experienced.

"I remember that shop," I said. "Aunt Julia bought her hats there."

"Aunt Julia!" Max laughed heartily to remember Aunt Julia, and he imitated her. "Do you think this is the zoo?" That was when I wanted my little dog Silky to be allowed sleep on my bed, during the annual holiday in Bray.

"Is she still alive?" Max asked. Aunt Julia had had a fatal stroke in the years directly after the war when Bray had been thronged with visitors from England and perhaps overwork in her guest house had killed her.

"You used to tell us that she was the stingiest old biddy on earth!" Max reminded me, smiling hugely.

"She was! If I were to tell you some of the concoctions she served her paying guests for dinner, you would think I was making it up!"

"Not now, Lia," Max said loyally and mischievously, "but if you had told us then, I would. You were a very dramatic little actress in those days!"

I was a little liar too in those days, but I didn't mention that.

"Max, Theo must have a hand in the furniture. I could never hurt him by not consulting his taste and judgement. He will insist on some antiques and perhaps a picture or two."

"All right then. We will buy the basic requirements. Maybe we'll have arguments about table-cloths—that would be healthy! And arguments about who'll do the cooking! Silkitoo can't cook, you know!"

This was a new Max. "I think you are getting better," I asked him gently. "Sleeping better?"

Max agreed. "For the past week, I have slept six or seven hours a night. Some bad dreams but no nightmares."

"Have you told your dad?" I asked.

"He knows. There were times I woke to find him sitting by my bed. I had been shouting. Sometimes I was crying. Sometimes Tadek was there in my room. Only a dream, I know, but he was very real."

"You never told me when that happened. He never came back to me, never, not even for a moment."

"Lia, some day I will tell you more about…about certain things…some day…when I can remember without crying out against horror and injustice. Not yet, Lia, not yet."

So many things I wanted to ask. Instead I put the important question. "So, has the time for the honeymoon come for us?" I wanted very much to be generous with loving him. So much depended on my forgetting Tadek and so much depended on my remembering him. All my life, all through boarding-school with the nuns, all through my days in the Abbey School of Acting, and in the dreary Land Commission, all through my engagement to Tony Lloyd, always, always I had to carry the image of Tadek in my very soul. He had enjoined on me when I was six years of age, never to mention his name, to remember his good name as a doctor, to protect his name as a Jew. Telling no one of the passionate love I felt in my heart had become second nature, the act of concealment was the same as drawing breath. Nothing had changed and I could never change. In the delightful Edwardian villa, in the garden going down to the trees by the Dargle river, would I be able to love Max with a physical response, and still not lose the beloved man who stood always in a shrine within me? Could I go on concealing from Max the fact that I worshipped daily at that shrine? I wanted to give generously for all the years that Theo had been my guardian angel, saving me even from myself when Burton had come back into my life. In a way, indefinable but certain, Theo had taken Burton's place, but without the aura of fear that was forever part of Burton. In Theo I had total trust. As time went on and Vasha became Theo's child there was never fear, never less than total trust. Vasha's coming was inevitably Theo's reward. Max must have his reward and I must not shirk that demand.

"Yes, our honeymoon," Max said. "Is a honeymoon a month? Could we stay away all of July? After that, we should discuss our future. I feel I have been idle and lazy for long enough." Now Max's voice was serious and his eyes were expectantly on mine.

"Max, it is wonderful to hear you say that—about your future. Our future?"

"We may have to go away, Lia. Perhaps in the autumn. I have been making enquiries. I do not want to go back to Vienna nor to Paris. There is nothing to be gained from staying in Dublin—psychology is in too early a stage here. Will you mind if we go abroad?"

"Of course not," I answered with certainty. My lot was cast in with him from now on. "Where is abroad?"

"I have been corresponding with colleagues in New York and in Philadelphia." America? Tadek had told me that he and I could have had a future in America. "Wherever you decide, Max. As it happens, I have a friend in Philadelphia, Berny. She too is married to a doctor. I was a bridesmaid at her wedding. I had a letter from her lately. I have been meaning to write to her." The day of Berny's wedding was the last time I had seen Burton. Berny had been in love with Burton. And I? I shuddered away from the remembrance. It has never been easy to forget Burton.

"Funny," Max said, "I think I would prefer Philadelphia to New York. I was looking at some pictures of it; it is less hectic, I think. The medical college of the University of Philadelphia might be a good place to re-enter my own particular stream."

"Have you been a fish out of water?" I teased, firmly putting away the vision of Burton in the bedroom of a hotel.

"But first our honeymoon!" Max was laughing and relaxed the way he used to be long ago when he and I spent hours talking what Tadek called "dog talk": Max's Toozy and my Silky. Now, in the afternoons when we pushed Vasha's perambulator around the long garden path in the back garden, we always paused a moment at the little grave of Toozy and Silky. Ted Levitsky had chiselled out the two names on a block of limestone, and planted mauve heathers in the earth. Silkitoo walked sedately behind the perambulator, and she paused too, her fluffy tail down as if in sympathy. It was always a happy coincidence that Max and I had this shared interest in dogs. We used to tell each other laughingly that we were dogs in a previous life. We never knew why it was that we could talk endlessly about dogs: our own dogs, other people's dogs, dogs we had heard about or read about. When we were young, Max had told me that his first choice of career would have been to be a vet, but his father did not think it suitable for a Jew, so Max chose medicine. That led on to psychology. Nevertheless, he had read enormously about dog medicine as he called it. We always called in a vet if we had a sick dog or cat, but Max would have diagnosed and prescribed correctly while waiting for the vet to come. He never failed to groom our dogs; that was a part of every day. There have been so many dogs, many little King Charleses.

In preparation for our departure, Shanlee was allowed to take over the bathing and changing of little Vasha, with Theo always nearby, his spectacles half-way down his nose, as he made sure that Shanlee did things exactly as Lia did. Shanlee was the most patient of women. She knew everything, yet she submitted pleasantly to Theo's meticulous instructions. When he was quite satisfied that Vasha would not suffer in any way from our absence, we were encouraged to load the car and set off. The phone had been installed in our villa, and we could be home again within an hour. I wondered if Vasha would miss me; we had happy little times together but even as I was hugging her good-bye, her dark eyes were watching Theo, and when I handed her into his arms, she pressed her little face against his coat as if to say: this is where security is. I loved him too much to be resentful. A lot of my security was vested in him too.

We took the old familiar road from Sandymount by the sea to Dalkey, and down into Shankill. This pretty village has always had special memories for us. Then we turned off right and a couple of miles more took us to our house beside the river. I realise that I am lingering on these early days, that I should hurry along, because I am setting out to tell the story of forty years, and so far I have covered only the first year. Those early days set the tone of our life together. There was happiness later; there was never Camelot again. Every detail of those years is clear and lovely to me, the never repeatable years, the years of all the firsts.

The first time we made love was in our villa that first night of our first holiday, our honeymoon. Someone has written truly that comparisons are odious, so let me not compare the first night of trying to make love with Max, my wedded husband, and those nights of passionate ecstasy with Tadek, in the mountains. There can be no comparison, there was no similarity. Tadek and Max were close friends since boyhood; faithful companions, heroic comrades; each would have given his life for the other. But they were two very different men. For Tadek and Lia there was a culminating unity, a once-and-forever perfection. Perhaps on that first night with Max, there was more love than passion. Perhaps I was afraid to show the urgent need that had been building up in me, and when the moment came I felt guilt. Maybe in this year of grace, women ask their men if the act has been satisfactory. Maybe, how should I know? Forty years ago women were apprehensive, a little fearful of being thought forward. A forward female was a very pejorative term for a woman then. The everyday love stories in womens' magazines were bland and non-exploratory of married rites.

"Lia, you are very quiet. You would tell me if I hurt you?" He had not hurt me. He was gentleness itself. I seemed to sense that he was an experienced lover, prepared to prompt. I longed to cooperate vitally, enthusiastically in his meaningful caresses. I was torn between the longing and the fear of losing his respect. So the first night and the second night must have been a disappointment to him.

"Would you prefer to sleep alone, Lia?" Max asked.

Perhaps that was the third or fourth night.

"Oh no, no, no! I love sleeping with you. Do you want me to go into another room like in Terenure?"

"I hated that arrangement. But I am afraid now of distressing you. You do not respond to me."

"Oh I want to," I whispered, "I want to but I am afraid you would think me bold—or forward. You know?"

He took me into his arms. "Please be forward, Lia— if you are not, I shall think I am in competition with a memory that obsesses both of us."

"I love you, Max. Honest, honest, honest, I love you very, very, very much."

"Then just be conscious of me, darling, only of me." He was thinking of Tadek, and I, like a guilty schoolgirl, had been thinking mainly of myself—a prudery never present in my love for Tadek.

"Max, were you in love before?" He paused, as he always did, determined to give a truthful but unhurtful answer.

"No," he said slowly, "I am in love for the first time, although I always loved you since the first day I saw you with Tadek. But I have had women. The girl in Vienna. In a way, she was special—very sweet. We were together for several years. It was neither love nor lust, but necessary. That is how some men are—most, perhaps."

I wondered if she was the lover who had shared Max's ways, and gestures such as Tadek had never revealed to me. Perhaps in the mountains our innocent loving was all either of us knew.

"And," Max continued, "there was a girl in Auschwitz. She was only sixteen. Lia, don't be shocked or hurt, please don't. Life in that place cannot be described in normal terms. She was four months pregnant by me when she went into the gas chamber. Her face, her shaven head, come back in dreams." I remember we were talking in the garden, watching the sun slanting off the river. He took off his heavy glasses. I think that was the real moment of my falling in love with Max. I wonder now if we had had to clear the air. He had witnessed my love for Tadek in the partisans' camp. I had made no effort to conceal it. I had been able only to wonder about Max. That night we loved as we had not loved before, and every night after that was beautiful, fulfilling, satisfying. For me at last there was a future. It was not the future I had longed for during all the years of growing into womanhood but it was a future full of close security. I was humble in the face of such bounty.

CHAPTER SEVEN

So that was how it was in the beginning: a slow exploration as it came to us that while we had loved each other in a totally familial way for many years, we really did not know each other at all. We had a love of the child, Vasha, in common and, we had to admit a little shamefacedly, close on that we had a common affinity with dogs. Our choices in reading we were never able to share, although we wanted to discuss with each other the books we read. Max adored classical music and opera; I loved romantic musical comedy. His father's eclectic taste in antiques, painting and sculpture had not been passed on to Max but when I was with Theo I was an avid listener and learner. All three of us loved the theatre, whether Irish, English or European. We went regularly to the Abbey, the Gate, the Olympia and the Gaiety, arguing the merits of acting and play most enjoyably. We loved dining out, and finding new places, new chefs. Forty years ago, there were not so many such places as there are nowadays. Money was not plentiful in Ireland in the fifties nor in the early sixties. Few enough could spend money freely as Theo Randt could. The discovery and sale of a single picture made an income for him in an hour that the majority of people, then, had to live on for a year. Perhaps it is only now that I am fully aware of that fact. I lived in an enclosed world in Terenure. I scarcely realised how pampered and cherished I was. All I ever needed was security and friendship of a very particular kind. Those elements were mine at last. How lucky I was in those years!

Phyllis and I had always kept in touch. She was self-conscious about writing and spelling, so mostly she scribbled regular postcards. I have always loved writing letters and looking forward to replies. With Berny also there was a regular correspondence. Neither of these friends knew that I was expecting Tadek's baby when I went to live in Terenure and became Max's bride. Berny, always the perceptive one, would know very well when I wrote to tell her of Vasha's birth. Phyllis had an in-built Dublinesque distrust of Jews—she would have to be bamboozled with dates. To discover that I was pregnant by one Jew and married to another Jew would fill Phyllis with foreboding. So I wrote my news to Berny and postponed telling Phyllis the real news to a later letter. Berny was quick to reply: she wrote that she knew very well I was pregnant on that last visit to Terenure. "I really thought you had done the deed with Mr Randt. I remember saying you should move in with him; he obviously adores you. But Max? Come on, Lia, I know very well it's not Max's baby—he is not the kind of person to get you into that sort of trouble, and I am fairly certain you didn't go to bed with that hunk in the Land Commission—Tony something. Still the same old Lia, full of secrets. We always knew you had a hidden idol—Lucille and I guessed that when we were in third year. You used to go "absent"—eyes all dreamy and sometimes I used hear you have a little weep in the bed next to me in the old middle dorm. It couldn't have been Burton, could it? I'll go mad with jealousy if it was! No, couldn't have been—I don't think you ever saw him after the day of the wedding, did you? Me neither—but I have never forgotten him—was he ever a man! Some day, will you tell me? What's all this about the possibility of Max coming to Philadelphia? All of you?"

Phyllis's letter had its own special message. It was almost a real letter, written on notepaper headed with the name of their hotel in Siena.

"Isn't this nice notepaper? Luigi says it is only for hotel business but I wanted you to see it and also I want to tell you that I am going to have a baby. I think I had a couple of false starts, not exactly miscarriages. I told Luigi and he told the doctor here about what happened to me in Holles Street—losing the child, and being so sick. I thought Luigi would be mad that

I had not told him before but he didn't say anything mad. Anyway the doctor here, who is very nice for an Italian, said there was no reason except my age—into the forties, like. Ma wanted me to come home to Ringsend and she would look after me. But you know what, Lovey: I have every comfort here. A woman in the kitchen and a woman to clean. A queen I am. I waited to tell you until I was absolutely sure and now I am. In four months. Say a prayer to St Jude. I have great faith in St Jude. There's an altar to him in the cathedral here and I light a lamp for the new baby every Sunday. Maybe next year you and Max will come to our hotel when it's all in going order and have a holiday. And sure, Lia, you never know you might have a baby of your own by then…"

My baby would be a year older than her baby—I should have made my confession long before. Somehow I had not thought of Phyllis's having a baby. I should have. Never, never had I breathed the name of Tadek after the very first night he had climbed in through the window. I was six then and full of delight to find a friend in my abandoned plight. Phyllis had (as she imagined) laid a solemn promise on me that such a dreadful thing would never happen again. "A young fella in a little girl's bedroom! Swear on your word," and I swore. Oh Tadek, Tadek, I would have faced a battalion of warriors carrying spears just so I could see you for a little while in that dreary bedroom. I used tell lies to Phyllis with my fingers crossed behind my back.

I showed Phyllis's letter to Max. Little by little we were sharing our past lives with each other; little by little we were growing closer; little by little there was less to misunderstand.

"You will have to write, not a letter, but a story, for Phyllis," Max said smiling. "All those little fibs you used to tell would come as a shock to someone who trusted you."

"But she was sorry for me, too," I told him. "Every night when she brought me over to Hastings Street, she used to say how sorry she was for me. She knew it was very lonely in that horrible little bedroom. And Tadek couldn't always come. He had to study for exams."

"How many years were you sent there for the night?" Max asked.

"It ended when I was nine. That was when my mother bought the house in Sandymount."

It was not my mother: it was Burton but his name was impossible for me to toss out easily.

"Nine!" Max took my hands in his. "You were nine when we played mad cricket on the strand."

"I think that was later," I said. "Or was it?"

"You were such a little thing," Max said, "with

curly hair flying in all directions!"

I made fifty attempts to write a letter to Phyllis but I could not. It was too close to Tadek's death to start explaining him away. When I tried to put his name on the notepaper, the tears started from my eyes. Bearing his child, learning to be at ease with the person of his friend, being happy in the life assigned to me—none of these had covered over the raw place where Tadek had dwelt within me for so many years. Trying to write the letter to Phyllis laid bare afresh the memory of the camp.

"It is too soon; I cannot," I told Max. "She is too far away. Writing is impossible. She would never understand. I want to settle to my life as it is. She is a dear good person, but she is another person, almost a pair of prying eyes—although I know that is unfair. Perhaps I could talk, not write, but that too is repugnant to me. I want you and Vasha and Theo to be my life, like the characters in a story which is not, and must not be, a ghost story."

"Come here, Lia," Max said. "Let me take on the role in your story. Never forget, because neither of us ever can, but re-cast the household for the continuing plot. The grandfather, the husband, the wife, their child. In your mind, there is a husband and a father. You cannot deal with double characters, not now. And neither can I. When we are alone and we need to mourn our dead, we will call Tadek to us and we will weep together. Lia, remember his message: you are to be happy. He would not want to destroy our marriage and it could happen if we harp on tragic memory."

"Do you remember your father's toast when we were reunited with Tadek?"

"Yes, I remember. He said, 'To happiness, the gift of the gods.'"

"Max, do you think he knew? Do you think he knew how things would work out?"

"He could not have known about Vasha. That is a miracle perhaps even he does not understand. You know, Lia, you have been his youth restored, his image of beauty since a number of years—ten, twelve? Instead of yourself, you have given him Vasha. The restoration begins again. But, darling, that does not mean you lose your little daughter." But I knew it did. There was no way I could begrudge.

So I wrote the letters, carefully couched, because I was too grown-up for deliberate lies. As Max had put it, there was a grandfather who was Theo, there was a husband Max and his wife Lia, and their daughter Vasha Victoria.

Phyllis never commented but she may very well have divined the derivation of the name Vasha. As for Berny, the name of Tadek Vashinsky was unknown to her. Neither was that beloved name known to the wide circle of friends and colleagues into which I was gradually introduced by Theo and by Max.

Here I am, still only at the end of the first year. I must hasten on. Our days rolled away, summer into winter. Christmas came and another year began. Max was spending time now on study. Letters from the medical college of the University of Pennsylvania had come to confirm his admission into the department of psychology for a course in his own particular subject. He had put on weight; he was sleeping well. His intention was to record, totally, his experiences with the partisans before and after Auschwitz. A correspondence on that subject was building up.

In April, to our joy and delight, I became pregnant. Need I record the number and variety of Theo's toasts? From the first skipped month, he was convinced that the new arrival would be a son. He laid down a case of special wine, perhaps it was champagne, carefully labelled for this son's twenty-first birthday. Giving me flowers was an everyday occurrence. Now he was enlisting my help in deciding on indoor plants for the neglected conservatory. He and I pored over books and pictures of exotic blooms. There was no central heating in the house; so now this became a big project. For part of the upheaval, we moved to the villa in Bray, Theo and Max and Vasha and I. Although I found the villa spacious and airy—especially I loved the riverside—Theo was cramped. He worried about his books and his pictures, although Ted and Max, helped by Shanlee, had moved the principal items into the storage of the basement. All other precious pieces and the furniture had been wrapped in gauze and protective sheeting. Theo would undoubtedly have stayed in Terenure, enduring the dirt and the noise, but he did not wish to be without the precocious presence of Vasha. Her rapid mental development was fostered by him, never forced but gently encouraged. In his arms, she made the tour of all his pictures, perhaps every day. Long before she could pronounce the name of either painting or artist, she gave signs of recognising the sameness and the difference. He would guide her tiny hands over a priceless piece of sculpture as she sat in his lap. He would read aloud to her for a short period every midday. She would watch his lips forming the words; perhaps in Hebrew if that were the language of the book; perhaps in French, which literature was his favourite. I often trailed along with them, still trying to learn all I could, but there were times I worried. "Do you think it is too much for her little brain to grasp?" I asked Max.

"Well," Max smiled, "my father did the very same with me. He was always so kind that I used hide my boredom—quite often I fell asleep. In those days, he used travel a great deal, buying and selling. Sometimes

I would forget most of what he had taught me by the time he took up his instruction again. Eventually, he wrote me off as a dunderhead!"

"But you do know a great deal—sometimes you let your knowledge slip out—as when we walked around the National Gallery the other day."

Max laughed at my serious face. "Some of my father's endless lectures must have rubbed off on me."

In September, the house in Terenure was fully centrally heated. It was restored to its former glory of creamy paintwork offsetting the burnished patina of the furniture and the pictures in their carved ornamental frames.

"He is not going to admit it," Max said to me, "but my father got the idea of electric heating from our little villa." I was so pleased for Shanlee. There would be no fires to light in the big rooms on the ground floor nor in the bedrooms. She never complained, and she never accepted help, but the work load she carried was unchanged in forty years. It was Victorian. She loved to go shopping down in Rathmines where there was a greater variety than in Terenure. She left her list of groceries in Findlater's, and in due course all the goods, beautifully packed, were delivered to her kitchen. The Merville Dairy horse-drawn carts brought milk at the dawn hour. Some goods in which Mr Randt took a connoisseur's interest were purchased from Smith's on the Green. Theo called this big food store the epicure's shop. Tea and coffee always came from Smith's. Chickens and some varieties of meat came from a shop in Clanbrassil Street. Looking back, it seems the even tenor of Dublin life, unchanged since the end of the Great War, continued on into the early sixties. Money was real. People used the phrase "value for money" and meant it then. By the standards of today, the comfortably off of those times had not big salaries, and yet they could afford a servant and a gardener, and (the luxury of it now!) a nursemaid for the children. The servants and the gardeners and the nursemaids were the poor of that time. Their wages were in shillings, not in pounds. Theo was always aware of the economic climate, and we were meant to appreciate each comfort and what it cost. My gran, in her very straitened circumstances, was like that too and I was accustomed to Theo's philosophy.

It took the year of my second pregnancy to realise that the logical method by which his father evaluated money irked Max.

"I wish there were only the two of us, Lia. Or even the three, or four of us. I wish we lived in the villa all the time, you and me and our children."

Secretly I agreed with him but I adored Theo. Not for all the gold in the world would I wish to hurt him.

"But we cannot live in the villa, Max darling. You

are going away soon. I must stay. You wouldn't want to take us with you—you will be very preoccupied—Theo says so every day."

"I hear him," Max said shortly, "but I don't listen to him. I'll have to eat and sleep, won't I? Lia, you wouldn't want me to sleep alone, would you?"

"Nor eat alone, either." I smiled at him. "But your first three months will be over by Christmas and the baby is due at the end of January. Then, big decisions!"

And that was how it worked out. Max went away to Philadelphia at the end of September. Because I was expecting the baby and already under a doctor's care and, indeed, already booked into the "Hatch," it was clear that he must go along. We exchanged letters every day, sometimes only a line or two. Those letters were so precious to me that I have treasured them all these years. I had never received a letter from Tadek. There was never need. Yes, each little batch of Max's letters is tied with blue ribbon, now slightly faded. They are letters full of the very essence of the man who wrote them, letters of tenderness and letters of lonely, fervent longing. I should love to set them down for all the world to see but I will not. A note here and there tells a little of his new life: "Your friend Berny had me over to dinner last night. She is looking forward greatly to when you will be here in the spring. Yes, Lia, in the spring. I do not know how I got the idea that she has a family. There is one boy only. He is a very handsome child, maybe eight or nine, tall and well-built. B's husband is very good-looking, very military, a good deal older than she. He talks of early retirement from the army—I think he specialises in tropical diseases. We drank so much I have a headache all day today. I think you will admire their home; I got the impression they are both free to come and go..." I remember pondering over this letter, and thinking about Berny. Was this husband a twice-divorced man before they wed? Or three times? Berny had had innumerable boyfriends. Even when we were in school, there was a new and violent and irrevocable love affair every summer—each lover the acme of perfection. Lucille, who was devoted to horses, used to jeer at Berny unmercifully but I, who believed in love, was ever a sympathetic listener.

CHAPTER EIGHT

Max came home for Christmas, our second Christmas as a married couple. He was amazed at the change in Vasha who was now two years of age. The years of her being hand-in-glove with Theo had begun. She had been told that I was expecting a baby, and every day (as Theo had instructed) she asked, "Are you well, Lia?" She never used any other form of address than Lia, while Max was Daddy-Max, and Theo was Daddy-Theo. She was a good little girl, happy, contented, self-sufficient—almost one could say, for so small a child, she was dutiful.

"I am glad she is so devoted to my father," Max said. "I do not have to share you with a demanding child. I have needed you so much, darling, I want you all to myself."

But I had missed out on being necessary to my child. I tried to explain that to myself, to Max but never to Theo. Even when talking to Max now that he was home, I had to be careful. He must be made to know, because it was so, that the thought of the coming baby, ours, his and mine, made up for any left-out feelings I might have.

"Vasha is very free with her love and kisses to all of us," Max said. "Are all little girls like that? I was half expecting pouts and sulks because I was coming back to re-possess her mummy."

The word "mummy" did not exist in Vasha's vocabulary, unless Theo had happened to mention Egyptian tombs. Max was re-observing the state of affairs to which I was used, although not hardened. That never came to be my attitude, no matter how I tried to rationalise. For Max's sake, I did not wish to dwell on the subject.

"Child psychology is a fascinating study," Max said. "There are more thousands of volumes on that subject that I had realised. I read recently that jealousy of siblings can permeate a life in no healthy way. It is a good thing, Lia, you and I have no siblings!"

"We are about to provide one for Vasha," I told him.

"I shall have to read up on contraindications," he laughed, "built-in safeguards! Do you think Vasha will be jealous?"

"Theo will see to it that nothing in her little world will be allowed to disturb her. We can always trust his judgement, can't we?"

We were talking in bed on Christmas night, nearer to the birth than we expected. "Lia, does your doctor listen to the foetal heartbeat when he is examining you?"

"With a sort of trumpet-thing, you mean? On my stomach?"

"Well, yes," Max answered. "Although that sounds a bit primitive. Has he said anything about the foetal heartbeat?" Max scarcely ever talked medicine. He sounded curious.

"He writes things down," I told him. "He doesn't say much. Why do you ask?"

"Of course I could be wrong," Max said, pausing as he always did. "It was when you fell asleep last night. You were in my arms. The night, the room, were still and soundless. I could feel your heart beating steadily under my hand, and my heart thump-thumping solidly. Then far away, the tiniest sound I ever heard. I could hear the infant's heart. I let my hand travel slowly until it was directly over the sound, an infinitesimal sound like music from another planet. You never stirred."

"Max, how wonderful! That is the loveliest thing you have ever said."

"Lia, there is something more. Perhaps I should not tell you, but I want to."

"Please tell me—even if it is bad, but by your voice, I think it is not bad."

"I could be wrong. I felt so heartbreakingly close to

you last night after all the weeks of being far away. It could be my imagination—it was a tremendous experience for me—but in that small frail thread of music there was a double beat. I strained my ears, striving to make my hearing move down my arm into my listening hand. There was, I am almost sure, a double beat."

"A double beat!" I echoed. "A little heart working overtime?"

"I think, I think, I am almost sure I heard two hearts. Then, as if tumbling over, the sound was gone. The general small turbulence continued, so all was well. Lia, should I not have said?"

"Of course you should! Whatever is in there belongs to both of us. Would you be pleased, as a doctor, if you are proved right?"

"That means little; but would you be pleased to have twins?"

"Oh, Max! Twins!" But I did not believe I could be so lucky. My age was into the thirties. To be given two babies for one pregnancy would be a prize beyond belief. Then I remembered. "Gran! She had two sets of twins! Oh, but she told me one set died."

"That was a long time ago, Lia. Infant mortality in Ireland in the last century was very high. If you and I produce two little children, they will not die. I promise you that. And this time, I will be with you right through."

"Maybe that very stiff head nurse won't let you stay." But Max smiled. He was a big man. To oppose him on size alone would take courage. Perhaps nowadays, expectant mothers know, or are told, everything. One hears of antenatal scans, analysis of amniotic fluid. Forty years ago, a woman went into labour with the feeling she would be lucky to come out alive.

Christmas Day was not ever a special day of celebration in our house in Terenure. Vasha had not been told the story of Nazareth. There was no more extra greeting, or giving of presents, on that day than on other days. Theo celebrated love of family in a thousand ways throughout the year. The day after Christmas Day was always a bank holiday, which was a holiday for everyone. We had planned a little visit to the villa on that St Stephen's Day. That was the day my twins chose to be born. They told me every year, after they understood, that there was never a chance their birthday could be overlooked, the day after Christmas. They need never have worried. I remember every moment of that day, a day of joy, pride, delight, a very happy day. If there was pain, it is forgotten, but I do not think there was any pain. Max stayed with me simply to hold my hands, tell me how beautiful I was and how proud he was. The two little boys slipped out into the world within ten minutes of each other. They were so tiny, one was four pounds and one was three and a half pounds. They were not identical, but they were alike enough in looks to confuse a stranger. They were olive-skinned and dark-eyed. They had wisps of tawny curly hair.

"This time it is I who am very proud of you," I told Max. He could not stop smiling. He had reported that the babies were perfect in every way, just as Vasha was. "It is too late tonight for her to come in. Has Theo told her?" I asked.

"I phoned him. He will tell her in the morning," Max said. "Was he pleased?" I had a fierce feeling of possession about these two little sons.

"He is overjoyed, Lia. I am sure he has Shanlee and Ted and the wine up in the long drawing-room."

I held out my arms to Max. "Hold me very close and tell me these babies are ours—yours and mine—and no one else has a claim."

"With Vasha it was different," Max murmured against my hair, "but we can always take her with us. And we are going, my love—you and I and the children. Tomorrow we will begin to plan. Just as soon as you are strong, we are going to be a little family on our own."

There have been so many times when I have thought: this is the happiest day. When I was young, there were hundreds more happy days than sad days.

Perhaps the hour in which my two little sons came into my life was the happiest hour of all.

Vasha was very articulate. "You not tell Daddy-Theo you have two babies? Why?"

"Lia did not know." Max was quick to defend me: "Only I knew."

"And you not tell?" Vasha persisted.

"No," Max smiled at her, "I like secrets." I see now that the lines were drawn early. There would be no secrets from Theo.

"What do you think of your little brothers?" I asked her. She considered the two little mites snuggled spoon-like into the cot. Theo was holding her hand, and watching her lovely little face. Her hair was very black and formed a glossy frame for the huge eyes arched over with Tadek's expressive eyebrows, now quirkily raised.

"I like them," she said. "When will they be awake and talk to me?"

She did not climb on my bed and snuggle. She did not ask such questions as when would we all be home again. She did not offer kisses to the babies, although she was usually generous with goodnight and good-morning and greeting kisses. She sat sedately on Theo's knee and listened with a kind of respectful wonder to all his enthusiasm for the newborn babies. Her delicate eyebrows remained raised as if in slight disbelief. Afterwards we talked. Max had also noticed.

"She is quite the young lady already." He smiled to think of it. "And she is only two."

"What my gran used to call 'old-fashioned.' I don't think she liked children to be too old-fashioned."

"Neither do I!" Max laughed. "I feel I am being sized up!"

By the end of the first week of the new year of 1951, we were all settled back into the house in Terenure. Theo had a nursery ready for the twins, quite different from Vasha's nursery, but just as well appointed. However, Max was now in charge and he said the babies would sleep in our room, either in his or in mine, but with us. They were very small and would need our joint attention. After six weeks of breast-feeding, Max gradually introduced them to bottle-feeding. I seem to remember it was a formula called Sister Laura's Food. Vasha took a mild interest in all the events to do with the babies. We were slow to choose names for them, and Theo left it to us. At last we decided on Stephen, because he was born on St Stephen's Day, and Theoderic, because of our beloved Theo. From the day their names were given to them, Vasha called them Stefan and Deric, and into those names they grew.

No time flies away more quickly than the growing years of our children. It is as if our states of being young are reversed. Our youth had lasted for ever; each day was a golden plum ready to be picked and tasted. Overnight, the signs of autumn appear. There are russet leaves on the tree. Now we see the children reaching out for the experience of what was once our forbidden fruit. Time passes, as my gran often said, "like a shout on the wind." Gran loved to get hold of phrases that were expressive, and that one appealed to her. Another of her pet sayings was: "So long as you have a man at your back…" That I understand very well now.

Max proved to be a born diplomat when the time came for the departure to Philadelphia. Vasha had watched the preparations, very often from the security of Daddy-Theo's lap. I made motherly overtures to her, enlisting her interest in folding little garments which had been hers, knitted jackets, little night-robes, vests, socks and bootees. "It is wonderful to have all these lovely little things for the twins to wear as they get bigger. It is so good of you to give them!" She held her distance; her eyes told me she was reading my frenetic gratitude for what it was, a ploy to make her ask if she was coming too. I wanted her to ask. I wanted her to come of her own desire. In the two years since her birth, the silken rope that was woven in her through me and from Tadek had become a fragile thread. Almost as if Tadek lived on within me without benefit of her existence. As if, I sometimes thought, she had come directly out of my love for Theo, out of his vigilant care of me, out of my gratitude to him. I came to realise that I must not, dare not, assume that Vasha would be with us in the new life in Philadelphia. Vasha, who was Tadek's child.

"You know, Father, I have been thinking that perhaps we will leave Vasha with you until the summer. What do you say? Would that be too much to ask?"

I wondered how Theo would receive this from Max, who rarely made suggestions of any kind.

"I am accustomed to this little burden," Theo answered smoothly. "But shall we not ask the child if she would miss her mother, and two little brothers now to play with?"

"Who, of the three of us, should ask her?" Max enquired.

"You should, Max," Theo answered. "You are the least involved." There was no sting intended in that answer and no hurt was taken.

In due course, a suitable opportunity came to question Vasha.

"Are you looking forward to the aeroplane trip, darling?" Max asked.

"Aeroplane trip?" she repeated.

"That is what we are packing for, Vasha. We are all off to Philadelphia, like in the song, 'Off to Philadelphia in the Morning!'"

"Daddy-Theo, too?" she glanced up at him but Theo shook his head. She put her hand in his.

"Not Vasha! Vasha stay." Theo disengaged his hand, and stepped back. He asked her, "Will you start to cry when Lia goes away with Max and the twins?"

Her eyebrows arched disdainfully. "Vasha stay!" she repeated. There was a firmness in her display of character that did not then, or ever, brook opposition.

"We will not be coming back until the summer, darling," Max said. "That is a long lot of weeks." Her hand had gone back into Theo's hand and with her other hand she had closed his fingers. "We take Silkitoo evening walk?" she lifted her face to Theo and they smiled together.

When the two little boys were three months old we set off for Philadelphia. Berny and I had been on the phone half a dozen times. She was full of enthusiastic cordiality for this renewal of our relationship, now at close quarters. She had vetted the house which Max had rented. The furniture had been thoroughly gone over by a contract cleaner. The house was warm and dry and centrally heated by oil. She had engaged a woman to come in daily. "She is black, Lia, but they all are and she is well recommended." A strange new world was about to open up for this little gurrier from Ringsend. Now indeed did time begin to race away.

CHAPTER NINE

Tadek had told me that in America a married couple of mixed religion, Catholic and Jew, would not be noticed for that fact as they would be noticed, maybe shunned, in Ireland. Tadek had never lived in America. Max had a different viewpoint. He found he agreed with Tadek overall. "But people do not live 'overall.' America is an enormous continent but a family lives in a place. Each place is a microcosm of the whole. People of one nation, of one religion, of the same customs, who have come into America from far away over the sea, tend to drift into each other's company just for the sake of a friendly face, a familiar language and similar roots. Thus are ghettos formed. The word was *borghetto*, probably Italian. *Borda* is a Latin word for a dwelling, I think. The *borghetto* was traditionally the part of an Italian city into which Jews were confined. Who knows why, Lia. It goes back to early Christian times in Rome. Maybe the Italians feared the Jews or the new Christians hated the Jews. Although, let it be said, in more recent times, Italy has persecuted Jews less than other nations have."

Max never made long speeches. What he had to tell me came now and then, a little at a time. I had been instructed by Theo over many years. The history of the Jews was perhaps more familiar to me than the history of the religion into which I had been baptised. Max and I had plenty of time on the journey for talk because we did not go by air. Theo was still a little apprehensive about long air travel. We went by ocean liner. We had a luxurious cabin; so we had good comfort in looking after our little boys who were now over three months old.

"There are Jewish ghettos in Philadelphia, and rich Jewish communities. I chose carefully the house which may be our home. That is if you like it, Lia, and if my prospects are good. Perhaps a year from now we could decide."

"What do you mean by you chose *carefully*?"

"I chose a mixed suburb," he replied, "about twenty miles from the city centre, fairly bourgeois. There is an Episcopalian church and a Quaker hall. No synagogue, no Catholic church."

When I was a child in Ringsend, and Phyllis was our servant-girl, she instilled into me a fear of Protestants. Jews she dismissed. "No God-fearing Catholic Dubliner would associate with Jews. But Protestants you better beware of. They were all English and they were put there to grind down the poor." Phyllis's young brother called the Protestants Proddy-dogs, and thumbed his nose at the Protestant church. Of Episcopalians I had never heard.

"You are telling me, Max, that we will not be, nor be forced to be, of any religion at all?"

"Do you still think I am, or our marriage is, worthwhile enough to abandon your faith?" Max was very serious.

So I asked him, "Suppose people, in your work for instance, question you, Max? After all, I'll be safe at home but you will have colleagues, and although you do not look as Jewish as Tadek, your name is Jewish and maybe our boys will look very Jewish. It is distinctive, after all."

"I will never deny that I am a Jew but the handy word is 'non-orthodox,'" Max said very firmly.

"One last question, something I have thought about from time to time. If you had married a Jewish girl, a girl devoted to her religion, what then?"

Max laughed at me. "The wonderful ifs and wherefores of life! Lia, if you had refused me, I would have shaved my beard and become a Buddhist monk."

I smiled with him. I had my own thoughts. The main thing in family life is harmony. I had occasion to recall with sad regret the bitter rows that were made over the choice of school for Lia's education, screaming rows leading to brutal beatings, rows that broke my mother's mind and sent her to her death. The choice between the convent boarding-school and the masonic boarding-school? Now, here I was, quite happy to follow what Max termed humanism. The word seemed to explain itself, so I did not question it. Would it have come between me and my peace of mind if I had been told that a humanist is one who denies the divinity of Christ and holds him to be a mere man? Would it? I don't think so. I remember Theo, anguished by the massacre of Jews in Germany, crying out at the malevolence of so-called Christians, "What a following he has, he who was a Jew, perhaps the cleverest Jew of them all! What power! What might! What an establishment!" For Max, humanism was associated with the humanities: Latin, Greek, poetry, rhetoric. For me? Human love was my ideal.

Berny and her husband met us and escorted us to our new home. She fell in love with the twins. She would dearly have loved a big family, she said repeatedly. Her husband had several daughters by previous wives and they had one son of their marriage. It was some months before we had settled down sufficiently to accept a dinner invitation to their home. I was quite overwhelmed by its size and magnificence.

Berny's husband, Denis Lowry, stood at the massive hall-door to welcome us. He was not as big a man as

Max (and ten years older) but he was very handsome. Berny had never been a beauty; yet her clear candid face held much appeal. She always knew exactly the colours to wear. Her manner, like her face, was frank. Instinctively I had always trusted her. Indeed I had acted on her counsel more than once. On that first dinner-party night, I was to receive a shock for which nothing had prepared me. She was conscious that I would be shocked. She did not allow our friendship to falter.

"Come," she said, "and meet my son. It is not quite his bedtime yet." And, with my eyes taking in the profusion of rich draperies over stained glass, I followed her up the stairs.

At the door of her little boy's nursery, she turned to me. She put her fingers on her lips. It was a warning sign. "We will speak later," she said. I was almost afraid when she opened the door that I was to see something deformed, crippled, retarded. I felt faint-hearted. Berny signalled for the maid to leave. Then I saw the little boy. He was playing with Lego, a toy new to me. He was constructing a little castle. He jumped up and rushed across the room into Berny's arms. I thought at once, this mother and son clearly adore each other. I saw his face and his figure in the full light as he hugged his mother. I recognised him immediately, although I could scarcely believe my eyes. There could be no mistake: this child must be Burton's son. The sturdy build of his body, the firm set of his shoulders, the dark brown twinkling eyes, the chiselled lips, the way his thick hair grew into curls on the back of his neck. I held my breath for fear I should call out.

Denis Lowry was handsome, he had a good carriage, and attractive brown eyes. If I had never seen Burton...But I had. I had slept in his bed, against his naked body, when I was the age this chid was now. I knew terrible things about Burton, I had seen his savage temper. I had hated him and desired him madly in the same moment on the day of Berny's marriage. Burton was married to my mother. He had broken my mother's spirit. It had never entered my head that Berny was pregnant on her wedding day. Berny had lovers. She knew the score. The marriage had been planned for months before. She was slim as a wand in her white dress, her veil encrusted with shining pearls. Everything about her was splendid, a brilliant young doctor about to be married to a very rich American, with whom she was deliriously in love—she had said so.

I was introduced to young Frayne. I would be Aunty Lia. He was polite and amiable. His mother promised to come later for a goodnight kiss. He clung to her and she smiled radiantly. Then we were in her bedroom.

"You knew, of course?" She had always smoked cigarettes. Now she took time to light one. "I went to him the night before the wedding—his hotel room—in Belfast. I never saw him alone again." Her breath caught on the last word and her voice came out in a whisper. "I must have wanted it to happen."

What could I say? My brain teemed with memories. I was remembering her on her wedding day, the brightest, happiest girl in the world. What year was that? During the war—we were twenty-four, twenty-five? Some grand hotel, a crowded reception, music—what was that music? Oh yes, I remembered: "Always," and Berny floating past in Burton's arms, her handsome bridegroom looking on.

"Oh Ber," I whispered, "I was the one who brought Burton into your life. I am so sorry...I..."

"Don't ever be sorry, old chum." Her blue eyes were clear again. "He was the greatest thing that ever happened to me—from the first night in the Hibernian Hotel. From that night, he always called me Frayne—never Berny Frayne, just Frayne. Look, I am still wearing his bracelet, the bracelet he bought for you, and gave to me that first night. If I knew where he is now, I would fly to him! Oh God, he was incredible. I had him hundreds of times and every time was better than the time before. You must know that!"

I stared at her, her wide blue eyes full of freedom.

"No," I said, "I never had him." I could not take my eyes from Berny's face. She had spent the night before her wedding in Burton's bed in that hotel; yet on her wedding day, Burton had attention only for Lia, his deep brown eyes holding a seductive flame as he waltzed her to some romantic music. And after the wedding reception, that flame had drawn her to his hotel room ready and yearning for the promised seduction. That hotel room where, only yesternight, Berny the bride had given Burton the rights he had established long before. How old was Lia then? Twenty-four? She remembered Burton's voice. "She is insatiable, your little friend!" Was he smiling that quizzical smile to think of the insatiable Berny of the previous night? When she was twenty-four, Burton was still entrenched in Lia's sensuality, unassailably entrenched despite all else.

"No, I never had him!" I repeated more firmly.

"No?" Berny was lightly disbelieving. "No? He was crazy about you. A thousand times he told me that you were the only good and innocent person in his life. I always assumed he had enjoyed your sweet innocence for himself."

"No," I told her, "but not because I didn't want to."

"So now you know about my adorable little Frayne. I named him for myself. Are you going to tell me about Vasha?"

"I will," I answered, "but not tonight. Not tonight, please not tonight, Berny." My brain seemed impaled on one thought: The night before her wedding to Denis Lowry! The night before!

"I must put my arms around you, Lia. We must always be friends, same as we always were. I need you. Promise? I am glad you know. I wanted you to know."

We went down to the magnificent dining-room where Denis was telling Max that these rich possessions were inherited from his grandfather and his father who had been high personages in the political world of the United States early in the century. They had lived in Virginia where Denis owned much land and property.

Max looked relaxed and at ease with Denis Lowry. He had dined here several times in his first few months in Philadelphia.

When we were at home, Max remarked on my silence. "What happened when you went up to see the son and heir? Handsome little chap, isn't he? You looked pale or shaky or cold when you came down. Are you all right now, Lia?"

Strange as it may seem, when I look back at those sunlit days of being their little friend and playing with Tadek and Laelia and Max on Sandymount Strand, it is only now I wonder how I managed to keep all my secrets separately. Later on, I passed Burton on to

Berny but I never mentioned the name of Tadek Vashinsky to her or to anyone. Tadek was my very heart and soul, the very blood in my veins. He knew of Burton but only to shield me from possible hurt. He saw him once without knowing who he was. He never knew that his sister Laelia lived with Burton and had Burton's child, a boy who was adopted or got rid of in some way. I could have told Tadek in the partisans' camp but I did not. Our time together was too precious. Theo knew many things but in his discretion there was wisdom. Max never asked questions; he never initiated enquiry. We talked together of Tadek, allowing no other name to intrude. And our talk of Tadek was for us alone—his memory was not shared.

To tell Max now that Berny's little boy was the son, not of the high-born Denis Lowry, but of a scoundrel named Burton who had been married to my mother, who had...who had...who had...No, I had to go on keeping secrets. I was a woman who was living in the times when there was much shame in intimate relationships. After all, Max had rescued me. He had taken on my illegitimate child out of brotherly love for his friend. I did not intend to sully his marriage to me by bringing up the name of Burton: Berny's secret, Laelia's secret, Lia's secret.

"Maybe I was cold," I said lightly, "but I am fine now."

In our new home with our own two little sons, thriving mightily, we delighted in learning, each from the other, our capacity for a deeply satisfying sexual rapport, highlighting our warm friendship and our love of family. Max was able to sleep in contentment. There were fewer and fewer dreams. He was amassing material for a book on the Jewish massacre. He was studying in the university. There would be an appointment to his own clinic at the end of the year. Deep inside myself, I buried this unwanted knowledge that wherever Burton might be then, he was living on in the person of a small boy named Frayne Lowry.

We began to meet the Lowrys more frequently, our acquaintance growing into a close friendship as the years passed. I saw young Frayne ever more clearly. My gran used to say, "On a good day, Burton would coax the birds out of the bushes—poor Marie, she can't resist, she can't say no." I saw the same persuading charm in Berny's son. He never gave trouble. He never had to kick up a scene to get his own way. He had conquered his mother and the rest of the household in the first years of his life. Everyone was in thrall to the charm of young Frayne, long before his twelfth birthday. That was the year Theo and Vasha came to Philadelphia for their first visit. We had gone home frequently: Easter, Christmas, summer. Home for us would always be Dublin, no matter how long we lived in the United States. That was a glorious Philadelphia summer. Stefan and Deric were going to be five and soon to start school. We had watched Vasha grow more pretty, more poised, more intellectually capable under Theo's care. With him, she was at ease and utterly content. We had said a year but we knew she would stay in Terenure. We talked of it sometimes. Max worried for fear I had been cheated, deprived. In time I became less unhappy about the situation because we were in constant touch with Theo and with Vasha. In between our visits she wrote little letters to both of us and to her brothers. She had started in a small private school when she was six. Ted Levitsky took her and brought her home. She was undoubtedly cosseted; yet she never showed signs of being a spoilt child. Remembering my own long friendship with Theo, when I thought of him as "the old man," I knew how delightful his company was, how serene he made one feel, how one always aimed to please him and how benignly he smiled on even the smallest effort. In that summer, when Vasha was presented to the Lowrys at young Frayne's twelfth birthday party, she was soon to be eight years of age.

CHAPTER TEN

Theo and Berny were old friends. Since Vasha remained in Theo's care, Berny had concluded he was Vasha's father. Her candid smile often revealed her thoughts. We had "evened up" she surmised and did not refer to it. I left it at that. She would say nothing to her husband. We had, she thought, established a solidarity.

"Mr Randt, how do you do it? You have not aged a day! And this lovely little girl is Vasha. Frayne, meet your new cousin, Aunty Lia's girl all the way from Ireland. Denis, isn't she adorable!"

I was watching. I always watched Frayne and I always saw Burton. In Frayne's eyes was that quizzical smile I remembered so well—the smile of conquest. Ah! what have we here! A very pretty little piece!

"Are you a colleen?" he asked. Vasha took him in, from the tip of his head, down his white T-shirt, white shorts, brown legs, white sneakers. Then her dark eyes travelled back up to his face. Her eyelashes flicked in dismissal.

"*Cailín*," she said distinctly, "is the Irish word for

girl. Yes, I am a girl."

Being put down never fazed Frayne (or Burton). He revealed a perfect set of teeth. "Ah, now I know an Irish word. Perhaps you will tell me some more?"

I am glad she is only seven, I thought. Instantly I remembered that I was only six when I gave my heart to Tadek. I took Vasha's hand. "Come and talk to Lia. It is months since we had a big long gossip. How is Silkitoo?"

But I could not keep her by my side all day. There were a lot of boys and girls at the party. They were mostly of Frayne's age but some smaller children had been invited to play with Deric and Stefan. Those two were a pair of rascals, up to mischief all the time, daring each other, egging each other on: "a handful," as my gran used to say of anyone's naughty children. The Lowrys' garden (or "yard" as they called it) contained a hard tennis-court and a big lawn for baseball. Soon, Berny and Denis were organising tournaments and team games and Max was given a whistle and a stop-watch. At the edge of the yard, there were tall birch trees, and here I walked with Theo, my arm tucked into his. We talked a little, feeling very content in each other's company. I saw Vasha watching the tennis game in which Frayne and three others were playing. Something about his smashing and volleying made me think he was showing off. I wondered if her eyes were intent on him and not the game.

I looked up at Theo. "Perhaps it is as well I am not Vasha's everyday mother, Theo. I would be too possessive."

He pressed my arm reassuringly. "Mothers and daughters! The same the world over!"

"Do you feel nervous about her?" I asked.

"Of course," he said. "Increasingly. She is very, very special. But may I say, she has a higher estimation of her own value than you ever had of yours, my dear Lia. When you were young, when you first came to me, your self-esteem was low. You look surprised? Why did I never chide you for that? You loved everyone, Lia, and you never guessed how many people loved you."

"You always treated me with love, Theo, but that was because you are so gracious and kind."

"In the beginning, it was your beauty—it still is—and your youth. Your youthfulness was a gift you brought to me. In a little while, it was because you *are* you. I love you for the best of all reasons: I cannot help but love you. Max and I have that same weakness," and he was smiling down at me.

"And Vasha?"

"For Vasha, I thank the gods every day. And I thank you. On every hour, I think of you. You are happy now with your little boys? And with my son?"

"Very, very happy, Theo. Max is a darling."

"And Stefan? And Deric? Do my grandchildren make you happy?"

"They are little monkeys!" I told him.

"All the better for that," he laughed. "They will get it out of their systems while they are young."

Even in small things, I do not like giving and taking back but Theo guessed my need to have him say more of Vasha.

"Yes," he said, "her estimation of her own value is very high, naturally so, and I encourage her (as do all of us in the house) by giving her the security of our affection. It is important to give affection to a young child and expect no reward for the giving. The child is not aware that affection is for trading. The child thinks as a child thinks. Children take all things for granted except fear. We give our affection to Vasha, freely. All of us, Ted and Shanlee. Silkitoo. All of us. From now on, we will make closer the bonds with her brothers." I listened and stored away his words.

In a little while, he spoke again. "There will be no boarding-school, Lia. Are you in agreement with me on that? There is an excellent girls' school in Earlsfort Terrace in the city. I do not approve of co-educational schools such as they have here in the States."

"Oh, why is that?"

"For exact biological reasons: both sexes perform less well educationally and both sexes are less appreciative of the other sex. School is not the end of youth, not the beginning of life."

"Will you encourage Vasha to appreciate the other sex?" I asked lightly. Or would he be possessive?

"I shall not oppose her appreciation. However, I hope to make sure her judgement is sound."

How would he do that? There was no chance that day for further conversation. Max and I helped with the party, especially with the smaller ones. All the young people were gathered around a big table on the lawn. Frayne played host to perfection. Vasha was easily the most delicious little piece of femininity there and the American boys were quick to notice her. She distributed her favours, smiling and accepting from all, making sure to talk to the other girls, never being less than sweetly polite, as if she had the experience of a young lady rather than of a little girl. Yes, my gran would have said "old-fashioned."

As always, Max and I talked over the happenings of the day in our own room. Max asked, flipping imaginary dollars through his fingers, "I suppose we will have to start giving parties in the American style for Stefan and Deric?"

"Luckily," I reminded him, "their birthday comes at Christmas and we are always at home then."

"But they will be accepting other kids' invitations, and we must make a return, mustn't we?"

"We'll manage," I assured him, "even though there will always be a double-up of friends!"

"Did you notice," Max asked, "that young Frayne was quite smitten by our pretty little Vasha? Denis remarked on what a little beauty she is. Lia, wouldn't Tadek have been proud! She behaves so politely! She stood out from all those other kids—they were strident compared to her!" I said, "Aren't you tired, darling? Shouldn't we go to sleep?" I lay beside him and I stared into the dark room. I pondered the idea that Frayne Lowry had found Vasha so pretty. Did Theo remember the day he had stood outside Laelia and Burton's apartment, waiting for me on the pretext that our travel arrangements had changed? He had stood there, framed by a long window, a silver-haired angel of rescue. He had watched us walking up the corridor from the lift, our hands clasped. He had all the time in the world to assess the big man who was Burton: the athletic build, the twinkling brown eyes, the crisp crinkly hair and the chiselled lips which could smile so beguilingly. Yes, those sensuous lips. Young Frayne's lips were exactly the same. I sought around in my memory for any recollection of what Theo would know about my friend Berny, the medical student. The dinners in the Shelbourne long ago? Berny, on every occasion with a new boy-friend. No, I was always intensely loyal. I would never have associated Berny's name with Burton's name. No, not to Theo. Not to anyone. But, to anyone who had looked on the face of Burton, young Frayne Lowry's resemblance was startling.

In the very same way that Vasha was a feminine re-creation of Tadek, surely Theo must have noticed young Lowry's features. Berny was, in her natural style, at ease with Theo. She knew nothing of Laelia, she knew nothing of Tadek, yet she thought she knew it all. I felt like a person in a maze. Would Theo cross-question me? Would Theo say anything about young Frayne? We were to be invited for a formal dinner in the Lowrys' before my visitors went back to Ireland. Perhaps many of my fears were groundless, but how to be sure? The dinner passed off without incident.

The previous summer, when we went home to Ireland, we had at last been able to travel to Siena. Each year the arrangement had been made and something, on one side or the other, had happened to cancel the plan. In the twins' early years, we spent a lot of our holidays in our Bray villa. The summer was high tourist season for Luigi and Phyllis in their hotel, still new then, still finding its way. Phyllis's baby was a son, a year younger than Vasha, and in his first couple of years, Phyllis guarded him day and night. St Jude, she wrote to me, had looked after her, but there would not be another child. Now St Jude was the guardian angel of her son. She had named him Anthony, both for her father and for another favourite patron saint, but of course everyone called him Antonio, and in time this was shortened to Tonio. He was like Luigi in looks, very Mediterranean, but like Phyllis in build, tall and strong. Even at five years of age, when we first met again (after years of letter-writing, letters telling of our lives in Philadelphia and hers in Siena), Tonio was taller than Vasha. Not that Vasha was with us on that occasion. Stefan and Deric were still too young to take away with comfort. We left them with Shanlee and Theo. We would have taken Vasha to Siena, had she wanted to come. She had become a seasoned traveller with Theo. They had been to Paris, to Rome and as far east as Istanbul. She elected to stay and help Shanlee. I always felt sad when she rejected my company. But, as Max said, her reasons, never stated, may not have been rejection. Perhaps she gave us to each other for our enjoyment, even though to all intents and purposes we were her mother and father. She saw Theo, and only Theo, as being the arbiter of her daily life. There, I have made that point enough times—I must not go on about it for ever. Max and I went to Siena on our own at last, and we stayed for three weeks. In later years, we often stayed much longer. I remember best the first time. "I must tell you about Catherine of Siena," I said to Max as we sat in the back of the cathedral, "because she always gave me the creeps."

"This should be good!" Max smiled.

"Every year in school we had a week's retreat. We all meditated in silence and were allowed one book to read. It was called a 'spiritual' book. If the weather was fine we walked around the pleasure grounds, in full view of the nuns on guard, and we turned over the pages of our books. If the weather was very bad, raining, we sat in our classrooms turning over the pages, and there it was possible to pass notes to each other."

"Forbidden, I suppose?" Max was amused. "And you did that for a whole week? In silence?"

"An endless week," I said, "with endless dull sermons and plain food, for the good of our immortal souls!"

"And where does Catherine of Siena come into this?" Max enquired, gazing at the glory of her church.

"Well," I said expansively, "I had discovered in the early years that the spiritual books were very dull, until I happened on the life of Catherine of Siena. Just think, the popes had left Rome and moved to Avignon in France. Catherine did not approve of that; she strove mightily to get them back to Rome."

"We must be coming to the creepy bit!" Max teased.

"We are," I told him. "She never took off her clothes for years and years as a penance, so that Pope Clement, or Gregory (I forget how many popes), would leave Avignon. The penance was to live in dirty garments without even washing! The book was full of descriptions of the lovely women in Provence, who were living in the pope's palace in Avignon, clad in silken robes, and drinking Burgundy wine. Catherine went to Avignon, in her own clothes I suppose, and she went into a daily trance after communion. The pope's women pierced her body most irreverently with needles, to see if the trance was genuine. I told Berny about this find of a book in a note, and we swapped books. Then we told Lucille, but she said it made her feel sick. And she re-christened the saint, 'Catherine of Senna Pods.'"

"When you talk about Lucille, I feel I missed a real innocent," Max said. "I would have liked Lucille."

"Well, lucky for me," I told him, "Lucille always said she wasn't gone on fellows! But you are right, she often comes into my mind. She was an innocent, always in trouble with the nuns for such silly things— never really bold."

The first of many holidays in Siena began a tradition. Max and I wandered around the city all day, every day. The colours were of the sunset—a city of yellow ochre and rose-red brick. Now Siena is changed, and I have seen it change, but thirty-five years ago it was a lovely medieval town, scarcely touched by time, and not too much by war. Tuscany is still the most beautiful part of Italy.

Luigi was a typical Italian—is there such a generalisation possible of any nationality? He seemed so to us. Early on in our traditional holidays, we noticed he had a quick eye for the young ones, and Max believed the Italian climate aggravated the temptations to *amore*. We thought he pleasured himself accordingly. However, Luigi's mother was never very far away, and *la madre* recognised in Phyllis a wife beyond compare. So an equilibrium was observed. Within the household of the hotel peace reigned, and the reigning queen was Phyllis. Sometimes she let slip the mask: "You might say, Lovey, that I came up the hard way. I deserve what I've got and I intend to keep it. There are always things one has to offer up for the things one has to suffer. My son Tonio will get the best. I was going on forty-six years of age when he was born. St Jude's miracle baby. I'll live to see that he gets everything I never had. No hotel lackey for him. I'll see to that, Lovey!"

In the early holidays in Siena, we used think that Tonio was a little rapscallion, an imp of devilry, but we did not understand then the freedom of Italian children—certainly of boys in the cities. Tonio was born there, his school pals moved up along with him. The friars with whom he was educated provided an excellent curriculum, the university was open to all who could afford it, and it seemed many could. We observed that Tonio was surrounded by friends and he was first in all things. Like his mother's family, the Dalys, he was a natural musician. He accompanied himself on the piano, not taking it seriously, not bothering to learn to read music. Stefan and Deric were enchanted with Tonio. He was like their great big brother. He let them go everywhere with him. They loved their holidays in Ireland, but the real holiday was in Siena. Stefan had a flair for music. He picked up very quickly from watching Tonio. Deric had inherited Theo's love of the beautiful. Siena was heaven to him as he grew older, with the libraries, the art galleries, the museums and the easy run on the train to Florence.

CHAPTER ELEVEN

I n the family, the years were always recalled by the birthdays. In the year 1957, Theo would be seventy in August. From Easter onwards, Max and I and the boys talked of nothing but the birthday party we were planning for Theo. In January of that year, Vasha was nine, and the two boys, who were born on St Stephen's Day in 1950, would be seven and a half. Shanlee and Ted, who had been in their early twenties when Max was born, were beginning to feel their years. Max and I wanted to appear young for the children's sake, but we too had passed the prime.

Berny's father had died a few years before. She still went home to Belfast most years for her mother's sake. The troubles in Northern Ireland were always kept hidden from the outside world until 1968. In the late 1950s and into the 60s, Ireland was always a peaceful place. The pace of life had not changed, we thought, in a hundred years. For Theo's birthday, Berny would come south to Dublin, and young Frayne would be with her. I had asked Phyllis to fit in her annual visit to her parents in Ringsend with the birthday party, and to be sure to bring Tonio for the special delight of Deric and Stefan. I knew August was a difficult month for her to leave her hotel, but it was now very prosperous and Luigi made no objection. As Max smiled over Phyllis's letter, he said, "Luigi is not a farmer but no doubt he'll make hay!"

Early in June, Berny arrived at the house unexpectedly. She had received a letter from a firm of London solicitors asking her if she could forward to them my address. The matter was to do with the will of Mr Jack Burton, who had been a client of theirs. We were both mystified. We never realised that Burton could be dead. This seemed incredible. We neither of us revealed our emotion but we knew that we had thought of him as monumental, immortal.

"How did they get your address, Ber?"

"That's easy," she said. "I have never stopped writing to him."

"Did he answer your letters?" I asked, although I did not want to know.

"No, never," she said, "but that didn't stop me. And I think you know why." I had seen Berny cry once. It was over Lucille's death. Now she did not cry. I wonder did she mourn for Burton afterwards when she was alone. Or when she looked on the face of her son. What hopes had taken refuge behind that free and easy way she had?

"Do you want me to write to these solicitors and give your address?" she asked, a little coldly, in the tone of a woman by-passed.

"I have never talked to Max about my strange relationship with Burton," I said slowly. "I merely told him that he was my stepfather, a long time ago." Had Theo told Max about Laelia, after London, when we were in Paris? Berny was unaware of a woman named Laelia. For all I knew, Burton may have continued to see Berny in London. But maybe his affair with Laelia was all over long before. Of course, it must have been. When Laelia's (and Tadek's) mother died, we heard no more of Laelia. Gran never had letters from her. I knew that she was now an internationally famous opera star. The newspapers carried her picture constantly.

"He must have left you something in his will," Berny suggested, still with an aloof voice.

"If that is all, perhaps that could explain away Burton to Max," I said, but instinctively I feared. "After all," Berny continued, "you were his dear little stepdaughter. He never knew I had a claim on him."

"Don't, Ber, please don't! I have no idea what this is about. As you said, you never told him because when you discovered you were pregnant, you could have been carrying your husband's child. When you saw little Frayne, you knew. When I saw him, I knew. Burton did not know and now he never will. So just let's be the same as we always were."

The bitterness was not gone. "You know what we always were, don't you? Me—a big mouth, full of advice. You—silent, full of secrets."

I was beginning to be angry and I detest anger. "All right then. But I'm good with secrets. I keep yours as well as my own." And then we were hugging each other, each loath to let the other escape from the precious net of friendship that had enclosed us since we were children.

"I'll tell you. Whatever it is I'll tell you, I promise. Berny, you know I'll tell you."

"Are we shedding tears for Burton?" she asked, and our eyes were ready to do just that. I remember we made coffee. Everyone makes coffee. Coffee never alters anything but the word is magic. Some time later that night, in time for the daylight hours in London, Berny phoned the solicitors and gave them my address. The time had come to see how much Max knew. I chose my moment to tell him that solicitors were looking for Burton's stepdaughter. I dreaded this intrusion of an alien force into our cherished and intimate understanding. I knew to go on much further with concealment could bring me close to untruths. I took the long, slow curve, unable to be blunt.

"Max, do you remember when you were in Vienna, and Laelia was there on her first music scholarship, and I asked you if you two saw each other? I was still in school then."

"I remember the time but I never saw much of Laelia. That was peacetime. Vienna was a very gay place. There were many girls."

"Did she have boyfriends?"

"I don't know, Lia. We lived on opposite sides of the city. She was a very serious student and very poor."

"After Mr Vashinsky's death she lived in London," I said.

"I thought she went to Italy. I seem to remember my father telling me in Paris that after her mother's death, she had a man in London. He said it was someone you knew, Lia."

"It was my stepfather." Now I rushed out the words: "They had a child, a boy."

Max looked surprised, not shocked. "If I was told that in Paris, I have forgotten it. I do not think my father mentioned a child. So many things crowded into our lives when war came, and at that time, 1938, Tadek was already in a labour camp. He spoke fondly of Laelia. He hoped for great success for her. But that was later, surely, when I joined the partisans. He certainly never mentioned a marriage, or a birth. I am sure I would remember if he had."

"My stepfather may be dead. Perhaps, I don't know. I think they were putting the child for adoption."

I spoke very fast, without emphasis, to cover the emotion that threatened to choke off the words. "In some roundabout way, the solicitors got hold of Berny's address. My stepfather was a guest at her wedding to Denis in Belfast, where I was bridesmaid. The solicitors wanted Berny to find my address—they mentioned a will." Max did not ask questions about the roundabout way.

"Don't be upset, darling. He was probably quite old, your stepfather, and had had a good innings. There, there, now, take my handkerchief. Shush."

Theo had said very little, it seemed. I should have known. He would fear to take away from me the shelter his presence had given me that day in London. I had never told Theo that Burton was at Berny's wedding. Guiltily, I remembered now that when I got off the train at Amiens Street Station, Ted was there, as always, with the limousine, and the old man was waiting in Terenure to hear about my day in Belfast, a city he cordially detested.

"So will you get in touch with the solicitors?" Max enquired.

"Perhaps I should let Berny give my name and address, as she received their letter. They will realise I am married." I had stopped the tears.

"Very much married," Max smiled. "I am sure my father would deal with the solicitors more easily from

Dublin, if that would save you any distress. We could phone him—their evening meal time in Terenure—maybe have a word with Vasha also?"

"Perhaps, Max, we should just wait and see what the solicitors' letter will have to say."

In due course, the solicitors' letter arrived. They made apologies for the long delay in contacting me. This was due to many difficulties, apart from the final difficulty of lost addresses. Their client, Mr Burton, was not an established client of theirs, having come in off the street, as it were, to make his last will and testament. Customary in time of war. There was the possibility that the apartment block in which he resided may have been bombed out during the London V-bomb raids. Lists of deaths were often mislaid. Their own strong-room had been damaged similarly and it had taken years to restore their files.

Their client had left a sum of money on which dividends had accumulated. However, there was another matter on which their client had in his will importuned the help of Lia? (now Randt), in the event of his death. It would be of advantage if this matter could be discussed on a personal basis. They were prepared to travel, or was Mrs Randt prepared to travel?

Max and I conned this letter, he with great cheerfulness, I with a sinking heart. Sometimes when he was tired from his day in the university or from the correspondence in connection with the proposed book about the partisans, Max would lie back and take off his heavy glasses, running his fingers through his now greying hair, and he would yawn apologetically. Always, at that moment, I loved him best of all. Then he was defenceless; he needed me; he replaced all other loves in my life. There were times, less often when we were older, when Max held love at bay— sometimes for days and nights. I learned to recognise these times and to associate the searing frustration which invaded his soul with his unwanted memories of Auschwitz. I redoubled my love and tenderness at those times. "Not so sophisticated after all, Lia, am I? Once a Jew, always a Jew." He was trying to keep sadness at bay. We decided at last that as our annual trip to Ireland was almost due, I should write to the solicitors and arrange a visit to their London office in July.

"You will come with me?" I asked Max.

"Of course, darling. You are not going to the Tower of London! They are only solicitors. There is nothing to worry about. Will you apprise my father of this! Would you wish him to come along since he knew about Burton and Laelia and the birth of a son?"

"This time, just you, Max. I will write to him about it before we go to Ireland, but shall I say to him we have told the solicitors you and I will be in London?"

"Take that serious frown off your lovely face, Lia. There is nothing to worry about. Of course, just you and I and a few days in London. A little visit to the Burlington Arcade?" He was always one, and Theo also, to promise a special treat.

Some doubt that stirred deep within told me there was something to worry about. I began to count the days on the calendar, the days until the long summer holiday in Ireland. I had done this every previous year with joyous expectation: the hills of home, the streets of Dublin, the house of beauty in Terenure, Theo taking me into his arms, hugging Vasha, kissing Shanlee and Ted and Silkitoo, Stefan striking chords on the grand piano, Deric in search of new pictures, new pieces of art, the first day of homecoming, the dinner that Shanlee had prepared, the little bit of jet-lag so Max and I could sleep late in the lovely room that was my own in Theo's house and seeing again my Murillo picture. I struck off the days on the calendar and the feeling that that year was of doom. What would I hear in the solicitors' office? What help was I to give? This holiday of 1957 that was to be so special a holiday. Theo's seventieth birthday party. Berny and Frayne. Phyllis and Tonio. Nothing must be allowed to spoil the birthday party. The image of Burton had not troubled my conscience for years. Even when I looked on the handsome features of young Frayne Lowry, I could push the thought of Burton into the background. That was Berny's secret. Now Burton was at the edge of my thoughts a hundred times a day. In a solicitors' office, some guilt in me was going to be laid bare before my husband's eyes. It became an ever-present dread.

"Lia, how abstracted you are these days. Do you feel off form?"

"No, no, I'm fine. What did you say, dearest?"

We travelled to London the day before the visit to the solicitors' office. I could not sleep in the hotel bedroom.

I lay still as a statue for fear of waking Max. I could not finish even a cup of tea at breakfast.

"Darling, you look very pale," Max said, "Are you headachy? Let me order some fresh tea. Or coffee."

I tried to smile for him. Would he look askance at me in a couple of hours? Would I turn out to be not the Lia he thought of as his wife, but some remnant of a woman who had been caught in a strange liaison with a man no woman should have loved and yet so many did? And I did—long ago.

"Look at me, sweetheart. Lia, if I could get a drink this early in the morning, would you have a little brandy? You are shaking, darling."

In the solicitors' office, I had to take a firm grip on

myself because I could scarcely hear his voice. It appeared that yes, Mr Jack Burton had left money to his stepdaughter. It had been accumulating interest since he had deposited it in the National Westminster Bank. The solicitor mumbled on about bank deposit numbers. He fumbled about with documents, reading fuzzy words. Maybe he was not mumbling or fumbling, maybe that was my lack of concentration. Suddenly I heard Max's voice call my name rather sharply. He was staring at me. "Lia, the solicitor has asked you if you would allow him to read a letter written by his client, Mr Burton? Lia, Mr Ormsby wishes to read this letter."

I stared back at Max. Was that the usual look of concern in his eyes? I looked at the solicitor. He held a document up for me to see. This was it, then. I nodded my heard in resignation.

Dear little Lia,

When we met at Berny's wedding, I realised you are the only one I can trust in this world. I have asked, begged, implored Laelia to cooperate with me in helping our son. She has received my letters. She does not answer. She is married very well, and her life has changed. Please, Lia, if I do not survive this endless nightly bombing of London, will you take him out of the orphanage—even if only for holidays? I am leaving enough money for his education, and something for you, which takes care of all I have,

*right now. I know I can depend on you, Lia. I loved
your mother, no matter what way it looked. Since
then everything went wrong. If I get free of this
uniform and the war is over, I'll take care of my son,
and of you, too, if you need me.*

Reading this short letter now, I see it is not the letter
of an educated man—so many little repetitions. And
he was not educated, he was just very smart. He could
pass for a duke, my gran used to say. His build, his
height, his looks were all magnificent. That day, in the
solicitors' office, I heard the words through a haze of
grief and, may God forgive me, relief. He had written
only what was necessary. It is very strange, and difficult,
to realise that underneath that brilliant, masterful
front, there beat a heart that loved a little boy and a
small girl he had wronged. Who would have suspected
that! Not Phyllis, who never trusted him. Not my gran,
who hated him. Not Berny, who never received a reply
to her cries for help. And then I remembered Mama
saying, "He is soft-hearted, really. He would cry over
a puppy."

"My wife believed that Mr Burton had put this boy
up for adoption," I heard Max saying.

"Apparently not," the solicitor answered. "The
name of the orphanage is Casa Santa Maria, Via
Alessandro Poerio, Rome. His name is Alessandro
Vashinsky." No marriage certificate—the mother's

name—no choice—the name of the street.

"But what year was that?" Max asked. "The boy must have been born in 1939, and you are not certain if your client was killed in the bombing in—when?"

"Mr Randt, from June to September 1944, we were hit by the V weapons. London had been blitzed earlier."

"Have you been in touch with this orphanage?" Max asked.

"We were waiting for Mrs Randt's permission. In effect, Mr Burton in his will has stipulated that she take charge of the boy and of the money for his education. I read that to you in the will."

"Yes, so you did," Max replied. "I was calculating that the boy must be eighteen years old now—some of his educable years are over. He was five or six when this will was written."

The solicitor waited, tapping his pen gently on the paper. Max took my hand. I whispered to him, "What are we to do?"

"May I use the telephone, Mr Ormsby? I should like to bring my father into this matter."

Mr Ormsby pushed the telephone across the desk. "Take your time, Mr Randt," he said courteously, as he closed the door into another office.

I heard Max telling the bizarre story to his father on the telephone. An eighteen-year-old son of Burton in

Italy! And I was thinking: a thirteen-year-old son of Burton in Philadelphia! I remembered Francesca— who had been raped (was it rape?) by Tony Lloyd and lived with Burton in the ENSA headquarters in the Isle of Man. Were there other children?

"My father believes we should discuss this entire affair in Terenure. Meanwhile, he suggests we allow the solicitor to proceed with the legal formalities."

"Do you mean I am to accept responsibility for the boy?" I was hardly able to speak. Another Frayne Lowry? Tall and splendid, those chiselled lips? That unconcealed sensuality? "Of course we will accept, *balibt*," Max said. "A stepfather is family."

The son of Laelia and Burton was born in London on the day I went to their apartment. I had gone to tell Laelia of her mother's death, never dreaming that Burton was with her. All too well I remembered the date of the death; so a week later it was the middle of April, in fact the fifteenth of April 1939. Theo and I went on to Paris. Max was there but Tadek was already with the partisans. Max said the words in greeting, "Spring in Paris, Lia," and my heart longed for Tadek.

"Yes," I said slowly, like one working a way out of a maze. "He would be eighteen."

The solicitor had come back into the office. He asked, "You made your phone call? I may go ahead?"

"Did you say when the will was made?" I asked; the

dates were becoming clearer.

"Yes, Mrs Randt. The will is dated in the first week of August 1943."

I thought, a week after Berny's marriage. He never answered her letters. But then she was a married woman. The Burton I remembered did not know the meaning of discretion. Was this another secret that I must keep from Berny? He had lived long enough to answer.

"Did Mr Burton come again to your office, Mr Ormsby?" I asked.

"No, Mrs Randt. The one visit only. A very tall man, if I remember correctly. But those were troubled times here in London, when whole families were wiped out, when legal offices disappeared from streets on which they had stood for centuries."

We asked many questions of each other, Max and I. We wondered if Burton had visited his son in the first five years of his life. Then Burton was never seen again. What effect did that have on a child of five? Or maybe when Laelia and Burton put the child in the orphanage they clanged the gates and forgot about him. Perhaps the boy knew only the nuns in the orphanage in Rome.

"You know, Lia," Max said, "I think that when Burton met you at Berny's wedding, you struck a chord in his heart!"

"I never thought Burton had a heart," I said, and I wondered if I was speaking truthfully.

"He probably remembered you as a little kid, and how they used to send you into that dark cold room every night—all the sadness Tadek told me about in Auschwitz. How you cried with loneliness and fear—and seeing you again at Berny's wedding filled this Burton with remorse, making him think of his own little kid in an orphanage."

"Maybe that was it," I wondered aloud. "And he went back to London and made the will and wrote the letter."

I did not tell Max that the room in Hastings Street was not Burton's idea; it was my mother's. I had become an intrusion in her life with Burton—he was forever catching me up for kisses, racing up to the bedroom in Sunrise, and playing with me while she raged at him.

"I think you must have reminded him of your mother, Lia. He became remorseful about her too—because she had died."

"How will we explain the lapse of years to the boy?" I asked, to get away from the mention of Burton.

"I was thinking of that," Max said. "My father has fluent Italian. Either you and he will go to Rome or all three of us. What do you think?"

It had been decided. Like father, like son. They

assumed they knew my mind—how little they really knew.

"Maybe the boy has grown up and left the orphanage," I offered.

"Well then," Max said, "the nuns will know his whereabouts. They will have kept in touch if he was there since he was a baby."

CHAPTER TWELVE

In Dublin, Theo listened carefully to the story again and asked for several parts of it to be repeated. He said, "Going to Rome presents no difficulties if Lia has decided she is prepared to take on the responsibility of an eighteen-year-old boy who has, we presume, never lived in family life. There is the option of putting his money in trust until he is of age. In my view, the important thing is to let the boy know that he had a father who cared for him."

I had had time to let the idea sink in. Any decision of mine would be based on that pathetic letter. The more I thought of it, the more I pitied the man who lived inside the magnificent Burton. The more I pitied, the more I had to help. The more I longed to help, the more I dreaded the taking of another Burton into my life, into my home, perhaps into my love. How would I feel when I met this boy, and saw again the face of young Frayne Lowry? I was convinced that just as Tadek had re-created himself in Vasha, so it was with Frayne, and so it would be with this boy. The thought that was crushing my spirits was that Vasha and

Alessandro would be mirror-images if the boy were like his mother, Laelia, who had borne a very beautiful feminine likeness to her brother Tadek. If he were like Burton, he would be like young Frayne. I grappled with this bewilderment of looking-glass pictures while Theo and Max made their plans.

Theo was constantly in touch with Rome in his business. He made the necessary phone calls. Four of us would go: Max and I, Theo and Vasha. It was never even hinted that we should shirk this family matter.

"The time may be at hand now," Theo said to me in a quiet moment, "to acquaint Vasha with the fact that Max is really the friend of her father, and you are her widowed mother." "Widowed" was to be the story?

"Oh no," I said, "I think she is still too young."

Theo held me close to him. "Lia, age has a strange way of catching up on us. There is scarcely ever a gap in the years, but this may be one. We will say nothing until Vasha meets the boy. I know her. I will judge if the time is apt. They are first cousins, this boy and my Vasha. As I said to you ten years ago, her name will lead her into a knowledge of who she is. If the meeting with the boy comes to nothing, if he wishes to remain aloof from us, or we from him, then the name Vasha will continue to be associated with the name of Max's friend."

I lay against Theo's shoulder. Much as I loved my husband, indeed more and more with each passing year, I never failed to find strength and comfort in Theo's arms.

"Your spirit is weary, *balibt*," Theo said. "We have been given a distortion to set right."

"I heap so many troubles on my friend," I said to him sorrowfully.

He kissed my head, left and right. "You know, *balibt*, it is only the delight you have brought into my life—only the joy, only the pleasure."

Stefan and Deric were left with Shanlee and Ted. The preparations for the birthday party were to go ahead. Shanlee had planned all the cooking she could do in advance and store in the second, bigger refrigerator, which was Theo's latest addition to her kitchen.

Max had arranged for a hired car at the airport in Rome. Theo sat in front as navigator. In the back of the car, Vasha put her little hand in mine. "It will be nice if you smile, Lia," she said. I had not realised I looked so preoccupied. "I know the hotel we are going to," she continued; "it is nice, *bellissima*."

"Do you know much Italian?" I asked her.

"Oh yes," she said, "Daddy-Theo allows me to order in the *ristorante*, or the *trattoria*. If I say, '*E troppo. E troppo caro!*' he always smiles, and then frowns. We pay anyway!"

"What did it mean—what you said?"

"It meant they were charging too much. Daddy-Theo never questions *il conto*—that is the bill." She chattered on, very pleased to be so knowing.

"All the other motor-cars are hooting their horns. It is very noisy," I said.

"Oh," she said with a delightfully superior little smile, "that is because Daddy-Max is driving so slowly. In Rome it is *fretta! fretta! presto! presto!*"

I have had evenings in Rome many times since then and consider that the colours in the sunset sky are incomparable. I remember nothing about that first evening, although there is so much I should like to remember. I was poor company, I fear. Theo made phone calls. He talked to friends. He made dinner dates and gallery dates. The second day we would visit the nuns in Casa Santa Maria. Memory begins again as we are driving through the high iron gates of the orphanage and seeing them being closed behind us, the car pulling in on a gravel drive, the engine going silent. And Theo turning to speak to us who were in the back of the car.

"As we arranged, Lia, you and Vasha will go into the convent. Vasha has sufficient Italian. The nun will bring you to Alessandro and you must then play it by ear."

He had arranged this? I looked helplessly at Vasha; her lovely little face was bright with expectation.

We were met at the door by an elderly nun. Her face was kind. "*Prego, signora, signorina,*" she asked, to which Vasha replied, "*Grazie. Buon giorno.*"

"*Buon giorno. Posso aiutarla?*" the nun enquired.

"*Alessandro Vashinsky, per piacere,*" said Vasha.

The nun nodded her head. "*Ah sì. Alessandro è fuori nel giardino.*"

We followed the nun along a windowed corridor. Vasha took my hand. "He is in the garden," she whispered. At the head of some steps, the nun left us. The sunlit garden was full of colour. There were groves of trees. Vasha ran into the trees, calling out, "*Le arancie*, Lia, orange trees!"

I stood on the steps and looked at an Italian garden, a convent garden, reminiscent of Cluny. I had never gone back to the convent in which I had spent ten of my young years, but I had never forgotten that garden of childhood, the tall multi-coloured tulips and the scent of the old-fashioned roses. Roses of Provence, Sœur Norbert named them. I had asked to spend my life there, in that very special convent garden. The nuns refused me and the refusal was crushing. I understood at once why guilt flooded into me there on the steps. I had reneged on the teaching of the nuns, rejected their precepts and found solace in a kind of negation which we called humanism. Had I much choice? Had I forgotten that I had free will? I stepped down, pushing the guilt away. The momentous task of meeting the son of Jack Burton took all my resolution.

There were no signs of workers in the garden. I had assumed the boy Alessandro would be employed as a gardener. I followed Vasha down a long shady grove. There were no voices, no sign of life. Then we saw a man seated with an easel in front of him. "Shall we ask him if he knows where Alessandro is?" I said softly to Vasha. We moved forward and she approached the artist. "*La disturbo?*" she asked in her clear childish voice. "*Scusi.*"

The young man stood up and turned to us. My impression was instant and my heart flooded with relief. He was himself a picture, a picture that was hanging in Theo's study, and which Theo called *The Levantine Jew*. I heard Vasha murmur the name, because she had seen this picture every day of her life. "*Lei è Alessandro?*" I heard her say, then very politely she added, "*Permetta che le presento mia mama, Signora Randt. Sono Vasha Randt.*"

"*Vasha!*" he repeated, smiling. "*Mi chiamo Vashinsky, Alessandro Vashinsky.*" Then he indicated the chair to me. "*S'accommodi, signora. Prego, si accommodi.*"

The gesture told me what he meant. I sat down and looked at the picture he had been painting. I could not see among the trees what I saw on the canvas. The colours were as vibrant as if growing in paint. My mind had stopped whirling at the instant the young man turned around to us. "Please return to the car," I said to Vasha, "and ask them to come here with you." This conversation was for Theo, who had the language. Vasha smiled up at the young man as she tripped round the easel. "*Mia papa, e Daddy-Theo, sono nell' auto. Vado a prenderli,*" and she ran away happily. I knew I was silent. I knew I was still staring at the picture. I wanted to say something while we were alone, something welcoming.

"I speak a little English," he began. "I learn in the café where I work at night, to buy... he indicated the paints and brushes...money to buy, *questi*."

"Your mother was my friend," I said slowly, "my dear friend."

"*Comprendo,*" he said. "My...father?"

"Your father loved you very much, but he..." I could not say Burton was dead. I think I looked up to the sky, to Heaven, as people used to do to indicate death.

Alessandro nodded his head in comprehension. I wanted to put my arms around him. How could I even have hesitated? It felt like a meanness in me that I had not rushed to this place the moment I had read Burton's letter. Had Burton strode under these trees when this young man was a little boy? Max and Theo were coming down through the orange grove.

"Well, Lia?" Theo asked.

"Yes," I answered breathlessly. "Yes. Yes. Yes."

"Theo Randt," Theo said, stretching out his hand. *"Ecco mio figlio, Max Randt. Lei è Alessandro Vashinsky?"*

"Sì, signore. Felice di conoscerla." Alessandro was polite, but puzzled. He took some garden chairs from a hut among the trees. We all sat down and Theo launched volubly into the story. The young man's face remained grave, occasionally answering whatever Theo said. I had no way of knowing what slant Theo was putting on the letter or the will. After a while, Max took Vasha's hand and they walked away among the trees. Vasha's treble laughter seemed to catch high in the branches, and once or twice Alessandro glanced in that direction. When Theo seemed to come to an end, the young man asked some questions. Most of them needed a simple *"sì"* in answer.

Theo turned to me, but he spoke slowly out of deference to Alessandro.

"Alessandro has no recollection of his mother. I told him quite factually that she married and has an illustrious career in opera. He remembers his father, and he has letters his father wrote. The nuns told him that the war kept his father away (which is no doubt true), and they received money from his father but not since 1944. I told him there is now money. He would like to recompense the nuns." Theo continued, "He has finished secondary school this year. He is eighteen. He has qualified for university and the nuns have applied for a grant for him. They have told him he could obtain his degree free of charge were he to enter a seminary. He thinks they are making what he calls 'novena' for him to consider the priesthood. One of the nuns is artistic and she has shown him the use of these brushes. It is for him, he says, a recreation."

Theo looked more closely at the painting. "The university first, I think, but he has a certain feeling for the paint!" He questioned Alessandro again, and the young man smilingly shook his head.

"Not the seminary, it seems! But he is very interested in French literature." This would please Theo, I knew. He read in French a lot of the time and in Hebrew when the Jew in him was uppermost. Theo talked again to Alessandro. "He tells me the nuns have a good library. He has read many interesting books on the history of art. I have mentioned some and he is familiar with them."

Alessandro watched my face as I listened to Theo spacing out the words. He said something very hesitantly. Theo smiled. "He asked would it be correct

for him to say he would like to attempt your portrait?"
I had almost been holding my breath, so anxious was
I that this interview would bring good results. What
was I hoping for? I suppose for Alessandro to be drawn
into our family circle, for him to feel free to come and
go in all our homes, in all our languages. Could I now
let the muscles of my face relax?

Vasha and Max had come back. She stood in front
of Alessandro, the "Levantine Jew" she named him.
He was equally quick: "Madame Récamier," he retorted.
Theo was very charmed. "He is right, you know. And
I never thought of it. Yes, Vasha is Madame Récamier
in the Gérard portrait. Clever of you, Alessandro. You
have been studying to advantage." Alessandro seemed
to understand but Theo repeated in Italian.

"Daddy-Theo, you have no Gérard."

"I had once: my father bought it in an atelier
auction in Paris, fifty years ago. Gérard was a pupil of
David—a better painter, but a poor politician; he fell
out of favour. My picture was not *Madame Récamier*,
but I know her, and yes, it is Vasha. I sold my Gérard
years ago."

Later, when Max and I talked over our day, we saw
that Theo was taken with Alessandro. We found
ourselves marvelling at the bright precocity of my
little daughter.

"I was never clever like that," I said dolefully. Max

hugged me. "I think you were. I heard you were a great little actress if you could only put your mind to it!"

"Now you are teasing. Suppose I say all the funny things Shanlee tells me about you!"

For the rest of our stay in Rome, Alessandro was with us all the time. Max and Vasha collected him at Casa Santa Maria each morning. Theo made money available. Max went along with him to buy some clothes, although he appeared to have jeans and shirts which were always fresh and clean. Max reported that he was very careful with money. He avoided shops on the Corso, which Max favoured, and knew shops of better value in the Piazza Navona. We had lunch in the hotel and then we went sightseeing. A little of that in the heat of the sun was enough for Theo, and Max was not a great sightseer. He, in fact, believed in the siesta—in Siena he and I were much given to the tranquil love-making of that shady time. Now, my first time in Rome, I never felt tired. There must be four hundred churches in Rome—at least it always seems like that when one goes in search of the masterpieces in the dark corners. I kept a supply of coins to light up the pictures. It was Alessandro who introduced me to Caravaggio on that first visit to Rome. Now he is my favourite, a source of endless joy. When I rhapsodised to Theo about this artist, he told me the story of a life spent among riffraff, the man often infected by venereal illnesses, untreatable at the time. Caravaggio, Theo said, although largely limited to religious pictures beacuse of their saleability, and short of money to pay models, managed to make his own place in the history of painting, by the introduction of the device of theatrically spotlighting his subjects. I asked Alessandro to indicate this to me. In careful English, he said that Caravaggio's treatment of human skin was unique in its transparency. His favourite picture, he said, was in Sant' Agostino, the Madonna showing the Child to the pilgrims. Her face is floodlit so the light shines through the skin. He was always surprised that so young a child as Vasha could be so absorbed in the explication of a picture. He brought us to the David and Goliath painting in the Galleria Borghese. "Look on the head of Goliath," he said. And when we saw *The Calling of Matthew*, Alessandro had us note the lighted colouring of Matthew's face and the colouring of that of the young boy. In a crowded picture these two faces are picked out, age and youth thus contrasted.

"Whose is the last face," Vasha asked, "the face that owns the calling hand? It is a face I like."

"That is Jesus," Alessandro said.

"I am glad you know who is who in all the pictures," Vasha said brightly; "that way I understand there is a story."

"It is the gospel story," Alessandro said.

"I must read it," Vasha promised. "Could you say if the Flight into Egypt is in that story?" That day we were in the Galleria Doria Pamphili. We sat down and gazed a long time at this strange picture. I could have told the story. I was well instructed in the gospels but I was a woman who had embraced humanism, so I said nothing.

"*Sì*, I can explain." And half in English and half in Italian, he told the story of the picture. "Herod would kill all the boy children in Judea. Joseph took the child and the mother and with their few possessions loaded on the donkey's back, they escaped from Herod into Egypt."

"Yes," Vasha said with delight. "I see the donkey's big eye. I see the old man holding the music. I see the mother, young and beautiful, and the little fat baby. But who is the creature with the wings playing the musical instrument? He is highlighted by the artist like Daddy-Theo said, and he has hair like Stefan, but how could a winged musician be there under the trees, wearing no clothes?"

"I should like to see this favourite picture of yours, Alessandro," I said. That day, Max drove us to Sant' Agostino. It was a very dimly lit church. Even so the Madonna's face has skin as soft as reality. "Madonna dei Pellegrini."

Alessandro smiled at us. "*Scusi piede sporco,*

perdonare." Vasha said brightly: "He is asking you to excuse the pilgrims' dirty feet." She pulled Alessandro by the sleeve. "*Madonna similarita Lia?*"

"*Sì sì*" he replied. "*La madre è più bella che la Madonna.*" And Alessandro took my hand. Vasha said, "He thinks you are like the lady in the picture, but even more beautiful!"

"And what do you think, Vasha?" I asked.

She considered the picture when we put more coins in the box. "Sometimes you look just like that; mostly you are just pretty." Alessandro, still holding my hand, now pressed it as if his English had failed but not his warm reassurance.

"Enough pictures for today," Vasha decided. "Let's go and eat ice-cream and coffee cake."

Ah to be young again and to look like the Madonna dei Pellegrini! When Max had gone away that evening to take Alessandro home to the convent, I listened as Vasha related the account of our day. When she said, "It is in the gospel story. Do you know that story, Daddy-Theo?" Theo's eyebrows lifted in question, his eyes now on my face. I shrugged slightly to indicate to him that no great harm had been done, but later, when she was asleep in bed, I found myself apologising for Alessandro.

"How could it occur to him that we are non-denominational?" I pleaded. Theo took my hand, always a sign of peace between us.

"Sooner or later, Lia, all the history of the world will flow towards Vasha. Her brain, her mind, her imagination, all alert and inquisitive and interested. Eclectic—but only for the rare."

"Your training, Theo?"

"Not so," he answered. "She brought her quality with her into the world. As do we all. You know my theories, Lia. Only on what we have been given in the womb can we be invisibly moulded. It is a deeply internal process. You and I have talked of this many times long ago. Environment, education, upbringing, can act only on the material which is there. There from a thousand forebears."

"I have often though of it," I told him, "and I have wondered if an influence could come suddenly into a life and change a personality?"

"Oh yes," he answered, "in the same way as a thunderbolt can wreck a house, leaving only a ruin."

"An influence for good?" I questioned.

"An influence for good can be assimilated by the tendencies which stretch out for good, and such influence is gentle, slow-growing like a tender vine. An influence for evil shows, not its tendencies, but its tentacles, very fast. Its roots are stronger—because evil is seldom fought; it has had time to go deep. Its surface rewards are more quickly apprehended and to succumb is easier."

It was these times of listening that I missed in Philadelphia. "I often wish to be with you, Theo, when I am on the other side of the Atlantic. Just to hear your voice."

"What was it James Joyce called the Atlantic: 'that bowl of bitter tears.' Come closer then and I will hold you."

"I am not unhappy," I said, "but I miss you."

"And I miss you, *balibt*." He smoothed my hair.

"Even though you have Vasha, Theo?"

"Even though, *lyubenyu*. You will always be first and most dear." He placed my hand on his chest. "This heart beats for you, Lia."

I thought then it was written in the stars that Vasha would be given to Theo for the joy of his declining years. Vasha and not I. There were moments, before custom became habit and habit became irreversible, that I knew pangs of a strange jealousy. Strange because it was equally divided between the need for all of Theo's love and all of Vasha's love. Those moments recurred but more rarely with the passing years. From that first visit to Rome and the first sight of Alessandro the scales seemed to balance more evenly. On which stave he was placed, however, I was not ever to be sure.

CHAPTER THIRTEEN

The nuns were concerned, Alessandro told us, lest they relinquish him into the hands of people who might perhaps ill-use him or even rob him now that he had money.

"Yes," Theo responded, "I am aware of this. My son, Max, will drive me out to the Via Alessandro Poerio tomorrow. I will bring with me a solicitor, recommended by your mother superior and we have the letters of your father's solicitors. Alessandro, you will need your birth certificate and various letters, so that you may acquire a passport, if you decide to travel with us."

So Alessandro went to the civil offices for his birth certificate, while Theo and Max went to the convent. Then the young man came back and sat with Vasha and me under the trees in the garden of the hotel, while we waited for the others to return. I realised now that, in fact, Vasha could not sustain a long sentence in Italian but she could help herself out (and me too) with phrase-book tags. Alessandro was a rapid learner, if a little self-conscious at first with pronunciation, and he was very quick to catch a meaning. Vasha, I had noticed, never let Daddy-Theo escape too far from the nerve ends of her telepathy. Now she was telling in great detail all our plans for Theo's seventieth birthday party. She explained the functions of Shanlee and Ted. "They are not servants, you know," she said, "although they do the work for Daddy-Theo—cook and drive and things like that. And we have a woman, Nelly, who hoovers and washes and irons. She comes on Monday and Wednesday and Thursday. She has a husband and he cuts the grass. And Silkitoo is our dog. He is a King Charles."

Alessandro lifted his eyebrows in my direction. "Oh, no," Vasha said, "Lia comes only on holiday. Lia and Daddy-Max live in America with my two brothers—oh they come on holidays too. They are Deric and Stefan—yes, they are nearly seven now, the same age as each other."

"You do not live in America?" the young man enquired of Vasha.

"I live in our house in Terenure with Daddy-Theo. He is my friend as well."

As well? Vasha always chose her words even in chattering. As well as her father? Was she old enough to think out such things?

"*Non capisco*," Alessandro smiled. "Why not all the family live together?"

"The Lord ordained it!" I said quietly.

"Yes!" Vasha agreed. "The Lord ordained it! Would you like to come with us to the birthday party?"

Alessandro lifted his face to mine in question. I answered at once, slowly so there could be no mistake, "Alessandro will be very welcome to come to Terenure in Ireland, to Siena to meet our friends, to America where we live. He will be very welcome to stay, to come and go, in all the places we live. Alessandro, we are more closely your family than you know. Theo will explain, perhaps tonight. You will have dinner with us, and after dinner, then, perhaps…"

I would tell Theo that, as he had foreseen, the right moment had come. I could see so clearly as I looked at them, that Vasha and Alessandro were two of a pair. It was imperative that they should know they were first cousins. His mother and Vasha's father were sister and brother. Now was the time to tell them. He could not be hurt, could he? Could Vasha? Theo, who understood all things, must summon this little family conclave. Then, at last, I would feel that I was out in the clear. Vasha would lose the father-figure of Max, whom she loved very much but she would be given the grave friendship of a first cousin. I, who had buried and cherished a secret passion all my life, did not want her risked into such a position of coming close enough to love yet never to take on love. It was improbable; she was only nine. But then, I was only six in Ringsend. First cousins they were and Theo would establish that basis tonight. Of course, I reassured myself, Alessandro would stay in Rome, Vasha in Ireland, years could pass. Ireland, Rome, America. Distance lends enchantment to the view, an old proverb, and could I apply it in this case? Let them stay unchanged, under a spell which could not be broken. I see now that I worried always.

Alessandro was speaking to me. "*Per piacere, Signora Lia, che cosa desidera? Un gelato? Un tè?*"

"A little pot of tea would be lovely, Alessandro. Out here under the trees." He was bending over me, and I held his face with my finger-tips, the way my mother used to touch my face for her rare kiss. I kissed his smooth cheek. His skin had that identical perfume I associate with Burton. So it was real, after all! There was an unaccountable surge of joy in my heart.

I had not imagined it—that scent of roses, of good soap, something masculine, some unforgettable aroma that was Burton. With him, the years added the whiff of cigar smoke, port wine, some unknown essence of cologne. Alessandro's tanned cheeks had the perfume of meadow flowers in summer. Nothing had yet been added. Alessandro's gift of skin was quintessential Burton.

Over and over again I have failed to understand

myself. I have met men and women who believe in fidelity, faithful to one and excluding any other. They cling on, long after they have ceased to love. The virtue is in fidelity when love itself has evaporated. I am constantly dragged back to that one first altar of adoration. Yet I loved my husband, holding nothing back. I loved Theo, who gave me more of love and strength and comfort than any other man ever gave. The thought has been there. I have not played with it, neither have I denied it. If Max had never returned from Vienna, would Theo have taken me to bed? He moved me, often, to offer something reciprocal, but the inner strength of the man placed that stepping stone between us. There was a space within which our spirits merged—but there was a ravine, too perilous to attempt. And yet, even now, I know how much I could have loved him—had I been given the chance. And Burton? Ah, that story is different, compounded of a strange masculine perfume. The ancient Irish legend of Diarmaid and Gráinne tells us that Gráinne could not turn away from Diarmaid because on the skin of his shoulder there was a smooth brown aphrodisian circle, the impress of a son of Aphrodite. This impress excited sexual desire which no woman could resist— there were many before Gráinne. She was the queen and her husband Fionn hunted her and her lover Diarmaid to death on the mountain top. In a thousand years, will another legend have been added? One that will tell of the impress of perfumed skin and the desire it creates? All over Ireland there are ancient caves, the marriage beds of Diarmaid and Gráinne, Ireland's Héloïse and Abélard. Sometimes I get lost in old legends, and the Hunt of Fionn and the Fianna is a favourite.

To return to the hotel in Rome: when Theo came in that evening, we all talked together about the visit to Casa Santa Maria. No, Alessandro *listened*. Whether he smiled, or looked sad, he was always handsome. He was undeniably a Jew, yet none of his features was pronounced. Although there was a certain resemblance to Tadek, and therefore to Vasha, it was remote. Her looks were vivacious, his were grave. She was outwardly assured although always courteous. He had an air of inner security, but too much protocol puzzled him into silence.

"It is the convent upbringing," Max considered. "A little of the outside world and he'll get the hang of the correct pecking order. Although, I must say I liked his deferential manner. He knows he has a lot to learn. We'll get along."

Theo had now explained the situation to the nuns. He told them Alessandro wished to pay them in gratitude for the years they had treated him as one of their own family. An amount of money was worked out and Theo gave the reverend mother a cheque.

"If you wish to continue to live in the convent, Alessandro, make a suitable arrangement with them. They would like that, if you decide so. Mr Ormsby will lodge your money in court until you are twenty-one if that is the court's decision. I have no doubt there will be interest available to you in due course. In the meantime, Signora Lia is empowered to offer you the hospitality of her house, my house, all our houses. I have lodged money to your name in the Banco Nazionale."

This was told to Alessandro in Italian and repeated to us in English. He looked from one to the other of us.

"He is coming to the party, Daddy-Theo! Aren't you, Alessandro?"

The young man inhaled a deep breath. He wished to speak to us in English, directly, without translation.

"*Per piacere*—if you please—my father—the money—*sì*. *Capisco*. *Comprendo*. Not more—*sono*—I am... I am... *estraneo*. Is it a stranger in *la famiglia*?"

Theo looked at me and I nodded. I knew *famiglia*. We must close this circle now. And so I began, "Alessandro, and Vasha, this concerns both of you. I will go very slowly; if you do not understand, please ask me. Alessandro is older, so first Alessandro..."

Vasha settled into her chair; she loved a story, an adventure, a project. I hoped with all my heart she would accept what I was going to say. I, too, took a deep breath to control my heartbeat.

"Vasha's father and Alessandro's mother were brother and sister. They were Tadek and Laelia." I felt Max's arms coming around my shoulders. I tried to smile at him.

"From childhood Tadek and Laelia, Max and Lia were the closest of friends." I was very conscious this could be told only once. I must get it right: here and there Theo supplied a word in Italian.

"Laelia was very beautiful and very talented. We were all poor and needed friends. Laelia wanted a career in music and she was helped to achieve this by Jack Burton, who was my stepfather. Laelia and Burton fell in love and Alessandro is their son. A few months later, the war started, and it separated them. Laelia's career took her far away and Burton was killed in an air-raid. We do not know what lovely things could have happened to them and to their boy Alessandro if there had been no war. None of us ever knew that Burton was dead until a few weeks ago. His will revealed Alessandro to us."

Vasha had perched on the arm of Theo's chair and she was watching me intently. Her great dark eyes were waiting for her part in the story.

"If there had been no war in 1940, I would be married to Tadek. The war came and Tadek went away to join the partisans. Vasha is our daughter. Tadek died in a concentration camp…" I had to put my head into Max's shoulder, my voice almost gone. "Max and Theo gave me and my child shelter, and a name."

Vasha slid down onto Theo's lap, and he folded his arms around her small body. Only her eyes spoke and they clearly said: "I am Theo's child." It would be a long, long time before she spoke of this night.

Theo said, "All good stories should have a happy ending! This calls for a toast. Max, *mio figlio*, touch the bell. We will order champagne."

I had left something out. Blankly unthinking, I had left out the name of Burton's other son. I had promised to tell Berny what was in Burton's will. "I'll tell you everything," I said to her. How could I have said that? How could I not have the sense to remember there could be a child involved? The child that Laelia said would be adopted. So lightly, so carelessly, she had said that. Laelia who was my lodestar of beauty for so many years. How, this very day, had I pictured Alessandro at Theo's birthday party, and never thought he would be face to face with his brother, Frayne Lowry. For a day, my spirit had soared free. I had imagined recompensing Alessandro for the years in the orphanage. It would lift the burden of my own childhood years. The weight descended again. In Frayne Lowry's face, Alessandro would be able to see the masculine beauty of his own father—were he to be told Berny's secret. My silence had made it my secret now. The free and open cordiality within Berny's marriage to Denis, the undoubted adoration of Frayne for his mother, both were protected by this secret—and maybe others, in all of which I longed to have no part.

In that moment, I would have been happy to see Vasha hug me, kiss me, even say some little thing like "poor Lia!" It was Alessandro who took my hand in both of his. "*Grazie, grazie, signora Lia. Grazie per tutta la sua gentilezza.*"

"Alessandro, look on me as a sister, and call me Lia. Or Aunt Lia if you prefer."

"*Permetti* that I call you *Madre Mia*?" he asked. Max was beside me. "We have acquired a son." He clasped Alessandro's shoulders. "Welcome to the family, Signore Vashinsky. Your Uncle Tadek is the reason I am here, in good health this night. He saved me from certain death."

Alessandro's eyes shone. "You will tell me?" he asked. "And you will tell me about my mother?"

"I will," Max said, "and you will read about the partisans in my book. Tadek was my brother before God."

Now I saw Alessandro smile, totally, for the first time. His face was lit from within, his eyes glowing, his lips glistening. I was to discover that he believed profoundly in God. Brothers before God was a powerful image for him. "And I can come to your house?" he asked.

Max laughed. "And sample the American way of life—what they are beginning to call the American dream! You will be part of the family—no special treatment."

I think my eyes told Alessandro that for him everything would be special.

"You'll have to endure the twins!" Max said.

"The twins, *comprendo—Stefan e Deric*."

"Right! Stefan and Deric—a couple of scamps."

Vasha was over with us now, while Theo talked to a waiter. "'Scamps' means *ragazzi cattivi*, Alessandro. But you are coming to Daddy-Theo's house first."

"No," Max said quietly. "We will have a week in Siena when we leave home. The passport will take a few weeks. You will return with Daddy-Theo to Dublin, Vasha."

"Oh yes," she said, "the preparations for the party. And Alessandro will come with you when you come?"

"If he would like," I said, and Alessandro gave us his luminous smile. Of course that smile reminded me of Tadek, and a little of Burton. I was going to be very careful. I turned to Max and kissed him with a lingering and loving kiss. He was, and would remain, the important one in my life.

"Lia was always star-dazzled, a lady who is not growing old quickly enough. A lady of secrets. A lady full of unfulfilled eroticism. She must be taken in hand!" Who said those words? Theo's eyes were on me but he had not spoken.

CHAPTER FOURTEEN

"The next time I come to Rome, I want to stay much longer," I said to Theo on the last morning.

"For the first time, Lia, four days is enough. Four weeks and you would never leave, perhaps, and become disillusioned. The magic is so strong an elixir, that gradual inoculation is necessary. You do want to live in America, don't you, my dear?"

I glanced around but Max was deep in chat with Alessandro and Vasha. "Only because it is expedient," I told Theo. "But Siena does not hold me in this way, and strangely, my first impression was that Rome was noisy."

"Which proves the potency of this city—because the Romans are exuberantly noisy. Some ancient wit said that Rome is the centre of the universe. A learned Greek, or a Chinese mandarin, would disagree."

"But you would not?" I asked him. He looked very thoughtful. "So much of the glory of the world has been set down here and thrived. I have reflected on the enchantment of Rome since I was a boy. I have come back again and again and longed to stay. It is the climate, the surrounding hills, the scent of the Mediterranean, the marble, the rose-red brick in the houses, the fountains, the frenzied clamorous Romans, their uniformly brown eyes. So many of the citizens have stepped out of Florentine paintings that one lives daily in an art gallery. What do you think, Lia?"

"It is the balconies in the sun, the glimpses of gardens, the roof-tops from the Spanish Steps, the antiquity that has not been oppressed by high buildings." But that, I thought, is only architecture.

"Is it the papacy?" he asked. "The popes have endured for two thousand years, despite their riotous behaviour in the middle ages. They must own a lot of the ground we walk on. Is it their compelling power hidden by the piety of pilgrims?"

"I have to admit," I told him, "I have not felt more of an Irish Catholic here, rather the reverse." Theo smiled down at me. "Ah," he murmured, "more pagan, more romantic, more in love with life."

He liked to read my thoughts. When I recollected that first visit, always longing for more, it was the hidden places that fascinated: the glint of a white statue in a courtyard seen in a flash between narrow streets, the face of a stunningly beautiful woman quickly withdrawn from a curtained window, a handsome man carrying flowers into a dark hallway.

Was he visiting his lover in the mid-afternoon, or was he bringing flowers for a death?

Theo said, "Rome quickens the blood and electrifies the imagination—you will come back, and it will happen again. Never stay. Like the Romans, you would become immunised." He was smiling.

Max had decided he would keep the hired car for the continuation of our holiday in Siena. While we drove to the airport with Theo and Vasha for their flight home, Alessandro was in the orphanage gathering up his possessions and saying goodbye to the nuns. He promised he would see them again, he told me later. They understood, they said to him: all children leave home and go out into the world. Theo had given him instructions that he take with him his paintings, even if unfinished, and had provided a large flat case for this purpose. "We will look at your work together," Theo said. "If you decide by the end of the summer that you are going to art school, you will need a portfolio. If you decide on university, you may need another year at school."

"I hope Alessandro will not have to go back to school," I said to Theo. "He seems too adult."

"It may be worth his while," Theo said. "He has two European languages, and certainly in French he is widely read. Soon he will read in English. He is quick. A couple of years at this stage of his life is no matter—

after twenty-two it could be something of an imposition." Although I felt very close to Alessandro, I knew it would be Theo's decision, and I would not voice an opinion.

"Will you miss Rome, Alessandro?" I asked when we were settled into the car, and on the road to Siena.

"*Sì, Madre Mia*, I will miss the garden of the nuns. It was my home." Perhaps he was more at home in the garden than in the small bar-room beside the convent chapel. He would be at home in the household of Phyllis; she was as ardent a Catholic as in our early days in Ringsend. Luigi, who believed in his own fluency in English, referred to himself as a "free-thinker." This, Phyllis said drily, absolved him from going to Mass.

"Phyllis will give you a big welcome, Alessandro," I told him, because I had asked her on the phone to do so. "She remembers your father very well. She will tell you what a fine-looking man he was." It was easy for me to talk like this, leaning forward to speak to Alessandro in the passenger seat beside Max. Max was always a great moral support, although I had never been open about the rigours of Ringsend, nor had I ever taken anyone's good name away. He may have known a little from listening to Tadek when they were in the concentration camp, but there were so many worse and urgent things then (and it was clearly necessary for them to remember happy days). Max was too contented with the present now to enquire about the past. It was, moreover, in my nature to gloss over the events of earlier times. In talking to Alessandro, I glossed mightily. My stepfather was his father—no more than that. It was in the best of our interests that the young man would think highly of his beginnings, despite the years of being an abandoned orphan. Theo had spoken to me of this at the airport. "Alessandro's self-esteem is now in your hands, Lia, and you know how important I consider self-esteem. As you say, he seems adult. He has a good promise of becoming a worthy one but eighteen is still quite young. And he more that most."

Alessandro blossomed in Siena, as did everyone under Phyllis's care. Tonio, a tall ten-year old, and he were brothers in their language, and of course in their religion. Tonio would drift away in time and away from Phyllis's watchful eye but for the moment he was being taught with the local priests and serving Mass in the cathedral. To a boy who had lived among nuns, Tonio was easy and acceptable. Tonio's popularity reflected on Alessandro, brought him out of himself and established him among the youngsters. It was a week of holiday all the more serene for me because I was watchful of this transition stage in Alessandro's life. We had our little chat, and our affection was growing but to see him "out and about" was a bonus. As Max said in his favourite phrase, "He's getting the hang of himself, getting the hang of things." For a psychologist, Max delighted in family-language: the good old words were adequate. Unlike Theo, he never needed to expound, or, as he often remarked about Theo, "to quote chapter and verse."

In a week or two, Phyllis and Tonio would be joining us in Dublin for the party, so when goodbye time came there was only laughter. Alessandro was as excited as a four-year old about his first flight in an aeroplane, and he enjoyed it, especially the clear view of the world below. We saw the Alps and the lands of Provence. We touched down in Paris and transferred to the Dublin flight. Ted was at the airport, as always, to meet us. In 1958 Dublin Airport was still a small arena with comparatively few operations. In those days, it was like flying in to one's native place, which of course it was. Nowadays it is becoming impersonal, very like any airport in any country. That long-ago time when Alessandro was eighteen, a boy with great shining eyes, the country of Ireland was a step into fairyland. For the young sensitive artist, the house in Terenure was pure heaven.

Theo toasted Alessandro's arrival in a wine that I recognised as a very special one, less often broached than his favourite champagne. Shanlee and Ted were very impressed with the new arrival. Shanlee walked around and around, admiring him. Later she told me he reminded her of a little brother who was only five when she left Zamosc. She never saw him again; perhaps he was dead. Master Theo had written many letters, made many enquiries, but her family had disappeared. The little brother's name was Joshua and he had eyes like Alessandro. Vasha led our guest into the reception rooms. He admired every work of art, being knowledgeable about many of them. He stood for a long time in front of the portrait in the silver frame: Lia in the wedding dress she was to wear as the bride of Tony Lloyd. This very flattering portrait was hanging over the fireplace in the long drawing-room. Theo's armchair was placed to look at the picture in a good light from the west window; at night it was lit by amber bulbs. Theo was very fond of this picture. It rested him, he always said.

"*Non ha molti anni*?" asked Alessandro.

"Perhaps eleven years," Theo answered. "I shall commission the mature picture very soon." It sounded like an invitation, or a promise.

"Of course," added Theo, "the sitter would need to be nearer than America!"

The dreamy dalliance that had invaded my imagination in Rome had disappeared. We were all down to earth again. Max was off playing golf with a couple of old school chums. Theo was engaged in conversation with Alessandro about Theo's future hopes and aims for him—and Vasha was listening in to their plans. I took the boys shopping for winter things. The jerseys and shirts were different in Dublin. In Philadelphia all the shops would have the same run of teenage attire. Stefan was interested in clothes, whereas Deric was indifferent. They were growing up all too fast and growing into different ways.

"I thought they would always be close," I said to Max, "like a solid block against the outside world."

"Yes, it is strange," Max agreed. "When you think of one infinitesimal cell holding these two little giants, you would assume they could not grow away from each other. Every day they are further apart."

I asked Theo about this. "It is good the way they are," he said. "They strike sparks off each other. Do not fret; if one needs the other's support, it will be there." They would be seven at the end of that year.

I wish I could set down the menu for Theo's birthday dinner. I am sure it was splendid. Apart from the family, Theo, Max and I, Vasha, Stefan, Deric and Alessandro—and of course Shanlee and Ted, and even Nelly who brought her married daughter to help— there were Phyllis and Tonio; Berny and Frayne; Chersy and her husband Denis from the old Land Commission days, with their teenage son and daughter;

half a dozen of Theo's business acquaintances complete with wives and children of the twins' and of Vasha's age. Vasha counted up to thirty guests. When I look back, I see only my own beloved faces, merry, laughing with each other, Theo toasting everybody.

"Why don't we ask Phyllis to sing for us," Theo said. "I hear she still does sing for special nights in their hotel."

"Who told you that?" Max enquired. "Young Tonio—he plays by ear, he tells me, although his *madre* wants him to have lessons." Theo would be all in favour of lessons, whether in painting or in music or in acting. "There is a basic theory in all art," he used to say; "even if you never paint a picture, you will have learned how to understand, even judge."

I hoped Phyllis would not sing the old melody whose words I could not bear to hear: "She is far from the land, where her young hero sleeps." That was the song of exile when the lovely Sarah Curran dreamed again of her hero, Robert Emmet, but for my heart it was the song of a man who had given his life for his fellow men and now lay in a desolate grave in the Matra Mountains. Phyllis sang other well-remembered songs: "Believe Me if All Those Endearing Young Charms." My gran used always ask for "Believe me..." After that, she sang another old favourite, "The Snowy-Breasted Pearl." I caught sight of Frayne's handsome profile. His eyes were fixed on his mother's face. Berny's fresh candid gaze was rapt with attention for the Irish songs we sang in school when we were young. Yet I thought the tears in her eyes were bitter rather than sentimental. There was a silence on Phyllis's last note. With a streak of the old gusto, she suddenly struck up "Phil the Fluter's Ball," and soon everyone was joining in and smiling at the words: "With a toot on the flute, and a twiddle on the fiddle-o."

Phyllis had sung the first two songs with a great deal of the old emotion, her voice pure and full. Tonio picked out the melody delicately and with such sweetness in the chords that he seemed like a great little professional. He was to go on to conquer the world with his music—different music—for a very different time.

Am I writing now with hindsight? Did I actually see that Vasha reacted to young Tonio that night? Herself destined to be an achiever, she was attracted to talent. Or do I imagine she played for his attention so early as the night of Theo's seventieth birthday? Among the children and couples dancing, did Vasha sway towards Tonio, catch his hands and whirl him around? Did Frayne Lowry catch her on the rebound and tease her, telling her she was only a child, while he was dancing in a jiving fashion just then becoming popular again? Did Tonio, young and naïve, fail to notice her, and did she turn to Alessandro as a little sister to a protective brother? He was constantly at her side, but then he knew so few others. Tonio, relieved by Phyllis from the piano, pranced around vigorously, enjoying the party, unconscious of personality. It must be hindsight. I could not really have been filled with uneasy apprehension as I watched Vasha and the three boys. Surely I was filled with happiness that night? Yet, now I think the pattern was set then; a kind of ritual with rules which, all unaware, we followed in our separate ways.

Was it that night, or in any one of several nights in the years that followed, that I asked my husband if he had forebodings when these young people were together? I used to think that psychology was akin to necromancy. He always smiled at this, and often he gave the same answer. "Do not worry about Vasha. She will be given chapter and verse by my father. She will toe Daddy-Theo's line—as do we all."

But will Theo always be there, I wondered.

CHAPTER FIFTEEN

That summer was full of plans for Alessandro. Edged on by Theo, he returned to Rome. He would be accepted by the University of Rome on the strength of two papers he had submitted on Italian and French literature. He would take history of art and ancient civilisation. It was in all a four or five-year course.

"Have you written to the nuns?" I asked him one day. "Will they let you have your room and board?"

"I have written to them," he said, "but I am not to stay at the convent. I am to stay with *la famiglia Delgardo*; Uncle Theo…arrange it. It is *una pensione per studente, una pensione completa*. I have *una camera commoda*."

"Are you—*felice*—with that?" I was getting an Italian word here and there, and very proud of myself.

"*Sì, Madre Mia*, happy. Uncle Theo, he will—*ordinare*—is it to arrange, again? *Sì*, for *i giorni delle feste, Natale, Pasqua* and the summer—in Siena, in Ireland, *forse* in America?"

"I understand, Alessandro, we will have you for

holidays—the time in between will not be so long."

"*E mi scriverai?*" he asked, smiling at me. "Of course I will write, Alessandro, but it will have to be in English."

"*Così va bene, Madre Mia.* It will be, *migliore*, is best for my English!"

Year after year after year, I waited always for Vasha to say, "You are my mother. I want to come and live with you." Now that she knew her father was dead since before she was born, would she say it to fill that place always empty in my heart? No, those words were never said. We loved each other, were gentle with each other, admired each other, as we watched life taking on the gradual process of ageing. Certainly I admired her beauty: it was rare and unique. From time to time, she would remark, "You are a pretty lady, Lia."

That year of 1957 I had acquired another son, and the farewells at the airport were warm and loving and lingering. We were all reluctant to part. It had been a lovely, lovely summer.

"In a week you will be going back to Rome, Alessandro. I wish I were going with you." His eyes flickered over the boys and Max. He knew I had another life and the wish to go with him to Rome was as fleeting as a quick kiss. He was perceptive.

"I am writing to you everything I do, *Madre Mia*," he said, "and I will make a big advance on my English."

"I will be very far away, Alessandro. Please, *per piacere*, if there is a...problem, write to Uncle Theo—*prometti?*"

"*Prometto, Madre!*" he smiled. Our names were called for the flight before we could all stop hugging and kissing and promising. "*Natale! Natale!*" the little boys shouted.

Although Berny had come to Theo's birthday party in Terenure and visited the house on several other occasions, we had agreed to postpone our serious talk about Burton's will until we were both home in Philadelphia. She had returned with Frayne to Belfast for a last visit with her mother and sisters. And indeed, it was a last visit. Her mother died in January of the following year.

When we spoke, it was with the freedom we had known long ago in Cluny.

"I think, Lia, that for once you could open up and talk. I think I deserve to know. As you admitted yourself, you were the one who brought Burton into my life. And I never regretted it until this orphan from Rome turned up. You listened to me confessing. You never said a word about this Alessandro. You knew, didn't you?"

"I didn't know, Ber."

"Oh for God's sake, don't tell lies. You and Alessandro were like a pair of cooing doves—you were like a long-lost mother to him! Is he yours? And Burton's? When?"

I forced myself to stare at her blankly, but I knew that I could have carried Burton's child beginning on the day that Alessandro was born. Nothing could erase from my mind the memory of the lust that had invaded my body on that day. Burton and I had sat drinking in a pub in London while his beloved Laelia was bringing Alessandro to birth. He had caressed me in a way to put the idea into my mind and that damned longing for fulfilment into my heart. Going up in the lift to his flat, he had held my body against his so that I must feel his urgency, as he must have felt my response clamouring for satisfaction. And, there in the corridor, Max's father, ever vigilant for me, stood waiting. And Burton pushed a hundred pounds into the pocket of my coat. "I'll be waiting," he said. I had cried salt tears of humiliation in the old man's arms, not caring that he saw my tears. I remembered now that he had asked about Burton. What was it he had said: "A fine-looking man—hitting up to fifty." I had thought then that Burton could never grow old. Now Burton was dead.

"You may well stare, Lia. You listened and said nothing when I told you I had gone on writing to him, writing, writing, writing. What sort of letters do you think I was writing if they weren't love letters? Where are they now? Did that solicitor show them to you? Have you got them? Well, read them, read them and you will know what possessed me. I poured it all out, all the stuff I could never say to Denis Lowry, all the passion for Burton that wells up when I fake the orgasm for my husband. It is like torture—like being burned at the stake..."

Her voice had been labouring and then she collapsed.

She let me hold her in a kind of desolation that was heart-breaking. I had to wait a long time until she calmed down sufficiently to understand and accept my role in the story. There was no need now to keep back the name of Vasha's father, although that secret had been so precious that still I wanted to hold it. It was hard for me to give up my secrets.

"Berny, please believe me when I tell you that Burton never made love to me. I wanted him to. He wanted to. Some sheer accident always stopped us. Please, please Ber, accept that. Sheer accident— someone interrupting—some misunderstanding. Another love was always there since long before I went to Cluny—think back on how I was and you will know I am telling the truth. That love was Tadek. You must remember when you came to my gran's house to tell me of Lucille's death that I told you I had broken off with Tony Lloyd. I was pregnant then with Tadek's child. It happened when I went with Theo Randt to find Max and Tadek in the partisans' camp. Ber, please listen, please. Long before you ever knew Burton he lived with Laelia. She was the sister of Tadek—please listen: Alessandro was born before the war and Laelia did not want to keep her child because she was at the very beginning of her career in opera. I think Burton must have thought Italy was a safe place to put the child, because I remember he said to Mr Randt that war was coming...That day in 1939 when we went to London to tell Laelia that her mother had died. I never dreamed that Burton would be there, in her apartment. I never dreamed we would find her pregnant. That he...That he..."

Berny had stopped shuddering. "Go slowly," she said. "I am confused. Didn't you have to tell the brother of his mother's death? Was he there with Burton and his sister?"

"No. Burton and Tadek never met, not even when I was a child. That day, Tadek was already a victim of the Nazi war."

"How was Tadek in the war before it began?" she questioned.

"There were labour camps and concentration camps in existence years before 1939. Perhaps people did not know."

"But Vasha is only nine," she persisted.

"That is so. Vasha is nine. When the war was over, hundreds of Jews went into hiding: Polish Jews, Russian Jews. There were years when we thought Tadek and Max were dead. Max's father did not give up hope. At last, we found them in a partisan camp."

She seemed to be assimilating the facts of the story. I could not go on elaborating. I had learned not to dwell on the bitter pain. "Just one thing, Ber—about myself. I did not tell Tadek that he had given me a child because he was not going to live...to...to..."

"And Max? Was he your lover, too?"

"Max was our friend. We married a couple of weeks before Vasha was born. His father knew, of course. Now you know."

"And, Lia, I hate asking, but what about my letters to Burton? Maybe you don't think that is important, but..."

"Berny, be very calm now and listen. We are never going to have this conversation again after tonight. Hold my hands. I want to keep serenity in my life and I cannot if we have to keep going back on the past. Bringing Alessandro into our lives has been an upheaval. Luckily for us all, he brought his own love with him—it could so easily have been different. To tell you the truth, I had a terrible fear that Burton might have reproduced himself, maybe re-created is a better word, in Alessandro as he did in Frayne—that we would have two boys identical in appearance. Had you thought of that?" For a few moments we stared at each other numbly. Berny's face, her wide blue eyes, her hair all ravaged, filled me with pity. I held her closer and kissed her poor forehead. Then I took up the question that was troubling her. "Your letters? No, the solicitor did not say how he got hold of your address. Burton made the will and wrote the letter about Alessandro a week after your wedding, Ber, and it is just possible he mentioned the wedding in Belfast to the solicitor. Burton never again came into the solicitor's office. The place in which he lived was bombed. Apparently it took years for lists of people who lost their lives in the bombing to be made and traced. The letters you have continued to send have been addressed to an address that has not existed for many years—maybe since your first letter. I am supposing you do not put a return address on your envelopes. They must just go into a lost department."

She shook her head. "No, I do not put my address nor my phone number on the letters. The night before my wedding—oh I told you, Lia, I went to Burton in the hotel in Belfast. Oh God, I wish I had not done that, but I knew—I knew—I knew—I had to give him up. He told me so but I wanted him for one last time." I thought she was about to crumple up again. Emotion was spent, dried up, as if her spirit had withered. After a long time, she said, "I knew the future address, the future phone number. I knew the whole dreary rotten future. I wrote it down in his address book. Lia—give him his due—at first he refused me. He never had before. It excited me and it wasn't that hard to break down his resistance. We had been lovers for so long. I knew how to get to him, how to work on him. That night there were no precautions. That was the way I wanted it—for the last time."

"Was it worth it, Ber? All those unanswered letters?"

"Oh God—it was unforgettable. Worth it? Yes, a thousand times worth it. And I have Frayne, in his image and likeness. Lia, there is nothing of my Burton in that Roman boy. Nothing."

If that pleased her, if that gave her satisfaction, if that helped her, let it be so.

"So it would seem," I agreed.

"He is not, not in any single way, like Frayne," she said vehemently.

"Then let us forget that they are brothers." I made my voice like a request.

"Half-brothers, you mean," she said, still sobbing.

"Berny, we are going to forget we ever had this conversation. You will allow me to resume my secretive life—as you always have. Oh Ber, stop crying."

"Lia, don't be angry with me. I have been going through hell. Oh God—if I had never gone on writing letters—so many times I have thought of divorce and then I would look at Frayne, or he would look at me, and I have gone away and written another letter. I was always thinking if only Burton could see Frayne—he is like a young god, his face, his body, his hair, like Burton must have been—if he could just once see Frayne, he would catch us up in his strong arms and race away with us." Her face was excited, exalted and then miserable, pitifully miserable. Poor Berny, then and later. Long ago in Cluny, Lucille used to jeer at Berny for her crazy infatuation with boys—so many boys—so long ago. She had even forgotten that Burton, were he alive, would be getting old now. He was never meant to grow old.

"Oh Ber, please don't cry again. Don't! Your eyes are all swollen." She was pitifully distressed. She who was highly competent in her everyday medical world now looked woeful, foolish.

"But don't you see, Lia—don't you see that will never happen. How can I go on enduring—living with a lifeless sot who knows nothing, understands nothing!" I thought fleetingly of the much-married good-looking wealthy husband with his soft-spoken Southern courtesy, his magnificent home, the adored son. I said to her, "You will find the strength to go on, Ber. I am sure you will."

She twisted her hands into the folds of her skirt.

"Imagining Burton, dreaming of Burton. Remembering his glorious f..." She was about to use a word I hated but she saw the quick turn of my head. "Sorry, Lia, how he, how he, how he...so gloriously. That is how I endure Lowry—Lowry goes mad for response; it makes him feel he's made it. A rag doll that's all I am—a puppet who endures. Never again. Not any more. Oh God...when I think...never again to knock on Burton's door..."

I listened to this glorification of Burton's prowess until I couldn't listen any more, and now I do not want to remember. Much of what she said was incomprehensible and outrageous to me. Then, in 1957, such revelation was offensive. Women did not discuss sex. The sexual act was the mysterious side of love—not an act apart. That night I sat there until Berny was exhausted. I longed to go home and unburden my mind to Max. Once more I had to store away a guilty secret. Not mine, and yet mine. In my furtive heart, had I also not yearned for Burton?

CHAPTER SIXTEEN

It seems to me now that the years of my life until 1960 were the medieval times of this century. There were several wars, and I supposed that was how history was made, to afflict people. My father had fought in the Boer War and then in the Great War of 1914. Millions, and he among them, had died for freedom. There followed a tenuous peace of twenty years during which people dared to hope that the weapons were laid away. All unbeknown, the weapons were being reshaped and resharpened with an amazing headlong technological precision. All unbeknown. Then came the war of September 1939 which continued until the Japanese surrendered in August 1945, and it is impossible to guess how many more millions, among them my beloved Tadek, had died for freedom. As I write, history is being faithfully enacted in wars all over the world, supervised and organised by superpowers.

The war that came in the middle of the century, after the statutory twenty years of hibernation, was the war of the sixties. It was not a war of weapons but a war fought, none the less, for freedom—now called liberation. The sixties were synonymous with liberation. Women were liberated by the growing concept of feminism; student unrest flourished and liberated the young; priests and nuns and old-time sins were liberated by Vatican II. New sins were uncovered: drug-taking, abortion, contraception, pederasty, quick divorce. All the new sins were strangely linked to human frailty. Gone were the days of murder on a grand scale, as war had been. With the coming of television, public debate was liberated to discuss sensitive and arcane topics which had been safely buried under all the wars. The dogs in the street, Theo said, and the children in the play-pens could write treatises on sexual aberrations. The sixties changed everything for Theo, not slowly but as an opened floodgate. He resented television although at first welcoming it. He had a set installed in his study. Many of the programmes were, he wrote to us, in appalling taste. In one of his letters, I find the words: "Lacking a war, there has to be a blood-letting. The gods ordain this chronology." Sooner this time, not quite the twenty years.

In Philadelphia, we were aware of the gathering momentum of day-to-day change. Stefan and Deric absorbed the American way of life in their school. They were both bright and outgoing; they made friends easily although their friends were not the same friends, and rarely mixed as a group. As little boys, they had quarrelled noisily but this was a thing Max would not tolerate and they had learned to sink their differences, at least within our hearing. Deric would look on with mild contempt while Stefan was twisting frantically to Chubby Checker but even Deric was impressed when the Beatles performed on the "Ed Sullivan Show." I think that was in 1964. It seemed as if every teenager in the States was squealing with joy when the Beatles shook their glossy heads in rhythm. I noticed a big change in girls: "Gidget" became a word to describe all the girls who came to the parties and began to join the boys in the yard. They were undistinguishable lookalikes, following the fashion set by Mary Tyler Moore, with flicked hair and wide white smiles of fifty teeth—the Sixties also made American dental history. Max brought home a new book, *Sex and the Single Girl* by Helen Gurley Brown. "This could be significant," he said.

"Single girls are not supposed to know a bookful of sex, are they?" I queried, holding the book with my fingertips and miming prudery.

Max smiled at my gesture. "Changed times," he said. "Before this decade began, any single girl who admitted a close acquaintance with sex would be assumed to have picked up the knowledge in a bawdy house."

This book became a best-seller internationally. It was made into a multi-million dollar film. The book and the film were part of a mighty watershed: the de-mystification of the role formerly known as romantic love. Max and I were fascinated by the catapulting of young America into the speech and habits of four lads from a working-class background in Liverpool. Being English was ultra-fashionable. John Lennon's accent might as well be the same as the Prime Minister's for all the kids in Philadelphia knew or cared. We could not know in our first few years in Philadelphia that the sixties, begun in a spirit of gung-ho revelry, could turn into dreadful years of mayhem. The assassinations of the Kennedys and Martin Luther King, the endless count of the body-bags from the jungles of Vietnam; bloody murder in the struggle for civil rights, rioting in city ghettos and on college campuses. I have described the sixties as they appeared to me, and I have left out the Flower Power people because it did not seem then that they were set in motion by the drug barons. They were a fringe culture, following the troops like the camp-followers of a war. The Flowers wilted and withered away, but their seeds grew multidinously into drugs. I was to learn about drugs. The sixties was the background against which our children grew into adulthood. There were quite a few of them before the sixties came to an end: Vasha and Alessandro, Stefan and Deric and Tonio; Frayne Lowry and Francesca's daughter whose place in the story is still to come. Francesca's daughter was not fathered by Burton, as perhaps I had suspected. She was totally legitimate, her mother assured me, and she was guarded always by an older brother, jealously guarded. And he was, his mother again assured me, the son of Tony Lloyd. "You forced me into that, Lia!" Francesca said, "Your money paid for it."

That was Theo's money: "Buy a trinket, Lia;" he had said and given a cheque so she could celebrate the certificate for acting awarded by the Abbey. That cheque was all I had and I gave it to Francesca. Because I was Tony's girl, I felt guilty and I was desperately sorry for Francesca who, of all of us in the school, showed the greatest promise. Frances Doyle she was then although she had re-christened herself Francesca and now she was Francesca D'Oyly. She had fulfilled the promise. Her name sprang off every theatre and film page, and reporters always referred to her somehow-connection with the D'Oyly Carte name. I was to learn that the son she had borne to a man she scarcely knew was the son constantly by her side, the guardian of his adored film-star mother, and the proud possessive brother of the starlet daughter. In true Francesca fashion, she had named her son Ramon, and her daughter Cherita. When this family came back into my life in all their larger-than-life sparkle, I could not but reflect that Tony Lloyd never knew he had a son. Tony would have made a good father, kind and upright, whereas Laelia who had lived with Burton in a rapturous love-affair (it could not have been otherwise with Burton) had relinquished her son without ever holding him to her breast. Burton was not a good man: let me not condemn him further; let me say only that he was not a good man but he had cherished his son. He had bequeathed Alessandro to me.

Alessandro had his twenty-first birthday in 1960. Theo arranged that the special present would be Christmas in Rome.

"You love Rome, Lia," Theo said. "The weather is usually good—get you away from the Philadelphia winter for a while. We will invite young Frayne Lowry to keep Vasha company. They can play tennis while you and Alessandro visit the churches; give you a chance to renew acquaintance." The plan was revealed in a long telephone talk.

"Vasha likes the churches, doesn't she?" I asked.

"Christmas is different," he said. "She can see the pictures another time."

"Do you think Vasha will like the idea of Frayne being of the party?" I asked this because Vasha monopolised Theo's company and never seemed to need any other companion.

"Oh I am sure they will be delighted to see each other. They are pen-pals, you know. They write all the time. He is asking permission to come. Berny will get in touch with you any day now."

Was that the moment to tell him that Frayne Lowry was not the son of Denis Lowry? The resemblance of Frayne and Burton to each other had never been perceived. But then, Theo had seen Burton only once and then briefly. It was I who remembered Burton in all his glory when he courted my mother in the room above the shop. Young Frayne was the living image. Every day, Berny looked on the features of the man with whom she had fallen in love when she was twenty. And, I thought, continued to love in the person of her son.

I listened to Theo elaborating his Christmas plan. He had told it to Alessandro, sending him a birthday card which was a reproduction of the famous painting of Madame Récamier. Theo was very pleased to come on it in Combridge's in Grafton Street.

"They had three the same," he said, "and I bought the three. A rare stroke of luck! I bought a picture as well, an Irish artist. It is your Christmas present, Lia. Just wait until you see it! He is good."

Say nothing, I decided. It is Berny's secret. It would

upset Theo to hear me unravelling old stories about people of whom he is so fond. Let Christmas come and go. Let everyone be happy.

"What will my husband, your son Max, be doing while I walk around churches with Alessandro?" I asked lightly.

But Theo had everything arranged. "He needs to do research for an hour or two every day. He told me so." I smiled at that. Max had agreed to say what Theo prompted. The research could be done in the racquets club with a few doctors of his acquaintance.

"And who will do all the dangerous driving around the churches?" I insisted. "If you're not directing the traffic, Theo, you worry."

"Not any more," he told me and I could almost see his smile of relief. He detested the speed of Roman traffic. "Alessandro is very accomplished with all the lessons he has taken."

"When did Alessandro acquire a car?" This was news.

"Almost a year ago," Theo said. "When I was in Rome last month he did all the driving, and very excellently. He purchased a second-hand car, and has since replaced that with an almost new Fiat. He looks forward to being your chauffeur. Max will hire a car; he trusts nobody in that traffic."

"I know to what place Max will be driving, and

other people will be playing tennis, but what will you be doing?"

"For me, a holiday," Theo said, "and I have some old friends to visit. Of course, we will all dine together, Lia—all of us." When I put down the phone, I went in search of Max.

"Who are the old friends to be visited by Theo in Rome?" I asked. Max laid down the pen and held out his arms to me. "That was a long phone call; I was beginning to miss you."

"He has always spent all his time with us. I did not know of old friends."

"You love my father more than you realise, Lia. He is a man like other men. Rome is one of his oases. Paris is another. I do believe he has been close, maybe platonically close, to a very attractive Roman matron for some years. She is a painter."

"Maybe he would prefer Christmas in Paris?" But why was I resentful?

"Apparently he considered Paris and decided against it because of all the recent student upheaval, the marches in the streets. He wanted to introduce Alessandro to the Louvre. He thinks that Alessandro knows the galleries of Rome off by heart."

Alessandro had been to our home in Philadelphia. His coming had filled my heart with contentment. His nature was full of affection, tolerance, compassion. He was undoubtedly Jewish in appearance, and handsome with it. Contrary to his looks, his upbringing from babyhood to manhood had been severely Catholic. This stern adherence to his faith was the dominant feature of Alessandro's personality. The strands of his discipline were composed of unswerving ethical belief and simple touching faith. From very early on in our shared life, Alessandro worried that I had reneged on the religion into which I had been baptised. He loved to hear all about the nuns in Cluny. We had a similar childhood in so far as all convents are somehow similar. He understood the reasons why I could not go to Mass with him. He was always circumspect in his bringing up of this subject. Nothing was said in the presence of Max nor of the boys; he mentioned it only when we were alone. I knew his concern came out of his love for *la Madre*. He could not think of her eternal damnation. He had always a little homily for me: "You are so good, *Madre Mia*, you are a perfect soul...*se non serviamo Dio...con spirituale...pregare insieme io e tu?*" Italian betrayed his tenderness of heart.

I did not say that some day in the future we would kneel down together and pray but I longed to say it. I had never forgotten the early days in Cluny when I discovered that I belonged to a faith, that I was part of a worldwide cherished community. Nor had I forgotten that airy over-the-moon release coming out from confession, being blessedly ready to receive Holy Communion, that martyred delight of fasting from midnight—the sheer lovely goodness of it all. There is no other feeling in the whole world to equal that feeling. Many times I longed to go, hand in hand with Alessandro into the utter peacefulness of shared prayer. I missed prayer more and more as time went on. Just as I accepted him totally and never questioned his integrity, just so must he accept me. He spaced out his little sermons but he made sure that I was aware he prayed for me. There was an abundance of meaning in his dark eyes each time we entered a church in Rome, I to look at pictures and he to reverence God.

Rome at Christmas time is a very different Rome from the Rome of the high tourist season in summer. It is Rome for the family. Everywhere there are parents and their children visiting *i presepi della Natale*. There are so many churches to visit, so many cribs. Yet each crib is different. A side altar is given over in every church for the presentation of the Christmas story. The artists who make them may take inspiration from a famous painting of ancient Rome or of medieval Rome or they may model Rome as it is today complete with this century's architecture. Against this backdrop, the poor stable of Bethlehem is built. The Virgin and Joseph, the shepherds and the animals, are grouped around the straw-lined manger in which the Baby is placed. Film is used to show the heavenly choir of angels in the sky above—a painted sky of eastern sunrise or a Roman sky of drifting clouds. Suitable soft music fills the air all around. Crowds of families gather at every crib. Fathers lift small children on high to view and to listen, the whispered questions are answered with a repetition of the story of Bethlehem. Over and over, one hears in Italian the words "no room at the inn." They were poor; there was no room in the inn; they were allowed only a stable.

I said to Alessandro, "I become a Catholic again when we follow the families to the crib, and not when we go to the Vatican."

Alessandro understood. "It is because, at the crib we return to the birth of Christianity and to our earliest beliefs. We had no doubts; we did not question then."

"Do you question, Alessandro?"

"*Madre Mia*, everyone questions. Italians have to prove to each other (how is the word? *accorto*?) yes, how shrewd they are. It is *più facile* to question than to put our trust in mystery. *Perché? Perché?* Always the question. Always to suspect and never to accept."

"I do not mean to let credulity drain away when we go to the Vatican," I told him, "but it happens."

"*Comprendo*. It is the magnificence presented to our sophisticated gaze when our childish eyes saw only poverty and obscurity. And we ask ourselves, is this the same Jesus?"

"And is it all necessary?" I added.

"*Sì*, it is necessary. It is the build-up of many centuries. In Rome, the family grows strong to endure. The family builds a large enduring dwelling. The Christian family began here, replacing the pagan emperors. The popes used the marble of palaces to build their churches. Roman marble endures, *Madre Mia*, as faith endures and as family endures. Look around you at the Roman *palazzi* built for the Borghese, the Colonna, the Farnese, the Medici. Are there not bishops' palaces, and basilicas in Ireland?"

We were viewing Rome from the Capitoline Hill. "Nothing like this," I answered, "all in one place."

"Ah!" Alessandro smiled down at me, his voice proud. "*Ecce signum! Ecce Roma!*"

Why did this innocent arrogance remind me of Tadek, who had said: "I am a Jew. Jews are set apart." Alessandro was the son of Laelia; the same blood ran in his veins. He was born to esteem that of which he felt himself a part. And he made it clear in his twenty-first year that although he had never known a house complete with parents, he was a citizen of Rome. Rome was his. And there he belonged.

"Do you sometimes remember that you have Jewish blood?" I asked.

"*Sì, Madre Mia. Ebreo*, that is the Italian for Jew. Sometimes I laugh at the mirror when I am shaving. '*Ebreo, tu*,' and then I laugh again and I say, 'Welshman, *tu*.' When my father came to the convent, we walked in the garden, and he told me that he came from the country of Wales."

"I thought he was English."

"That is what he said and he said it on all the occasions he came and he said not to forget that. I did not know English to understand what he said. Sister Amelia always walked with us so she could translate. She was English when she was young. Sister Amelia was the nun you met. She showed me how to use paint. She spoke of my father when I asked her to. She said he had *presenza magnifica*. Do you agree, *Madre*, with Sister Amelia?"

"Oh yes," I answered quickly, always a little afraid to dwell on the recollection of Burton. "Yes, he was very tall, very attractive and wonderful."

"Sister Amelia always said that the war was not his fault." I wondered if Sister Amelia had felt the magnetism of Burton, she who had been English before she entered the convent. I wondered if she had been so drawn to the little boy because of the *macho magnifico*, so drawn that she wanted to take Alessandro in her arms and be his mama. He was only four when he last saw Burton.

"Was Sister Amelia kind in a loving way?" I asked. Alessandro was surprised; he answered in Italian and then he translated. "Those nuns are not allowed to touch nor be touched. She was kind to the degree allowed. I never wanted to kiss her because she was ugly; but yes, she tried to be kind."

"You like only pretty women, Alessandro?"

"Only beautiful women, *Madre Mia*. In the world now there is only one beautiful woman. It is you."

I was happy to be flattered and complimented and admired. The Italian sky fosters such delightful felicitations. Phyllis's Luigi was an expert in this and I never took any of it seriously.

If Max could have a favourite, it had to be Stefan. That Christmas in Rome, father and son drew together in a shared love of sport. Stefan went everywhere with Max: playing squash, watching football, pony-trekking far out at a mountainy farm owned by a psychologist friend of Max. If the weather had not been like a June day in Ireland, their pursuits might have been frustrating. Deric searched out galleries not previously explored and pondered over catalogues with Theo. He found small cinemas in dark alleys, and he sampled films he would not have been allowed to see in Philadelphia where Max vetted the entertainment. I questioned this obsession with what Deric called *avant-garde* cinema but Theo was adamant that both boys were now into the teens. "The more open the view of life," he told me, "the better for the emerging man."

"And what about the emerging young woman?" I also remarked to Max. "We are all so occupied. Isn't Vasha thrown very much into the company of an immensely attractive young man?"

"Immensely attractive!" They were agreed on that. "Yes, indeed, they complement each other in looks, don't you think?"

"I didn't go out with a boy when I was sixteen," I said to Theo. "My gran would have had a fit."

Theo looked at me very seriously. "And what would she have had if she knew that your tender sixteen-year-old heart lusted after a hidden love? I, too, prefer the old ways, my dear Lia, but we are now in the sixties. We must not create hoops of solid concrete for the young people to crash against. Hoops, yes, but for them to jump through..."

But I persisted. "Theo, isn't there such a thing as young people being unable to resist temptation?"

He said, "There are some sweets of temptation which are rightly irresistible. Vasha will recognise the rim of the hoop."

I could only hope that Berny had instructed her good-looking son in the philosophy of hoops. As it happened, Vasha did not view Frayne as a prime temptation, only as a very good tennis player. And he knew enough to keep his views to himself for that Christmas.

We would spend three days of New Year with Phyllis in Siena. Alessandro did not come with us because he had examinations in early January and he was intent on study. I was disappointed.

"*Madre Mia*, this is your last day in Roma. May I take you to my special church, one you have not seen?"

In the car, he told me that he had thought a lot about the way my beliefs edge away when I enter an enormous showpiece of a basilica. I had said that I felt more urgent faith within me in an unpretentious little chapel in the west of Ireland. It was, I realise, a stupid thing to say. Suitability is all. We drove through a squalid district of factories and gas-works. Alessandro saw my dismay. I had grown accustomed to fountains and terraced gardens.

"For centuries, this was a place of pilgrimage. The pilgrims walked beneath a canopy, a colonnade over a mile long, upheld by eight hundred columns of marble. All gone now. Ah *qui sait*? To the right, beyond those walls, is the Protestant cemetery where are the graves of Shelley and Keats."

I remembered some Shelley—was it from "Adonais?" Aloud I felt for the words: "'When hope has kindled hope and lured thee to the brink...Or go to Rome which is the sepulchre, /Oh not of him, but of our joy...They borrow not/Glory from those who made the world their prey...And he is gathered to the kings of thought...'"

Alessandro glanced at me in admiration. I smiled at him. "I was an utter romantic about Shelley when I was at school. And even now! Perhaps because he died so young (not quite thirty) and so tragically. He came to Ireland once—in 1818, so long ago! And to think his bones lie nearby."

"Also, St Paul's bones lie here," Alessandro said. "The legend tells us that when he was savagely beheaded, three places that his head hit the ground, three fountains sprang out of the ground, and in the early times three churches were built. We are going to Tre Fontane, *Madre Mia*; perhaps there a prayer will rise from your heart."

The church we saw is not the original church which was, it is written, magnificent...and burnt to the ground in 1823. Shelley would have seen that wonder-of-the-world basilica, Shelley who was so marvellously in love with Rome. The present church dates from 1854, and is very beautiful.

"Now Tre Fontane," Alessandro said taking my elbow gently in his hand. "This way." Leaving the church, we stepped through a door into cloisters. The monks were chanting their office. Alessandro whispered, "They are the Trappists. We will sit here and listen." In the half-light from the high stained-glass windows, it was easy to slip back a century into meditation. I remember that my eyes closed humbly. Some prayers of childhood can never be forgotten. Slowly I whispered the Our Father, the Hail Mary and a fervent Act of Contrition. In the gloom, I saw that Alessandro's eyes were shining as if in gratitude. Holding my hand, he added the Salve Regina to my prayers. Then we kissed solemnly the way Theo always kissed, on each cheek. In a little while, we left the cloisters and the church.

Alessandro was happy. He chatted as we walked under the trees to the car. "In early days, all here was a swamp." He pointed up at the eucalyptus trees. "The monks distiled a potion from these leaves, to cure the mosquito bites. The bites were poison, and the swamp was named *Mal Aria*. Do you suppose that is malaria?"

Other words of Shelley persist now in my mind:

> *Like a child from the womb, like a ghost from a*
> > *tomb,*
> *I arise, and unbuild it again.*

CHAPTER SEVENTEEN

Everyone has come to know a great deal about psychology in the last forty years. Child psychology has altered and improved parental attitudes. At the time of Vasha's birth psychology, although Max's chosen profession, was a mysterious science and never a topic for discussion. When Vasha entered the teens, I began to have doubts as to the wisdom of relinquishing my role as her mother, as a mother with top priority rights in her life. Never for a single moment did I see Theo's influence over Vasha as other than benign. And so it was from the first moment to the very end. Nevertheless I had lost out on the most precious link there can be, that between mother and daughter: your daughter is your daughter all your life; his very first girlfriend snaps the cord that had held you as the woman in your son's life. And that is as it should be. But in the very first moment of Vasha's life, I had given her up. I lived to see the folly of that surrender, and yet I know I could not have acted otherwise. In that time of her birth, recompense had to be made to the man who had led me to that precious event.

Without Theo, Vasha would never have existed. I was about to leave him alone after our years of needing each other. For him I would come to love Max. That was Theo's desire, happiness for his son. To have kept me and the baby with him in the house in Terenure would have meant forsaking his own son. Max's need of loving care was extreme then and for a long time after. The hell of the concentration camps was relived in a delirium of tortured dreams. My weak attempts to forge a separate life for myself and the baby were easily foiled. The luxury of the house in Terenure could not be resisted, and I loved being with Theo. I adored the man. Pleasing him gave me infinite pleasure—very especially in the months after Vasha's birth when Theo was arbiter and monitor of each action in my life, and in hers. It is impossible to forget the deep pleasure of his holding the baby to my breast in the dawn hours. Our eyes would meet above her tiny dark head, and in that meeting of the eyes our hearts would acknowledge our utter devotion to each other. "You are sure it does not hurt?" he would question softly. "You would tell me, Lia?" When I said, "It comforts me," his dry papery fingers would stroke my arm and the gladness he felt for me would shine in his glance. The tenderness with which he held the small baby was wonderful to behold. At any time Max, being a doctor, was quite matter-of-fact about the baby, confident that she was healthy and could survive a bit of tossing-up or a fit of sneezing.

"A hard-hearted wretch!" Theo would call him to which Max always retorted, "I keep my tender feelings for the poor mother—she is not giving trouble!" And very tender he was. Yet, disloyally, there is an intermittent thought: the psychologist in Max never warned me not to give my child away. Did he ask himself? I will never know now since I never asked when I could have. Max prised me away from his father after the boys were born; he bonded me to himself. Perhaps settling in our house on the Dargle River might have been a better idea than going to America? His father was obsessed with the baby but he would have given her up if Max had brought out the big psychological arguments. Perhaps we were of the same mind that, in ways we could not fathom, his father and my child belonged together. We did not question. The year was 1948 and psychology in Ireland was associated with the madhouse; it certainly was not used as a source of ethical advice.

Let it be said that I was never, in my own mind, separated from Vasha. There was a continuous exchange of phone calls, letters, gifts and many holidays. There was a loving amity between her and the two boys. They spoke proudly of "our sister in

Ireland and our brother in Italy." The accepted custom of living in different countries never raised questions.

I have described the way our time was divided. That delightful pattern of life changed scarcely at all until the year Vasha became seventeen. That summer she had taken her Leaving Certificate examination and was choosing her courses in university. Stefan and Deric would graduate from high school the following year and their decisions were already made. Deric would follow Theo into fine arts; nothing else was ever considered. Theo had built a little empire and he was well pleased to hand over to Vasha and Deric. Stefan talked only of the science of travelling in space. When he was eight years of age, he surprised us with the statement that the earth was 92.9 million miles from the sun. I remember the way Max laughed, asking: "Why not ninety three millions?" and Stefan replying: "Point one of a million is a lot of miles, Daddy. The travellers must calculate their rations for an exact number of days!" In the background was Deric, tapping his finger to his forehead. "Gone nutty!" he said in his clear childish voice, but Stefan looked very superior— he had read the book and could quote it at length. Ten years later he had not changed his mind. Space was the big preoccupation. Frayne Lowry, six years older than the twins and soon to be qualified as a doctor, shared Stefan's fascination with space travel. The idea then mooted of sending men to the moon generated waves of excitement in which adults were involved, proving to Stefan that he was definitely a young man of his time, if not well ahead of his time. Deric was utterly scornful of this "moon idea" as he called it. "Suppose they get there," he argued; "they know already that it is not another living world—only ashes and craters!" But Stefan and Frayne argued that it was the getting there that was important—the opening up of space.

I always kept a little diary and I find the question written there: "Are people trying to get into space so they can leave this unfinished world and start on a new one?" The diaries of the sixties show a great deal of uncertainty throughout. Happy events are barely noted, not expatiated on as in earlier years. Questions abound and are unanswered. One little piece of writing is many times repeated as if for reassurance:

What great good luck had given me a husband beyond compare, two handsome sons whom I love very much and a wonderful, beautiful, talented daughter who is safely in the keeping of the man I loved best in my life.

Everyone loved and appreciated and cherished Theo. He is part of that inner shrine of secret worship— perhaps the greatest part now after all the years have passed and only the shrine remains.

We all assembled in Terenure for Theo's birthday

in August. The year was 1965. Alessandro was twenty-six. He had taken his degrees several years before. He was a junior professor in the history of art and ancient civilisation in the Gregorian University and he taught English in the French School of Languages. He had used Burton's money to buy an apartment in Trastevere. There was a large balconied room under the roof which served as his studio and there was a ready sale for his drawings of the city. The balcony looked down onto the grey Tiber, and away into the distant Nieme Hills.

I had been many times in this apartment, always bringing with me some small gift that he could use: a cushion, a jug, a painted plate. He got much pleasure unwrapping my gift and adding it to the colourful clutter with which artists surround themselves. I was always eager to visit Alessandro and in a sense I was more securely part of my whole self with him than at any other time. When he embraced me, that magic perfume of his skin never failed to enchant me. I was a child again in Burton's arms in the big front bedroom in Mama's Sunrise. All the childish stirrings of sensuous arousal which Burton had created and fostered were there under Alessandro's warm lips ready to flame into passionate response. Always I had to remember that I was not a child any more. Circumspect and dignified, I would withdraw quickly from the embrace. I would move around the studio to inspect his sketches. I would walk out onto the balcony to admire the view. One can admire distant vistas for minutes at a time. There was the ever-present fear that I would embarrass Alessandro by a display of nostalgic emotion which he could not be expected to understand. Sometimes, he caught my hand and drew me close to him again. "*Madre Mia, io la conosco, la capisco.*" What did he know? What did he surmise? Then he would release my hand, and we would smile an acceptance without words.

On holidays in Dublin, we two would go off on sketching expeditions. As in Rome, his interest was in older parts of the city. My role was to drive the car and provide a flask and sandwiches. Max had enough of drawings all his life; to him Dublin was a golfer's paradise: so many clubs and all so accessible. Sometimes, Deric came sketching with us. The lunch-break was always in St Stephen's Green even if it was raining and we had to sit under umbrellas. Sometimes Alessandro made hazy drawings of my figure in a summery dress. Theo had forbidden any attempts at a portrait: "I will pay you handsomely to paint Lia's portrait when your skill matures—and when you equate your understanding of her with her beauty, more exactly." Alessandro often stood gazing at the Lia picture in the silver frame. "He is right," he would say, "but soon I will do justice."

The birthday party was as successful as ever and always. Perhaps that was because we changed neither the formula nor the friends, nor (I should add) the food for the party. That was delicious and memorable. The next day it took all of us all day to put the big house back to rights. Theo kept to his room for this busy day, under strict orders to rest. With so many of us, the work was easy and enjoyable. There was much laughter and snatches of song and exchange of news for which there had been no time between the feasting and the dancing. Frayne danced back and forth while dusting the furniture. He was everyone's favourite. They said he was a perfect specimen of magnificent American youth. I, alone of the happy crowd, knew he was his father's son—not American at all but Welsh-English, the living image of Burton. I was always careful to bestow the very lightest and airiest of kisses on Frayne. I did not want to know and I never did know if he also had inherited that delicious skin aroma so special to Alessandro, the perfume that blossomed under a warm kiss and lingered in a caress. Some precious pieces of sculpture were always removed for the party and it was my special task to replace them, polishing each with a chamois.

"Did you know that Tonio is not going on to college? He has got his own band together and they are going to tour."

"Has he told his mother? She will never approve."

"Why not?" This from Frayne; and from Deric, "Phyllis wants him to be *professore musicale* in the university—special degrees, special qualifications." And Vasha said brightly, "What does he need qualifications for? He can play four instruments as well as the piano. And he has written several songs." I could hear the proud admiration in Vasha's voice. It is always a strange thing that no matter how clever a person is, another's talent is the one he craves. Just as there is no success in life unless the best friend fails.

Now Deric was asking, "Is it all decided that you are enrolling in the University of Perugia?" To which Alessandro put in: "Perugia's history department is reputed to be the best in Italy." And Frayne, waving the yellow duster like a matador, teased, "She doesn't know enough Italian to go to an Italian college!"

"Oh yes, I do," she retorted, "and Daddy Theo has checked them all and decided on Perugia. You can come and visit me, smarty big head. I will introduce you to a gorgeous *signorina*—if you are a good boy!" Stefan wanted to know, "Is Perugia one of those tourist places by the Mediterranean?" Alessandro told him that Perugia is up in the hills mid-way between Rome and Siena. "Tonio is coming to see me at weekends," Vasha said jubilantly.

That was the moment I had misgivings. I began to long for a closer association with my daughter. I wished I were the mother in harmony with Vasha's inner dreams. We had become surface people. It was a sad thought.

"You will like Perugia," Alessandro told Vasha when we were taking a break for coffee in Shanlee's kitchen. "The nuns in the orphanage took us on pilgrimage every year to Assisi. They are Franciscan sisters and they have naturally great devotion to St Francis."

"Who was St Francis?" queried Stefan. The others looked at Alessandro, and he looked at me. "Didn't you ever tell the boys about little Francis who talked to the birds and met the angels of God on the hills?"

"You tell us," Vasha asked.

"Well, you will not be able to escape hearing all these tales when you are in Perugia, because Assisi is only down the road. The countryside in Umbria is wonderfully pastoral and almost untouched since the middle ages."

"Please go on, Alessandro," pleaded Deric who loved antiquity and was not unwilling to get a break from the big tidy-up. Deric was a little bit lazy and he was happiest curled up with a book. Alessandro smiled at us. He loved to talk about Italy whether about the towns, the mountains, the poetry, the music or most of all about the painters. "There is a strong sweet wine in Umbria, *la schiacchetria*, the word means 'chatterer', and Umbrians drink *la schiacchetria* the way we drink coffee. Stories are on everybody's lips, and Francis who founded the order is still alive in Umbria, quite often spotted at the corner of a street! He was not a poor boy; he was the son of a rich merchant—who was a *bon viveur* with money to indulge himself. The boy was taken prisoner in war, and he came under the influence of the monks. He was the friend of the poor and of animals and of the birds. His poetry is very sad and moving—the earth, the trees, the fowl and helpless suffering humanity were his intimates."

"Did they kill him?" asked Ted who was listening and whose own history told him that the followers of the Jew Jesus were killed in the early days.

"It was his death wish that he be buried with the criminals who were executed on Infernal Hill. And he was, but the pope ordered the name changed to Hill of Paradise. A great basilica in his memory is built there and Assisi is still enclosed by ramparts to protect it from heretics."

"I will go to see it," Vasha said. "Is there a picture of him?"

"There are thirty frescoes to show the scenes of little Francisco's life. The frescoes are attributed to Giotto—and they are certainly typical of Giotto's school. *Madre Mia*, did I tell you that this little saint invented the very first *presepio*, what is called the crib, on Christmas Eve in 1224? In the Alps, and in Rome, there are many of great antiquity and of great beauty."

"I remember, Alessandro," I said. "That lovely Christmas five years ago."

"And what about Perugia?" Vasha asked, a little impatiently.

"Being the capital of Umbria, it is a dignified town. It is medieval and of much interest. It is a town of churches; St Peter's and St Dominic's are authentic middle ages." He noticed Vasha's rather quiet face, usually so sparkling. "But do not worry, Vasha, the students have a lively time in Perugia! *La schiacchetria* is plentiful and available to all. There is much river activity. The Tiber rises in the Umbrian hills and flows through Perugia under bridges unchanged for centuries."

So we had been given a picture of the Italian town which was to be Theo's chosen cradle of culture for Vasha. He had mentioned Perugia but as being among several choices. Later that night, the entire scheme was presented in family council, but so persuasively that neither Max nor I could find a reason to demur. Like all of Theo's plans, he had decided before he had consulted. On an earlier visit to Rome, he had journeyed by rail to Perugia and here he called on cousins he had not seen since before the war but with whom he had corresponded now and then. In their house Vasha would have accommodation. They would be in constant touch with Theo: "And of course, with you and Max, Lia. We will have a full circle of contact by the telephone. I have it so arranged."

"Who are these cousins?" Max enquired. "Did I ever meet them?"

"They are also Randt," Theo said. "My father and his grandfather took the name legally in Paris. Why? Because it was the name over the shop which they rented when they arrived in Paris from Zamosc. My father set up a bookshop. It prospered; he bought the premises. It is still mine, and now it is a gallery. For years, Maurice Randt rented it from me. He specialised in school and college books. Did well until the war."

"I remember them now," Max said; "their eldest was my age. What was his name? Why are they in Perugia?"

"His name is Maurice, the same as his father. They got out of Paris in June 1940, four days before the German army came in. And the same day that Italy declared war. They crawled practically all the way to Milan, a few miles every night, their possessions in two baskets. Six of them, four children. They had lost all. With only their knowledge of books they started again."

"And the children?" I asked.

"They survived," Theo replied. "The two eldest teach in the university, the youngest runs the shop and the girl is married. She lives in Genoa."

"Will I like them, Daddy Theo?" Vasha asked.

"They are good people," he answered, smiling fondly at her, and adding mischievously, "Will they like you?"

Looking at Vasha, I had the certain feeling that she was aware of her own strength. I remembered what Theo had said about her self-esteem. She gauged the effect of her beauty on those around her. Her shell was not full of chinks as mine was. I wondered if she had a soft heart, or if her head ruled. It was sad to know so little of so fascinating a daughter.

After all the talk and all the planning and the introduction of strangers into our lives, I could not sleep that night. Lying awake in the bedroom, that luxurious bedroom which Theo had made for me in the house in Terenure, I was thinking again how little I knew about Vasha. It seemed only a year ago when she was a small girl welcoming me home from America, looking at my dresses, fitting on a necklace and smiling into that mirror, and I was catching my breath to see again how like Tadek she was in a bewitching little feminine way. Were there boys in her life? She had lots of girlfriends and Theo gave her absolute freedom. Ted had taught her her how to drive and she now had a full licence. Theo would give her a car if she expressed an interest in having one. Ted had taught me to drive and suddenly I remembered Tony Lloyd's fury when Theo wanted me to have a car. Tony Lloyd! I hadn't thought of him for years. Now I wanted Max to make love to me for a total reassurance that I belonged to only one man in the world. But Max was sleeping soundly, his breathing soft and even. I crept out of bed to curb my restlessness. I sat in the big chair by the open window; the late summery sky lit the room with shadows. I could not get away from the unwanted thoughts of Vasha. She was emerging into womanhood as mysterious a person as when I carried her within me. If I could live that time all over again could I, and should I, have acted differently?

Max had missed my presence beside him. Now he came and sat on the floor beside my chair. Not wanting to blame me for disturbing him, he said sleepily, "I had too much wine at dinner." I kissed his head. "And I should have let you sleep it off. Sorry, darling."

"I am awake now," he said. "Want to talk?" He nestled his head against my knees. "A cigarette would be nice but it is too much trouble! Is it about Vasha?"

"Mind-reader! Maybe we could talk tomorrow. It is all so hazy."

"Tell me, anyway. Share with me, sweetheart."

"Max, would I be supposed to have a mother-daughter talk with Vasha? She is unexpectedly so grown-up now."

"It is a bit late for all that facts-of-life stuff, Lia. She will have asked Theo and he will have had someone competent give her the biological data, probably when she menstruated for the first time. She would probably smile at you if you supposed her still innocent."

"I have been left out of an important part of her youth. I forfeited the right."

"Forfeit is a tough word, Lia. We did what looked best for both of us, for the baby and for Theo."

"Yes, I suppose so. But for the first time, I feel discarded. A bit forlorn. A bit at a loss."

He was silent for a while, and then he said, "I do, too. It is the price we have to pay. I would like to have a role in Vasha's life. But, if I know my father, he is feeling a let-down also. She has grown up and soon she will have grown away. I know he is sad to be losing her."

I said, "Why could she not do her degrees in Trinity, the same as you did? And live at home here in this comfortable house? Why a *pensione* in Italy?" I could see no reason for Perugia.

"If she had lived with us from the start, my darling Lia, we too might have chosen Perugia. It is a magnificent seat of learning; the ambience will be right for her. That will be my father's first consideration. His instinct tells him that she is now a woman. It is time to back off now she has proved she can handle freedom."

"Max, has he said this to you?"

"No Lia, but I read him. His work is done. His age is catching up. He will still be the guiding spirit. Vasha will not want for anything."

I sighed. My little girl, Tadek's gift to me, was passing out of my life without ever being in my hands. The price to pay?

"I shall never know her inner dreams." And I realised that I had never had anyone to know my dreams. They had to be secret.

"Come, Lia." Max was standing up and gathering me up into his arms. "A massive build of a lad," my gran used to say. "Women," Max said, "should share their inner dreams with their husbands." And that was not all he said. His love-making always began with words, declarations, promises and wild, wild flattery. His kisses were slow and exploring; his physician's hands understood how to caress most expertly; his seduction was gentle and withheld until pleaded for. Now his urgency grew faster and his final demanding entry was utterly satisfying. Max had perfected his own technique. It was exquisite.

CHAPTER EIGHTEEN

If I thought of the 1960s as the Middle Ages of my memory I see the 70s as the later epoch, a point in time when an event set off a new reckoning date. Afterwards we would say that an event was "before we left America," and there would always be a small note of yearning in our voices as if the years in America had been our golden age. In my heart I knew that those years in Philadelphia had high moments totally unconnected with Max and the two boys; yet, over all, the picture of our home in Philadelphia is in spirit the same as the unchanging tranquil Constable landscape which used to hang in Theo's study. That picture fetched a great price in Theo's auction, and perhaps it is the auction in New York which was the mark of the beginning of the later epoch.

When a letter came from Theo instead of the usual cheery phone call, we looked at the envelope with some trepidation. Max and I were now alone at home. Stefan had been accepted as a cadet in the American air force and he was now well advanced in his brilliant career. Deric was a final-year student in *L'École des*

Beaux Arts and learning his trade in Theo's *Galerie Randt* in Paris. Vasha, still the darling of all hearts, was ready to leave Perugia for Theo's *galleria* in Rome. Frayne was very much part of our family; Berny and Denis were still our closest friends although not each other's closest friends at times. Frayne was in the American air force too, a recognised consultant in the medical side of space aeronautics. Alessandro, handsome and brilliant, still lived in his studio apartment in Trastevere. His exhibitions were regular events in a busy social life. He knew everyone and he was very popular. We waited always to hear that he had fallen for one of the many glamorous girls of his circle. His early and continuing devotion to his Catholic faith seemed to bind him into a fairly disciplined life-style, never detracting from his tolerance and his charm. He and I kept in touch by telephone and letter, and exchanged regular visits. Max often said that he could be jealous of Alessandro—his devotion to me and mine to him—were it not for the fact that jealousy needed such a lot of energy more suitable to youth and, anyway, Max always added, Alessandro was the very nicest person on earth. Of Tonio we heard constantly from Phyllis but mostly from Vasha. She was extremely proud that his *banda musicale* was making a name in Italy. She sent us records of his music and his songs but we acknowledged to ourselves that we would need to be thirty years younger to appreciate them. Tonio had not lived at home since he was sixteen. Luigi's hotel was now very prosperous. We understood that Phyllis had to (as she said) "keep the hard word up to him" since his old mother had died. We knew Luigi alternated between ardent devotion to Phyllis, and roué-style amorous affairs with (to quote Phyllis) "young wans," and but for the fact that (again quoting Phyllis) "he knew what side his bread was buttered on," there might have been a split-up.

And now back to Theo's letter, and the beginning of the later epoch. "I wondered why my father did not ring last week," Max said as he opened the letter. "He must have forgotten." An inward pang told me that Theo would not forget. I knew we were both filled with apprehension to see a letter. Theo's phone calls could last an hour.

"Max, read it out loud so we both know it at the same time," and Max read slowly:

Dear Both of You,

Do not be disturbed. I am better now. On Thursday last, I experienced what our doctor called a fibrillation in the heart. (Max will explain that to Lia.) It was painful, but perhaps not serious. Confined to bed, I am taking stock of my situation...

"Max, Max," I interrupted, "is that a heart attack?"

"No," Max said decisively, "not a heart attack, Lia, but a warning, a strong warning. No, no, do not be alarmed—a warning to slow down. All this travelling! At his age! Wait, let us see what he has written. Do not look so frightened, *balibt*. Come, sit beside me." He put his arm around me. Now I could see the writing, still beautiful, but I imagined it shaky. Max held the pages between us:

Now I have time to notice that this big house and an old man in bed are too much for Shanlee and Ted— even with the help of missus Nelly and her daughter, and this year, a boy for the garden. Even so.

As Lia knows, my usual way is to make all the plans and then, like a conjuror, take the result out of the hat. So, be surprised: I am about to lay out the design and invite your comments. Firstly Shanlee and Ted should be retired to a little place of their own with no heavy work involved. Lia, would you rent to me your house in Bray for the duration of their time or their ability. We drive out there occasionally. Sometimes on a fine day Shanlee dusts and we make coffee. They like that place. They like the river.

I have taken an option on a house in Merrion Square. The sunny side of the square, Lia! There is a lift to the first floor in this house. A firm of auctioneers leases the ground floor, and an engraver of my acquaintance is in the basement. The upper

*two floors were set in flats. Empty now but in a
disgraceful condition. The day of these houses
finished with the end of cheap domestic labour. In
the city they are fetching low prices. I paid £800 for
this house in the suburb in which I live, and my
neighbour sold for £30,000 recently. It is to be
subdivided. If Max agrees—it is his house of course—
I will put it on the market. I should do even better
than my neighbour! So what do you think, my son?
An upper-floor fortress in Merrion Square or your old
home next to a block of flats..?"*

Max stopped reading. "I thought he would never
leave Terenure. I thought *that* was his fortress."

"Would Shanlee and Ted be lonely out in Bray
where they do not have the few old friends who live
on the South Circular Road?"

"A lot of them are dead now," Max said. "They have
each other and they have peace of mind. They have
terrible memories of the long-ago times in Zamosc,
Shanlee especially. When I was a little kid, she used to
tell me and she used to cry."

And I remembered Tadek's father in their kitchen
in Ringsend telling me about Zamosc, their houses set
on fire by the cossacks. He had burned his hands
pulling the balalaika out of the fire.

"Yes," Max said, "Shanlee will be glad to pass her
days with peace of mind. When we are old enough for

change, we welcome it." He continued reading:

My hope is that your work in Philadelphia will soon be completed. You will have compiled all your research for your books and all the interviews you have told me about, and you will be aware of the effects on those lucky enough to have escaped the Holocaust. I know you are planning a separate book about the partisans now endeavouring to live normal lives. You will write great books, Max. The point I am labouring is: could you write your books in Dublin—in Merrion Square? I know you have given notice of your last term in the college. So, is the time ripe for a move?

For a little while there was a pause. We would not have the same reaction, of that I was sure. I would be ready to fly immediately to Theo, to comfort him, to nurse him, to humour him, to be at his beck and call every minute of every day in the very same minutes of every day that I always missed him. Theo was my god of wisdom, of love, of tenderness. He had made himself the enchantment, the magic, the pleasure-dome of my existence. In the weeks approaching our holiday in Dublin each year, my spirits lifted with the joy of seeing him again. When we parted, my heart pained for many days. I adored him.

Max knew all of this. He rejoiced openly when we were again together, all on our own. "I want you for myself, Lia. When my father is around, you are mesmerised." But he loved his father: he was proud of him; he referred to him constantly. The actuality of living with him might prove to be tedious. I recognised that as a fact of life: when he was a child, he lived as a child and when he was a man, he needed his own space. "Please go on reading, Max," I said, although I could read the letter: it must affect us both at the same moment. Max turned back to the letter:

Being practical, I must consider the escalating cost of insurance. Within the last year, Vasha and Deric have compiled an inventory, not only here in Terenure but also in Paris, Rome and Lisbon. From this inventory, we have decided on an auction. It will be held in New York by Christies in conjunction with their New York agents.

Max put down the letter. "All this without a word to us! No wonder he nearly gave himself a heart attack! Did Vasha mention this?"

"No, but it would seem to her a part of her training. The talk is always of artists and paintings. And didn't Theo say at Christmas that he was grooming Deric? He said that several times. Deric never discusses what goes on in Paris. He is sort of secretive."

Max smiled. "Well, we know where he got that!"

"Please go on reading. You are nearly finished."

"Right," Max said. "Where was I? Oh yes, he is

going to have an auction. Oh here it is:"

*And now, Max my son, I am going to ask a favour.
If you approve of my plans—I am depending on
your, and Lia's, approval—could Lia come to me
while you wind up your affairs in Philadelphia?"*

I read the last line:

My love to both of you,
Theo Randt

I remember we stared again at each other, trying to
read each other's thoughts because we knew they were
opposed. The long slow look would conceal us, my
secretiveness and Max's open-mindedness. I rejoiced
that Theo had sent for me. I would rush across the
world at his behest though it meant leaving my
husband. Max spoke first, one half-note higher than
usual. "He has not left us much choice, has—no, Lia,
don't say it, I know he wouldn't write if he did not see
the necessity. But I do not, and never did, fancy the
idea of a *ménage à trois*. No point in protesting; so
please don't. No, please don't!"

I knew he would regret being angry and indeed
anger with him was very rare. I knew he would take
back those words. He would invite me to laugh at him,
later, in the bedroom. His love-making would be
pitched to reassure himself that he was my own
husband who came first in my own world, and he
knew I would give caress for caress no matter how

insistent. I had learned all the initiations and all the responses over many years, and it was easy to refine and revamp and re-create, to go ever further in giving because he was a man so easy to love, a man ever grateful for intimacy.

Max was not the one who counted the days when the Dublin holidays drew near. He always showed amusement to see the calendar exxed off day by day, but a later frenetic passion betrayed the cool smile. From time to time, he used a phrase: *a twelve-year start*: "My father has a twelve-year start on me in your affections, Lia. Yes, it counts. Those were your impressionable years." And I would always tell him that it is now that counts, now his father was getting older and we must give him more. At times he was persuaded; nevertheless his delight was unmistakable each time the Aer Lingus plane took to the air and the twins waved goodbye to Dublin—his beaming smile told its own story.

The day we received the letter, he waited for a suitable hour to put through a call to his father's doctor who was a close friend of his. They talked and I waited in fear for the outcome of the talk. Perhaps the letter had not told the full truth of Theo's attack?

"Yes," Max reported sombrely, "my father has had a warning, but his general health is good. I told him last Christmas to stop acting like a thirty-year-old.

Apparently he was planning a trip to Mexico when the heart started acting up! He never learned to delegate! There are several of his people in Dublin he could send to Mexico! Dammit, there are people in Mexico who could come to him! What's in Mexico for godsake?"

There was no doubt at all left in my mind by this explosive speech so unlike Max. There was cause for concern. We would be going back to Dublin and there would be no delay in doing so.

As it turned out, Alessandro was the one who went to Mexico. Theo valued Alessandro's judgement ahead of any judgement not his own. Just as I had always done, Alessandro took every word from Theo's lips and stored it away, augmenting Theo's knowledge with wide study of his own. His mother's genius for music was in him—a genius for great art. I, who knew, saw in him his father's genius for turning to personal account every chance that came his way. Some earlier gene had endowed Alessandro with a soaring generosity of spirit; there was no trace of Laelia's self-serving nature. For Burton I suspended any final judgement. He had bequeathed Alessandro to me for love of the child. It is a lifting of pressure to write now and freely of a time when all these events and the thoughts connected with them were buried still in the secrets vault of Lia's heart. I saw Alessandro in his relationship with Theo as a part of my recompense. The satisfied

enjoyment of Theo at Alessandro's many achievements
(not the least of which would be the famous auction)
compensated if only a tiny part for the unexpiated
guilt of desiring Burton. Unexpiated. Unatoned. The
trouble was there when my lips touched the fragrant
skin of Alessandro's face, and with yet more guilt, I
would not have wished it otherwise. It was only, I told
myself, left-over guilt. It was not infidelity.

A private art collection in Mexico City was about to
go on the market. Alessandro went direct from Rome
and returned there, so, although I was in Dublin we
did not meet. We always exchanged letters and
colourful cards. Reading those notes now, our main
concern was for Theo's health. There are some
references to the teeming population, the poverty and
the wealth. Theo knew the paintings and the antiques
on which Alessandro was to give an evaluation. On
Theo's agreement, he purchased and these would be
for resale in the forthcoming auction of Theo's own
collection.

I went to Dublin ahead of Max who had to
superintend the packing of his papers and reference
books, and for this he had the help of his organisation.
He had almost finished his lectures in the college. We
had added very little to the furniture already in the
house and the rent had been paid to the end of the
semester. I would have been glad if Stefan and Deric

could have been at hand to pack their own accumulation of cluttered memorabilia. All that stuff was packed into cartons and despatched overland. I remember that those cartons lay unopened for many years in a spare room in my house by the river in Bray. What had seemed so precious to the boys growing up became so much junk requiring too much energy to re-assess. Ah well!

My last two weeks in Philadelphia rushed past in the race to get ourselves up and out. Max was very careful not to let his frustration disrupt our days. He was being deprived of his accustomed routine, and resentment showed in small ways: jocose asides at which I smiled but which I knew were not meant to be funny at all. Over the years of our contented married life, our love-making had fallen into a pattern of peaceful play and innocent fulfilment. This changed abruptly and became like the night of his father's letter when he was unsure and insistent. Genuine tiredness from the day's toil of packing was not allowed to stand in the way of an ardent response. "You do still love me, Lia? I am not too old, am I? Tell me you will miss me, tell me, *mayn lyubenyu*, tell me that you will miss me." I must rouse myself to whisper back all the encouraging assurance I could think of, knowing all the time that yes, I would miss him peripherally being so used to his amiable presence. But also I would treasure the chance to give my total comfort to the one who had named me solace of his spirit, yet who never demanded solace, who had never asked and lived only to give. Submerged in my husband's re-awakened desire, my thoughts were far away across the Atlantic, every breath was monitoring Theo's house in Terenure. Prayers, so long unsaid, were flooding my heart. Oh Lord, let Theo live. Ask anything else, Lord, only spare him. Please, Lord, even for a little while.

The prayers were echoing through my mind at the airport when Max's arms clasped me close to him. "Never forget you belong only to me, Lia, only to me." When the plane lifted into the sky over the verdant tree-lined city of Philadelphia, I sighed with relief that I was safely on my way to Theo. The thought that Max could be jealous of his father struck me and in the same instant I remembered that I, at times, had been jealous of my daughter's place in Theo's life. I let both thoughts slip away. To oneself one must remain always a mystery. There was more consolation in prayer. There has always been more consolation in prayer.

CHAPTER NINETEEN

When Ted was at Dublin Airport to meet me, I had the immediate reassurance that although Mr Randt was still under the doctor's care and following the strict order to stay in bed, he was not in danger.

"Is he in pain, Ted?" That was my prayer all through the flight: Oh Lord, please do not let him suffer. I could see the anxiety lines on Ted's solemn face, but he assured me that the heart was not giving stress now. I asked no more questions about Theo, trying rather to enquire for Shanlee and Silkitoo-the-Fifth and the cats while, all the time, a new prayer was rising: Oh Lord, let Ted be telling the truth.

In all our years, I had never seen Theo in bed. His bedroom was in the front of the house. Mine and Max's were on a corridor overlooking the back garden. Ted announced my arrival and Theo called out to me, "Come, *balibt*." That lovely word means beloved.

Theo's bed was high and regal. He was a king receiving a courtier. For several years now, he had cultivated a closely clipped beard. A beard is a distraction so, at first, I could see no change. But he had aged, and when I saw his eyes without the reading-glasses, my heart contorted in pain. He knew that, as he knew everything.

"Lia will have jet-lag," he said very softly. "Come, stretch out on this eiderdown and share my pillows." I slipped off my shoes and obeyed. My prayer had been answered by the merciful Lord.

"Ah there, little one. I have told Shanlee we will have a couple of hours for you to sleep off your jet-lag. Then, if you are equal to it, Lia, we will have Shanlee's lunch. In the afternoon, we will talk. No, *balibt*, not now."

"What a very grand eiderdown," I murmured and he murmured back, "It is Persian, very valuable." This was so inimitably Theo that I just had to smile up at him. He took the outer edge of the quilt in his hand, and drew the downy softness over me; he let his hand remain on my hand. "Rest, little one," he whispered. "I am here."

Have I already written it too many times that, with Theo nothing was theatrical and everything was. He was the consummate creator of an unforgettable moment which he could conjure into an hour, into a week. In my case, into forever. So, restful sleep was conjured up for Lia to slip into a dream of being always under Theo's wing. In the dream, Theo was an angel. When I woke up to feel Theo's hand on mine—and it could be no other hand; I knew those delicate papery fingers—it was as if I had returned to the day I recovered consciousness in Tadek's poor room in Ringsend and felt Tadek's hand holding mine. I remembered I had the childish thought that if I were struck blind I would always know Tadek's hand. The dream and the memory had fused and there was pleasure in the fusion of Theo and Tadek. I forgot that Max had warned me, "Remember you belong to me." I turned to Theo and his arm drew me upward to his bearded face. He kissed me as he had always kissed me, on the left and on the right of my head. "We have always known it, Lia. From the first day. Then, there was Tadek. For a while, there was Tony Lloyd. And now, there is Max. But we have not changed, *balibt*. We cannot."

I breathed the words against his face. "Is it enough that we know it?"

"It is enough," he said and he released me although he must know that I was lying in the place I had coveted for years. Is coveting one of the deadly sins? The instant feeling was that we had recognised a brink and stepped back. Perhaps the recognition was only in me? Theo had always been aware and that reverential stepping-stone was not crossed. I had a new and wonderful secret to hide in a wayward heart. We knew. We both knew now.

I went away to shower and change. I found myself choosing a silk blouse because Theo had said, so many times: "There is something special about a woman in a silk blouse." It was not new that my attire should be chosen to please him; only my recognition was new. We had lunch together in his bedroom, and then we began a long rambling conversation about his letter. It would be six months at least, he said, before the auction. He would not put this house on the market until he had completed the purchase and the renovation of the house in Merrion Square. Max, he said, must approve the sale of this house because the house belonged to Max: it was Theo's wedding present to him.

"You will be in agreement with my plans, Lia, when I explain? You will, won't you? You will be the mistress in Merrion Square. A square you have often admired, yes? You are accustomed to my son, but tell me, how would you feel taking on the father? The father-in-law?" So many questions, so special a pleading, called for special reassurance. It was not at all a question of how I would feel, but rather would Max be amenable. And Theo knew that; his glance was trusting and almost dependent.

"Is it a very big house," I asked, "as big as the Land Commission offices!"

"Well now," he smiled, "I was never in the Land

Commission which is possibly two or three houses run into one to make a Government department."

I recalled the Land Commission as a huge, dreary place full of unexpected corridors and stone stairways with black iron railings.

"This is a single house, Lia, not even double-fronted. It was built in an era when Dublin was the second city in the empire. The Georgians loved terraced squares and ornamental centre gardens. The one I intend to buy has had the lower staircase destroyed by the inclusion of a lift. However, the lift stops at the first floor and the beautiful staircase, from the first floor to the attics, is quite restorable—costly, but possible."

"Attics? Are you going to store pictures in the attics?" I began to see this venture down into the city as a challenge he was setting up to take his mind off the declining years. I was wrong.

"No more pictures, little one—unless one or two of our favourites for the rooms of the apartment. I am tired of paying heavy insurance so that one old man can walk about his private gallery. I am very tired of the fear of loss."

"So tell me, Theo. There is an upper floor and beyond that there are attics. I can see you have made your plans."

"Only if you think we can happily coexist, Lia? You and Max and I?"

I made my smile as confident as I knew how. I put the love of both of us into the smile. Theo said, "For a few days I thought I would never see your face again. Your smile is giving me a new lease on life." And I answered bravely, "When Max arrives here, you will get yet another lease, even longer!" Theo had said, "It is enough that we know." It was an ultimatum to me and maybe to himself: thus far and no further. It was time to keep Max's name in the forefront of every topic. I would let Theo weave his enchantment in whatever time there might be left; he had earned that right. As for me, I would practise smiling gracious acceptance and hold myself back from wanting more than the abundance I already had. I was optimistic of fulfilling my proper role.

"You are adept at describing houses, Theo. Tell me about this apartment on the sunny side of Merrion Square. You said that in your letter—unless this talking would tire you?"

"Come here, *balibt*, and lie beside me on my precious quilt, and I won't have to talk out loud. You like this Persian antiquity? You are Scheherazade, I am the Sultan Schahriah and we are in a fresh instalment of the *Arabian Nights*. Yes? And I may hold your hand? Thus? Now, are you comfortable, my dear? So let me begin. These auctioneers and estate agents, a reputable firm, are known to me for many years, as is the engraver, a Dublin Jew like myself. When I take over the premises (after you and Max have given it a favourable inspection) we will be responsible for the whole building—over all—fore and aft." Now Theo was enjoying himself. This was like the old days in the 1940s when we used sit in his library and I used drink in his knowledge of everywhere and everything. Theo talking this way was a Theo I had missed in Philadelphia.

"Leases will be arranged for the business conducted on the ground floor, and in the basement which is ground level at the back, a long narrow strip of rubbish dump at present, but it will look very well tarmacadamed. Now we come to the first floor and the attics, and for this we have the lift which we must always maintain in good condition—the stairs are still partly there but I am beyond climbing stairs."

"Theo, I don't believe that. How many rooms in the apartment?"

"Plenty," he answered. "Three bedrooms with bath *en suite*; another possible guest-room, maybe two. A large Edwardian drawing-room across the front—facing south-west, Lia. It has a good fireplace which we will electrify. Central heating would be the thing. Which type would be best? That requires investigation. These things are changing; meanwhile electricity for heating and cooking. There is a large room in the attic which

I would like you to give an opinion on. It would make a kitchen/dining-room, properly designed. I am sure you have American ideas, Lia? And the big fanlight dormer windows give a view of the Dublin Mountains."

"That is the very first view I ever saw," I told him, "from my mother's sitting-room over the shop in Ringsend. I asked Phyllis if the mountains had names and Phyllis found out for me that one of them was called the Three Rock Mountain. I thought she made that name up just to keep me quiet. She was so kind, she would even tell a big fib. But there really is a Three Rock Mountain, Theo, and a Hell Fire Club which Phyllis's da told us was the devil's gambling den when he wasn't in Monte Carlo."

He smiled sympathetically and kissed my fingers. "Would it give you bad dreams to see that view every day, little one?"

"I would like it," I told him warmly. I hoped I would. I heard the click of the swing-door from the kitchen into the hall. I moved off the bed and sat into the armchair, slipping on my shoes. The king and the courtier would please Shanlee. After nearly half a century in his service, he was still Mr Randt just as Max was Master Max. Shanlee valued respect and so did I. There was no need to say a word to Theo. He would understand my regard for Shanlee's sensibilities.

"This is terrible stuff," Theo moaned comically as

he sipped a glass of barley-water which Shanlee poured from a jug. "The doctor was kind enough to inform me that the plonk I drink clogs the system. I looked-up that word, Lia. It means cheap Australian wine. Australian! I may be a wine-bibber (another thing the doctor said) but it is the finest French wine."

"Your second glass, sir," Shanlee said.

"Poor Theo," I smiled at him. "As soon as you are up and about you will think of a toast."

"And it won't be in barley!" he rejoined. When Shanlee had gone, he whispered, "I don't think it was the wine, Lia. I think it was coffee. I had taken to making it for myself—too strong and too often. I was getting a guilty conscience! Now, where were we?"

"We were in the kitchen in the attic with windows."

"Ah!" he breathed out a long, sad sigh," the kitchen where Lia will make milk toast and weak coffee for poor Theo the Invalid! We are going to have dinner out, as we always did! Do not forget, my dear Lia, that Merrion Square is adjacent to the Shelbourne." For Theo, "dinner out" rounded off the day.

"But can we afford the Shelbourne when all your pictures have been auctioned off?" I queried mischievously.

The idea of not being able to afford dinner in the Shelbourne, or anywhere else amused him highly. "I have always looked forward to your finding new places for dinner, and you have always indulged me in those expeditions. You must not think I am suddenly an old crock."

I did not think that. I was rightly confident he was a strong man in need of a period of rest. I did not stay too long that evening. In my own room, I pondered. Despite his eager talk about his new plans was there a deep down shade in his voice? Was his enthusiasm actually banking-over a worry? Did I detect a passing shadow in his eyes when, in parting, he had said, "Tomorrow, we will talk all day about the family." Many times through the years Theo had said: "What a wonderful family you have given me." I knew there was something on his mind.

My habit of scrutinising Theo's face and voice went back a long, long time. I remember how I could read his face each Thursday evening when I came to Terenure from the Land Commission. One glance and I could tell if the news was good or bad, or if there was no news at all. During the war and for several years after, we waited always for some good news of Max. Should there be news of Max, there would be news of Tadek—or so I hoped, although I never sought to press my own particular interest. I knew the old man (as I called him in my mind) was spending a fortune in money employing people to track down his beloved son. Gran and I were as poor as the proverbial church mice. I was dependent on the old man for any whisper of news. I had enormous respect for him and, all the time, I was unaware my respectful dependence had turned not alone to loving him but to being in love with him. All I ever knew since I was a child was the enveloping cloud of loving Tadek. And all I ever knew later was the necessity of pleasing Theo by loving Max. And I did love Max. And I had loved Tadek all my life.

Until now, had I known the meaning of "in love"? It was an emotion of flame. I stood in the centre of the beautiful bedroom and let the flame envelop me. I am sure that every woman who comes to the realisation of "being in love" will recognise that wondrous first. All instincts ignite simultaneously: love, lust, longing, wondering, questioning, responding. Hundreds of lightning flashes are intent on illuminating the pedestal whereon stands the beloved. But this, all of this, was how the interior of my being had always been for Theo. Always, since the first day when I was less than twenty and he was well into his forties. Now I recognised the meaning of my seeking him and my obedience to him...add together the years wasted by war and the twenty years of happy marriage to his son. I was into the fifties and Theo was past seventy. The sum of our venerable ages must create the mightiest of inhibitions. I had thought of it fitfully here and there during our years: what if Theo had taken the girl (who had knocked on his door to enquire about a Jewish funeral) into his arms and into his bed instead of taking her to Paris to offer her to his son? Could that have been destiny? Or was destiny all that followed?

I stood in the centre of the room that Theo had created for me and I revelled in the emotion of reliving all that was Theo. He had followed up that first call on the door in Terenure. He had been by my side from that moment. Lia, admit it now to yourself: you gave him Vasha because you were in love with him. You had been given the gift in love and you passed on the gift in love. And Theo knew. He always knew. Today Lia knows. And he knows that the knowing will go into the vault of Lia's secrets. It will be as he has said: it is enough that we know. I thought of him sleeping beneath the magnificent Persian eiderdown. His heart at rest now Lia has come full circle.

It took a while for Lia's heart to beat steadily after this new admission. Steadily was the essential way for two ageing hearts to beat, steadily to take each day on trust that night would come without a change of rhythm. I was well practised in keeping secrets, my own and now Theo's.

CHAPTER TWENTY

I n the morning light, the previous day and the night had vanished. I was early down into Shanlee's kitchen. I kissed her in greeting.

"Shanlee, please let me help you. Allow me to carry the trays now; those stairs are tiring." I could see she was glad.

"I am full of joy that you have come, Lia. Mr Randt needs more hands than mine. It is yet too soon for his breakfast. Ted is with him now—Mr Randt does not take kindly to help but Ted can make up the bed and make sure he has no accident from slipping in the bath."

"Did that ever happen?"

"Yes it did," Shanlee told me, "and Mr Randt hurt his wrist. But now there is a rail on each side. If he will use it. He can be obstinate, like Master Max."

We smiled together; we knew: obstinate, stubborn, self-willed, even obdurate. They could be all of those things, but with our smiles each told the other we would indulge them a thousandfold. I sat with my cup of coffee and watched all the old familiar ways in which Shanlee moved around her kitchen. Max often said she used her kitchen as a religion, ministering to the pots and pans and preparations as if she were a priest in a temple. "And tell me, Lia, when does Master Max come home?"

"Home" for Shanlee was never Philadelphia. She loved Max devotedly. He had taken the place of the baby son who was snatched from her breast and flung into the blazing ruins of her house. Neighbours had dragged her back from the flames and hid her with them for many weeks. The rest of her family had been taken away by the Russian soldiers, to be shot in the marketplace of Zamosc. It was a long time before her husband found her again. Sadly, they did not have another child. She was fond of saying that God gave her Max, and Mr Randt. Always "Master Max."

I brought her up to date about Max. He had a few weeks to put in at the university and his colleagues were helping him fill crates with his books and papers. He would be on the telephone every day and she could talk to him—as she always did, asking his advice, usually on medical problems she had heard about or read about. A little chat with Max made her happy, like a grandmother with a beloved grandchild. Shanlee and Ted were almost as old as Mr Randt.

When Ted came into the kitchen, Shanlee had a small tray ready for Theo: just a pot of coffee and a couple of plain biscuits. She had put two coffee cups on the tray. "He will want you to join him," she said.

"Good morning, Theo!" He smiled benignly to see me, and his smile was almost back to normal.

"Ah *balibt*! So Lia is now my handmaiden!"

"How is my patient today?"Everything about me was normal because I had practised my smile *en route* to the bedroom.

"This is wonderful." He was sipping the coffee in between the words. "Why did I not think of getting fibrillations years ago!"

"While it is still early and we are full of energy I'll hold you to your promise that we would talk about the family. If I know you at all, Theo, I know there is something on your mind. You have given yourself a lot of things to worry about, the auction, the move. It is not that. Is it the thought of parting with all the lovely things you have lived with for so long?"

He had not touched the biscuits. Now he smiled at me. "Did you tell me once, a long long time ago, that there is an Irish proverb: 'May your wife eat biscuits in bed.' Lia, every day, a hundred times a day, there is some small thing to remind me of you. Something you said, some way you looked—maybe when you were very young."

One could only smile at such flattery. I took the tray. "I am taking this down to Shanlee. Ted will be up in a few minutes. Please wait for him and I will be back." He guessed at my thoughts. I was a little fearful of male bravado. The fact that I was here was not to be taken as a licence for Theo to decide he was completely back on his feet.

"I promise to be good," he said gently. All went well. I was able to settle in the armchair and we chatted away in low voices. At last he said, "You are right, Lia. I am worried about Vasha. I have been worried for several months."

"Why? What has happened?"

"Well, nothing actually," he answered slowly. "I hear it in her voice on the telephone."

"The thing you hear in her voice, Theo, is it excitement, exaltation, or depression, anxiety?"

He took time to consider. "I think it is uncertainty, insecurity." Ah yes, insecurity in Vasha would worry him to whom Vasha's self-esteem was of paramount importance.

"Was she ever lonely in Perugia?" I asked.

"No, she was never lonely. From the start she had friends everywhere. She acquired a little sports car and flew around the countryside. She adores the place and the people. She sees a lot of the Martelli family in Siena."

"Yes, I know about the car. She arrived in Siena when we were there. She and Phyllis are thick as thieves, so Phyllis says. And I saw her several times in Rome in Alessandro's place. She was always in top form."

"You did not think to go to Perugia to visit her, Lia? She mentioned that. I teased her about being jealous of Alessandro." From his high pillows on his regal bed, Theo turned to look at me.

"Jealous of Alessandro?" I repeated. "His drawings? His career? His life-style?" I sat up straight with indignation.

"No, no," Theo said, "of your affection for him and his for you." Dumbfounded, I lay back in the comfortable armchair and I considered what he had said. Vasha belonged to Theo. In a thousand ways she had made that clear as time passed. I had accepted his ownership without ever wishing it otherwise. Alessandro belonged to no one.

"One way or another," I said, "Alessandro never presses a claim."

"But Vasha wants everything both ways. That has always been her nature, and she always wins and she is always the popular winner. As a young woman, she may be irresistible. She has no reason for fear. Yet, there is fear in her voice when we talk, and the last time we talked was days ago. When I became ill, I gave Ted his instructions in the event of her phoning. It is usually I who phone her. In view of the auction, it was plausible for Ted to say that I was tied up with a client and not tied to this bed. Lia, my dear Lia, I have a favour to ask you. I want you to go to Perugia—no, wait a moment, I would not ask if it were not uppermost in my mind. She does not know that my case is such that I cannot fly out but she must know that I am worried because there has always been an acute telepathy between us. She has phoned and Ted has promised a reply but I have not replied. You must be my bridge to Vasha."

If you wait long enough, and patiently, for the heart's desire then it is sure your turn will come...Who said, "When the gods wish to punish us, they grant our wish"? For Vasha to need me was my dearest wish. Theo stretched out his hand to touch my face. "Would you contemplate going on Monday, Lia?"

Monday was only two days away. I could imagine myself in a plane high up over the Alps and worried to death about Theo lying in this bed in Terenure. I wanted to stay by him, watching over him to whom I owed all the good things in my life. When I was young and I thought of him as old, I used to promise myself that if ever he were laid low, I would give up whatever I had to nurse him back to health.

I queried very lightly, "Do you seriously think that I could take your place with Vasha?"

"No," he said and he smiled, "nor could she take

your place with me. But, all the same, would you go on Monday?"

Still in a light tone, I asked, "To prove that she has no reason to fear my affection for Alessandro?"

"No," he said again, "no, of course not—although she does—but for me, Lia. Because I feel some force has entered her life and I am helpless—helpless, obeying doctor's orders. For me?"

"For you," I said, "I would do anything."

"So tell me then, why did you never go to Perugia?"

I did not have to think about that. "The time had come to separate my life from Vasha's life. In earlier years, I had longed to have a close relationship with her. That faded. I would never have been on her level. In the first hour of her life, I knew that. Perugia was your choice and I knew nothing about Perugia. The choice confirmed your absolute authority. There can only be one absolute."

"Did you resent that choice, Lia?"

"On the contrary, Theo, I was glad of it. Just—a small human failing on my part—I could not face the concept of Vasha in Perugia. We have met frequently over the past three years, here, in Rome, in Paris. She continues to amaze and astonish me—her beauty, her brilliance. Perhaps you are over-anxious, Theo, simply because you are a bit down?"

"Perhaps, Lia, perhaps. So, to set my poor old mind

at rest, you will go on a little visit?"

"Would you be in the mood to prepare me for Perugia? Unless all this talk is wearying you?"

"I have been waiting for years to have your attention all to myself, little one. Perugia? One of the reasons I chose Perugia was so that *you* would go there. To visit Vasha would be a good pretext. I had hoped I might be the one to introduce you to Perugia and the hill towns all around. The opportunity was never ripe. In this family, there is always a circle around you."

"Just more of your flattery!" I told him. "But for Vasha, why exactly Perugia?" I drew my armchair very closely to his bed so that the timbre of his voice could be conserved. He took a long deep breath, and his eyes rested on my face.

"For Vasha, from the earliest days of her interest in art, her critical faculties have been keenest on Renaissance art and on classical art. She dismissed (a little unfairly) all the movements of the nineteenth century as so many futile rebellions: abstract art, expressionism, dadaism, pointillism etc. Of the French and German painters, she will tell you that each had one good painting followed by ever-weaker self-imitations. Of sculptors, she makes an exception of Rodin but insists that between him and the Greeks there is an empty space. She holds as fact that about the year 1520, painting reached the peak of perfection:

Michelangelo, Titian, Leonardo, Correggio, Raphael and a few others had abandoned the style of draughtsmanship of earlier centuries and ascended new heights setting standards which dominated Europe for the next three hundred years. Once into the late eighteenth and nineteenth centuries, Vasha loses interest. Deric, on the other hand, is a specialist in the many styles which took root in the mid-nineteenth century. In twentieth-century sculpture, and in the American school of painting, he is becoming an international judge and collector. Give him another ten years!"

I had heard most of this before. "And the second reason for Perugia?" I prompted.

"Ah Perugia!" Theo's voice softened with love. "Umbria is the green heart of Italy, scarcely touched by time. Christian art (to which we owe an immense debt) is preserved in Umbria in its simplistic entirety, its roots clearly seen as the source of its traditions. Umbria has architecture, paintings, mosaics, sculpture coming directly out of the Renaissance and it experienced the masters of Rome even before Christianity—as if, I sometimes think, Michelangelo betook himself to Spoleto for his retreats and left his thumbprint there for ever. Although Correggio was a man of Parma, many of his models have the look of Umbrian women. For example, his *Holy Night* has a virgin with the face of a young woman of Orvieto. I knew that young woman many years ago. Northern Italians (and Parma is in the north of Italy) do not have that rustic relaxed look, nor do Florentines whose features are often aquiline and intense. Ah Lia, there is a tenderness about Umbria, reflected in the basilicas and hermitages, which comes directly from the countryside. So many saints of the Roman Church have had their living in little Umbrian towns, like Cascia and Assisi, that it must be possible one could cultivate one's soul in serene harmony with the peaceful land."

"Did you ever think of living in Umbria?" I asked.

"Only for brief interludes, and that goes for Rome and Florence and very especially for Naples. They have, in Italy, every form of beauty—the men in the streets are models for Caravaggio—but their notion of plumbing has not moved with the times!"

"I never noticed that!" I said in wonder.

He teased my innocence. "You would not, in a good hotel! Nor in an expensive apartment! And even then..."

Now I teased him. "And where may I go, Theo, to see this Orvieto woman who posed for the Virgin hundreds of years ago?"

"Correggio's *Holy Night*?" Theo enjoyed being teased; his son Max did not. "You will find her in a gallery in Dresden," he smiled. I smiled back at him. "Maybe next year? I should like to speak to Vasha on the phone before I descend on her and I should like to tell Max of the proposed visit."

I had pleased him. "Yes," he said, "I would expect that. Ted is so accustomed to my trips to Europe he can deal with the itinerary and make the necessary booking. Vasha, of course, will tell the Randts that you are coming. Their guesthouse is nice and they speak English. You will like them."

Max would grumble at my sudden departure to Italy, and without him. So I rang Vasha before I phoned him. (A *fait accompli*, initiated by Theo would not so easily be ruled out of order.) She was at home and she seemed pleasantly surprised to hear from me; nevertheless I imagined a hesitant confusion in her voice.

"Are you all right, darling?" I asked. "You sound as if you have a sore throat."

"Do I?" she answered without further comment. "Are you going to Rome? Alessandro is going to Mexico but I do not think he has left yet."

"No, not Rome, not Alessandro. Perugia and you. This is the first chance I have had to come all on my own to see you. I am here in Terenure and Max will not be coming home for another few weeks. May I come and see you?"

"Why, Lia?" Was there a shade of suspicion in her voice?

"For the enjoyment of it," I answered sweetly. "That is, unless you are too busy for a visitor?"

"Why is Daddy-Theo not coming with you? He often said he would like to introduce you to Umbria."

"Well," I replied very cheerfully, "he is fairly immersed in this idea of auctions and inventories. Are you too busy?"

"No, I have been idling this past week. I defended my thesis. There are a couple of awards to be picked up and one last course, but I know the stuff backwards."

"And would I be a welcome guest, Vasha?"

"I would like to welcome you, Lia, but you will forgive me if I say you took your time." Vasha had always had a way of being cheeky without letting it get into her voice. I remained stubbornly cheerful. "Better late than never! The plan is for Monday and I am looking forward to seeing you."

When Max was on the phone later that day he had some trouble in hiding his anger, making remarks about the difficulty of my travelling alone. I had to make my voice sound flippant. "But my dear love, I am not travelling in a coach-and-four over the Alps. It is door to door nowadays, you know!"

"Not to Perugia, it isn't! I remember that place, all hills. There will be changes and you may have to carry your own luggage. Be sure you have plenty of enormous tips! I'll be over in a few weeks—this trip could wait until I come."

"Theo seems worried about Vasha," I told him.

"He has started to look for things to worry about," Max said. "It's his age. It's catching up on him."

I made a wry face into the telephone. Theo's age. My age. We were ancient.

"Max, I want to please him because he has had a bad fright, not that he will admit that. I just want to please him any way I can."

"Lia, you always wanted to do that. You are much fonder of him than you realise."

"I miss you very much, darling. I can't wait until we are together again. I miss you and I love you." I believed in my utter sincerity. Indeed I did love him, I depended on him completely. Until I would feel his strong arms holding me, I would not be at ease. At ease in Max's love was necessary; it was what made life worth living even though I had all the good things of life in abundance. Being in love with Max's father was a different love altogether, not necessary at all, not easeful. It was enough to know.

"Please take care of yourself, Lia. I walk around this deserted house hoping to find you hiding somewhere. By the way, Berny rings every day. She misses you too. They are all set for a great get-together when the auction comes off in New York. Stefan and Frayne have already put in for plenty of time off."

"But the date is not set! Theo says six months, Max."

"I told Stefan the auction will be this side of Christmas. I rang Christies and they say the last week of November has been set aside."

"So we will have the summer together, darling?"

"I am planning on it," he assured me, "and I am going to need a holiday. I did not realise what I was taking on with this last lecture tour in Canada. It is very hard to believe that there are people, at university level, who deny the Holocaust. Never happened, they tell their students. One of their arguments is, if such an event ever took place, there would be no survivors, none at all. Oh Lia, I miss you, you always listen so patiently. I know I go on and on."

"Keep the summer in your mind, sweetheart: just the two of us in our little house by the river. Maybe our last summer there; next year I hope to see Shanlee and Ted settled in and no more stairs for them to climb."

It was always hard to put down the phone on these exchanges which were our substitute for love-making. On the phone, we drew very closely to each other, there was a warmth in verbal intercourse almost more amorous than seduction...almost.

CHAPTER TWENTY-ONE

The wonders of the world of Umbria were not to be revealed to me after all—not on that first visit. The plane trip in the 1970s was not direct, but it was familiar to me: Dublin-London-Rome, where I was met by a pleasant-looking man holding up a small placard with my name on it. This was Dion Randt, one of the sons of Theo's cousin. Obviously, he was accustomed to meeting tourists. He chatted easily as soon as we were out of the environs of Rome. He taught English and French in the Franciscan college. His mother owned the *pensione*, and his father ran the bookshop. There was not much opportunity to view the scenery as the day was closing in. Although I had left Terenure at six-thirty a.m. it was quite late when we arrived in Perugia. Signora Randt and her husband were most welcoming. The *pensione*, prettily creeper-clad, was comfortable. Even by moonlight, I could see how well-sited it was to catch a panorama of rolling hills.

Signora Randt showed me into a nice bed-sitting room. She apologised for the absence of Vasha, who had unexpectedly to drive over to Foligno and must have been delayed. The kind lady brought some tea to the room and I sat down to wait. Although I thought I was not tired, I fell asleep.

The sound of an electric switch and the sudden light startled me awake. Vasha was there, standing a little way from me, waiting for me to recollect myself. She created the impression of having been blown in by a tempest. Her jacket was flung open, her black hair was streaming across her shoulders, her tanned skin had a blush on the cheekbones as if stung by the wind. Her always-brilliant eyes were not smiling. She had never rushed into my arms, and she did not now. It seemed an age before she spoke.

"Sorry I was not here when you arrived, Lia. I was delayed at Foligno."

"Don't worry, darling. I was well taken care of."

"Was Alessandro at the airport? It could be today he is leaving for Mexico."

"I do not know if he was." My voice was dry. "I did not look for him."

"You will be disappointed not to see him," she stated and still she did not smile.

"Oh I see enough of him!" I said carelessly, remembering Theo's remark about jealousy. In a lighter tone, I added, "I came to see you. How you are. Where you live. And, of course, to see the place while you are still here, if you have the time to escort me a little." She did not answer; she scarcely moved. I felt at a loss, puzzled, irrelevant. I too sat still, unable to think up any small talk. At last, she said: "Daddy-Theo sent you."

"If you think so," I answered, taking time to measure her lack of expression.

"Why?" she asked. There was no answer to that so I made none. She stood up and I noticed how tall she was, taller than I by several inches. She moved a chair nearer to me and sat down. Her attitude was coldly inquisitorial. "I asked Alessandro why you gave me up when I was born but he did not know the reason. I asked Phyllis; she did not even know who my father was and she knew you all her life. Is Alessandro my brother?"

I had not expected an assault on the citadel of secrets. As used to happen to me when I was young, my thoughts flew in all directions at the same time. She waited for me to speak but what was best for me to say? "When we found Alessandro, the story was told to you, Vasha: who you are and who he is."

"I was only a kid then and the story was never referred to since. And if I remember it at all, the story did not tell why you handed me over to Daddy-Theo. I asked him if he is my father but he shook his head."

"Vasha, the story you were told was truthful. Your

father was Tadek and he died. If he had lived, he and I would have married." This was very hard for me to say, as if I were in a witness-box.

"So I am illegitimate?"

"Yes," I answered immediately, "and so is Alessandro. But you are not brother and sister, you are first cousins."

"But his father was something to you. A lover?"

I wanted to hit her across the face, see her reel and hit her again. I was shocked at my reaction. I gripped the arms of the chair. Tears come easily to me and those tears were rising in the heart. I fought for control of my voice and got out some words.

"I am sure you are entitled to ask questions. I have said always the fewest words but I have not lied in your regard." The passionate love I had shared with Tadek in the camp on the mountains rose up into my throat, cutting off the words. Oh how well I remembered the ecstatic radiance with which we entered into the act of love to beget this strange gorgeous creature who would now sit in judgement on me. Whatever Max and his father Theo had witnessed in the camp, they had never questioned or condemned me. Max, who was above all a psychologist, surely knew that the sublime rapture of first sexual intercourse never happens again. Perhaps Max, who was generous to a fault, never looked for a repetition of the primitive ecstasy of virginal love.

"You are always so correct, Lia. I find it hard to believe that you would have a wild, one-night stand with a man and let an illegitimate child face into the world."

I gripped the arms of the chair harder. I was afraid I would lose self-control. Why must the secrets I had never told to anyone be dragged out to placate this girl? Was she, as Theo feared, under some sort of pressure? Certainly, this rough-speaking arrogance was never present in her before.

"Talk to me," she said, "all night if we have to!"

"Even if I am tired from travelling?"

"Even so," she said abruptly. "But I will make a concession. I will get some coffee in a flask, and you can get ready for bed. Get into bed if you wish."

I was tired of her uncouth manner and I was glad to get out of the clothes I had been wearing all day. I had felt like ordering her out of the room, but the normal resistance of my nature seemed to have drained away. I felt only disappointment. Something had gone wrong. My gran used to say, "Everyone knows their own know." I washed and sat on the bed brushing my hair. When Vasha returned with the coffee, I was about to protest that I never drink coffee late at night. I said nothing. I pulled the duvet over my feet and propped my head against the pillows. The coffee had neither milk nor sugar but I drank it.

Vasha said, "So tell me, once and for all, how did the very proper and soft-spoken Lia allow herself to become the mother of an illegitimate child? You said I had a right to ask."

"And what about my right to keep my own counsel?"

"When Daddy-Theo sent you here, Lia, he must have had a good reason. Why you? Why not himself?"

This I could answer. "I think he would have come himself because he imagines he has reason to be worried on your behalf. He sent me so that I could put his mind at rest about you. He did not come because he could not. His doctor has ordered absolute rest. He remains, however unwillingly, in his own bed in his own room."

Her manner had changed completely as I spoke. Now her features were softened with tender concern. "Is he going to die?" she whispered.

"I am sure he is not," I told her. "He has been doing too much and he needs only to let go. Max is in constant touch with his doctor."

"Are you sure he is not going to die?" She came to sit on the side of the bed. "Are you sure?"

"As sure as anyone can be about a man of his age." I repeated what Max had said: "His general health is good. His heart muscles were strained but he has not had a heart attack."

"Lia, was it any news of me that caused this...this stress. Did Mrs Randt write to Daddy-Theo?"

"All Theo said to me was that your voice on the phone was different and that worried him. I am inclined to think that was his reason for bringing me home from Philadelphia in advance of Max—his worry about you. I take it there is some cause for this worry which Theo does not know?"

"You are sure he will be better when he rests? Please tell me the truth, please Lia? I will go home tomorrow. I must tell him that there is no need to worry." Slow tears rolled down her lovely face, lovely again since the hard aggression had gone.

"Vasha, just tell me there is no need for his worry." I took some tissues from the box on the bedside table. Her tears were pitiable. I had got the instinctive feeling that the worry within her was a worry she was trying to unload onto a failure in me..."Illegitimate baby" sent echoes back across the years. An illegitimate baby was the worst worry a woman could have, and the most heart-breaking. I was given time to think my own thoughts while Vasha crouched there, silently blaming herself for some mysterious sin which had brought Theo close to death. Sin came into her anxiety, of that I was sure. Twenty years ago I had put myself beyond the pale of innocence. I had not forgotten the courage it took to tell Theo.

"Vasha, you wanted to blame me for whatever it is that is now causing you such anguish. Blame me. I am your mother and I love you. Trust me." It had been an effort to get the words out but once they were said, I rejoiced. She was shy in staring at me, the brazen light in her brilliant eyes was gone. "Ask me again whatever it is you want to know," I invited.

"Was it just a fling, or were you in love with my father?"

"I had loved him since I was six years old. That was when I asked him to marry me and he said I would have to wait for twenty years." She nodded as if in deep understanding and she smiled a little. "But he never did marry you?"

"The concentration camps, Vasha, the war, the partisans. But in the days before Tadek died, we were married to each other in the truest sense of the word." My voice was sad and lonely.

"Does it hurt very much to talk about that time, Lia?"

"Strangely not to you; not now to you."

"Did Daddy-Max know the baby was not his baby although he married you?" I marvelled at how little of the story she had understood. She, the clever precocious child, had not taken in the implications of the story when it was told in the hotel in Rome. Yet Alessandro, a newcomer to the family and with imperfect English then, had comprehended the essence of the relationship.

"Yes, he knew. And Theo knew. Max married me so that you, as yet unborn, would have an honourable name."

"But why then did you give me away?" I did not know then—then it was an instinctive act—but I knew now why I had given her to Theo and Theo had always known. She was the symbol of our love although she came out of another love.

"Vasha, tell me. Have you not always felt that you and Theo belonged together? That Theo's soul was the father of your soul a thousand years ago?" I remembered Theo had said that to me when I was Vasha's age. Was it on a train journey through France? "When you were only a few hours old, a tiny baby, Vasha, Theo held you in his arms and your eyes opened wide and gazed into his eyes. You recognised each other."

I had caught her interest. It was a new idea and she was considering it. At last she said thoughtfully, "Yes, it is so. I feel closer to Daddy-Theo than to anyone else on earth but there is also the obligation on me to prove myself to him. I love him to death but I will never level up. I dread to cause him pain, to let him down. And I know this sounds selfish but I wanted you as well. I wanted a mother to myself. When Alessandro came into our world, you allowed him to call you *Madre*."

"Darling," I said, "I longed always for you to call me Mama, or Mum, or Mummy or any of those names. Always and always."

"I wish I had known," she said sadly.

"You see, my poor love, I had to make a choice. And I made it exactly because I loved Tadek's baby so much. When I knew you were inside me and going to be born, I had nothing, nothing at all to offer a new life: no money, no position, no real qualifications. And the Ireland of those days was hard on an unmarried girl with an illegitimate baby. I wanted to go on alone, keep my baby and work for her. But work at what? How to feed and clothe and educate her? Most of all, how to protect her from the slur of illegitimacy."

"You actually wanted me, Lia?"

"Oh yes, oh yes, I wanted Tadek's baby with all my heart." Vasha's face was turned to me, her eyes open and candid. "You see, Lia, that is the difference. I am where you were. And I do not want this baby." For a second, I went into shock and then I took her into my arms. After all, she was my own child. I rocked her gently to and fro the way Tadek used to rock me all those years ago when I cried with loneliness and fear. "There, there, love. No need to worry any more."

Gradually the story came out. Although Theo had heard nothing and knew nothing, his protective instincts for Vasha were sound. "When I had your phone call, Lia, I had to act fast. I guessed you were being sent out because Latta Randt suspected something. Because I felt guilty, I was on edge. Today I went to Foligno. I had money for an abortion."

"Is abortion legal in Italy?" I asked, holding her closer and kissing her neck.

"I don't know," she said. "I wasn't going to a hospital or a doctor. This is a back-street abortionist all the girls know about. They call her *La Strega*."

"Is that her name?" I asked.

"It is what is written on her door," Vasha said. "*Strega* means a witch. I found the place easily—her name was there—but I could not go in. I turned back on the road twice but I could not face going in—fear, I suppose."

"I am glad you did not go in," I said, my own voice full of fear.

"Why? Why, Lia?"

"Because I fear a back-street abortion—girls get killed. When I was very young I used to hear our shopgirl, Daisy Emm, telling Phyllis about her friends who went to these places and Daisy Emm said they were "botched-up"for life or thrown into the river. It was the Dodder, then very dirty, and it came up into our cellar at high tide. Old sacks would float around in the water and I was frightened to death in case here were dead girls in the sacks. I am so glad you did not go into the witch's house today." I hugged her even closer until I felt her body relaxing.

There was no continuous narrative, no whole sentences that I can remember. The picture that emerged was the hyped-up music dementia familiar to me from the sixties in Philadelphia—familiar from television and newspapers and the talk of Stefan and his pals—now transposed into an Italian setting. Tonio's music, Tonio's world. If I had imagined that the Flower People owned the psychedelic culture and confined the drug-taking to San Francisco, I heard now of orgies so wild as to be more appropriate to pagan Rome, the Bacchanalia celebrated in cocaine rather than wine. For over a year, Vasha had been smoking some substance whose name I have forgotten, and which had become indispensable to her. She had lost all appetite for food and she had spent whole nights away from the *pensione* which had made Signora Randt very censorious. "She pried," Vasha said. Perhaps Theo was informed. Perhaps not. I shall never know.

It began to eat into Vasha's consciousness that the drug had taken over control. One day when she was driving to the college, she could not remember her own name. Until that moment she had never considered the possibility of losing herself to the drug. Everyone else but not Vasha and not Tonio. She had started to abstain for two and three days at a time when Tonio was away on tour. Enduring the dry retching, the perspirations and the awful headaches never lasted beyond the third day and then she went back on the drug. Then, two months ago, she managed to keep off for a whole week, at the end of which she travelled up to the *Festa Publica* in Milan. She had determined to be her own person again. Full of fervour to convert Tonio to her new way of thinking and full of the affection she had always felt for him she was buoyant with life and sure of herself as she had been in all her years of growing-up. Tonio would listen to her, he always had. How many times had he made up songs to tell her that they were destined for each other—a hundred, and more.

Perhaps Tonio had gone much further into drug-taking than Vasha knew, perhaps he used much more potent drugs. The *Festa* was an enormous success, Tonio would be acclaimed; he would net many millions of lire. The celebrations in the hotel room continued into the small hours. Vasha watched with clear eyes the strange antics of young people high on drugs. When she went to Tonio's room to say goodbye until they would meet each other again, he was injecting a syringe into his arm. "*La notte cominciare!*" He had had a long day; he had sold himself to millions of fans; he was never in better form. Laughing exuberantly, he repeated, "*La notte cominciare!*" She tried to snatch the syringe. Her protests were met at first by passionate persuasion. Her refusal to be held and kissed infuriated him. He warded off her frantic struggle to get the syringe by striking her across the face, and knocking her to the ground. He jumped on her in a positive fury of abandon. The struggle culminated in a violation of her body so torturingly painful that she was screaming in agony. He was choking her to shut her up but in the next room she was not heard, so uproariously loud were his musicians and his friends. He threw a towel across her and left her there. Somehow she made her way out. The last thing she heard was his guitar and his voice calling on the stars to witness his undying adoration. "Just like you said about my father, Lia: I had this childish passion for Tonio since I was a little girl and I saw him playing the piano in Daddy-Theo's drawing-room. But it was not the same Tonio; it had not been the same for a long time. Now I hate him."

I remember I drew her down beside me. I held her and she felt my tears sharing her tears. "He came every day. He rang every night. He sent jewels and flowers. I never answered his calls. I never took his gifts. I wake up in the night and think it was a dream—one of those awful dreams when you cannot cry out for help. For most of my life he created the magic and now it is over and there is only hatred. And his mother was my friend. She has a heart full of love and she cared for me very much. She always hugged me, the only woman who ever hugged me like a mother."

I thought of Phyllis. I remembered the letters telling me how devoutly she had placed the new baby, Tonio, under the care of St Jude. Some help Jude had turned out to be!

"I care for you, Vasha. I am your friend. Trust me."

"He kept up his calls for four weeks. Then he went on tour to the United States. I did not get the monthly and soon there will be another one due and I know it won't come." Poor sad despairing Vasha. She was quiet for a time, working up courage for a question: "Why are you not scolding me? Why are you not shocked when I talk about an abortion? Why, Lia?"

"Darling, when I was carrying you, no one ever scolded me. You did not ask for this baby. You cannot be blamed."

"Yes, I can. I knew I was playing with fire when I started the drugs. Oh I was to blame. To say otherwise is to call myself stupid and I know I am not. I should have foreseen this end. I saw others."

"Do not plan an abortion until you are very sure, very sure."

"I am sure," she said. "You said I am to trust you, Lia. I trust you never to tell Daddy-Theo any of this conversation. Can I trust you?"

"Be assured, on my word, I shall never report this

conversation to Theo." Theo's image of Vasha would go unsullied to the grave; on that she could be sure. I had never lied to him but I was expert at leaving things unsaid and I knew he relied on that. No thrusting questions.

"Will you come with me tomorrow? To *La Strega*?" Her voice was imploring.

I knew she was going to say this and I had been considering. "If you are adamant about an abortion then I will be at your side. But not in a back street. No, Vasha, No. Look, it is the middle of our night. This would be a good time for getting Daddy-Max on the phone. Vasha, trust me. I will do whatever talking is necessary. Please trust me. I am your friend. I will not betray you." I wanted to say that a child born into this world must come through an act of love: that is my creed. "This household is asleep. We could use the phone."

"Is there any way," she begged, "that we can avoid telling Daddy-Max? No matter what you say, he will know exactly what you are asking." The thought of being less in the family's regard than she had always been was too much to bear. "Oh Lia, that night of the *Festa*, I was like a teenager with New Year resolutions. Give up the drugs and give up Tonio. It had to be both. The drugs and his music and his tours are all one. I was being taken for granted, I was losing my identity and soon I would lose myself. Even tonight, coming from Foligno, suspicious of why you were here. I longed for, and knew where I could get, a few amphetamines."

"But you kept on going and here you are." I had no way of knowing if she felt, as I did, all the love of the lost years now welling up between us. Her voice murmured on for a long time the need to confess. I could only repeat, again and again, "I love you, Vasha. I am on your side." And at last, huddled up together, we fell asleep, she still in her outdoor clothes.

CHAPTER TWENTY-TWO

In the morning we were calm and open with each other. We made a great fuss of showering and choosing pretty clothes and brushing hair and using make-up. We had breakfast in Signora Randt's glass veranda. There were other guests and pleasantries were exchanged with them and with each other as if we had slept the sleep of the angels. Vasha went into Signora Randt's kitchen. They conversed in Italian which always seems excitable and controversial but is usually just talk. Then Vasha took my hand and led me upstairs. She said, "I told her we had so much to talk about that we would stay in your room for an hour or so."

Vasha flew around the room, straightening the bed and folding away a few clothes. This was yet another aspect of Vasha—Shanlee's example? Theo's training? "I think Latta is mightily relieved that my responsible mother has come on the scene! Evidently she was very curious about you and she is quite impressed!"

"Vasha, while we were eating breakfast, I had time to think. Let me tell you. My code of ethics is bound to be very different from yours. Different, that is all. I could not begin to offer advice. I wish to respect your adulthood. No matter what you decide, I would wish to play a practical, helpful part. I woke up with the knowledge that I love you. Very deeply, Vasha."

We gazed into each other's eyes. The flawless beauty of Vasha's face, while not like my mother's face, still reminded me of her: the gleaming smile that was Tadek's was Vasha's also, the perfect arch of her dark eyebrows, the fathomless depths of her eyes, the delicate shape of her nose, the curve of her cheek, the tan colour of her skin against the blackness of her hair. I loved what I saw. And yet it brought back my childhood.

She asked, "Is it foolish or wise not to waste time? When I got your phone call, I panicked. I realised that I would not be able to do anything to change my condition while I was squiring you around the tourist trail. That is why I went to *La Strega*—the days slipping past."

"Vasha, time is urgent. If you have thought it all over thoroughly and made up your mind, there is not a day to be lost. But not *La Strega*. This is a little country place where everyone is watching everyone else. As you said, all the girls in the college know about the witch. Your, or our, going into that house would get back here within the hour. From here to Dublin is a telephone call."

I was certain that Theo would not countenance abortion and I knew Max saw it as a last resort in a medical emergency. He had witnessed forced abortion on women in the camps and he had never forgotten their mental devastation. When I thought of phoning him the previous night, I had the hope that if I asked for help, he would fly to the rescue. In the morning light, I knew that indeed he would, but not to abort a baby. Just as Vasha herself had been taken into the care of Theo and Max, so would her baby be. Max could sustain this shock but Theo could not. All his loving ambitions for his beloved Vasha would be overturned. He would feel he had failed. I could not bear it for him that he should have failed...not now when he was struggling to get back his strength.

"Lia, is abortion murder?"

"That is Catholic teaching, yes." Maybe all Christian teaching. Maybe all teaching, ethically, medically.

"I know girls in college who had abortions," she said and added, "It didn't seem to worry them." I wondered if she could see into the depths of reaction in another girl's spirit.

Vasha had brought a satchel from her room. She took out a small paperback. "These are available in some stalls," she said, handing the book to me. "Lists of addresses where students can get help but there are none in Italy. I looked."

I read the book through carefully. Although the word rape had not been used by Vasha, that was the scene lodged in my mind: brutal rape. That it was which strengthened my resolve to go along with her wheresoever she could get help to blot out the horror of that scene. The conviction in my mind was not that the life given by God was sacred but that the life put into Vasha's body by a raping beast was not sacred. So far as I could reason it out, then and now, the only woman ever to have conceived a life given by God was the Virgin Mary, and we believed that because a pope had made it an article of faith. All other women had taken a life into the womb by an act of man. There was an upsurge of feminism when I lived in Philadelphia which urged on women the right to choose. In the seventies, women were slow to be liberated. Now, everything has changed. When I talked to Vasha across the paperback lists, I never mentioned the Virgin Mary nor any other idea I might have liked to discuss. I said only, "It seems fairly clear that one could have help available in Holland," and I had promised myself I would not offer suggestions.

"Let me see." She took the book. "I was looking for addresses only in Italy. Yes, Amsterdam. And there are private clients. Phone numbers also."

Of unspoken accord, we stood up and walked over

to the window. The view of the gentle hills and the red-tiled houses held us in deep contemplation. I guessed she was working out a plan. It must be her plan and only hers.

"I have not even been seen by a doctor," she said softly. "Could we phone one there, get a number from one of these referral agencies?"

"I do not want to make any phone call from here to an agency. When you are firm in your decision, we will phone Theo, enquire for his health, tell him we are well and are moving out all on our own."

"He will demand details, Lia! You know how he is." Vasha's brain always moves in fast-forward. "There is a gallery in Amsterdam, the Rijksmuseum, which I have not visited, although I gave a lot of space to the Dutch School in my thesis. I know I was chancing my arm. The middle seventeenth century has Vermeer, Van Ruisdael, Jan Steen and Willem Kalf. These artists reflect daily life on the streets and in the Dutch homes exactly in the manner of the Renaissance artists. I should see them. Vermeer especially; he breaks up the light. He must have studied that in Rome—pictures did not travel further north than Provence at that time." Her face was alive with enthusiasm, her anxiety banished for a moment.

"I take it, then, that we will tell Theo we are going to Holland?" Now she sighed. "He will think I am selfish. For ages and ages, he has been talking of bringing Lia to Umbria."

"Yes, I know. But Umbria won't go away. Maybe next year." And I enquired, "Which of us will talk to Theo?"

"Oh Lia, let it be you. He has told me that you are the solace of his spirit. Isn't that a lovely phrase? Do you know, when you are far away in Philadelphia, he will sit for an hour gazing at his painting of you in the silver frame. Did you know that? Was that a wedding dress?"

I smiled at her. "Yes, a silly old wedding dress chosen by Theo for the painting." Tony Lloyd was another story there was no need to tell.

"You are more beautiful now, Lia." And that was the most cherished compliment I was ever given.

Even on the phone, Theo's voice brought me comfort. "Ah *mayn lyubenyu*, I have been watching that telephone beside my bed and willing it to ring."

"How are you, Theo?" I quelled my anxiety and put a smile into my voice. "Tell me in detail how you are. In every detail." I imagined his smile; I could see his reading glasses laid down on the Persian eiderdown. "Already I miss you, Theo."

"Then you must not stay too long away," he said. "Tell me about Vasha." I had prepared this in consultation with her, and my only fear was that he would hear the lie in my voice. If my voice betrayed me, surely he would understand I was acting for Vasha? Surely we shared Vasha?

"She is fine, Theo. Just a little run-down after a hectic year. She is anxious about you. So tell me everything."

"I, too, am fine. In another week, I may be allowed up to sit at the fire. Isn't that ridiculous! No stairs for a week after that. And, worse again, only one hour a day to work on my catalogues. Tires the brain, the doctor says. Boredom tires it worse. The day is endless! When I have read *The Irish Times*, I try to settle to a book, but I get restless."

"Restless is good, Theo. It means that energy is building up, ready to be released."

"Do you think so, Lia?" His voice was pleased. "So are you setting out to begin with Perugia today? Vasha should be an excellent guide. But I do not like that little care she has. Hire a comfortable car, Lia. Spare no expense; the hill roads may not be too good. If I were there with you, I would be the best guide." And if I were there with you, Theo, safe in Terenure, I would not be afflicted with guilt.

"Theo, I am not going to be shown the sights of this city today. Not this trip. Vasha has left work undone on the Dutch School and we are contemplating a little tour of the galleries in Holland."

"Holland!" He was astonished. "Holland! You don't have to go to Holland—she can read it up. Is she there? Let me talk to her."

"But Theo, it would be nice to have her company, to get to know her. And she may be a little weary of Umbria for the moment. Holland would be a change of scenery."

"Holland may have had scenery a few hundred years ago. Now it is a glorified car-park stacked up with bicycles!" I heard the edge of anger in his voice. "Put Vasha on the line, please."

"She has gone out, Theo. She did not know I was going to phone you at this moment." I hastened to add, "She is in fine form. She may be packing. I haven't even unpacked."

"So? And when are you leaving there for Holland?" I heard the doubt in his voice.

"Quite soon! Perhaps today."

"I see," he said. "Then will you please come direct home from Holland. If Vasha is unwilling to show you around, then, well, then…Well, I am surprised." The doubt in his voice was unmistakable. He would expect me to query the doubt and I couldn't.

"I will see you in a few days, Theo. Please take care of yourself." He grumbled a bit at this drastic change of his plan and then we said goodbye. Perhaps his doubts would fade with the slow realisation that Lia must be doing what she thought was best. Or, maybe not best but expedient. I would depend on him not to question me on my return to Dublin. He would know I could not tell lies face to face.

Vasha explained the situation to Signora Randt. I spoke to Alessandro on the phone. He expressed no surprise on hearing of the unexpected flight to Amsterdam. That afternoon he was leaving Rome for Mexico city. He would like very much if we would overnight in his apartment. Vasha had a key, and in any event the caretaker would see to everything. There was plenty of food in the freezer, and if we would like to stay longer, he would be delighted. "Will I see you in Dublin, Alessandro?"

"Much later on, *mi dispiace. Come sta, Madre Mia*? I look forward to Dublin—September, *forse*?" He had not made any direct enquiry as to Vasha's well-being. I wondered how much he knew, or guessed perhaps, of the past year.

Soon we were on the afternoon train for Rome. A *tassi* took us to the apartment in Trastevere and Vasha arranged with the *tassista* to pick us up at nine the next morning for the airport. I found that Vasha was very efficient and a cheerful companion. She had either put her own heartbreaking worry to one side for my sake, or she was steadfastly setting out to solve it. For my part, I kept up with her, interested and sociable.

Inside, I was cringing with guilt. If Theo knew! If Max should find out! Should I be counselling, pleading, imploring? Every so often, I could feel the tears behind my eyelids. This all-too-convenient shedding of new life! Was I about to abet a murder? But there had already been a murder of a girl's love, a faithful love for many years. Looking back, I could see it all so clearly: the holidays, the birthday parties. Vasha and Tonio had never made a secret of their attraction for each other. How much did Phyllis know? She would have to be shielded, kept outside the secret of which I was part. Her deep religious faith would not permit a condoning of that to which I was now committed. Maybe, just maybe, she would have a certain amount of relief if her dear Tonio broke up with the beautiful young Jew. Phyllis had never accepted the idea of a Catholic-Jewish marriage. Fond and all as she was of Vasha, to Phyllis Jews were alien creatures best kept to themselves. If Lia had not dated back to when Phyllis was twelve years of age, then I too would (to use a phrase of Phyllis's) "have been shown the door." As it was, she always made a point of telling me that she prayed for me: "Lovey, I never forget you at Jude's altar."

As I said, Vasha was a good travelling companion. From her earliest years, she had gone everywhere with Theo. She was fluent in three or four languages and had enough of the rest. It seemed only a few hours from Rome until we were established in a hotel in Amsterdam and on the telephone to the addresses in the little book. She chose a French clinic because it was the most expensive. The date was set for Friday. They would wish her to be examined physically and interviewed by a doctor and a psychiatrist. I knew enough French to understand that she was insisting on the presence of her mother at all times. She repeated it determinedly: *"Ma mère tous les temps, toujours."* Apparently, this was not unusual although much more expensive. The extra cost was agreed without demur.

"This is not pleasant for you, Lia, but now that I have found you I can tell you that I am like a child afraid of the dark. Friday night at eight o'clock is the latest time the clinic operates. If they are otherwise satisfied, that will be the time set for my abortion"— her voice almost broke on the words—"and we will stay there for the night. I had to insist. Their domestic staff have the weekend off but we can pay. I said we would leave in the morning, Saturday morning, sharp at nine. They will have a taxi waiting."

I summoned up the strength to smile agreeably for her. I was determined not to say anything equivocal but the words came out. "So long as you are sure, my darling. You have all of Thursday if you wish to reconsider."

"Lia, if you knew me as well as Theo knows me, you would know I never change my mind. I had lost all my self-esteem. I was throwing myself away for a fool."

"But there was once love?" I asked softly.

"Childish infatuation for his music which I thought was him. It was his scene I wanted; without the drugs of the last year, I think I would have come to my senses but he made the drugs easy, always available. You know, he is the most talented among all the new young musicians in the world. He is at the top and he could go on to make the biggest business in Europe. His achievement blinded me from seeing his fatal flaw. One day in Rome, one single day, I suddenly noticed that Alessandro has no vanity. After that, I saw the vanity in Tonio all the time. It destroys all the rest—and then—that night!"

She paused for a long time, then spoke as if finishing the previous sentence: "A man has to be responsible for me. Responsibility complements all the gifts I could bring to a union." Her self-esteem was beginning to seep back. I pressed no questions on her conscience. I said all the small comforting words folk say at a wake in Ireland—that was how the night felt.

Maybe we went sightseeing in the Dutch streets on Thursday. Thursday is one of the blank days of memory. Friday was an endless grey day in an elegant grey clinic. We were paying for top-class attention, and that is what we got with the minimum of questions and the maximum of medical professionalism. The medical examination confirmed a positive pregnancy, a mere seven weeks. For the psychological interview, Vasha insisted I remain in the room and that the questions be translated into English. The questions were few enough and remain in my mind: Has your mother or your father influenced you to abort this foetus, unformed foetus is more correct a title, an embryo of an embryo if you prefer? Have they brought pressure on you to abort? Has the father, the natural father, done so against your own judgement? Is any other agency forcing you in this time? Have you given sufficient time to your own judgement to be fully formed? Do you realise you need not act so quickly? Do you fully understand that what will be done cannot be undone? An abortion is an end. Do you understand?

From my position in the room, Vasha was in profile, her head held high. I was struck afresh by her beauty and her seeming imperturbability. I wondered if her sublime beauty concealed a heart steeled to deny.

"You are completely opposed to carrying the embryo to full term?"

"Yes, utterly opposed."

"There is a wide demand for babies to be adopted." The doctor said this in a well-mannered enquiring way. "Even, perhaps, within your own family. Have you asked them?"

"Certainly not." Vasha's icy tone brooked no further enquiry.

Much later in the evening, this doctor came to our tasteful grey room. "Have you had a change of heart, my dear?" she asked. She repeated the question in several languages but Vasha was briefly adamant. A document was duly signed. I observed that Vasha read the document very slowly and carefully before she signed in triplicate, retaining one copy. Theo, I mused, had trained her well in business matters. Sadly, the question here was a matter for the heart.

"Then we are ready. Will you come with me, please." The doctor held open the door.

"And my mother?" Vasha asked, waiting.

"Your mother may come also, if you both want to have her there." I sat in the small operating theatre while the abortion proceeded. I sat far across the room and my eyes were tightly closed. Once again I found that old habits die hard. Prayers long unsaid were coursing through my brain and now the prayers were of contrition. God, I implore your forgiveness, I am heartily sorry for having offended thee. Please don't let Vasha die. She is sorry too. I know she is but she was never instructed. She does not understand about the giving of life. Maybe when she did not ask for it, but I understand and I should have tried. Please God take care of Vasha, I am sorry with all my heart...

This guilt in my soul was compounded with so many other guilts and now with a new and ghastly enforcement of secrecy. Theo, who could look clearly through the mirage of my emotions, he above all must be protected from this crime into which I had allowed myself to be catapulted. I was unwilling but I was weak. May God in his mercy forgive me. The abortion had become a crime when I heard Vasha's indrawn gasp of pain. Was the pain so sharp and bitter that it could penetrate the film of anaesthesia?

When we were back in our own room, and the nurse had gone away, I fussed gently around Vasha's bed, soothing back her hair and kissing her slender fingers. "I am so glad you are with me," she whispered. "Me, too," I answered tenderly. "Me, too."

She fell asleep very quickly, breathing easily and softly, almost, I thought, like a traveller relieved of a back-pack. Early the next morning, we returned to the hotel. It was soon time to keep in touch with Theo. "Theo, how are you today? It was a bit hectic yesterday. It got too late to ring you. So, tell me how you are?" He was very glad to hear my voice. We chatted for a few minutes: his health, the weather. Suddenly, he said,

"Lia, put Vasha on the phone." He waited, for about two minutes. I was holding up the phone to her like a question-mark. I heard his voice, "Give me your phone number, Lia, and I will ring back in ten minutes. Tell her."

In ten minutes, the call came. I stood up to leave the room but they were not speaking in English nor in French. Out of the long distant past, I realised Vasha was answering in Hebrew. The call was very, very short. She turned around to me. "I will tell you exactly what was said...he said he wanted no explanations, only direct answers. He asked was it a broken love affair, and I said yes. Then he asked if Lia had given me a solution. I said no, only consolation. He said, she is the only one who has the right; there is no blame to the mother. And it sounded as if he had slammed down the phone."

"Oh damn, damn, damn," I almost wept. "It sounds like a sleazy plot for one of those fifth-rate American films." Vasha hugged me and she was actually smiling. "In Hebrew, it sounded like a bible story, ancient and farouche—nothing at all like a French clinic!"

"Will I get away with it back in Dublin?" I asked fearfully.

"Without a doubt." And she was still smiling tenderly, affectionately.

When we were getting ready to go our separate

ways, Vasha spoke of the abortion. "Lia, please go on loving me although I have laid this burden on you. I know you were persuaded along because of Theo and…"

"No," I interrupted, "stop there! Theo comes into it, of course. I owe my life to him. I owe you to him. You are my own daughter and for you I would do anything. For Theo, but for you most of all."

"I think Theo would survive," she said slowly. "Theo is strong. What I have done, I did for me, and I will be the stronger for it. But also, I did it for Phyllis. If I went on to the end, she would know that the baby had come from Tonio. Her heart is broken enough between Luigi and her son—she knows the worst of both of them. I love Phyllis. I loved her all the time I thought you had given me away."

CHAPTER TWENTY-THREE

There is an apt expression, and those days in Amsterdam are exactly that, a blot on the landscape of memory. The incident may be assumed to be unknown to members of the family; on my return to Dublin, Theo said nothing to me about Holland. Max never asked "What took you two to Holland?" Later again, Alessandro failed to enquire. Between Vasha and me there was never a mention, never a sympathetic glance exchanged. The age-old friendship with Phyllis and myself limped on as it always had, propped up with the odd postcard, the odd visit, she and I too occupied with our own lives to have time for questions. Maybe, or so I suspected, Phyllis imagined that when Tonio broke loose from the fascinating Jew, his life would mend. Phyllis's real troubles still lay ahead.

Theo found his way back to health. When the doctor had made the final visit, we celebrated with one of Theo's toasts, this time in sparkling Madeira which Theo assured everyone was the lightest wine in the world. And we also celebrated the success of

Alessandro *in absentia*. His purchases in Mexico would bring enormous profit in the New York auction. He remained in Mexico for the supervision of the packing and crating of the pictures, and he supervised the transporting of them to New York. They would remain under seal until November. In Paris, Deric was completing a similar task of collecting sculptures, antiques and jewellery which Theo judged would fetch great prices in November. The Roman *galleria* was allowed to continue while the tourist season lasted to the end of September. Vasha came and went between Dublin and Lisbon. While his vacation continued, Dion Randt accompanied her. No one remarked on it. He was a young man of immense charm, and very helpful.

My own life locked back into position with Max's homecoming from Philadelphia. Rejoicing all day long in the certainty of Theo's recovery was exhilarating, but when night fell and the house was quiet, it was time to go into my husband's arms with the satisfied knowledge that I was free and at home in the place which was mine by law and by love. When Max told me, and he told me often, that I belonged to him alone, I was glad to assent. Passion came naturally even though another love lay elsewhere. Max's approach was of such a subtle amorousness, his technique so long established, that he found it easy to set the fires alight. It was clear he enjoyed his power. There was no guilt in my ardent response. I was his in the way he wished me to be. All alien desire was banished in the darkness. When morning came with Theo's breakfast-kiss, it was enough to bask in the secret; the basking tranquillity would last all day, and night would bring again the luxury of desiring and being desired. These were the days and nights of having the best of both worlds. Theo knew, and applauded. I discerned it in his glance. The very fact that he was still there every morning held all change at bay.

The days were full of practicalities. The preparation for the auction required the concentration of all the family with the exception of Stefan. He was engaged in top-secret training. Everything to do with the conquest of space was top-secret; his phone calls were much fewer, coinciding with his rare time off, and we could never phone him.

Theo had experts in every field: packers, removers, assessors, but before these men came to the house (and I presume to the galleries) the inventories had to be checked and rechecked a dozen times. The inventories for removal did not carry the values. There were separate lists of inventories for insurance. The inventories were also separated into schools and periods. We were started on the work by ten o'clock each morning and Max called a halt at six to the dot. We did not work on Fridays from late afternoon until dinner on Saturday at eight o'clock. It was a lifelong habit of Theo's to spend that particular twenty-four hours apart from the rest of us, in his study and in his room which adjoined. He ate alone and very little. We supposed he read and medidated; he never invited anyone to share this time of personal withdrawal.

In that long summer before the auction, Max and I gave ourselves that twenty-four hours for recreation. We drove out to the countryside, had a few drinks and sometimes dinner in a favourite place. Other Fridays we had a sabbath meal in Shanlee's kitchen, perhaps going to the theatre or a film later. Every third week or so, we drove down to our house on the Dargle River, planning to have our little second honeymoon there before the auction and before the final removal to Merrion Square. Theo had completed that purchase and the house in Terenure was now going on the market. Property prices were beginning to rise after the long slump. The beginning of the seventies showed a time of comparative prosperity. The Government had set up the Industrial Development Authority, attracting industrialists to Ireland with grants and tax-free allowances.

Theo often expressed gladness that, somehow, going into the seventies, Ireland had finally climbed the climbing wave of recession. He was glad but he was also foreboding.

"Ireland has no tradition in industry. The people will see the new masters from wherever in the same way the land-locked peasants saw the old masters from across the Irish Sea. All the trade unionism in the world will never convince the new factory workers that they are being paid enough—they have no traditional comparisons. They will never have heard that Moroccan carpets are made by the tiny fingers of six-year old children who are paid with a bowl of rice. Industry takes centuries to establish without an industrial revolution. There will be strikes and many of the new factories will close down, or move out to where the owners can hire cheaper workers."

Max was never averse to taking his father down a peg or two. He would argue crisply. "They won't be able to close down or move out until they had paid back the grants and allowances."

"By which time," Theo would rebut, "you think the factory workers will have adjusted? The centuries of subjugation to a landlord's whim will have been forgotten? But you forget, my son, that with the first wage-packet, the worker goes back into bondage. He must have clothes to work in, a house to live in, a wife to take care of him. Money and more money! He who walked free on his own fields will become an indentured slave."

Max was always nettled by such remarks. "You have not much faith in your fellow man, Father. Those fields involved hardship and tough work."

"But the freedom to be your own boss," said Theo.

"Maybe." Max enjoyed this argument. "Maybe there are many farmers' sons who would trade the harrow for a college degree?"

"I take that point," Theo would say, "and I have no doubt that there are many hard-working farmers who are putting their sons (and I hope, their daughters) through university. Making doctors and lawyers and architects of them is not the same thing as putting them into factories. Will those young doctors and lawyers stay here in their own country? Will the Government set up great teaching hospitals to enhance Ireland's fame in the medical world abroad? Will the teachers and lawyers and artists set up ever more schools and universities? Will they call out to the far corners of the globe: 'Here be learning!' We have talked of this, Lia—you and I. It was done in the seventh, eighth and ninth centuries—and how much more difficult it must have been then—before the Normans came to change everything."

"That's going back a bit, Father! This is the twentieth century. Different world."

"And differently opened up, a few hours' flying

time to anywhere! All those graduating scholars will
fly off to the ends of the earth, leaving Ireland in the
lurch, leaving the low-paid jobs mortgaged, as like as
not, for their education."

But Max was persistent. "And why should all those
highly qualified young people have to go, why not
good jobs here?"

"Because," Theo told him, "the new cock-robins in
office will be so busy feathering their own nests they
will not notice the flight of their kith and kin until it
is too late. The new mansions of the newly rich!
History repeats itself for ever. It is happening already."

When we were alone after one of these frustrating
talks (which Theo enjoyed and Max unwittingly
encouraged), Max would say to me, "I told you, Lia. He
is looking for things to worry about. You talk to him,
he will listen to you." Silently, I always agreed with
Theo's theories. I believed him wise and just. When
Theo philosophised, there was an echo-chamber in
my mind.

I cannot now recall any change in the deep-set
relationship between Vasha and Daddy-Theo. I have
read over the diaries and the notebooks, all of which
were given into my care and which lay for years in
their marked boxes in the spare room of my river
house—referred to always as "the famous spare
room"—and I see not the slightest reference to a

shadow left over from the Amsterdam episode. Knowing my own tendency to leave cryptic messages in the diaries about things I did not wish to state clearly, I see nothing to indicate displeasure or confusion. My lifelong habit of respecting secrecy is apparent in these diaries; and even in this chronicle there may still be that need.

At the very end of August, Max and I had our holiday in Bray. Silkitoo the Sixth came with us. All the Silkitoos down through the years were totally happy with Shanlee and Ted until the moment I came across the threshold, and then whichever little dog was there became my shadow. The others always teased me about that, and Deric used to rattle out a song on the piano, "Me and My Shadow." Always a King Charles, although I never ever told anyone that the King Charles was the pet chosen by Burton for my ninth birthday, and he had suggested the right name, Silky. But I did not linger over Burton's image when I petted Silkitoo Six; for many years Max was the one identified with the need to have a small dog about the place. Equally we shared this devotion to dogs, never missing the big dog shows in Philadelphia and, when we were there, in Ireland on St Stephen's Day and St Patrick's Day in the RDS. We made two expeditions to Crufts, always promising ourselves we would go again the following year.

I remember every detail of our holiday in the river house. There was a sunlit enchantment about the river that year. It had been a dry summer and the water was low, lapping over the brown stones all day and sending the same lullaby through the open windows at night. We made excuses of shopping to go into the town every morning. We bought the paper, always *The Irish Times*, and once a week the *Wicklow People*. There was a home bakery for bread and chocolate eclairs. In a different shop we bought milk and eggs and cheese, in yet another, freshly caught fish; and in a butcher's shop we made hectic decisions between lamb and beef. Nowadays in Bray there are supermarkets and shopping centres. For me, shopping has become impersonal, indifferent. And alas, nowadays, there is no one with whom to share the small adventure. Then it was so enjoyable. After the shopping, we drove down to the sea front, and took Silkitoo for her daily walk along the promenade, almost deserted now the holidaymakers' season was over. We walked the full length from Marine Terrace (never forgetting that James Joyce lived there long ago) all the way to Bray Head. Bray was so essentially part of our shared history that, each day, we were drawn ever closer together in memory. My gran and Aunt Julia had their names invoked with laughter, but often we were more easily able, on that seashore, to bring back Tadek and Laelia.

I told Max how I had felt the first premonition of future sadness when Tadek took me up along the Cliff Walk to impart the news that he had got an internship in a hospital in Bournemouth and that he would be gone far away for three years.

"I know," Max told me. "He took you off on your own because he was afraid you would cry your heart out at the news. He always dreaded to see you cry. It unmanned him."

"Was that really what it was?" I asked. "Unmanned? I was always a little bit afraid to cry because Tadek could become so withdrawn. There were so many long partings in those days and somehow, I needed to cry about the loneliness."

Max hugged my arm in his. "I knew that, and I wanted to comfort you, buy you iced caramels. But I was only a Johnny-Come-Lately and we both respected Tadek's opinion in everything."

It was just as well that Max had not tried to divert me with his comfort. On those little holidays in Bray, away back in the 1930s, one person only existed in my world. Max was only a shadow in another's shadow.

"You had to wait a long time in the queue," I smiled happily at him, "but when your turn came, you made up for everything. We, Max and Lia, have got to the happy-ever-after days!" Max looked so pleased and proud. Although it was not then the done public thing, we paused to kiss for a long, long moment, savouring our deep contentment with each other. I clasp that sunny moment always in my heart, and I thank God that our futures are hidden from our eyes. The countdown to the end of the happy-ever-after days was already written into the calendar ahead.

It is possible to put unwanted thoughts into the back of one's mind, and that is surely what I did with all thoughts of Vasha. The guilt that would never go away found a cavern within. The guilt for what had been done or the guilt of concealment from Max and from Theo: I could never resolve which was more bitter. Max was all truth and open-hearted. But Vasha was my child and she had asked for secrecy. I could never betray her trust. Few enough in those days and fewer still in the time to come were the occasions when Vasha and I would come close enough to embrace. I read the diary and I see the forked pen with which I wrote. Max also kept a diary to annotate his progress on his studies and books on the Holocaust and the partisans. He drew a firm black ink line across the two weeks' holiday by the river. On the line he wrote: *I have died and gone to paradise with Lia*. I am infinitely glad now that I did not disturb his paradise with a sordid story of abortion. I suppose I had long practice in keeping secrets.

After the auction, the river house would be home

to Shanlee and Ted. They were looking forward to this retirement while doubting if anyone else was capable of taking Theo into proper care. To please her I watched Shanlee preparing the dishes to which, she said, the master was partial. *Borsch kholodny* was one, and *polenta grassa* was another. I wrote everything down in a notebook and read all the measures and directions back to her. Theo scolded her gently for fussing and then he praised her cookery. Again he scolded her so that she could be sure he valued her. And indeed, he did. His preparations were thorough and far-seeing. Ted would be provided with a small car, and it would be brand-new. He would have his own bank account in Bray organised by Theo. He advised them to put their savings in a separate account in a different bank, and also to make their Wills and indicate their wishes for their burial should they go before Theo. They were proud to make their Will so that Max would inherit their money and possessions. Max was equally proud to know, as he told them, that he was their sun, moon, and stars. Shanlee's eyes shone each time he said that.

Theo Randt's antiques and fine art company was not exactly world-wide. Nevertheless he had many more outlets in places than I had previously been aware of. Max had said his father never learned to delegate; yet he had been delegating for a year before he told us of his plans. In fact, by the end of that summer, almost all his treasures had been packed and insured and despatched to the warehouse in New York to be held in readiness for the sale in November. Max worried all the time that Theo was overworking. Every night he complained about his father's lack of caution. "Lia, couldn't you have a word with him; he will listen to you. He will bring on a heart attack. It is ridiculous the way he is carrying on. Why has he got to sell everything as if he were due for incarceration in a debtors' prison? Speak to him, Lia, for godsake."

Theo was thriving mightily on the operation. When I tried a little gentle remonstrance, he said, "I have always seen the culmination of my life's work in exactly this way. Just suppose, Lia my dear, that I dropped in my tracks, and left you two and the youngsters to wind up the business! None of you could run it—you and Max know nothing of market values. Vasha and Deric are still learning. They will be good in their separate ways, but they will need guidance. Now I can give that but without carrying the whole load. You understand me, Lia?"

"So, it is a promise, Theo. After the auction you will rest and read and sleep?"

"Come here, little one." He held me in a gentle way. "We will do more than that. We will go out to dine. We will have a night at the theatre. On your birthday, we will walk down Grafton Street. Yes?"

In the middle of October Alessandro arrived and my world was complete. He had a very tender way of murmuring, "*Come stai, Madre mia?*" This small enquiry was meant for my ears alone. It demanded a recognition in his own language, equally tenderly: "*Bene, grazie, e tu?*" His response to that was always the same: a gently smiling, "*Madre mia bellissima.*" Alessandro had a superb command of English, but for me he used little Italian phrases, establishing our intimacy. We managed to have a few exchanges bringing us up to date in small everyday matters. As I have already written, I waited for him to mention Umbria or Holland, but he did not, nor did I. Most of the time, he was deep in consultation in Theo's study. Within the next week Vasha arrived from Lisbon, and Deric from Paris. They both disappeared into the study for many hours at a time.

Earlier in the year, Stefan had written vaguely about Apollo 16. Now we understood that in December it would be Apollo 17, and there was a possibility that he would have some part to play. If so, he would not be meeting us in New York; training would prevent his leaving the base. His letters are brief and scribbled but the excitement in them is insuppressible.

We learned that when the auction was over by December, Theo's empire would be divided three ways. Vasha would get Lisbon which had the most magnificent gallery near the Pina Palace and had living-quarters attached to it. Deric would run the Paris gallery as he had been doing but now he would own it. Alessandro was given the *galleria* in Rome retaining the present *direttore* until the man wished to retire. Alessandro had frequented the gallery since his schooldays and the *direttore* was a respected friend. For Stefan, Theo had made ample provision which he would inherit when he would be twenty-five years old.

"I am giving them equal shares to build on," Theo told Max. "When I go, it is all up to them."

Max said to me, "He will go sooner than he thinks if he doesn't calm down. Speak to him, Lia. I am sure his blood-pressure is up." He allowed Max to check his blood-pressure and smiled when it was found to be normal.

Now Max and I were assigned our job which was to send out the invitations for the auction...hundreds and hundreds of them. These beautifully engraved cards in their linen-like envelopes were sent to all parts of the world. Very many of them went to strange addresses in the Middle East. At that time, I had yet to become accustomed to the idea that Arabs were not barefoot Bedouins in the desert, but multi-millionaire oil-sheiks who must be interested in acquiring art treasures of a different, though not an older, culture.

"Have they palaces or art galleries or museums?" I asked in wonder.

"Probably all three," Max told me, "now that every Tom, Dick, and Harry has a car needing petrol."

Theo praised our diligence with the invitations. "Your reward will be great in New York," he said. "I have engaged a penthouse suite for the family. It is the Fabergé, French of course, so we will be assured of good dinners and excellent wine. Alessandro has inspected the suite, and he has sampled the cuisine." Theo smiled. "You will all agree that Alessandro is a good judge?" We teased Alessandro that he must be careful not put on weight. Now Theo sat down beside me and looked at my heap of envelopes. Always a one for praise, he said how clear and clean my handwriting was.

"But I am much quicker," Max claimed. "Look at my big pile of invitations!"

"Illegible!" Theo smiled at both of us. "Totally illegible! Doctor's scrawl!"

CHAPTER TWENTY-FOUR

Theo had instructed Christies to purchase hundreds of yards of plain matt material in three colours: grey, black and sage green. In the three storeys of the warehouse the walls and windows were covered in this material. Theo decided that the lighting should be artificial rather than risk variable daylight. Important pictures could be subtly highlighted, and precious antiques spotlit in their glass cages. The auctioneers brought in their own hanging experts, although Theo made sure to have the last word. The effect of the three floors of treasures was stupendously beautiful. The photography was all done days in advance of the auction. The day before opening for viewing was a day of locked doors while the catalogues were checked against the inventories, and rechecked several times until everyone was satisfied.

Hundreds of list catalogues had been sent out in advance. The catalogue on sale at the entrance contained stunning pictures of many precious items and centrefolds of the three wonderfully decked floors. Theo was very pleased with the descriptions in the

newspapers: "unsurpassed display of costly art,"
"glorious," "fabulous art for the fabulously wealthy,"
"one for the connoisseurs who do not count the
shekels." This last caused a wry comment from Theo:
"If we escape with no worse than that little chip of
anti-Semitism, we will be doing well." References to
"Aladdin's Palace of Wonders" restored his high good
humour. The press had certainly hyped the viewing,
and the crowds who thronged to the huge warehouse
caused traffic jams. The auctioneers had insisted on a
very expensive price for the catalogue so that only
genuine buyers would attend. There had to be a
rushed reprint of the catalogue. I am sure it is still on
many bookshelves; it is on mine. In itself it is a lovely
work of art. All else is gone but the catalogue remains.
It is a thought which accompanies me into the National
Gallery in Merrion Square: the artist is dead and gone
these hundreds of years, but the boys and girls, men
and women, who posed for him have taken on lives of
their own. They endure: they are real people and in the
years to come they will live on and on...

Theo had indeed done the family proud with the
accommodation he provided. The suite was
commodious and very comfortable. Ted had come to
look after Theo but not for driving; rather to see that
he was not worried about all the grooming deemed
necessary for this last appearance in the public world

of the big dealers. "After this event," Theo told me, "you will find some comfortable silk shirts for me to lounge in. Try the Russian shops in New York—scarcely imported but maybe good copies—must be silk." So there were the three of us, Vasha and Deric, and later Alessandro came. Berny and Denis Lowry had booked into the same hotel and Frayne joined them. Although we were all roped in to give assistance for the first couple of days, we had the relaxed feeling of being about to begin a holiday. Dion Randt had come from Italy to be with Vasha. He stayed with friends in Manhattan. When Theo saw the two of them together like close friends, he raised his eyebrows expressively at me, and I could only murmur, "Just friends, I think." Theo took another look, and said, "She has everything. Why does she need moral support?" Luckily we were interrupted. When Theo asked for information, he waited for an answer. The interruptions were frequent, and the question was forgotten.

Walking with Theo later, we watched a family admiring a group of statuary. The woman was very beautiful, and with her was her son, tall and dark as she was, and a much younger pretty girl. All three were fashionably dressed. They stood out even in the milling crowds. When the woman turned her head, I recognised her. Whether by the good start given her by nature or by the clever art of a beautician, Francesca had aged scarcely a day. Involuntarily, I uttered her name, "Francesca!" I must have aged, or changed. It took her a moment to remember me. "It is Lia, isn't it?" Although we had parted most uncivilly many years before, we now embraced like two long-lost cousins of a fond family.

"Of course I remember you, Mr Randt. Who would forget those luscious dinners in the Shelbourne? We were only poor students and you were our rich and fatherly patron of the arts."

I thought that was a neat twist, especially the emphasis on the "father." Would she so handily remember the cheque I had given her, which had been this rich patron's cheque? She remembered. She fixed her actressy eyes on my face and said, "My son, Ramon, Mr Randt. He is quite old enough for Lia to have met him but I do not remember if she has. No? Well, here he is." I could not mistake her meaning. "And this is my daughter, Cherita. You may have read in the news of my recent divorce? No? Here in the States they made a big thing about it." Handshakes all round, while Francesca made sure that her voice carried in a wide circle. There was no need but she probably never stopped working at being a star. I did not like her any more than I had done long ago. To my dismay, I heard Theo's voice. He was turning on the charm. To him, she was another bidder who had bought the expensive catalogue.

"I believe I have seen your name in lights on Broadway, madame. Before we leave New York, we are to see your play. I hear you have a *succès fou*—as, I am sure, with all your work. There is a film also for us to see?" It was best to smile as radiantly as possible and appear to agree. He was always a step ahead with his invitations. Now, he was showing an obvious admiration for the pretty daughter and Madame Francesca was very responsive to Theo's talk of a supper-party. "Lia will exchange telephone numbers with you. It seems I am being called away." Instinct told me to get out of an arrangement. Francesca was bad news for me whenever our paths crossed long ago. I remembered Phyllis telling me about Francesca and Burton in the Isle of Man during the war..."All eyes turned to follow them, Lovey! Everyone said she was an Italian princess and he was all puffed up in his British uniform like a general—masses of gold braid! But I remembered her in your plays in the Abbey and I knew she was from Ardee Street. Her mother worked in Jacob's." I smiled with pleasure (as taught in the Abbey School of Acting) and a supper party was set for the following night in Theo's suite. As they moved away, I wondered if Francesca knew that Burton was dead? Or, come to think of it, did Burton ever tell her he was my stepfather? Or, come to think of it again, what of Tony Lloyd? If she even knew his name. Far removed from Ardee Street was Tony Lloyd. Chersy had said then that Francesca had acted out the Rosy Redmond prostitute and provoked Tony into a similar response. Poor old Tony! Chersy said he was as drunk as a coot. And so was Francesca. She had blamed me because I had pleaded with her to go to the party, and then had failed to show up, leaving her at the mercy of my druken boyfriend. That was the day when Tadek's mother died and I was in Creighton Street with Gran.

I watched the beautiful family moving through the crowds. The son was very protective. He took his mother's arm and his admiration was in the very curve of his attentive shoulders. Tony Lloyd's son, the very build of Tony with Francesca's dark eyes and straight black hair. In some recent visit, Chersy had told me that Tony, now a commissioner in the Land Commission, never took a proper lunch hour but went down instead to Clarendon Street Church and spent the hour in prayer. "But, Lia, wasn't he always a class of a Holy Joe!" I remembered I used to tell her how respectful and restrained Tony was even when we went swimming and lay in the sun. She used to answer, "Hah! He's getting it somewhere!" But I think he really was a rigorously correct man. He never meant to rape. Poor old Tony.

So, without going into the historical details, I told Max that the famous actress Francesca D'Oyly was coming to supper by Theo's invitation, also her son and daughter. I rang down to Berny's rooms to ask her to come and persuade Denis and Frayne also. Latterly, Denis retired early but when he honoured a party, he was always the most popular guest.

"Francesca!" Berny exclaimed. "I never thought we would see her again! Is she really the same—the famous film star. Honestly? The papers were full of her divorce a few weeks ago."

"The same," I said, "complete with son of thirty odd and a very pretty daughter of less than twenty."

"A son of thirty? Are you trying to tell me something?"

"Could be," I said, remembering Francesca's eyes.

Berny was laughing on the phone. "That was the first time I deflected an abortion, I often wondered. I don't remember everything in life but I remember her. I took her over to the gynaecologist's office; I knew there was no one there—it wasn't their hours—and I did a pregnancy test on her. She went down on her knees and begged me to do something, anything. She said her mother would kill her. She was too far gone, and the way I saw it then, I was the one at risk. You gave her money and we gave her an address in London.

I used to wonder for years what had happened. When we were coming back to where you were waiting she swore at me that you had landed her in trouble and that I could help her if I wanted to. I told her I couldn't. I swore on my honour I couldn't. She dragged at my face with her nails. She said that she would get me some day."

"Well, she didn't, Ber. Looking at her today, I am sure she has often thanked you in her heart. She has a gallant, handsome son and all the fame she could have craved."

When I put down the phone, I could not help but let my mind go back to that time when we sent Francesca to a convent in London and we never got in touch, never troubled to find out what way she was. Surely we were not so helplessly heartless? We forgot Francesca and we got on with our own lives. I could never like her, but she had the courage to survive. It cannot have been easy. There was the war, rationing, bombing. Little children were taken away for evacuation. I did not honestly want to know in what way she struggled but I deeply regretted my part in that struggle that was forced on her. It was good that she was so beautiful and so talented.

The supper-party divided like a tournament with Madame Francesca a royal reigning queen. There were courtiers and knights in just the way Theo liked his guests to behave at his parties. Frayne and Ramon and Dion were like the knights of Vasha who was fully aware of the effect of her beauty, aiming her brilliant glances like lances at the knights. Ramon was the unknown. With him she was provocative—all in good humour—to make the night lightly interesting. Theo was in fine form, directing quite outrageous praise at the lovely actress. Deric may have left his heart in Paris, but he was not averse to chatting up the extremely pretty Cherita. Sensing a rival in the newcomer, Frayne soon sent sparks flying in all directions. Frayne was no mean wielder of a courtly lance. Moreover he was (as I am sure I have remarked before) a truly magnificent specimen of young manhood. In all the years of his growing up, I had often caught my breath, so alike was he to the Burton I had worshipped long ago in my mother's "Sunrise." Max and I assumed that Frayne felt he had first rights to Vasha. They had been unswerving friends, intimates, since childhood. We all knew that Frayne encouraged a following of adoring females. So many people said to him, "You should be in films," that given the touch of arrogance in his nature, he would fail to imagine Vasha looking at any other man. His distinguished career in the air force made him a favourite in Theo's eyes. As for Dion, it seemed to me that, all unknown to those of us who had not lived in the household of Perugia, this very personable Italian had assumed the role of protector. How much, or how little, he knew of Tonio Martelli, I could not guess. There was a definite calm assurance in his attitude, his smiles were tinged with amusement.

Max was a student of human behaviour and he often drew my attention to small but telling incidents. He noticed that each time Deric, no doubt attracted by the delicate flower-like grace of Cherita, bent his head closer to speak, or listen, to her, an imperious note in Ramon's tone of voice reminded the girl that big brother was watching.

"I think your old friend has a firm grip on her children!" Max remarked. "Deric is not making much headway with the child-star!"

"Anyway," I reminded him, "hasn't Deric got himself nearly engaged to that lovely girl in Paris?" Max was always more deeply into the boys' confidences than I was.

"Oh, I almost forgot to tell you—Marie-Claire ditched Deric for a multimillion Japanese industrialist. He told me this afternoon." I was amazed. Marie-Claire was so aristocratically upper crust, so very French. "You can't be serious! Marie-Claire married to a Japanese?"

"What have we got against the Japanese?" Max smiled at my indignation. "I am not sure if she has married him, but our dear Marie-Claire is in Tokyo with Mr Woo."

We laughed together. "You made that name up," I accused him. "Mr Woo!"

"Take a peek down the table. Would you say that Mama is re-placing the steel handcuffs on the son?"

We were rising from the supper-table, and Ramon was hastening to his mother's chair and she was rewarding him with a maternal smile of such purity as only an accomplished actress could produce. One supposes that young people, attracted to each other at a party, will find ways of keeping in touch and furthering their initial acquaintance. As we were parting in the foyer of the hotel, I happened to notice that Cherita slipped a small card to Frayne. I noticed it because I was surprised she did not slip the card to Deric, with whom she had flirted prettily all evening. I think that because Deric was not involved, I promptly forgot the incident. No doubt there were phone calls and meetings but, as a family, we were caught up in the frenzied atmosphere of the auction. Max and I were constantly present to guard Theo who was in danger of overdoing his attendance on the hundreds of bidders and buyers known to him over fifty years of dealing. Vasha and Deric had to be there all the time, and Dion had been roped in to render further assistance. Francesca had deputed Ramon to bid for several pieces of sculpture and he took it for granted that Vasha would give him advice. Frayne was never far away and Cherita liked to link his arm and gaze up at him in admiration. That was my impression in the fleeting glimpses of all of them among the throng. On the fourth day, Alessandro joined us from Rome. Theo welcomed him with open arms. He poured out on Alessandro a totally uncomplicated love, almost as if he were a son. It had been so from the beginning and had deepened with the years as their mutual interests grew. His emotional feeling for Alessandro showed itself in a much easier style than his unfathomed affection for Vasha. As with me, so it was with Vasha: a torrent with stepping stones was Theo's love for his women.

Alessandro's arrival, his tender *"Come stai, Madre mia?"* set the seal on my days. I should describe Alessandro; it is a joy for me to remember his looks. He was a Jew. There could be no doubt about that; he was more like Theo than Max was. Well above average height, he carried more weight than would ever be considered fashionable—in that he was also like Theo. He was Italian in the colour of his skin, the texture of his wavy hair, the attractive shape and depth of his eyes. His eyes were the eyes of men in Florentine paintings. The young Vasha still called him "the Levantine Jew" after the picture in Theo's study. Describing him cannot begin to evoke the charm of his presence.

His coming seemed to quicken the excitement of the auction. Discerning bidders flocked around him. He was a known envoy of Theo's and he was a known artist in his own right. Max observed to me that Ramon was, or appeared to be, put out by the extravagant way in which Vasha twined her arms around Alessandro when they talked together. They kissed and hugged and whispered like lovers—it was the Italian way.

"Shall I tell Ramon that Vasha and Alessandro are first cousins?" I asked Max.

"Tell him nothing," Max said. "This time next week, we will be, all of us, back on the other side of the Atlantic and, what's that line, 'not a trace left behind.' Personally, I can't get back soon enough."

Not a trace left behind. Tadek used to find an odd line to quote—did Max remember?

We had seen nothing of Francesca since the night of the supper-party. She was appearing in one play and rehearsing for another. Now we were getting ready to go to the theatre.

"I hope no one is going to get hurt here," Max said. "Such a carry-on down in the auction rooms today. Daggers-looks!"

"I do not think it will be Vasha," I said, "and I hope it won't be Deric—another let-down after Marie-

Claire."

"It could be Frayne," Max was thinking aloud. "The way he toys around with that kid, Cherita!"

"From what I saw," I said, "I think he was trying to fob her off."

"The two of them were missing. The brother asked me if I had seen his sister. I wish Frayne would get it into his head that he cannot take a girl like Vasha for granted. He thinks that when he gives the signal the wedding bells will ring."

"Do you see Frayne as her choice?" I asked.

Now he was reflecting. "It is a strange thing about Vasha here in New York. This place has an effect on her. It is as if 'virtue had gone out of her.' A different Vasha. Strange!"

I was sorely tempted to confirm his intuitive instinct. I said nothing. He continued musing: "I used to think she was weighing them all up...and that other young fellow, Tonio. I thought she would make her choice known to us. That is the last thing in her head now. She is in the mood for play-acting, shuffling off any thought of responsibility. Theo would like to see a brilliant engagement. I don't think it will be Frayne."

"What about Dion? He has been there in Perugia for all of her three years. What about him?"

"Dion will hang on in—he is strong enough to give her all the rope she needs. He is a Jew; he can assess value and not arrogate it to himself."

"Are Jews cleverer than other people?" I teased.

"But you know they are," Max smiled, "and they are able to endure long waiting. It is in their blood."

Hindsight is an easy way to write a story because the writing is tempered by what memory knows in advance. When we gathered in the foyer of the theatre, all I saw was a group of superbly attractive young people, all single, all successful, all shining with an opulent contentment. Theo was proud of our togetherness. I saw his fond glance as he admired each face, each evening dress, each tuxedo. The auction had passed its fifth day without slackening. The prices he had gauged were never less than, and in many cases far exceeded, his expectations. His health, jealously watched by Max, was fully restored. He said he had never felt better.

I was immensely impressed by Francesca's acting and by her beauty. The role revealed her as a voluptuous and yet delicately sensual woman in her middle years. As I had known when we were students she was pliant, malleable, utterly teachable. With a producer to mould her presentation, she was adorably convincing. I found myself hoping that, with all the wonderful roles she played, she had grown within into a woman who was deeply loving and tenderly fulfilled. An instinct which might be jealousy, or begrudgery, left me unconvinced.

She learned by rote; underneath she was unchanged. Her aim to succeed was gigantic, and let it be recorded, that ambition served her well to the very end of her career. That night in the theatre I sat next to Berny and in the intervals we walked the corridors. We could not but observe how all the lovely women turned to admire Frayne. Berny would tip my arm and give me a tiny blinking wink. I could read her thoughts of absolute pride. In her eyes was the message, as it had been so many times before: "If only Burton could see his son tonight. Look at him! The pride of it! Isn't he magnificent!" And in his full-dress uniform of a lieutenant-colonel in the American air force, he was indeed magnificent.

CHAPTER TWENTY-FIVE

We were due to leave New York on Monday. The Sunday would be busy all day for Theo and all his assistants wrapping up the business of a complete sell-out. The Lowrys would leave on the Sunday, and Frayne would be with them. Apollo 17 was now in the news and we gathered that, whatever about Stefan, Lieut-Colonel Lowry would be a very important part of this great undertaking in his capacity as a high-ranking medical officer. Late on Saturday, Berny and I were having our last little chat and our last cup of tea. The talk was about Frayne and that was natural because I was the only person in the world with whom Berny could talk openly and unashamedly about her adored son. Somehow, with Frayne supplying their link, she had managed to keep her marriage going though she had never felt desire for her husband. From time to time, she formed sexual liaisons with strangers but, she said, Burton had forever spoiled her and nothing lasted. She preferred to go home and admire her beloved image-son. I tried to change the subject.

"Honestly, Berny, I thought Frayne would be

married by this time. He is getting on!"

She smiled brightly. "He can't leave his mother! But, actually, as you probably know, he has proposed to Vasha at least six times."

"And did she turn him down?" I enquired. This was news to me.

"As if you didn't know, Lia! Still good at the secrets? Last year, she was madly in love with some Italian. A musician. Frayne thinks it is over for the last couple of months. He doesn't think she is serious about this present guy—this Dion. Anyway, she tells Frayne that they are distant cousins—same name."

"So is Frayne still in with a chance, do you suppose? That would be nice to look forward to, Berny. Are you in favour?"

Berny was always candid. "I am not so keen on her being a Jew. Jewish wives and mothers are very possessive—he likes his freedom. But I am keen on her for herself, and her looks are a good match for his. What *I* think won't be the deciding factor! Vasha's ideas are her own. I have never understood why she does not take Frayne's proposals seriously. Is she a bit spoiled, Lia? By Theo, I mean. I'll say that girl, Cherita, is thoroughly spoiled. She doesn't seem to know when she is not wanted. Frayne had hoped that this week in New York would deliver Vasha into his hands but between the auction and that awful Ramon she has her hands tied…has she said anything to you? What about tonight? Do you know if they are meeting? God, will you look at that weather." We both walked over to the windows and gazed out at the heavy snow. "I hope Frayne has not gone out. I never trust New York in snow. It turns into a blizzard."

At that exact moment, the phone rang. "Denis here, Lia." The punctilious courteous voice had a tremor. "Apparently there has been an accident. If Berny is there, may I speak to her? Thank you." I listened to her staccato replies: "A shooting! The ambulance! What hospital? No! Wait for me!" She dropped the phone and without a word she fled out and down the corridor. Through the open door I saw the second's pause at the lift down to their rooms. Denis had said an accident. Was a shooting an accident? I had glimpsed Berny's stricken face and I knew the bad news involved Frayne.

The following hours were a mad jumble of messages and phone calls and taxis crawling through blinding snow. Max came with me and we judged it better to leave Theo with his accountants and mentioning only "an accident—bad weather." He had got through a grinding week and we still had to get him home. The weather was appalling and even hardened taxi-men were reluctant to drive—double and treble fares had to be paid. We were told that New York could come to a full stop and that included electricity and phone lines. As the night wore on, all these hazards were making it harder every minute for us to have any hope that Frayne could last the night. He had four grievous bullet wounds in his body. Max assured me that Frayne would get the best care possible. Maybe he and Berny and Denis could assess Frayne's chances—they were doctors. I saw him on the point of death and, as always, I started in to pray with all my might.

When Alessandro joined us at the hospital, I got new hope. I whispered to him, "Will you pray for him? You are a special friend of God. Please Alessandro, you have never done anything to offend Him. Please." Max and Denis had been admitted to some inner room with Berny. Alessandro folded his arms around me and we sat side by side on a long bench with other people who were waiting for their own bad news. Close to my ear, I heard Alessandro's low voice murmuring one prayer after another. What matter that the prayers were all in Italian and that I did not understand many of the words. They were prayers and, when all else fails, there is no comfort to equal prayer. I know I have said that many times. I have come to need prayer.

"*Madre mia*, you are shivering. I should get you back to the hotel. The best possible care is here for Frayne. He is no ordinary patient. Come, let me take you back. If Theo is there he will be frantic with worry."

But I would not go; it would be like desertion. "Berny is my friend since the first day in school. If I went away while she is keeping vigil and Frayne died it would be my fault. Please stay with me and go on praying." That was many years ago. I cannot forget that I used the words: it would be my fault. And I have faltered over the thought and bowed my head in remorse. Unfortunately I was the one who had brought Francesca into Berny's life and unthinkingly I had brought her back again. Was it my fault? Not because of evil intent. Rather because such things were written into the map of my destiny. It might have been better had the nuns accepted me into the convent and locked me away from all harm. They did not so choose, alas.

Alessandro kept the enquiring police at bay during that long night by repeating, "*Non capisco. Non capisco*," followed by a stream of Italian until they gave up. Against my head, his lips murmured, "*Non parlare! Non parlare! Silenzio!*" When the police had moved off, Alessandro apologised for commanding my silence. "If they think we know anything, they will bring back someone to translate. We know nothing but they are hard to convince. In Rome, the same. Any name will do for the notebook."

Early the next morning everyone was questioned and hectored by the police in Theo's suite. Alibis were produced and accepted. Finally, our party were all allowed their right to go about their business. Theo and Max, Vasha and Dion, Deric and Alessandro were booked to leave Kennedy Airport for Shannon. Theo decided it was best for my own peace of mind if I remained in New York for Berny's sake, until her son was at least out of intensive care—and that was very uncertain. He had been shot four times and the bullet at the top of his spine was causing extreme anxiety.

We learned that Ramon D'Oyly had made a statement to the police in a very straightforward manner immediately Dr Max Randt had telephoned the terrible news of the shooting to their apartment. He was aware that his sister, Cherita, had been seeing Dr Frayne Lowry. She was very young and she had taken a shine to him. So far as Ramon knew, they had had breakfast together a few times. On the day of the tragedy, his mother had forbidden Cherita to leave their apartment because of the blizzard. He had driven his mother to her rehearsal and had remained to drive her home, again because of the bad weather. If his sister had any tryst with Dr Lowry, she would have phoned to cancel. But she had not made a date. Cherita made a similar statement. She had met him but not on that day.

The police had checked the place where Cherita and Frayne had met previously. Before the shooting, Frayne *was* there. The waiter said, "Once seen, never forgotten." On account of the weather the place was half-empty. The man waited about twenty minutes and then he went into the phone booth and then the shooting must have begun. The noise was not heard because there was music and radio and television in the background. A barman carrying drinks had seen the man slumping and then he had fallen out of the booth. No one saw anyone nearby nor anyone running away.

I have copied that from a yellowing newspaper. The account is all the more ignominious when one remembers Frayne.

Berny never left the hospital. Denis had to endure an endless interrogation from the New York detectives called in when Frayne's rank and importance were uncovered. There were questions that Denis could not answer. Who would want to kill their son? Had his life been threatened? Frayne's murder (his death was imminent) must be tied in with all the secrecy surrounding Apollo 17. Apparently the police questioned people of all ranks on the base where Frayne would have been if he had not been in New York. The police also told Denis a fact which he had always known: men, and sometimes women, were killed every day on the streets of New York. Four bullets was a fairly clean way to go if you had a choice. One detective volunteered the information that blizzards and heat waves brought out the loonies.

When I sympathised with Denis for having to put up with the illogicality of the police interrogation and the crudeness of their observations, he sighed heavily. "I am weary of listening to them," he said, "but in a city of this size with the teeming millions of mixed races there probably are gangs of crazy gung-ho criminals out there. However, it is my private belief that many, very many, of what look like random killings are inside jobs. They call the perpetrators hit-men. They kill for money and the victim is designated to them—no personal acquaintance necessary. It is easier that way."

We were sitting in the Lowrys' room. I was keeping Denis company; Berny would not leave the hospital. Denis had had a slight coronary the year before and his rising blood pressure was giving concern. He was utterly devoted to Berny and to Frayne. He was the proudest father in the whole world. He believed Frayne was the living image of himself when he was young. He said so constantly. He loved his son very deeply and he was grief-stricken that this horrible thing had brought his son to the verge of death. Denis was a gentleman of the old school; his southern courtesy is unforgettable. Despite the possibility of impending tragedy, he was graciously thankful to me for my concern for him. He was glad, he said, not to be left alone and I was glad to be of comfort. "It will be best," he said, "that Berny should believe murder can occur for no reason in New York at any time, on any day. Should my son die, New York must take the blame. Should my son die, she will not want to live." It was heartbreaking to see so impressive a man so close to tears but he held himself back. He would not forget his duty to a visitor. He even tried to smile.

"There is a thing I must ask you, Lia. Although, if you do not wish to say, then let it go."

I held my breath. There were things I would not wish to say. Never. And I would not say. I was not good at dissembling. Silence was my chosen cover. Lies face to face would be difficult.

He continued, "Berny mentioned that she had met Francesca D'Oyly briefly many years ago. Is she a close friend of yours, Lia? If I may ask?"

I breathed out a long sigh of relief. "I knew her in the Abbey School of Acting when I was seventeen. She was never a special friend. Neither Ber nor I has seen her since the day she left Dublin. We were students then."

"So all this friendly intercourse of the past week is merely coincidental with her stage appearance and the auction being in New York?"

"Just the merest coincidence," I told him.

We were (I thought) companionably quiet for a long time. I was beginning to wonder if he should, perhaps, be left alone to take a little rest. At last he spoke as if after deliberation.

"When Frayne was going out...how many days ago?...that day of the awful weather, I asked him was it necessary to go out at all. He said he would not be long away; he had had an urgent note from a friend. We all chivvied him about his admirers and I said something to that effect. I remember his sober answer: This one is very young, Dad, and her brother is giving her a hard time. Look at the snow, I said. Wait until tomorrow. Tomorrow we will be gone, he said. Berny had gone down to have tea with you, Lia. So I lay down to rest. I probably dozed and then I heard the phone ringing."

I thought it helped him to go over the ground again, and once more the sympathetic silence took over. He was choosing his words. "When we were having breakfast that morning he brought up a subject about which we had never talked, although as doctors we face the problem often. That is incest. He asked us, if we were counselling, what would be a good approach? The conversation was brief. We both recommended certain books which, in general practice, we had found useful."

It was fairly clear that there was more to follow and I waited. If Berny were here to help his inward debate, I supposed she would understand him better. I was a poor substitute.

"In the hospital," he went on, "we were given Frayne's wallet and his watch. They kept his various cards and his clothes which were bloodstained very badly. However, I requested a thorough examination of his clothes before I let them be taken away—I presume to forensic. His wallet contained some money, not a great deal, but we neither of us carry much money since credit cards were invented. It was not a case of robbery. His watch, for example, is worth several thousand dollars. It was a twenty-first birthday present."

He appeared to sink into himself. Then with kindness, he said, "Am I keeping you, Lia?"

"Oh no, Denis. I am not going anywhere until it is time for us to go to the hospital, in an hour's time."

"Then may I finish what I wanted you to know?" And while I sat there nodding my head I prayed inwardly that Fate had not handed me any more secrets. "When I took the wallet and the watch into Frayne's room to leave on his table, I found these." From his pocket, he took several notelets of the sort one sends brief messages on. "They were thrown on the table; no attempt at concealment. They were of no personal value to him. Take them, Lia."

Two notelets and on them was written in the childish script that all American children seem to learn in primary school:

Please, Frayne, help me. Advise me.

Cherita. At Clary's.

Please, Frayne. It is desperate.

Cherita. Same place.

"This is unbelievable, Denis. What help? What advice?"

My view of Cherita was of an amazingly pretty girl, who was surrounded by the love of a mother and a brother and indeed by every luxury that money could provide.

Denis's voice was very low and reluctant. "Frayne said her brother was giving her a hard time. Those were his words."

I had thought that Frayne was playing his usual role of the gay Lothario to the prettily flirtatious Cherita. I was unable to imagine any serious conversation between them. I was staring in disbelief. Then Denis took another notelet from his pocket. "And there was this," he said. This notelet was crushed and scribbled and not signed:

Please please please Frayne same place.

Denis said, "It was thrown on the table like the

others but I don't think it is like the others. I think Frayne went to the meeting. The girl did not come. He waited twenty minutes and then he went to the phone booth. It is in Clary's vestibule."

I waited for him to tell me that he had called, or was going to call, the police. But he said nothing. His face always so patrician, so proud, was crumpled and old.

I found it hard to speak. "What about the police?" I mumbled. "And what about Berny?"

"In this country," Denis said, "you make an instant report to the police, or you are the one who is concealing evidence. You may even be accessory to the crime. Time for reflection is not allowed. And when you have called the police, your life will never be your own again. Frayne's life if he is spared to us, Berny's life, my life. We are doctors who have made our marks. Besmirching is not of our choosing."

"Denis, perhaps you should say no more. Whatever you are thinking, whatever you decide to do, it is best you keep your own counsel."

"I am taking you into my confidence, Lia. For one thing, I prefer a witness. For another, Berny has always told me that you are the only trustworthy person she has ever known, and she loves you as dearly as a sister."

Denis took my hand in his two hands. "First then as a witness: you will remember what I have allowed you to know of my fears and suspicions. Despite the fact that I will destroy what might be evidence. On my oath, if Frayne does not survive, I will hound Ramon D'Oyly to the death chamber. But Lia, if Frayne does survive, there will never be any suspicion beyond the known possibility that New York is a dangerous city."

He placed the notelets into an ashtray and set them alight. When they had burned down to nothing, my voice came out in a whisper: "I think you have a strong hope that Frayne will pull through?"

"I have," he replied and his voice was braver; "more by instinct than by knowledge."

It was three weeks before Frayne was pronounced out of danger. His convalescence was slow. His looks were not impaired, he did not lose the mashed fingers which had been holding the telephone receiver, he walked again, he played tennis again, but the damage to his personality was severe. Frayne became introvert, a very closed-off private sort of person.

Three weeks after Max and Theo had left New York, I arrived back in Dublin, and my poor old native city looked mighty good to me. I walked around the streets and felt the freedom of this eleventh-century village tucked in between the mountains and the sea. I had been away before and I had been glad to come back, but never so delightedly glad as this time. There was an old song very popular then, and I heard myself

humming it as I turned off O'Connell Bridge, down
George's Quay, and along the Liffey wall past Creighton
Street:

> *Dublin can be heaven with coffee at eleven,*
> > *and a stroll in Stephen's Green...*
> *Grafton Street's a wonderland,*
> > *there's magic in the air;*
> *There are diamonds in the lady's eyes*
> > *and gold dust in her hair...*

I was happy with the sense of relief to have escaped
from New York. Deep regrets for what had happened
would flood back later. Just for the moment, to be in
Dublin was enough.

"New York was very good to us!" Theo said. I never
gave him a rough answer and I did not now, but I had
to say, "You can have New York and everyone in it."
Theo looked disappointed. "I thought you were
enjoying yourself—except for the accident."

"Well, yes," I said to please him, "except for the
accident." I see it written in my diary that Max had not
allowed Theo to hear the full extent of the shooting.
At another time to keep Theo from full knowledge of
any event would have been impossible but the night
before they left New York was a night of reckoning
with accountants. They, all of them—Theo, Max,
Vasha, Deric, Dion and Alessandro—had a bare three
hours of sleep before they went to the airport. The full

impact of what had happened to Frayne was not fully understood until long afterwards. Why the shooting had happened was never revealed.

Soon we were on our own again, the three of us. Max had to drop a lot of his own work to fit in with Theo's plans. There were already enquiries from prospective buyers for the house in Terenure. It was urgent that we go ahead with the full decorative renovation of the Merrion Square house. We would move just as soon as it was ready and we had installed Shanlee and Ted in the Bray house.

Theo talked of getting a regular woman to help. He had grown used to the look of Missus Nelly and her daughter but they lived in Crumlin. Then Missus Nelly came one day with the news that the daughter's husband had walked out, leaving Emily and their three kids. I am not sure how it was arranged but in a small city, it is helpful "to know someone." Nelly and Emily were given a corporation flat in a new building in Townsend Street, five minutes from Merrion Square. When Theo enquired about the missing husband as to where had he gone, Missus Nelly told him laconically, "Foreign shores!" Max said that meant England but Theo preferred the romantic notion of the Amazon Basin. When he further enquired about the departure Missus Nelly spared a few further words to tell him, "It's the nature of Dubbalin men!" Theo regaled us with this. It was so unexpected that he was highly amused. "They will be hard up without a man's wages; so I gave them a cheque, but, Lia, you must see to it that they have beds for the children. There is a lot of stuff here that is never used now."

Shanlee knew all of Missus Nelly's requirements. She had taken an interest in Emily since she was twelve years of age. The flat in Townsend Street probably ranked top class for beds and bed-linen, not to mention all the wardrobes and mirrors that were not sent down to Ellis's auction rooms on Usher's Quay. Shanlee did not want those heavy items. She was content with the furniture Max and I had put into the river house when we honeymooned there the first time. Theo kept on inviting her to choose pieces in Terenure but she was happy with the minimum, as always. Ted had the new car which Theo said should keep him happy too, but Ted worried about the Master. Max was anxious that Shanlee and Ted would settle. He talked to Ted: "We don't want to have to keep on about you and Shanlee. It is time for you two to take it easy, Ted. No more big car to take care of; no more stairs; no more grounds, just the bit of lawn— and don't start planting vegetables and digging. That is over. There is only the two of you now and there are nice vegetable shops in Bray. You have the car. Don't be carrying heavy loads." Theo had contractors down in Bray to build a wall in case the river would flood. None of us had ever lived there in wintertime. Ted and Shanlee had the phone and they were under strict instructions to pick it up if there was the slightest need.

All the moves were made at last in the month of May. We established Shanlee and Ted in the house by the river. As was his lifelong custom, Theo had brought along some special wine to toast their new dwelling. The house was full of evening sunshine and sounds of rippling water. The house itself seemed to be welcoming them. I was sure they would be well contented in a little while. Two days later, we left Terenure. Theo had not allowed my bedroom to be disturbed.

"I made that room for you, Lia, and I want you to sleep your last sleep in it exactly as you will always remember it."

Theo, Theo, Theo. What an amazing man he was. I have never forgotten that lovely room, nor have I forgotten that last night in it. It is poignant now in my lonely bed to remember, if only for a passing moment, the love-making of my husband on that last night in the house which had become my home. A passing moment is all because, like a dream, the memory fades into the dark. Theo knew it had to be a special night because he knew Max and I had found each other in that room...and there we had found the perfect way of making love so that, in our moment of climax, we recognised each other. Lia loved Max and Max loved Lia—no one else. In that room we had banished the ghosts.

There was an intensity in Max in all his dealings, and that intensity came across as an inexorable passion of loving, an unyielding insistence that drew forth an orgasm unforgettably sweet. We did not sleep at all. We wanted that last night to go on for ever. We murmured love-words to each other, endearments, half-memories, phrases of gratitude. We caressed and kissed in ways that seemed new and different only to remember how we had discovered and said these things when we first went to Philadelphia so long ago with our two little sons then only three months old. Then again, the warm murmurs ceased and we entered into yet another surge of giving each to the other. We stood at last at the window to watch the May dawn come out of the eastern sky and etch in gold all the chimney pots of a Dublin suburb.

Max held me comfortably against him. "Will we ever know another night like this?" I asked him.

He smiled down at me. "The problem is," he said softly, "in Merrion Square we will have to break-in a brand new bedroom."

CHAPTER TWENTY-SIX

From the very first day, the house in Merrion Square was all that Theo had dreamed and planned, a vision fulfilled. We were, all three of us, at home and at ease in our new abode. It was even easier in this grand setting to be in love, in communication, in total friendship. There was a fresh pride in ourselves. Theo had more free time than he had ever had and more time for me. He and I made all the special expeditions we had promised ourselves. The brief moments when I had come so close to him during his illness were old dreams suspended in mist—some day to be taken down and rewoven. It was my daily task now to run through the rooms to make sure nothing was neglected, although Nelly and Emily were thorough in their three-days-a-week care. When summer brought warm sunshine, I was the one who folded away the Persian eiderdown beneath which I had once rested with Theo. It did not hurt to remember. It seemed that Max had come into his own kingdom at last. He never said now, "You are fonder of my father than you realise—he has a ten-year start on me." We had time and to spare for each other, father and son, Theo and daughter-in-law. Max was pleased beyond his expectations that Theo found so much pleasant pastime in my company. Writing absorbed much of Max's day. He had two preliminary studies published, and now the main book was almost ready with his publisher waiting. He had found a business shop in Westland Row where they typed and copied his manuscripts.

"I am glad to keep him occupied, Lia. How you listen to the endless repetition of his ideas I'll never know!"

"I could listen for ever, and it is not repetition." And that was true. We discussed the daily news, watched television, took strolls through the square or through Stephen's Green, had coffee in the Austrian Kaffee. Theo rested in the afternoon. We became no more intimate than we had ever been; we were completely open and affectionate as always. The reverential stepping-stones were back in place across the deep unknown tide of emotion. On a rare occasion, he would hold me at arm's length and look into my eyes. "What is ours is ours," he would say softly. I bent my head to acknowledge this truth. I owed him my life, my husband, my children. If, down deep, some rebellious instinct turned away from such dependence, I was only remotely the owner of that instinct. Human love remained always the uppermost ideal. I knew then, and I know now, that I adored Theo. That Max was my beloved husband kept me safe.

We had some very grand occasions in Merrion Square: as when all the family assembled for Theo's birthday. It was always his seventy-fifth. We did not let it go beyond that. We said we had lost track, preferring it that way. In truth, and I mean it, he never looked much past sixty. His hair had been silvery since the first time I saw him. It was still thick and always groomed. We thought he would shave the beard after his illness, but he had grown used to it. Every week, his barber came in to trim the beard closely and tend the hair. Theo would never allow the growth of hairs in his ears or his nose; that would be gross. I presume the barber attended to these concerns also. Theo's showering and grooming took several hours of every morning. He liked to emerge, he said, "as fresh as a daisy." His handkerchiefs were scented with cologne. I saw him quite sad only once in those days: that was when his dentist died suddenly of a heart attack. Theo had thought him such a healthy man.

Max said, "He'll think nothing is safe now—especially his teeth!" I reminded Max that Theo and his dentist had been friends for fifty years. "But only because he was the best dentist in Dublin," Max scoffed. I always supposed that sons feel free to poke fun at their fathers—Stefan always did and sometimes even Deric.

We were not always alone. Deric came from Paris fairly frequently. He had always a hundred questions for Theo. Max was very happy when Stefan came; writing was dropped for the duration of the visit. They went fishing; they played golf. Stefan often proclaimed that he was looking for an Irish girl. He did not look very hard, so we presumed he had half-a-dozen girls back in the States. For Deric there was Marie-Claire. She had tired of the Japanese businessman. Deric was a bit like me. One love in a lifetime would have been enough if the vagaries of Fate had left us alone. Vasha's visits were spaced out to coincide with events of interest and, as time went on, the spaces were further apart. I was a little ashamed about that. It seemed ungrateful. Theo had given her so much. Once or twice, I tried to bring up the subject. Theo listened to me patiently. One day when I faltered to a halt, he crossed the drawing-room and sat down beside me. He held me in his arms, as he often did, tenderly and gently.

"But hasn't it all worked out as we would have wished, *balibt?*"

"No, Theo. I think Vasha should be remembering and recalling all you have been to her. A father, a patron, a benefactor, a friend."

"Vasha knows she would embarrass me with a

constant barrage of gratitude. I have always preferred that she take me for granted as she would a father. She knows me since she was an hour old. We understand each other."

I persisted: "Surely you expect her to show more..." He stopped me. "Lia, have you not always known that what was done was done for you—and for Max and for your life together?"

"Yes, but..." I began.

"Lia, yes is enough, no buts. Vasha is wonderful. The pleasure of watching her grow up gave my life a dimension totally unexpected and undeserved. I owe that to you. It is I who am grateful. Vasha and the boys...things have come full circle. And I still have you, *balibt*. Nothing has changed. What is ours is ours." "Coming full circle" was a favourite phrase of Theo's. He was utterly important to our comfortable life. We watched him. We compared notes. We dared not fuss about him because he would resent that; it would emphasise his age. His health was marvellously perfect.

Now I must come to talk of Alessandro in those days. He brought with him from Rome so special an aura of concerned love. He stayed every summer for the whole month of August. The horse show in the RDS was an annual delight for him. I have kept his sketches of horses and women's hats. Sometimes the horses are wearing the hats. I remember his dry humour. Between Theo and him there was an affection most joyful to behold. They gossiped and argued in Italian so vociferously that they sounded as if they were disagreeing dangerously. My Italian had progressed just a little beyond the small phrases which Alessandro expected in response to his tender enquiries. It was usual in those summers for us to go on sketching trips together but not so far as we used to. If Max was writing, he would have the study door firmly shut. His father could kill time his own way but Alessandro remembered Theo and did not want him to feel left out. Theo knew all things. He did not begrudge me Alessandro.

In April every year there was an exhibition which Alessandro laughingly called *I Pittori Domenica*, the Sunday Painters. He was both patron and organiser of this flourishing show. Even when we lived in Philadelphia, Max and I always spent a few days in Rome for this event. Vasha and Deric came too. Often it coincided with Easter. When we moved to Merrion Square, I went on my own. Theo reserved his visit to Rome for the high season when Max would go with him. These visits on my own were very special, very precious, although they lasted for only a few days. The balconied apartment had become home and the sunsets never failed me. There is no comparison between the sunsets in Ireland and in Rome, although I admit we have colours in the Irish sky seen nowhere else. In Rome in springtime, the horizon flushes up a russet sky to frame the huge golden orb sinking slowly like another and more wondrous planet than the one we live in.

There was always an essential call to Tre Fontane—this was my annual pilgrimage, Alessandro said. As on the very first occasion, we would go into the dim cloisters, timing our visit to hear the monks chanting their evening office. We sat close together to join our prayers now that I could say them in Italian. Then we would whisper together as we listened to the monks.

"You think, Alessandro, that always provided I make my annual pilgrimage, you and I will meet in Heaven?"

"I do not care if you make a little fun at me. Having you here now reassures me in the months ahead that you are safe. You are ready for Heaven."

"Is it as easy as that, *figlio mio*? Just one act of perfect contrition?" And he would nod in solemn agreement.

Leaving the cloisters, Alessandro would stand for a moment before he let the heavy door swing shut. He always looked back into the darkness. "They are men of God," he would say. I was always glad to get out into the sunshine, to get well away from the sadness of sanctity and to chat happily as if I were totally

untroubled by pangs of conscience. But had I let slip
the claim to Heaven? Was it enough to be a humanist?

The oppression disappeared very quickly in
Alessandro's apartment. He was the centre of a bright
social scene and every evening his friends congregated
to drink wine and smoke and endlessly discuss their
interests. He kept me always by his side as if I were his
most prized possession. Italians are accustomed to
matriarchy. They assumed I was his mother and were
fulsome in their compliments. Alessandro constantly
drew attention to some aspect of my looks. Later, I
would smilingly rebuke him.

"You do not seem to have noticed that my hair is
beginning to go grey! Alessandro, please do not say
those things. I'll admit I love compliments but you
know, *figlio mio*, I passed the half-century some time
ago. As my gran used to say, 'She will never see fifty
only on a hall-door!'"

"And you are embarrassed, *Madre mia bellissima*,
because you are still beautiful? It is so and I must tell
you."

"All right, all right. But only when your friends
have gone home!" Saying goodbye to him at the
airport was always a bit tearful and I knew it was
because the perfume of his skin brought back my
childhood...and susceptible memory. I could see
myself riding high on Burton's shoulders across

Sandymount Strand, my face quite close to his tawny hair, my small hands holding the collar of his coat and all around me in the air the exquisite masculine aroma of his skin. When Alessandro hugged me and kissed me, I wanted to stay within his aura for ever. For a few days he had lifted all care from my heart. We were two different people: a youthful mother and a young son.

On the plane journey home, I upbraided myself roundly. I was getting old and Alessandro was no longer a youth. The illusion was a transient magic— my real life was in Merrion Square and that is where I wanted it to be. The strange tormenting desire which Burton had inflicted on my soul would never completely vanish. Perhaps Burton in the nether world had ordained this perpetuation and so had given me Alessandro. When the Aer Lingus plane hovered over Dublin, I shook myself free of these unwanted ideas. Used Max wonder at the fervour with which I rushed into his arms? He was delighted of course; but did I see a momentary question in his eyes? Theo had no such question in his eyes. He received me back into his familiar embrace, kissing my head and murmuring Yiddish endearments close to my ear, *balibt, balibt*. And oh, I was always so glad to be home with my two men. Surely this was where the heart belonged.

Almost four years slipped away in the happy routine

of our lives. One day Theo asked us, "Have you stopped to think that soon we will be into the eighties? In 1980, we will be twenty years away from the millennium!"

Max looked up from his papers. "What brought that on, Father? Are you feeling all right?"

"Fine!" Theo answered. "But I doubt if I will be celebrating the millennium!"

"I hope you will," I said loyally.

Theo laughed at my anxious face. "And be as old as Methuselah? What do they say...give me a break! Oh no, thank you!"

Max had now two books published. The third was in process of being accepted. His English publisher had a concurrent offer from America and one from Canada. For over six months there had been interviews and negotiations on both sides of the Atlantic. Max had decided there was nothing more he wished to say on his subject. The third book had much hard criticism of various governments. Max's legal advisers said he should accept the offer of television appearances to defend his thesis. His being on television would soften the blow, they said, because his appearance now was that of a benign patriarch: in height, breadth and silver beard he was a Biblical figure. There were twenty-two years between himself and Theo, but now they looked like brothers with Theo the younger. Theo had worked hard all his life at his chosen profession. He was widely known for the unstinting help he had given to young artists, financially and creatively. But Theo had made it a good life, with much ease, much luxury, great wealth. The time in the concentration camps and on the run with the partisans had aged Max. During these years that became apparent. His eyes gave him trouble; his hair thinned; his face was becoming very lined.

I have written "was becoming." The hardest part of this chronicle must now be written. I have let several years go by because I could not face this hardest part. I have to force myself to take up the pen. It is my task. I have got so far; it is best to finish and close down the shutters. It was easy enough for you, I admonish myself every day, when you were at the heart of the good times, rambling on about love and luxury. You were the luckiest woman who ever lived, cherished as you were. It is an axiom of living that all things have their price. To pay the price with head held high—ah, that is the trick!

Max was commiserating with himself. He was tired of having to make so many journeys, endure sleepless nights in so many ugly rooms, eat so many uneatable meals.

"Is there any way you could come with me, Lia—just to hold my hand and be there at the end of the day?"

We looked at each other helplessly. Theo could not be left. The divided longing: comfort Max or care for Theo?

"Could Shanlee and Ted move in for a week or so?" Max pleaded. But we knew Ted was not well. He had had a minor stroke and poor Shanlee was worried out of her mind.

"Would Vasha come over? We never ask for her help. Isn't it time?"

At that thought we gave up. Theo was the traditional Jew who insisted that the store must be minded. The Lisbon gallery was the pride of his life—*Galeria Vasha*. To have Vasha sitting in a Dublin drawing-room, no matter for what reason, would (we realised) get on his nerves. Deric had announced his engagement to Marie-Claire some months previously and we supposed the wedding was imminent. Stefan was in Hawaii. Recently he had had a big, big promotion. It was not a good moment to call him away. Hawaii, he had let us know, was the best yet: sun, sea, dancing girls. We thought of Alessandro but we hesitated. He was more helpful than our own sons at any time but he was under great pressure at that moment as his manager (*il dirretore*) had taken time off for a second marriage. He had been a widower for years. Alessandro was still involved with the university. Again we hesitated. I think we delayed long enough for Fate to step in. It is my sad experience that Fate will not tolerate a vacuum. Life goes on.

We had, of course, kept our deliberations low key. As I have said so many times, Theo knew all things. He was sensitive and intuitive. He would not allow us to worry on his account.

"Are you serious, my son, when you tell me that this will be your last trip to the United States?"

"Definitely. Absolutely. Without a doubt. And my last book. *Finito.*" Max's tone was adamant.

"Why don't I go with you, then?" Theo asked.

We must have stared in astonishment. Theo was always prepared for Rome or Paris or Lisbon. He averred he hated America. We were ready to tell him that he was not really able for such a journey, which included a visit to Canada. We could not hurt his feelings or be scornful of his desire to help Max. Again we hesitated.

"I never felt better," said Theo, "so no need to worry on that score. I was just thinking the other day that I was never in Washington. A city worth seeing, isn't it? Several times when you two were living in Philadelphia, I thought we could make an overnight trip. I suggested it, didn't I, Lia? It would be nice to see Washington."

I have no doubt, no doubt at all, that when neither Max nor I said anything to hinder her that day, Fate sat to her spinning-wheel again.

That is how it came about: Max and Theo flew to New York *en route* for Washington and Lia drove sedately home to Merrion Square. Smiling and happy and loving each other dearly, we three parted at Dublin Airport, never to meet again. A long time now to lay down the pen. Other words must suffice:

> *A complicated interlocking system of manoeuvres*
> *that are designed to maintain life in a human sense*
> *in spite of the fact that the person is wounded at*
> *the very core of her nature.*

CHAPTER TWENTY-SEVEN

I may have to let this newspaper cutting tell that part of the story about which I know nothing. More than ten years later I cannot set down in my own words the horror which came out of nowhere to shatter my life into a thousand splinters. There have been times in the passing years when I thought I had the jagged edges of my days reassembled into a smaller, compacted semblance of existence only to find that a sudden thought, a bar of music, could leave me again with only a broken mirror.

On the evening of February 23, 1980, a twin-engined Air Florida Boeing 737 took off from National Airport, Washington. There had been snow all day, and almost as soon as it left the ground, the plane began to stall; after only minutes in the air it lost height rapidly, sliced through the evening traffic and crashed into a bridge across the frozen River Potomac.

Ice was the villain of the tragedy. Although measures had been taken earlier to remove it from the airframe, a thin layer of hoar frost had formed on the aircraft's wings in the 35 minutes that

*intervened between treatment and take-off. The
hoar frost was as thin as a sheet of paper, but it was
enough to send the plane plunging down. Seventy-
eight people lost their lives.*

Over and over again when I try to think otherwise,
when I dream of a peaceful cemetery, a grave with a
marble headstone on which I have engraved the
names of my beloved dead, and when I see myself, as
in a vision, bringing floral wreaths to remember them
in every season, flowers of every recurring growth in
every passing year: daffodils and tulips; roses and
lavender; chrysanthemums and red-berried holly, over
and over again I am forced to admit there is no
cemetery, no marble tomb, no flowers. Seventy-eight
living persons went down into the Potomac River and
no body was ever recovered. The weather closed down
in Arctic cold and not all the technological devices
known to the experts could penetrate the broken
frozen hulk of the crashed plane nor release any of
these within it. For many weeks I held the hope deep
in my secret heart that the ice would keep intact and
hold together the people who had been pitched into
death. Hope died at last when I was told there were not
even broken bones. When the Potomac rushed onward
in the thaw, whatever was left was carried away more
than a hundred miles into the Atlantic Ocean. Someone
said, and it became my hideous nightmare, that this

river had massive falls in its course to the ocean.

The family must have assembled. Friends must have come from everywhere: business acquaintances, doctors, writers, many Jews whose presence was, no doubt, acknowledged but whose names were scarcely known to me. I see myself wearing a black suit, standing in the drawing-room, among many hands holding glasses of coloured liquid. To these hands I am extending my fingertips, my head is nodding politely. I am part of a nodding line: Vasha, Deric, Stefan, Alessandro. I see the broken face of Phyllis and I hear Frayne's voice telling someone to be careful: your mother is in a state of shock. In case I am the mother in question, and not wishing to offend, I make an effort with my voice and with my words. Someone is at hand with a handkerchief but my eyes are dry.

Those days must have ended. My family and friends must have gone away back into their own lives. I seem to have been kindly left to get on with what they surely thought was bearable in a rich house with no shortage of cash. Lonely for a time, of course, but she will get over it. She is a strong person. She will pull through. What did anyone know of the internal chaos of remorse which went on day after endless day, into endless sleepless nights. There can be no logic in grief. The unspoken words, the might-have-beens, the regrets, the repentance, are all illogical and all the more impossible to bear for that very reason.

I see myself, months later, pacing the drawing-room, papers in hand. I approach the telephone. I hesitate. I walk about again. I take up the phone and I put it down. What would they want me to do? For the rest of my life? They. They. They. They were there with every waking moment now. If I slept and dreamed, they haunted the dream. I could say their names in a whisper when I was alone. I was not troubled by money worries nor by loneliness. I wanted no one. Facing each succeeding blank hour was trouble enough. The restlessness was stupidity. It took a long time for reality to surface.

Nature has a way of calling up its forces. A day came when I dressed differently. I went down in the lift and I actually said a nice good-morning to the auctioneers' receptionist. I walked up Merrion Street and on to Stephen's Green. This is Dublin, I told myself. This is my city, the city of all who went before me to beget me into this city. My native city. There was comfort in this thought. A small comfort compared with what I had lost but there was warmth. I recited a familiar litany: Dublin is home and I know no other city more suited to being home. You could walk all around Dublin in an hour, and the city fathers cannot expand it because it was created too many centuries ago. There are rich streets and poor streets, posh people and beggars, the remains of colonial rule and the embryo of twentieth-century reassertion.

I have been in a few cities, I think as I walk around the lake in Stephen's Green. I admire Paris which is a city for lovers. Lisbon is full of lovely women and exotic vistas. London? Only Londoners born within the sound of Bow Bells could honestly love London; the rest just work there. Rome? Well, yes. Rome has a lot to offer. Compared with Rome, Dublin might look shabby, but all the more endearing for that. Dublin was named "Strumpet City" by several of our writers, and I understand that very well. She has been mother to bastards in the old sense, and she still is in the pejorative sense. A golden-hearted strumpet, though. Once she takes you to her bosom, you have the freedom of all her attractions—poor or rich, it's all one. That was the way I was thinking on that morning when reality finally surfaced. Was I thinking or was Dublin thinking for me? So it had been since I was a child in Creighton Street. The deep-down rebellious instinct that made me want to fight free of all ties was resurrecting itself again. Dublin does that for you when you walk its streets alone—it is Liberty City. No alien culture of slavery had a permanent abode in Dublin. Hordes of conquerors from across the seas had put this place on the anvil for centuries and hammered away to form the Dublin ethos. I felt it in the air of

Stephen's Green. Early summer flowers were colouring the grass. Winter was over. Soon Alessandro would be free to come and he would help me to sort out and rearrange. He and I had long ago discovered the essential reason he and I were kin. It was that early convent upbringing; it was the nuns. Ask any man or woman who has passed early youth in a boarding-school with religious; they recognise the fact in each other.

In the way Italians are perhaps more male than other European men, Alessandro was very essentially male: a little bit lazy, a little bit self-indulgent, a little bit dependent. Yet, because of those early years in a place that housed him but could never be home, he was all-round aware. Children get to be all-round aware when they eat and sleep with strangers.

So I did not turn to Vasha, nor to my sons. They were not all-round aware of my problems. I waited until August and I opened my mind and heart and soul to Alessandro.

"It is as well we have a whole month to talk," he said. "We have here a major revolution."

"It is all just finance, isn't it? You know all my reasons. I don't want ever again to ask any man to stand between me and the rest of the world. Only this time, Alessandro, I promise never again. I cannot face the family or the solicitors, telling me I am mad to throw everything away. Nor do I want sympathy. I have thought about it long enough. You will do the acting and the talking for me...I know you will not refuse."

"You want to get rid of everything? Everything, *Madre*?"

"Yes," I answered. "I do not want the worry or the responsibility of riches. Nor do I want to look foolish in the eyes of solicitors and auctioneers. You will shield me."

"*Madre mia*, would you consider letting another year pass before a final decision?" he asked. "You have been much alone since..."

"No, Alessandro. It is not shock. It is me, myself, I. So long as I can remember, I have followed the will of other people. Each time I was about to make a resolution for myself, someone or something turned me around. I never had the life I planned to have."

"You have not been unhappy, *Madre*. You have been loved by all. Your face is the face of a serene woman."

"Then my face deceives. Deep down there has always been a chained creature who longs to be free. Who longs to escape."

We talked and talked and talked. It was easy enough to convince him that living alone in a great big house in Merrion Square was not realistic. The place echoed emptily from Friday to Monday. Holiday weekends were endless. The upkeep of such a place would be enormous. Theo knew how to generate money. I did not. There is a type of executive woman today who would jump at the chance to take over the rents, the licenses, the leases, the bankers' orders. I was a woman of an earlier generation. I was not exactly averse to a certain amount of luxury but the nuts and bolts of securing it presented a picture in my mind which frightened me.

"Alessandro, do you remember in Rome one day when you were giving me a little lecture, you said always to remember that in the midst of life, we are in death?"

"Yes, I remember saying that, although I did not invent it, but I deny lecturing you. I was telling you how I think."

"You were proved right, *figlio mio*." I was always afraid of becoming emotional with Alessandro. In my heart we were very close. And I could not cry any more. Grief had to be secret. "And when it happens to me, in the midst of life, I must be ready."

"You think Theo was ready?" he asked.

"Spiritually he was always ready," I replied. "Materially I cannot pick up the pieces. And Max was only getting ready to live."

"Will it make it easier to be ready if you are poor?"

"Look at Shanlee and Ted. They get along on very little, saving their money to leave for Max. They thought they were ready, all plans made."

"Are they poor enough for you to live with them?" He looked surprised. Their grief was harder to bear than my own.

"No, no, no" I cried out. "They bring Max's name into every conversation, Theo's too. I cannot forget any single thing that has been but I must remember in my own way."

Alessandro knew I had to spill out all my ideas, crazy as they might seem. He knew I expected him to play devil's advocate, even though he understood me completely. By the end of a week, I had convinced him that my mind was made up. I would become an enclosed order all to myself, living frugally, dressing soberly.

Alessandro could scarcely endure the idea that I would make all these sacrifices and then come to regret such renunciation. I might turn away from poverty and be too proud to look for help. He lifted the edge of the silk scarf I was wearing, and pressed it to his lips. "I cannot see you as a holy nun, *Madre mia*."

"If I fail in this way of life, then I will try another way, but I will not fail." Only my voice let me down; it was sad.

"It is not right that I allow us to begin all these

negotiations for selling without informing the members of the family." He said this in several different ways and at last he made all the necessary phone calls. I agreed he could not take the responsibility and the possibility of being blamed for what the others would see as grief-stricken foolhardy gestures to be regretted as soon as made. They found I would not be deterred. Deric constituted himself the man of business. Theo always said he had a good hard-head. The date for his marriage to Marie-Claire had been set several times. Now it was to be the twenty-fourth of September to coincide with her twenty-fourth birthday. The two twenty-fours would constitute a good luck omen. I should like to record that indeed the omen worked its charm thereafter, but alas it did not. There was never a balance in their marriage—as far as an outsider could judge. Deric was too intensely demanding as a husband and Marie-Claire was too fly-away to be a submissive little wife. However, I did not set out to chronicle their marriage, so let it be. Suffice to say that Deric was there when his mother needed him.

Within a few weeks, Deric had put everything in the hands of solicitors and valuers. The Murillo painting, a copy on canvas but considered of value, was mine and the only painting I wanted to take with me into my reconstructed life. This picture of three little Spanish boys, although given to me by Theo, was not symbolic of Theo's taste.

I asked Deric to make sure that Shanlee and Ted were secure in their tenancy of the river house while they were able to go on living there on their own. For me to live with them would inflict on them the burden of reverting to being servants. That is how they would see the situation. The death of Max had a disastrous effect on Shanlee's health and, even though she was so poorly, she nursed Ted devotedly through his stroke. I would find a small place to rent, and some day I would go into the river house and make it home again...some day when I could live peaceably at ease with memory. After a year, that time had not yet arrived.

Following daily advertisements, I tracked down a little place in Chapelizod under the Knockmaroon Hill below Cluny. This area was familiar since schooldays but memorable only with teenage recollections. When Vasha saw it, she bought it.

"Renting is a fool's way of spending money, Lia," she said. "You are foolish enough; don't overdo it." She had taken on the mantle of Theo, but differently. As the next years rolled on, she counselled and advised rather than loved. Deric was warmer in his guidance but within a year his married life occupied all the time left over from accumulating wealth. That brings me to Stefan. Now am I being fair if I say he cut himself adrift when his father was gone? Is that what happened or is that how I see it with a tinge of jealousy? His career always had top priority. It is ten years since we have talked. I miss him. He was great fun and he is probably still great fun. A bachelor who enjoys life, I am told.

CHAPTER TWENTY-EIGHT

I spent the first Christmas of our bereavement with Alessandro in Rome. I was now the *madre* indeed, a widowed *madre*. In his apartment I was completely at home. I accompanied him to Mass. We made the pilgrimage to Tre Fontane. We did our tour of the *presepi*, my greatest enjoyment. We spent the traditional Christmas Eve session in the Piazza Navone, like a young pair, buying tinsel and tiny fir trees for the balcony. We were pretending tremendous Christmas happiness to keep each other distracted.

Alessandro came back to Dublin with me to assure himself that I was settled as well as I could be settled. He was not totally enamoured, he said, of the Chapelizod house but at least it was not overlooked. The river at the end of the garden was the Liffey.

"Not so nice as the Dargle," Alessandro said. "What I call a utility river. No brown stones, no hanging willows."

"But better than a closed-in yard?" I asked. Closed-in yards were an unforgotten feature of Ringsend.

I struggled through the seasons. There were days

when I persuaded myself, "I am over it." All I had to do was to repeat those words. Alas, there were days when I stood at the window gazing at the greeny-grey river moving slowly to the sea. There were days when I took a bus into Dublin and came back again as alone as ever. The small patch of ground never responded to my spasmodic efforts at gardening. The clay was damp and heavy.

In the summer Shanlee died and within a month Ted, too, was gone. All over again there was gloom and grieving. I locked up the house by the Dargle. It was still too soon.

"Aren't you being rather silly, Lia?" Vasha enquired looking around the place in Chapelizod. "This place reeks of self-pity. Depressing. I would be prepared to renovate it and sell it. Move to Bray. Altogether a better area."

I took a long look at her. She is spectacularly beautiful. Her clothes are fabulous. She permits her name to be associated with riches and titles. She has not married. Frayne Lowry is her close friend.

I said, "I will know when the time is right."

In December I went to Rome. Now again comes a hard part for me to set down in writing. I feel I should protest my innocence. Or was it the naïvety of approaching age?

We did all the things together that for Alessandro

and for me had become our traditional Christmas things to do. There was a calm quiescent composure in our days. Or so I thought. We were deeply affectionate in our actions, in our greetings, in our good-mornings and in our goodnights. We lingered lovingly over these salutations, caressing with fingertip caresses—a devoted mother and son. So I thought. I was conscious always of the aroma of his skin but that was a thing I never said.

The day after Christmas we were sitting out on the balcony, wine glasses in our hands.

"Would you stay here with me?" Alessandro asked. "And not go back to Dublin?"

I misunderstood the depth of meaning in his voice. "Until when?" I asked lightly.

"Until always," he said.

Still misunderstanding, misjudging, I said, "I could stay for another week if we change the tickets."

"I want you here always. I have wanted that for years. Now it is two years since..."

I interrupted. "Don't say any more. You know I could not stay. You have your own life—a wonderful life. Alessandro, my holiday is just a holiday."

"Would our marriage make it right and proper?" The tenderness of his voice echoed out into the evening sky.

My face must have been a study in sheer amazement.

Alessandro, my solid and reliable Alessandro, had taken leave of his senses. He bowed his head as if in dread of an angry rebuke. But I was not angry, only absolutely incredulous. At last I found a voice, and I made it gentle.

"Marriage is for lovers, *figlio mio*."

He looked up. "Marriage is for a lot of things," he said, "and I could give you all of them."

"Alessandro, please, please—we have a wonderful relationship." His handsome face was alight with feeling. "You are not my mother but I love you as dearly as if you were. I am not your son and that love is different. I want to marry you. There is no bar on us. I beg of you, *bellissima*, I beg of you, let us marry!" The voice and the attitude were tender and yet firm. He meant what he was saying. The impossibility of what he meant seemed to be unnoticed by him.

I tried again. "Surely you are mistaking your very real pity and sympathy for a quite different feeling?"

He stood up and lifted me to my feet. "You are the only woman for whom I feel love. From the first moment in the convent garden. Desire rushes through me when I see you. *Per piacere, per piacere*, please, please, Lia, do not ever go away again. Stay with me..."

Deliberately I lay against him and I, too, let all the almost-forgotten feelings of desire rush through me. Deliberately I inhaled the perfume of his skin. My entire life, my world, revolved on this erotic masculine aroma which was Burton's legacy to me. Deliberately I raised my face for his kiss. It was at once tender and passionate and searching. For five whole minutes, I loved and desired Alessandro with all the passion of a used-up heart. And how much could be left in a heart that had known Theo?

Then I stepped back, free of his arms. "That is it," I said softly. "That is all I have to give."

"That was only the first moment," he pleaded, holding out his arms for more.

"Alessandro, I am twenty years older than you. I stood beside your mother the day you were born. No, no, my dearest boy, if we must part, let us do so in love."

It is a great glory in a woman's treasure-chest, that ark in which she holds her gifts, to know that in her age she was desired by a kingly man. It is a glory she cherishes among the secrets.

"*Madre*, it is not only this desire which you must surely know you inspire in me. It is the love of many years, the love which will care for you and sustain you when you fail. I must be at your side when you will need someone to depend on and the others are not there. I have waited and waited without hope. And now I can ask—you must know this was meant to be— let me show you. Come, stay in my arms, *per favore*...stay." There was more, much more, and our tears flowed helplessly. "Let me go on loving you. What are the years in the future when I have waited all those years in the past? Let me show what desire can do. I worship you. Stay, please stay with me for ever..." The pent-up passion of many years came streaming out and most of it came in Italian supplications of such a fervour as perhaps is only possible in Italian.

I was tempted. I was sorely tempted. Not only did I love and need Alessandro: I need the consolation of loving. To the end of her days, a woman misses the warm comfort of loving; she misses a chosen man to complement her days and her nights. When I sit and think of Alessandro, I recall that he was quite a man. He was handsome and brilliantly gifted. He was sensitive and perceptive.

Oh yes, I was tempted. He pleaded his cause all the way to the airport, weaving the car in and out fearlessly through traffic, shouting over the strident klaxon horns. I heard his voice above the noise, "And I want to bring you back to your faith."

That too, Alessandro? But, my dearest son, I could not take advantage of you. That is what it would have been, taking advantage. I had worked myself free of ties of duty. I had no need to live up to anything, to measure up to anyone. For the rest of my life, I could be myself. After the goodbye at the airport, I was glad for the very first time to see Rome disappearing into the clouds. In Dublin I would be free.

Five Christmases later I went back to Rome. We all assembled for Alessandro's first Mass. He had become a monk in the monastery of Tre Fontane. After that first Mass he held me in his arms until it seemed that no power on earth could prise us apart. Then the gates clanged shut for ever. Tre Fontane holds the men of God in silence and in secrecy.

Alessandro, my darling, you have chosen the better part. Desire for fading beauty would be assuaged, and assuaged all the faster for the fleeting years. Holiness could be lost. We may meet in Heaven after all.

Once again, Deric was the man of business. Once again, Theo's empire was divided. Alessandro's share went three ways: to Vasha, to Deric, to Stefan. I took nothing. I wanted nothing. I had given the money from the air disaster compensation to Alessandro. He had given it to the nuns of the orphanage where, long ago, Burton had walked in the garden with his little son.

EPILOGUE

On one of those never-forgotten holidays of childhood in a Bray that has vanished in a world that has vanished, Tadek and I had our fortunes told by a famous fortune-teller, Mike Nono. Max supplied the sixpences. Tadek, who was poor and very slight, was wearing a hand-me-down blazer. His fortune was swift and abrupt: "Nothing much in life ahead for you. A quick end. Beware of the gallows!" I, on the contrary, was nicely dressed in whatever was the fashion for girls. "Ah!" said Mike Nono. "You have a prosperous future. Your last thirty years will be affluent." It is recorded in the inevitable little diary that I wished our fortunes were reversed. I see I looked up the meaning of "affluent." I am not rich but my life now would seem very affluent to Mike Nono in the crystal ball of the far-distant future. In 1937 we were all so poor, hoping for sixpenceworth of happy prosperity to come our way.

I was reunited with all the diaries and the souvenirs when, last spring, I took possession of my house by the Dargle River. Sometimes on a sunny afternoon, I spread out all these little notebooks on a garden table and I steep myself in memory, not all sad and not all heart-breakingly tender. There were lovely moments of sheer exultant joy—all faithfully written into the days now forever in the past.

I look down at the sunlit sand edging the lapping river. This was all I ever wanted. This quiet solitude to think my own thoughts; to people my own garden with my own friends who walk under the roses although their scattered bones may lie on other sand, in other earth, far, far away. I owe so much to them. I must honour their memory, and I am happy in this task. As Theo so truly said, happiness is the gift of the gods.

Also by
Lilian Roberts Finlay

Always in My Mind
A Bona Fide Husband
Stella

POOLBEG